"I am here to be bedded."

The bluntness of her words took him off guard.

He didn't like at all the singular purpose for which she'd come to his club, and the irony was not lost on him. He reveled in sin, enjoyed his role in introducing people to vice. What the devil was the matter with him?

"If you look closely, you'll see that some of the gents wear a red button on their left lapel. They will provide that service for you."

"I'm not interested in them. You intrigue me, Mr. Trewlove. You are the one I want."

"I do not involve myself with my clientele."

"I'm not asking you to involve yourself. I'm asking you to bed me."

Was it even possible to bed her without involving himself?

"We can stand here and debate or we can waltz and debate." Bowing slightly, mockingly, if truth be told, he waved toward the dance floor. "Shall we?"

By Lorraine Heath

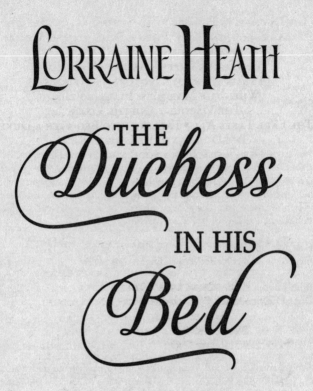

LORRAINE HEATH

THE
Duchess
IN HIS
Bed

A SINS FOR ALL SEASONS NOVEL

AVONBOOKS

An Imprint of HarperCollinsPublishers

THE DUCHESS IN HIS BED. Copyright © 2019 by Jan Nowasky. All rights reserved. Printed in the United States of America. No part of this book may be used or reproduced in any manner whatsoever without written permission except in the case of brief quotations embodied in critical articles and reviews. For information, address HarperCollins Publishers, 195 Broadway, New York, NY 10007.

First Avon Books mass market printing: September 2019
First Avon Books hardcover printing: August 2019

Print Edition ISBN: 978-0-06-267606-1
Digital Edition ISBN: 978-0-06-267607-8

Cover design by Amy Halperin
Cover illustration by Victor Gadino

Avon, Avon & logo, and Avon Books & logo are registered trademarks of HarperCollins Publishers in the United States of America and other countries.

HarperCollins is a registered trademark of HarperCollins Publishers in the United States of America and other countries.

FIRST EDITION

19 20 21 22 23 QGM 10 9 8 7 6 5 4 3 2 1

To Rosalyn Rosenthal
For her loving kindness and generosity

Acknowledgments

The British system of peerage and entailments is a fascinating study in primogeniture and can be rather complicated at times. I wish to thank Mr. Grant Bavister, Registrar at the College of Arms, London, for patiently explaining the intricacies of how the system works when there are no male heirs to inherit and a title goes extinct. In addition, he shared information on the distribution of entailed properties in the absence of a male heir. All the information he provided was invaluable. Any errors in understanding or interpretation are mine or a result of literary license.

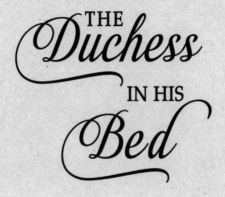

THE Duchess IN HIS Bed

*T*he Earl of Elverton scowled at his latest bastard, blotchy and naked, held aloft by a midwife, as though she were offering him a treasure discovered in the ruins of Egypt or Pompeii. He wondered if he should present this one to his wife, tell her to suckle it at her teat, and announce to the world she'd given birth to it.

Why the devil couldn't he get his countess with babe when he had such success at it elsewhere, with every woman he bedded save her? Perhaps if he were more enthusiastic when it came to the taking of her—

But she was a plain, docile thing, the daughter of a marquess his father had forced him to marry when he was nineteen. Naught about her made a man's cock stand at attention, although he did manage it. Yet still, after a decade, not once had his seed taken root.

He should probably rid himself of her. A trip down the stairs, a fall from a rowboat in deep waters, a tumble from her horse. He could make an accident happen. He had before with a brother who should have inherited the title ahead of him.

A *shooting accident* when they'd been out hunting

grouse. No one was surprised. The heir apparent had never been comfortable around weapons or truly mastered the use of firearms. "He tripped, his finger on the trigger," Elverton had told everyone. "The gun discharged quite by accident." No one doubted his word, no one suspected it had been *his* finger on the trigger that was responsible for his brother's demise, not when he blubbered and produced tears. He became the victim, the one everyone comforted, because he would have to live with the horror that he'd witnessed due to his brother's clumsiness. Fools all.

Now he slid his gaze from the bawling babe to the woman in the bed recovering from her ordeal, watching him, waiting for his decision. If he were to arrange to pass this by-blow off as his legitimate heir, he would have to dispatch her to a watery grave at the bottom of the Thames in order to ensure her silence. He was not one to take risks of discovery when misdeeds were done. While at present—with her bedraggled hair sweaty and her skin clammy—she wasn't much to gaze upon, when she was at her best, she was the most beautiful, exciting woman he'd ever plowed. She also possessed a luscious mouth that knew its way well around a man's cock. He grew hard just thinking of placing his once again between her luscious lips.

"Swaddle it," he ordered the midwife.

"Can I not keep this one?" his favorite mistress asked.

He glanced around at the lavish furnishings he provided for her in the fine town house he leased. "Not unless you want to keep it and yourself on the streets. Bastards are tiresome, a burden I do not tolerate."

"But you will ensure he is well cared for and loved, will you not?"

No good would come of changing his plans, but where was the harm in a small lie that would keep her enthusiastically welcoming him between her thighs? He gave her a much-practiced reassuring smile. "For you, I will do near anything."

Perhaps he'd even replace his wife with her when the time came, if it came, if his countess did not bear fruit soon.

Taking the boy from the midwife, he headed from the room. Because he paid for his bastards to be "put away"—*killed* in baby-farming circles—he preferred to spread them out, never using the same farmer more than a couple of times. He'd recently obtained a new name, a woman he'd not visited before. He'd gladly hand over the required fee to Ettie Trewlove to ensure he was never again inconvenienced by this brat.

Chapter 1

*S*he was in want of a man.

And not just any man would serve. She had a particular one in mind.

Standing in a shadowed corner of the Elysium Club, an exclusive gaming hell singularly for ladies, Selena Sheffield, Duchess of Lushing, watched as the club's owner prowled the floor with lengthy, lithe strides, reminding her of a large sleek lion, predatory and dangerous. His black fitted coat caressed his wide shoulders, as she suspected many a lady had. His black brocade waistcoat molded itself around his lean torso. His white shirt and knotted snowy cravat were pristine, a direct contrast to the swarthiness of his skin. He didn't appear to be a man who spent all his time indoors.

She'd first caught sight of him last summer at Lady Aslyn Hastings's wedding, when the daughter of the late Earl of Eames and ward to the Duke of Hedley had taken Mick Trewlove as her husband. Selena had known nothing about the Trewloves until that day, until she'd caught tidbits here and there as people whispered about the disreputable family that was naught but by-blows.

Then the Duke of Thornley had married Gillie Trewlove—a tavern owner of all things, for God's sake—and the whispers had turned into a dulcet tone of alarm. More recently, one of the Trewlove brothers had taken Lady Lavinia Kent, sister to the Earl of Collinsworth, to wife, and suddenly no one could talk of anything other than the Trewlove bastards and the swath they were rapidly cutting through Society like Genghis Khan's hordes intent on conquering what had once believed itself unconquerable.

She considered herself immune to their spell but had to admit to being intrigued by Aiden Trewlove ever since she'd seen him standing at the altar looking nothing at all like his brother, but then only God knew who had sired him, who had given birth to him. However, it had been more than the cut of his bristly shadowed jaw or his patrician nose or those full, sensual lips that had made it near impossible to take her eyes from him.

It was the way he'd seemed amused by the entire affair. Whenever he peered over his shoulder or faced the crowd of people who had packed themselves onto the pews, desperate to watch a lady of such a storied family marrying a man of such a scandalous one, he'd studied them through half-lowered lids, as though taking their measure and not wanting them to see exactly what he thought of them, of how much he found them lacking.

But when Lady Aslyn had glided up the aisle, the warm smile he'd bestowed upon her, expressing his acceptance of her and welcoming her into the family, had marked him as not only kind but immensely approachable.

And Selena was in need of a man harboring both characteristics in order to calm her fraying nerves and ease the guilt threatening her resolve. She was where she should not be, standing with her back pressed against a wall, wearing a gown of deep royal blue, a mask of the same shade, because Aiden Trewlove offered women sin and secrets. Not all the women hid behind masks, not the bold ones or those who had nothing to lose. She imagined the freedom one must feel to stride through the rooms unmasked, to be unafraid, to be liberated. But it was imperative that no one ever learn of her presence in the scandalous environs provided by Aiden Trewlove.

To women, he had opened the heavens where gods plotted and revealed the delicious mysteries within. A club they whispered about among themselves, a place unknown to fathers, brothers, and husbands. A domain in which women ruled and did as they pleased. He'd given them a paradise within the shadows of London that was theirs and theirs alone. He'd known what they wanted, what they needed. And he'd provided it.

A man who created all of this, who understood women so well and knew the entertainments for which they yearned, surely would not sit in judgment and would know how to provide a safe haven where a woman could do what she ought not without fear of her actions being revealed to others.

And so she watched as he whispered in the ear of one lady, making her laugh, while his words to another caused her to dip her head and blush profusely, a shy smile curling her lips upward. To various other women he nodded or grinned—the grin given slowly and seductively as though the one to whom it was given was the only soul in the room for whom he had a care. He placed his hand over one lady's, stopping her from moving a stack of wooden disks into the pile at the center of the table. Then, with a devastating wink that no doubt took the lady's breath, he tossed one of the chips onto the mound.

Then he carried on striding through his dominion— No, not *through*. Toward. Toward her.

Her heart kicked frantically against her ribs; within her gloves her palms dampened. She wasn't yet ready to step out of the shadows into the golden glow of the gaslit chandeliers above. She wasn't yet prepared to meet, to speak with this man who might prove to be her salvation—if only her courage would not desert her.

It was more than his good looks that unsettled her. It was the way he moved as though each movement was calculated to bring attention to him while giving the impression he wanted none at all. The manner in which he observed so keenly, so thoroughly, as though he could decipher all mysteries, make them blossom before him. Choosing him could turn out to be a colossal mistake because she had secrets to hold close. If she were wise, she would turn on her heel and flee. But if she'd never fled the circumstances of her marriage, she certainly wasn't going to run off now, simply because his thorough gazing of her was disconcerting in the extreme. No man had ever looked at her as though she were a confection to be nibbled and enjoyed.

He stepped from the light into the gray and

leaned one shoulder negligently against the wall papered in curlicues of dark burgundy and light rose. The shadows prevented her from discerning the exact shade of his eyes, but not his keen interest in her, not the slight tilting up of one corner of his mouth. "You're new here."

His diction was more polished and refined than she'd expected, not fully aristocratic, but close. She wondered if his father had seen him educated. Not that it mattered as his schooling wasn't a deterrent to her purpose, although her nerves were certainly vying for that role. Somewhere within the recesses of her soul, she found the wherewithal to shore up her confidence and force it into her words. "You can't possibly know that. I'm masked."

"I can identify the ladies who visit, mask or no. It is not only a face by which one might be recognized." Slowly his gaze roamed over her, not in an insulting or lascivious way, but with an appreciation that had her skin prickling as though it longed to be nearer to him. Then his eyes were back on hers. "What is your name, darling?"

She didn't want to remember how she had once longed to be someone's darling, to have endearments, not apologies, whispered in her ear. "Lena."

A shortened version of her name, a name no one would recognize her by should they hear it. A name she never used.

He cocked his head to the side, gave her another thorough going-over, shook his head. "I don't think so. Too simple a name for far too complex a woman, I wager. Helena, perhaps, Helena of Troy. Or something fancier."

Licking her lips, she glanced around nervously,

noting she'd snagged the attention of a few ladies, those not masked known to her, which meant she was known to them and probably to a few of the masked ones as well. She didn't want to consider the embarrassment and shame she would bear if her presence were discovered. "I don't wish others to hear my name spoken."

"It will be our secret," he murmured, his voice low and seductive, causing unexpected warmth to sluice through her, along with a desire to trust him completely, with everything, but she wasn't quite as foolish as all that.

"Selena," she whispered back, thinking no word on her tongue was nearly as sensual as any syllable on his.

"Selena," he repeated, his voice going even lower, a velvety caress that nearly had her leaning toward him, toward those lips that created such mesmerizing resonances. "I'm Aiden."

"Yes, I know." Did she have to sound so breathless of a sudden? "The owner. It's quite a spectacular place."

"How would you know? You haven't left this spot since claiming it after coming through the door."

Oh Lord, the man was too observant by half. Choosing him could turn out to be an error in judgment. Without another word, before she claimed another breath, she should take her leave, but his gaze held her hostage as though she were a butterfly beneath glass. "I can see the entirety of this room."

"Ah, but this room is only a small portion of what I offer." He held out his hand, ungloved, large, rough-hewn. It would swallow her breast. Where had that thought come from? Yet at that particular moment, she could envision those long, slender fingers doing little else than kneading what no man had ever touched. "Come, my lady. Allow me the honor of giving you a tour."

She almost corrected him. She wasn't *my lady*, but *Your Grace*. However, the less he knew of her, the better. In addition, considering the way he studied her, she wasn't entirely certain if he was addressing her with an honorific or claiming her as *his lady*. A silly thought. An even sillier one was that she wouldn't mind if the latter were the case, but it was imperative that he not have a care for her and she not have one for him, that tonight's little adventure leave behind no fond memories to be mulled over in the days and years to come.

Swallowing hard, she placed her gloved hand in his, surprised how the warmth of his burned through the silk. He tucked it within the crook of his elbow and began leading her out of the shadows.

"I'm looking forward to introducing you to the pleasures of sin."

AIDEN TREWLOVE ESCORTED the lady into the dim light where he could get a better look at her. In contrast to his, her hair was the shade of wheat with the barest hint of red, as though she'd eaten strawberries as a child and the fruit had become part of her. But it was her eyes that drew him in, the blue of the hottest flames dancing upon a hearth, and he had the unsettling thought that with her he could get burned.

Not likely. He was not one to become overly involved with a lady. Having watched as one had nearly destroyed his brother when they were younger, randy, and wild, Aiden had made a vow to never allow any woman to capture his heart. He would enjoy them, ensure they enjoyed time spent with him, but he'd walk away if he ever felt a spark that threatened more than a casual encounter, more than a frolic between the sheets.

He'd noticed this one the moment she entered his establishment, although he made note of every-one who came and went. It wasn't unusual for a woman, upon first arriving at his club, to be a bit shy, to hover in a corner, to be hesitant about going forward and embracing what he offered. But this one had been neither shy nor hovering nor hesitant. She'd been watching. Not the dice games or the cards or the roulette wheel. Not the well-dressed men walking through offering champagne, brandy, and port. Not the young bucks leaning over a lady's shoulder whispering tips on how to play and com-pliments into her ear. No, none of that had caught her attention or sparked her curiosity. She'd been watching him.

He'd felt the caress of her gaze like a physical force traveling the length of him, and the urge to preen had hit him strong. But he was not one for preening. She either liked what she saw or she didn't. Based on the fact that her hand was now nestled in the crook of his elbow, he assumed she liked.

He was desperate to see her without the mask that covered three-quarters of her face, leaving only her mouth and chin visible. Her chin reminded him of the bottom half of a heart, but more delicate, finely etched by fate's gentle hand. The gods had taken care in creating this one.

She had luscious lips, a rosy pink, not red. His

mind started to wander to other areas of her that might be pink, and he abruptly brought it back to the task at hand. Too soon to travel there. Besides, he didn't need to be walking about the place, looking as though he'd stuffed a tent pole in his trousers. He was introducing these ladies to sin, not decadence. "Do you have an interest in these games?"

"I wouldn't know. I've not played them."

"So you only have an interest in that which you know? Where's your sense of adventure, darling?"

"I'm here, aren't I? My presence must demonstrate I'm in possession of a great deal."

"But you're not entirely comfortable with your surroundings or your daring to come here."

"I suppose the mask was a hint, but no, I'm not. I had to give myself several lectures before convincing myself to come."

"Nothing will happen here that you do not want to happen."

She looked up at him, a bit of deviltry reflected in the blue depths. "So I will not lose my coins should I sit down at the tables?"

He laughed, grinned at her. "Point well made."

Her lips twitched and for half a heartbeat, he thought she might at least offer him a hint of a smile. He wanted to see the upward curl of her lips, the joy reflected there. A sadness, a sorrow, hovering about her was calling to his protective nature, the irritating side that caused him to make sacrifices regardless of the cost to himself. It was the reason he now owned this club, a gift from his brother Finn, for whom he'd once humbled himself before their maggot of a father. Finn had seen it as a way to repay Aiden for a debt Finn felt he owed in spite of Aiden insisting he didn't. But the tug he felt to protect this lady was far greater than anything he'd ever experienced before. Was ludicrous to the extreme. He didn't know her or anything about her. He couldn't imagine she didn't already have a protector.

She was nobility, that much he did know. Her fine threads and the cut of her gown hinted at it, but her diction clinched it along with the manner in which she held herself, as though accustomed to people bending to her will. He'd never much favored the aristocracy except for the coins they could place in his pockets. At nineteen, he'd opened the Cerberus Club intent on taking what he could from as many lords as possible, using them for his betterment. Certainly, the less affluent visited his gaming hell. He had no prejudice in him when it came to money. He'd taken it from sons, brothers, and husbands. Now, with the Elysium Club, he would take it from daughters, sisters, and wives.

Finn had made plans for this club before love diverted his attention away from it. He now lived on the outskirts of London, making a wife happy and raising horses. When he handed Elysium over to Aiden, barely a dozen women visited each night and it had been designed to reflect a bit more elegance and refinement. Aiden had made some adjustments in order to appeal to the ladies' hidden desires.

The addition of the masks had been his idea, because he'd known women would be curious, but hesitant to show their faces. Yes, those who came through the doors had to swear an oath of secrecy, but he was well aware that oaths were broken. Hence, he'd needed a way to protect those who needed protection, while at the same time offering them a sanctuary and a means to fill his coffers.

The gaming room through which he escorted Selena remained much the same as Finn had left it. All manner of gaming was to be found here, and it was here that the bulk of his income was earned.

"I'd not expected to see men playing," she said.

"They're tutoring their partners. These games are not what ladies play in the afternoon while sipping tea. Would you like me to fetch you a tutor?" Even as the words escaped his mouth from habit, his gut tightened with the thought of anyone leaning in and whispering advice into the delicate shell of her ear.

"I have no interest in learning card play."

He wondered where her interests resided but where was the fun in getting right down to it? He preferred keeping her at his side a while longer, learning more about her, discovering all the various facets of which she was comprised. "Perhaps this will interest you more."

He led her through a doorway into a room his brother had envisioned for elegant meals with white linen-covered tables and candles flickering on them. What use had adventurous women for such boring dining options? He still had the flickering candles, but they stood on tall pillars providing the barest of light over fainting couches and mounds of pillows where ladies lounged while men placed grapes between their lips or handed them glasses of wine. Young bucks knelt before them, holding a platter of food while they ate to their hearts' content. Some women invited the men to join them while they dined, some merely wanted to

be served. Whatever their pleasure, the gentlemen
were hired to provide it.

"Have you a hunger to be sated?" he asked suggestively. "A thirst to be quenched?"

"I have no interest in food or wine. Although I
am intrigued by the decadence."

She lifted those flame-blue eyes to his, and it took
every bit of resistance he could muster not to fall
headlong into the fire. Why was a woman with such
seductive powers coming to an establishment that
catered to the lonely wallflowers?

"Within this room, women are made to feel like
goddesses," she continued.

It pleased him that she understood the underly-
ing purpose of his efforts here. He grinned. "Hence
the reason we call it the Goddess Parlor."

"Did a woman help you design this place?"

He thought a touch of jealousy marred her tone,
but that could not be. They didn't know each other
well enough to spark emotions as volatile as that
between them. Although had she wanted to lounge
about within these walls, he might have found himself letting go any man who came near enough to
inhale her strawberry scent. "My sister-by-marriage
suggested the ladies would welcome being made to
feel special."

"Which one? Lady Aslyn or Lady Lavinia?"

Definitely nobility. She spoke the names as though
they were familiar to her tongue, and he fought not
to consider with what else he might wish to make
her tongue familiar. "Lavinia. Although she's dispensed with the use of *lady* before her name." Except
when she wrote scathing articles about the unjust
treatment of unwed mothers and children born on

the wrong side of the blanket. Then she embraced her place in Society, allowing it to serve her purpose and a greater good. "You seem to know a great deal about me."

"Your family is the talk of the *ton*."

"My family, but not me."

"Of course, you. How do you think I knew of this place? Why provide women with all this?"

"I have a gaming hell for men. Not as posh. Cards only. But every now and then a woman would come to play. Why shouldn't women have their own space in which to enjoy themselves? Why should they be relegated to evenings of needlework?"

"Because it is the proper thing to do."

"And you are proper, are you?"

"I have been. In the past."

"And now?"

"Not so much, obviously."

He detected a bit of remorse in her tone, perhaps even shame. It would lessen in time. She would become addicted to what he offered. He had yet to welcome a lady into his lair and not see her return. "You might not be in want of wine, but you should at least absorb the atmosphere of the parlor in a bit more comfort."

Chapter 2

$\mathscr{A}$s he began guiding her toward an immense ottoman in a back corner, she considered objecting, but her plans were dependent on retaining his interest. Besides, it would no doubt behoove her to become more comfortable with him. The velveteen-covered piece of furniture was larger than any ottoman she'd ever seen, designed to allow room for sprawling. He lowered her to its edge, and when she would have sat there primly and properly, he lifted her feet onto it, gently twisting her in such a way that she found herself lounging against a mound of pillows. She'd never been in a prone position with anyone other than her husband. "I'll get it dirty."

"It can be cleaned. Or we can remove your shoes." Unlike hers, his words came easily, as though he'd murmured them a thousand times.

She noticed then that several of the women had done exactly that, bare toes peering out from beneath skirts, stockinged feet clasped in attentive hands. "I'll leave them on." They wouldn't be here for long, surely.

He spoke to a footman before sitting so his hip

buttressed hers. She hated that she gave a little start at his nearness, wasn't acting nearly as sophisticated as she'd hoped she would.

"You're tense. Would you like me to rub your shoulders?"

Her gaze darted nervously to those large hands and strong fingers. "Not at the moment."

"Why are you tense, sweetheart?"

A different endearment, and she wondered how many he possessed, if he would use them all on her, if he used them on all the ladies, and she found herself wishing he would reserve one for her and her alone. Silly to expect to mean anything to him other than business. "The truth?"

"It's always easier to recall than a lie, should the subject come up again." He leaned back on his elbow, and with his free hand, he skimmed a finger along her calf. Only then did she realize her skirt had not fallen properly to cover her ankles as it should. Her first instinct was to shoo his hand away and tuck her toes up beneath the hem, effectively hiding what he should not be touching. But he would hopefully be touching a good deal more before the night was done.

Through her stocking she could feel the gentle and remarkably intimate swipe of his skin over hers. Swallowing, she strove not to become lost in the lovely sensations. She had to keep her head about her and not do anything improper in front of witnesses, no matter that she was disguised. "I've never done anything remotely naughty."

His gaze shifted from the exposed calf to her eyes. "Why tonight?"

Shaking her head, she was grateful the footman

interrupted the conversation by returning with a tray bearing a glass of red wine. Aiden Trewlove straightened, took the glass, and offered it to her. While she'd stated her lack of interest in it earlier, she decided a sip or two might go a long way toward calming her nerves. "Aren't you going to join me?"

"It wouldn't do for the owner to get foxed."

"I won't be getting foxed either." Still she sipped the wine, smiled at how smoothly it went down, how it warmed and gave her a sense of familiarity. "A fine vintage."

"My sister Gillie owns a tavern. She'd have my head if I didn't serve the best."

"She married the Duke of Thornley."

"Another detail with which you're familiar."

"As I said, you're all the talk."

He stretched back on his elbow. "Which puts me at a disadvantage as I know so little about you."

"You know nothing at all about me."

"I know you're someone's wife."

She tensed, but his finger again trailed along her calf, distracting her, easing her back toward a more comfortable place. "You're guessing."

"Although you're wearing gloves, I can see the outline of a ring on your left hand. You would have been wise to remove it before you came."

She should have, but she'd worn it for nearly seven years now, hadn't even thought about it. Unsettled to realize she hadn't taken the simplest of precautions to protect her identity, she took another sip, striving—

"A duke I'd wager."

And nearly choked on the wine. With a cough, she covered her mouth, barely aware of him taking the glass from her as she sought to regain control, to prevent the burgundy from killing her. Gently, he patted her back. When she was more herself, she took the glass from him, cautiously swallowed the rich wine to regain her equilibrium. "Why would you think that?"

"The manner in which you hold yourself as though everything is your due, the impression you give that you are in a place beneath you, a place in which you really have no interest, walking with a man who isn't good enough to polish your shoes."

"You are wrong there, Mr. Trewlove. I suspect you are applying your own prejudices to me. Not that I blame you, not if the rumors I've heard are true. They say your father is nobility."

On her calf, his fingers flexed as though she'd struck him a blow. "I don't talk of my sire. Ever."

So it was true. Noble blood ran through his veins, which worked well with her plans. "And I will not discuss my place in or out of Society," she said tartly. "So it seems regarding that aspect of our lives, we are of a like mind."

As he once more leaned back, his fingers returned to their trailing, going a tad higher with each stroke, growing dangerously close to her knee. So inappropriate and yet she sensed perhaps he was testing her, daring her to object. Or maybe he simply liked the feel of a woman's leg.

"If I were to extinguish the candles on either side of you, enshrouded you in darkness, you could remove your mask."

"Darkness is never absolute. Within this room, the mask remains. Besides, you'd be amazed by how observant some ladies are."

He studied her for the longest and then began working on the buttons of her shoes.

"I said they were to remain on." She would have kicked free if he hadn't closed one hand around her leg, just above her ankle, the moment she began to speak.

"You'll be more comfortable with them off. My floors are clean."

He glanced at her through half-lowered lids, just as he'd looked at the gathered nobility in the church, and she had an unreasonable desire for him not to find her lacking, not to think her a coward.

"When was the last time you went barefoot?"

Strange that she should recall it. "I was nine, and there was a field of clover that I simply couldn't resist." It had felt like running over velvet. She shook her head. "My governess had a time of it, keeping shoes on my feet."

But that day her mother had given her a blistering scolding, convincing her that she was too old for such nonsense. She'd kept her shoes on ever since. Disappointing her parents, disappointing anyone actually, had always made her feel rotten.

She sipped the last of the wine, finishing off the glass, and there was the footman offering her another. She took it, peered over at the man who seemed comfortable in spite of his awkward position, his feet remaining on the floor, and she wondered how he might react if she ordered him to place them on the ottoman, so she could remove his boots. Obviously the wine was having an effect on her, bolstering her courage. Although not completely. She gave a slight nod, and his fingers immediately returned to their endeavor.

When he'd removed her shoes, he handed them off to another footman who suddenly appeared. She assumed he'd somehow alerted the servant that he was needed although she'd seen no signal. "Give them to Angie, to be placed under my name."

"Yes, sir."

As the servant dashed off, Aiden Trewlove said, "You can pick them up in the foyer on your way out."

She'd left her cloak there on the way in, at a counter in front of a room teeming with wraps. The girl guarding things hadn't asked for her name but had merely given her a number. She wondered if they had a special place where they kept ladies' things that came to them in his name, wondered what items ladies might leave with him.

Suddenly she wasn't wondering anything at all as he stroked the side of his thumb along one instep before encasing her foot in both his hands, squeezing and kneading. So much better than clover against her soles. She rather wished she wasn't wearing stockings. Then immediately felt guilty for enjoying his ministrations so much.

"Where were you educated?" she asked, seeking to distract herself from the wicked way his fingers moved over her.

"The streets."

She shook her head. "You've had some schooling. I hear it in your speech."

"That's Gillie's doing. She's of the belief that speaking properly is the first step to moving up in the world. When we were younger, she worked for a woman who taught her how to rid herself of the Cockney. Gillie shared what she learned with all of us."

"If not for your reputation, one wouldn't know you came from the streets." She'd sought to compliment him, but he merely shrugged as though it was of no consequence to him what people thought. She wished she could say the same of herself. But her position in Society required that she care and never cause any embarrassment to her family.

"How is it that you chose to own a gambling hell?" She was truly curious about this man, who worked to make her feet feel lovely while never seeking to take his heavy-lidded gaze from her face.

"This evening is about you, darling, not me."

Those words melted her nearly as much as the press of his thumbs along the center of her sole. She couldn't remember the last time she'd been anyone's main focus, that her wants, needs, pleasure had taken precedence over another's. "If that is truly the case, it would please me to know your tale so surely you should share it."

He grinned such a masculine, sensual grin that she feared she'd find herself swimming in unchartered waters with this man. "That reasoning is a bit convoluted." With another shrug, he dipped his head to the side, held her gaze. "Ever played the shell game?"

"I don't believe so."

"The patterer—that's what you call the person who manages it because he talks the entire time—has three cups. He lets you see him put a pea or a ball or some other small object beneath one of the cups, then he starts moving them around quickly, talking, talking, and when he stops, he wagers an amount that you can't correctly identify where the pea is. You guess correctly, he pays you. You guess wrong, you pay him. Not a lot, usually. Three-pence, sixpence. Depends on the crowd, what it looks like they can afford."

"And you always guessed correctly where the pea was."

That grin again that did funny things to her chest, made it tighten until it was difficult to breathe. "I *was* the patterer and always knew exactly where the pea was. Right in the palm of my hand. So no matter which cup they picked, they were wrong. As I was lifting the cup under which the pea was supposedly hidden, I would slip it into place. 'Sorry, mate, here it is,' I'd say and collect the winnings."

"You cheated." She was horrified at the thought, even more horrified that she was impressed with his strategy and quick sleight of hand.

He chuckled darkly. "Of course I did."

"That's how you made enough money to finance your business? On ill-gotten gains?"

She seemed to be amusing him because his smile got even broader. "No. I had this rickety little table with one leg in its center that I carried around with me, so I was always on the move, going from one place to another. Had my three cups, had my pea. One day a crowd had gathered. This bloke comes up, dressed all fancy. Red brocade waistcoat. I remember that the most, being impressed by the waistcoat and judging him on it. I was eleven. Had been doing my trick quite successfully for a while, was full of myself. Decided this toff had money. I was going to take him for a guinea. I laid out my terms, and he agreed to them.

"So I went through my little routine. Showed him the pea going under the cup, palmed the pea, shuffled the cups fast, egging him on, 'Where's the pea? Where's the pea?' I stop. 'Where do you think it is, guv?' I fairly crowed. He lifted a cup, and damned if there wasn't a pea beneath it."

She released a quick burst of laughter, taken off guard by the profanity he voiced so casually in her presence—no one ever used foul language in her vicinity—and the self-mocking look he gave her, as though he understood he deserved getting caught in his arrogance. "He was a swindler as well?"

He nodded. "He grew up on the streets, knew the game. Brought his own pea and slipped it into place as he was lifting his cup. I couldn't very well call him out for a cheat without exposing my own trick."

"So you had to pay him an entire guinea?"

He shook his head. "He told me, 'Never let the mark lift the cup himself.' He'd been watching me for some time apparently. Introduced himself. Jack Dodger he was."

Her eyes widened. "Not *the* Jack Dodger?" One of the wealthiest men in London, in all of Great Britain for that matter.

He nodded. "Indeed. I went to work at his gaming hell, Dodger's Drawing Room, learning my way around proper gaming. Eventually I became a dealer, the youngest they'd ever had. But I wanted to be the one standing in the balcony looking down on my domain, not standing on the floor being watched. So when I was nineteen I struck out on my own. I didn't think it was right to go into competition against a man to whom I owed so much, so I opened the Cerberus Club in Whitechapel, more for the dregs than the posh, but dregs have coins, too. And not all the nobility is welcomed in the finer circles."

"And from there you decided women needed a place as well."

"I can't take credit for that. It was my brother's idea, but his heart was never truly in it, so he gave the place to me."

"Gave it to you? Without recompense? Just like that?"

"He felt he owed me."

"Why?"

"Ah, darling, that's another story entirely." Abandoning her feet, he straightened and leaned toward her. "Now you need to tell me a tale. What brought you here tonight?"

"A CARRIAGE."

He chuckled low at her quick response, her deliberate failure to properly address his question. This one was full of secrets. He'd wager the entirety of tonight's take on it. He couldn't figure out what it was about her that drew his attention, that kept him at her side. Normally, he didn't linger with the ladies, having no desire to make any of them jealous—jealousy was bad for business. But for some odd reason, he couldn't seem to tear himself away from her. Perhaps it was the sadness in her eyes, or her discomfort. Most women had excitement thrumming through them when they came here, but with her, it was as though she had no interest in the place but felt compelled to be within these walls. She was searching for something, thought she'd find it here, but he could have told her no treasures resided within these rooms. They provided only momentary escapes. There was value in that, but it was always fleeting. Which was the reason people returned. Because the joy they found here could not be taken with them. It always dissipated once they exited.

Which was good for business. Ensured they'd return.

A footman came by, refilled her wineglass, and went on his way. She didn't object, and he suspected she was beginning to feel a bit more relaxed. Reaching for her free hand, he began rolling her glove down past her elbow. Why did ladies wear frocks that exposed their arms and then add an accessory to hide them?

"What are you doing?" she asked, and he heard a measure of alarm in her voice.

"Gloves are a nuisance."

She closed her fingers into an ineffectual fist. "Please don't remove them."

He thought of the ring that might be recognizable to those who knew her. "We could place your ring inside one of the gloves. It would be safe there. We have no thieves here. Or I could tuck it into one of my pockets."

She shook her head, and he wondered about the man who had placed it on her finger, and how she wanted it to remain there. If she loved him, would she be here? Hell, Lady Aslyn visited on occasion and she adored his brother. Sometimes a lady just needed to escape for a while.

He rolled the glove back into place, trailing his finger along the soft flesh of the inside of her arm where the glove did not reach. "I'm waiting, sweetheart, for your story."

She brought the glass to her lips, delaying the telling, and he rather regretted not deigning to join her, but he did have a rule about not becoming overly familiar with his guests because fraternizing too much wasn't good for business. Like his siblings, he was very much aware that his fortunes rested on taking care of his enterprises. Those in his family were born of scandal, and it still dogged their heels, and while he sometimes skirted the edge of impropriety, he didn't do it here, never here. Yet she tempted him in ways no other woman ever had.

After licking her lips, she turned her attention to the shadows. "I told you of the clover."

"You've more interesting tales than that."

Her gaze swung back around to him. "Not really. It's the reason I'm here."

Not for a single minute did he believe she was as boring as all that, but he also knew when not to push. "Finish off your wine. I'll show you another room of entertainment."

He liked watching the way her delicate throat muscles worked as she swallowed. There was not a solitary aspect to her that did not draw him in. He wondered if he took her to a room cloaked in blackness if she would remove the mask and allow him to outline her features with his fingertips. He'd always had a knack for drawing things and thought if he traced her features, he could transfer them to paper.

She'd barely gathered the last drop on her tongue when a handsome lad—they were all handsome; Lavinia had convinced him the ladies would appreciate fine scenery wandering through the establishment—barely twenty was taking her empty glass and offering her a full one.

"We're done here," he told the servant, surprised by the gruffness of his tone, the curtness of it.

Jasper must have been surprised as well because his eyes widened considerably before he gave a quick bob of his head and made a hasty retreat.

Aiden felt her speculating gaze on him, more than he saw it. He had an urge to apologize to her, to the lad, but he was not in the habit of apologizing, and an apology might lead to him having to confess he didn't much like the idea of any of his lads fawning over her—even though that's what he paid them to do. Make the ladies feel special so they would return in order to feel special again.

"I'll need my shoes." She surprised him by her absence of a comment on his earlier reaction.

"No, you won't. As I said, the floor is clean. Why close those lovely feet in leather when there is no need?"

Standing, he took her hand and helped her rise to her feet. Without her shoes, the top of her head came to his shoulder, and he didn't want to consider how much he might like tucking her cheek into the curve there, an odd thought for a man who never tucked women in close. He liked them well enough, enjoyed their company immensely, but wasn't one for offering hugs when they were in need of them. Tears usually had him searching for the nearest escape. He didn't simply hold and comfort for the sake of simply holding and comforting. He liked having a jolly good time.

Tonight he was not acting himself: lounging about with a woman, giving her attention, excluding all others. Perhaps it was merely the mystery of her. But others wore masks and he wasn't slavering to know details about them. He should hand her off to one of the attention-givers but he feared he'd then find fault with how much attention the gent was giving her. If it wasn't enough, he'd be angry because she was doing without. If too much was lavished upon her, he'd be furious because he wasn't the one doing the lavishing.

If she was aware of his rioting thoughts, she gave no indication, merely tucked her hand into the crook of his elbow as though it belonged there. The wine had done the trick. She was more relaxed, more at ease. Strange how he was suddenly more tense.

Taking his time, he guided her into the next room, one that Lavinia had insisted would appeal to the ladies, one he referred to in private as the Wallflower Parlor, although to his guests it was merely a ballroom, like any other they'd visited before, but within these walls they were guaranteed a waltz with a charming gent. Although he'd have preferred to provide employment for the poorer among them, he'd needed fellows of a certain caliber to entertain his ladies, men who spoke with a bit of polish and knew how to dress to please in jackets, waistcoats, and cravats. Most of his visible male staff had been trained to take a position in some posh house as a footman. Here they earned double what they would have elsewhere.

"I'd not expected dancing," she murmured.

A few ladies lined the edge of the dance floor,

awaiting their turn, knowing they would soon circle about the floor. No female here was ever neglected.

"Perhaps you would care for a waltz?" He never danced with his patrons, but he wanted to hold her in his arms, sweep her over the polished parquetry. The fact that he'd never waltzed in his life would hardly serve as a deterrent to something he desired. Lavinia had taught him the basics, thinking it might come in useful at some point, that he might wish to dance with one of his guests. He hated to give her credit for being correct. While she was now his sister-by-marriage, he was still struggling to forgive her completely for the horrid past she'd wrought upon his brother.

Selena shook her head. "I am not here to dance."

"You have no interest in gaming, in feasting, in dancing. Why are you here then, darling?"

With a bit of obstinance and daring, she met and held his gaze. "I am here to be bedded."

Chapter 3

Growing up in the rookeries had taught him to never show exactly what he felt so he didn't allow so much as a muscle in his cheek to tic, but the bluntness of her words took him off guard. As did the fact that she continued to hold his gaze as though she hadn't said something outrageous. He wanted to tear off the damn mask and see if she was blushing. If she was, it was only her cheeks because her chin remained a pale alabaster, with no hint whatsoever of pink or a warming.

He didn't like at all the singular purpose for which she'd come to his club, and the irony was not lost on him. He reveled in sin, enjoyed his role in introducing people to vice. It was unlikely he was headed to heaven and so he fully intended to enjoy the ride that would deliver him to hell. He understood people had urges, had never understood why fault was found with people satisfying those urges—in or out of marriage.

Yet at that moment he wanted her to be more discerning in her tastes, her desires. He didn't want her interested in the act alone. He wanted her interested in engaging in the act because of how madly she was drawn to someone in particular, drawn to him. What the devil was the matter with him?

"If you look closely, you'll see that some of the gents wear a red button on their left lapel. They will provide that service for you." He said the words flatly and yet an unwelcomed tightness was building within him like a volcano on the verge of erupting.

"I'm not interested in them. You intrigue me, Mr. Trewlove. You are the one I want."

"Alas, I do not mix business and pleasure." It nearly killed him to say the words.

"Consider it all business."

"I do not involve myself with my clientele."

"I'm not asking you to involve yourself. I'm asking you to bed me."

He was accustomed to being the one in pursuit, not the one pursued. While he appreciated her boldness, was quite taken with it if he was honest, it did make him feel uncentered. It wasn't that he didn't *want* to bed her. It was simply that he was wary of her motives. Did ladies in whom he showed an interest feel the same, worry they might be left with regrets?

Was it even possible to bed her without involving himself? Certainly he'd had encounters that were designed to merely slake lust, but she seemed a lady deserving of more. Did she fully comprehend the loneliness that could strike when the body was replete, but nothing called to the soul? It was an odd thing, having just met her, to realize he didn't want to bed her and then be done with it. He wanted a bit more time to explore the possibilities of her.

"We can stand here and debate or we can waltz

and debate." Bowing slightly, mockingly, if truth be told, he waved toward the dance floor. "Shall we?"

"I'm not wearing shoes."

"All the better."

How OFTEN HAD she considered slipping off her slippers, certain the flow of her skirts would keep her bare feet hidden while she danced? She abhorred shoes, the manner in which they confined, often causing her toes to pinch. So the freedom she now had was as delightful as she'd always thought it would be, with her soles skimming over the polished wood as he swept her over the floor.

It didn't hurt that a handsome man whose gaze never wavered from her was the one doing the sweeping.

"I shocked you with my bluntness." Had shocked herself, truth be told. She hadn't meant to blurt it out, had intended to be a bit more subtle in gaining what she required.

"Not shocked. Surprised, more like. Certainly you're not the first to come here wanting to dive into the more unforgiving of sins. Unhappy wives, lonely widows, doomed spinsters. Why not spend a night dancing with the devil?"

"I don't believe the devil would have rebuffed me."

"I am too familiar with temptation, vice, and addiction. I do not gamble at my own tables. I do not drink of my own spirits. I do not lounge upon my own ottomans. Until this moment, I've never waltzed upon my own floor."

She offered him a small, tentative smile. "So you are open to making exceptions."

"It would appear so."

Laughter nearly erupted from her. It had been too long since she'd had a good laugh. "You don't have to sound so disgruntled."

"I'm curious. Have you ever been told you're beautiful?"

"So many times that the word has lost all meaning."

"Did you marry for love?"

"I did not."

"He does not satisfy you?"

"Can a woman be satisfied?"

"With proper bedding. And a proper bedding begins with seduction." With the slightest of pressure from his hand splayed over her lower back, he urged her nearer until his legs were brushing against her skirts and her toes were coming dangerously close to his boots, but she trusted him not to step on them, not to send her hobbling home.

"You've been seducing me since you approached me in the corner."

One side of his mouth hitched up. "Before that, I'd wager."

She smiled fully then; she couldn't help it. "Your earlier strutting through the gaming floor? Was that for my benefit?"

"You noticed me, didn't you?" He shook his head as a small self-deprecating grin formed. "You're making me break all my rules."

"You don't strike me as one who adheres to rules."

"I was striving to turn over a new leaf. To become respectable."

"Respectability is overrated."

"And you know that because you are so disreputable?"

"I know that because I *want* to be so disreputable. I have observed propriety my entire life. It grows wearisome."

"I have another rule, sweetheart. I don't bed married women. That one I have never broken."

"Fortunate for me, then, that I'm a widow." Not so fortunate really. If she wasn't a widow, she wouldn't be here, wouldn't have sought him out. She hadn't meant to confess the truth of her marital status, but even if he'd read Lushing's obituary in the newspaper, it was unlikely he would associate the duke with her, for surely he would not expect a woman only three days a widow to come so soon to a house of sin. Still, the less he knew or suspected about her, the better. She didn't know why she found herself telling him things she shouldn't. She'd learned early on, from the cradle, to hold her thoughts to herself and never reveal her true opinions or feelings, and yet here she was blathering on like a fishmonger's wife who wouldn't soon find herself facing consequences.

On the other hand, where was the harm in what she'd revealed? Even if he managed to discern exactly who she was, he didn't have the power to interfere with her plans. Besides, she was accustomed to having her way in most things. It was a privilege of her rank, and she'd discerned she wanted him. Why was he playing so hard to get? It was her experience that men were ruled by their baser instincts and nothing was baser than the need to see to their cocks. Why was he being so blasted difficult? Why hadn't he immediately escorted her to a darkened room and lifted her skirts? More irritating than his apparent lack of interest was the sympathy that plunged into the depths of his brown eyes.

"How long?" he asked.

"It's of no consequence."

"Do you miss him?"

At that particular moment, she missed the silence of him, the fact that he'd never bombarded her with questions in an attempt to discern every facet of her. "Have you no interest in bedding me?" Her voice held her impatience. She'd come here for a purpose, and he was delaying it.

His long fingers splayed against her back, dug in, and claimed as he brought her scandalously nearer, until his thigh was practically nestled between both of hers and she feared his feet might become entangled in the hem of her skirts. But apparently he was too light-footed for that disaster to occur, knew precisely what he was about, had calculated exactly how closely he could hold her without causing any mishap. Or perhaps it was simply at that moment they seemed to be one and the same. Strange how she felt as though she was sharing a familiarity far more intimate than anything she'd experienced in a bed.

"You deserve better than to be bedded." His low voice thrummed through every nerve ending she possessed. "You warrant a scandalous and thorough seduction."

His eyes locked with hers, offering a promise she didn't know if she had the courage to accept. She couldn't draw in a single breath. Suddenly coming here seemed an incredibly reckless venture, yet in spite of the pounding of her heart, which she was rather certain he could feel traveling all the way to her fingertips, she couldn't bring herself to break free and leave. She was all of twenty-five and not once, in all her years upon this earth, had she ever been *thoroughly* seduced. She couldn't even claim to have been slightly seduced.

The final strains of the tune wafted on the air, lingering like the scent of a flower whose blossom had closed up for the night. They ceased their movements, but he didn't loosen his hold one iota. "You don't know me." Her voice sounded raw, as though she'd not used it in ages. "You can't know what I warrant."

"Every woman merits more than a bedding. Each is deserving of seduction. All that said, I suspect I know you far better than you think."

She was grateful the mask hid her reaction, that he couldn't see how much she longed for someone to truly know her, to be aware of her thoughts, fears, and dreams.

"As for your earlier question regarding my interest in bedding you—rest assured it is strong and powerful. If you were to turn your attentions to another man here, I might, regretfully, find myself having to kill him."

She was remarkably ashamed of the satisfaction that swept through her because he might be jealous of another.

Another tune started up, and he was again gliding her over the floor. She had danced with gentlemen more accomplished and polished when it came to the waltz, but it had all been merely movement and motion, adhering to the formalities of the steps. His style was more feral, raw, and alluring. He held her gaze as though to look away would signal defeat. Their proximity to each other was scandalously close, not that it truly mattered here. There was an earthiness, a primitiveness to the way all the couples moved in tandem around the ballroom. Out of the corner of her eye, she could see how each of the other gents looked at his partner as though she hung the moon and the stars.

But Aiden Trewlove had perfected his regard to reflect that of a man truly smitten. Even if only for a moment, the length of a dance, a woman felt treasured. *She* felt treasured. She hadn't expected that tonight, didn't want it. It made her feel weak when it was imperative that she remain strong in order to do what needed to be done.

"Odd that you wouldn't remove your gloves, that you rejected the notion of my bare hands touching yours when you're here in hopes that my palms will caress all of you," he said quietly. "Imagine how much nicer this would be without the silk separating us."

Suddenly, she imagined it, wildly and provocatively. She rather feared her heart, which continued to beat erratically, might very well give out before the night was done. Her death would certainly serve no one, least of all herself, well. If anything, it would merely compound the guilt she would take with her to heaven. If that was where the angels carried her, although it was quite likely after tonight's escapade that they'd merely dump her in hell. Which she'd feared until an hour ago. Now, however, she found some comfort in the prospect of arriving there, because she was quite certain it would be his final destination as well. She could imagine him laughing uproariously, delighted by his surroundings, and driving the devil to distraction. She rather wanted to witness all that.

"One can be bedded without removing all of one's

garments," she informed him as haughtily and learnedly as possible. Lushing had certainly never required all garments be removed, so exactly how was Aiden Trewlove going to caress *all* of her? With those palms. The one that cradled her hand as though it were a fragile bird. The one that covered a good bit of her lower back.

His grin was saucy and daring. "Where's the fun in that?"

She almost asked if there was fun to be had in bedding. For her, it had always been more of a chore, a duty, a requirement of marriage. She was here hoping for something more but was at a bit of a loss as to exactly what that *more* might consist of. Caressing bare skin. *Caressing. Bare. Skin.* The words seemed trapped in her mind as though they were riding on a roundabout.

From the caressing and holding he'd done so far, she could tell his hands were roughened by his labors, whatever they might entail. But they were also clean, well manicured. He had a scar that ran along the side of his forefinger and onto the back of his hand. Thin, raised, white. He'd had it for a time. She wondered how it had come to be.

Would his seduction involve the exchange of more stories? She rather thought so, rather hoped so.

The music again ceased playing, a signal for others to change partners, while he simply continued to hold her, waiting patiently for when they could begin moving again. In a ballroom, three dances with the same gentleman would be scandalous. Here it was nothing at all. She was neither concerned about it nor worried over her reputation. "How many more dances?" she asked.

"One."

"And then?"

"I'm going to kiss you until your knees grow weak."

HER EYES FLARED slightly, her lips parted, and his cock reacted as though she'd reached down and slid her fingers along the entire length of it. Christ, what the devil was wrong with him? He enjoyed women but had never lost his head over one, yet something about her called to the baser instincts in him, the Neanderthal who wanted to claim and protect—and yes, strike down any other man who touched her.

He'd been a stranger to jealousy until her, and now that the emotion had introduced itself, he didn't much like it nor did he understand why it was gadding about. She was correct. He knew her not at all. To feel anything toward her other than mild curiosity was foolish beyond measure.

Other women wore masks in his place. A few had still never removed theirs. But the mystery of them didn't intrigue him. She did. Immensely. Irrevocably. Intensely. He wanted to know everything about her, inside and out.

No, he did not. He wanted to seduce her, bed her, forget her. As easily as she apparently planned to forget him. And there was the rub, the reason seduction was required—because he wanted her begging for it, recalling him with her final breath no matter how many gents came after him.

She claimed to want to be bedded, and the way she'd said it with no emotion whatsoever, as though it was a given that he'd jump to do her bidding, had at once intrigued and angered him. Aiden Trewlove did not bend to the will of the nobility. Unlike his mother, he would not be *used* for their pleasure. He might provide pleasure, but it was always on *his* terms and his terms alone. He knew nothing at all about his mother but had gleaned enough about his sire to know the poor woman probably had little say in the arrangement. The same could not be said of him. He was always in control, always in charge, always had ultimate say.

He might not have had any choice in what they did with him when he was born, but by God, he had absolute control now. No one dictated his actions, save himself.

He wondered if the woman standing before him had once had no choice either, if perhaps it was the reason she was here, because now as a widow she had the power to determine her destiny and her activities. So she sought what she'd never had: passion.

For surely she wanted more than an emotionless coupling.

"My knees are quite steady," she finally said, and he couldn't prevent himself from grinning at how long it had taken her to recover from his vow and to come up with a retort.

"I intend to turn them to jam."

Her pink tongue darted out and licked the lower lip he fully intended to devour shortly.

"You're quite cocky."

"It's the reason you chose me."

"I will admit to finding you fascinating."

"Have we met before?" He didn't think so. He'd have remembered that mouth, the shape of it, the full lower lip that gave the impression of being in a permanent pout, the bow shape of the upper lip, thinner, half the plumpness of the lower. Her mouth would provide a nice cushion for his.

"No, but I've seen you from afar, heard tales of your . . . prowess."

"I have a policy of kissing but never telling. I'd always assumed ladies, especially those who wandered about above the riffraff, kept their affairs secret."

"No one has ever spilled any secrets. It's simply the way your name is always spoken on a sigh that led me to believe you had hidden talents. Then, of course, there is all this. Why provide such decadence if you're not willing to partake?"

"Perhaps my preference is to simply watch from the shadows."

"An onlooker?" She shook her head. "No, I see you as an active participant. There's too much maleness in you."

AND THAT MALENESS was directed at her with a smoldering gaze that nearly had her tripping over her feet. She was accustomed to lighthearted banter and flirtation, not looks through half-lowered lids that had every pore in her body steaming, every inch of her skin sweltering, her nipples puckering, and the secretive place between her legs begging for her to crush it up against something, against him. His hand. His thigh. His crotch.

Dear God, where had those thoughts come from?

As though her body had written its needs across her pupils, he shifted his hand until the edge of his palm rested against the lower portion of her back and pressed her slightly, with just enough force, enough determination that she was keenly aware that his body was reacting with needs similar to hers.

Her earlier question was unerringly answered. He was interested in bedding her. Desperately, if the hardness that greeted her was any indication.

Then he eased away, leaving her to wonder if he'd been teasing her or staking a claim. The latter she decided. A man who threatened bodily harm to his employees was not one to reveal his desires unless he was assured that they'd be reciprocated.

The music finally came to a halt, and so did they. This time they didn't wait about. Instead, he placed her hand snugly in the crook of his elbow and led her from the dance floor, from the room, into a darkened corridor, and swept her along a maze of rooms, hallways, and passages. He was intimately familiar with every inch of them as he needed no light to guide him. Strange how she didn't hesitate to follow, how her steps were as sure as his. She trusted him. It was an odd sensation to give herself wholly over into a near-stranger's keeping.

She'd spent a good bit of her life wary of people's motives but had no cause to be suspicious of his. He might manage a den of vice, but he was honest in what he offered—and he'd been honest with what he was on the verge of delivering. No games from him.

She wished she could claim the same.

The echo of grinding metal alerted her he was opening a door. The action barely slowed him as he pushed the wood aside, creating a crevasse through which he pulled her into a dimly lit hallway. She hardly had time to note doors beyond them before he was escorting her up a set of stairs lit with sconces here and there.

At the landing, she could see more stairs beyond, but he ignored them and dragged her through an open doorway into another corridor and then into a room that contained a red velveteen fainting couch. He released his hold on her and she wandered farther inside. Paintings—nudes—of solitary women, solitary men, couples, and groups adorned the walls. Suggestive statuettes of naked couples caressing or kissing were nestled in the corners.

The snick of a door closing, being locked, caused her to swing around. His arms crossed over his chest, he leaned against the door and simply watched, waited.

She turned her attention back to the fainting couch. For some reason, she'd assumed he'd require a massive bed, that they would loll about in it and—well, her imagination had never taken her beyond the lolling. The couch seemed inadequate. Was it even called being bedded when it was done on a fainting couch? Or was it being *fainting couched*?

He was the expert, she the novice, in spite of her seven years of marriage.

"Not exactly what I was expecting," she said honestly, facing him.

"I thought you'd appreciate the couch when your knees give way."

"As I mentioned before, my knees are made of stern stuff."

His grin was cocky and all male. "Never challenge me, sweetheart, unless you're willing to deal with the consequences. Remove the mask."

"No." She stated it firmly, resolutely.

"There's no one here to see you, to recognize you."

He would see her, although he probably wouldn't know precisely who she was. Still, she suddenly felt a need to remain incognito. Baring her face would make her too vulnerable, would make her feel exposed. What she was doing was wrong on so many levels, and she needed to remain as secretive about it as possible. "I can't."

She'd expected him to give her an ultimatum, to force her to remove it in order to gain what she wanted. Instead, he merely pushed himself away from the door and prowled toward her, determination darkening his eyes.

Quite suddenly, she rather wished she'd moved nearer to the couch because the desire, the want, the need reflected in his expression already had her knees threatening to buckle.

Then his hands were gently cradling her jaw, his thumbs meeting at the shallow dimple in her chin, creating the top part of a heart turned upside down as he held her. It was silly to keep the mask on, and yet it afforded some sort of protection, some sense that she was in charge, when the reality was that she hadn't been since the moment he'd approached her. No, before that. From the moment he'd begun striding toward her. That was his power, his strength, his allure. He took command and held on to it.

That thought alone was enough to have her knees weakening. She'd never been so close to a man who seemed fully capable of ruling hearts. She would not give him hers. All she would grant him was use of her body, and in giving him that, she would be using him as well.

Holding her gaze, he lowered his head only a

fraction, and she ceased to breathe as her stomach quivered in anticipation. She licked her lips, taking satisfaction as his gaze dropped to her tongue, dampening what he would soon be tasting. Strange how the smoldering in his eyes made her feel powerful, allowed her to regain some control.

But when his mouth landed on hers, she realized it had all been an illusion. She had no control, whatsoever. No thought, no scheming, no goals—only taking pleasure from this simple exercise, a mating of lips and tongue, breaths and sighs. His fingers skimmed along her jaw, her chin, over and over, as though he sought to permanently embed their shape within his palms. Their goal accomplished, his hands glided along her throat, over her shoulders, and down her back, pressing her nearer as his arms cocooned around her. Hers circled his waist, her hands spreading wide over his broad back, and she resented the coat he wore that prevented her from outlining the corded muscles she was rather certain composed him. But that opportunity would come shortly, for surely he would at least divest himself of his jacket before taking her completely.

But that was for later. For now there was only the kiss proving all her previous claims regarding the makeup of her knees to be false as he plundered, slowly, sensually, thoroughly. The man knew his way well around a woman's mouth, knew how to explore, how to titillate, how to come to know it intimately. She suspected he could sketch the inside of her mouth to perfection should he put his mind to it. He left not so much as a hairbreadth unmapped. All the while, he gave her the freedom to learn all the textures that made up this one aspect of him.

Roughness, silkiness, hardness, softness. She took delight in each discovery as their tongues parried, not with animosity, not as though they were embroiled in battle, but as though they were engaged in an ancient ritual, the start of a journey that would prove them equals.

His actions struck at her poet's heart, brought to life yearnings she'd never before dared to awaken. She'd known they were there, but she'd hidden them away, forced them into slumber for fear she'd offend her husband if he knew the hunger that gnawed at her in the quiet hours of the night when she'd lain alone in her bed, after he left, when the tears would fall.

She stumbled because her legs, blast them, did give out. Without moving his mouth from hers, he easily lifted her into his arms and carried her the short distance to the fainting couch where he laid her down, knelt on the floor beside her, and continued to ravish her mouth. His groans echoed around her, reverberated through her as he held her with one arm positioned at her back so her chest met his, his other hand cradling her head to give him the angle he needed. She didn't want to consider how many women he might have kissed in order to perfect this move.

All she wanted was to take advantage of it.

She'd always thought kisses were a perfunctory thing, a greeting to the day, a signal one was retiring for the night. But he made it involve all the senses, all aspects of her body, not just her mouth and her traitorous knees, but her curling toes, and her dampening core, and her erratic heart.

He dragged his mouth along her face where

mask gave way to flesh, then along her throat, over her collarbone. She whimpered when he nipped at the swell of her breast. When he closed his mouth over her nipple through her clothing, the remainder of her body melted.

He went still, so still. She was certain he continued to breathe, because she felt his hot breath penetrating the cloth, moisture gathering around her nipple. Then he eased back, cradled her face once more, and held her gaze. "It's time for you to leave, sweetheart."

She shook her head. "But you haven't bedded me."

"How very astute you are."

"Isn't that the purpose of this room? Isn't this where the men with the red buttons bring the ladies to bed them?"

"It's where they bring the ladies who want to be kissed thoroughly. It's where they bring the ladies who want to be fondled."

"And those who wish to be bedded?"

"We have other rooms for that, rooms with large accommodating beds."

"So that's where you'll take me now."

"No."

"But I want to be bedded. I've told you that, confessed to it. I won't object to your taking me."

"You might want it, sweetheart, but you don't desire it. I won't take you to a bed until you do."

Chapter 4

$\mathcal{W}$hat he did do, however, was escort her to her carriage. It carried no markings, had been one her husband used on occasion when he wished to go someplace where he didn't want his identity or title known. Aiden Trewlove kept his arm around her the entire way, with her snuggled against his side as though he were reluctant to be rid of her. She liked thinking that perhaps he was.

He gave her another kiss, this one on the back of her gloved hand, before assisting her into the carriage where she settled in against the comfortable squabs. Lushing had been a stickler for comfort.

Aiden Trewlove leaned against the frame of the doorway and studied her. Or perhaps he was striving to find a way to invite her back in that wouldn't wound his pride. "If you still want to be bedded on the morrow, return here."

As though her request had been a lark and she'd change her mind with the arrival of more time. "You vastly overestimate your appeal, Mr. Trewlove. You rejected my offer. I'm not likely to come crawling back."

He gave her another one of those saucy grins that were beginning to irritate her, even as they caused her heart to flutter. "We'll see how you feel tomorrow after taking me into your dreams tonight."

With that, he slammed the door shut, shouted up an order, and the horses bolted forward. It took everything within her not to crane her head out the window and watch as her increasing distance from him caused him to shrink and disappear into nothing.

AFTER ARRIVING AT the residence, still in somewhat of a daze from the fervent kiss Aiden Trewlove had delivered, she removed the key from her reticule and unlocked the front door. The expanse of gardens, brick walls, hedgerows, and trees surrounding her would prevent any prying neighbor from catching a glimpse of her. Although at this time of night, it was unlikely anyone was awake to peer out of a window. The only ones who knew she'd gone out were her lady's maid, Bailey, who had helped her dress, and the driver who had taken her to the notorious club. She trusted them to be discreet and keep her confidence.

With the laces of her mask threaded through her fingers, she made her way up the stairs, her mind replaying those breathless moments spent within the arms of the club owner. Who would have thought that a kiss could be so encompassing?

She must have kissed Lushing a thousand times, but she'd never opened her mouth to him, and he'd most certainly never thrust his tongue between her lips and claimed everything within, claimed her. Was it because Aiden Trewlove was a commoner that he took such liberties? Were those in her station simply too civilized to respond in such an animalistic manner?

Opening the door to her bedchamber, she walked in, closed it, and leaned against the mahogany, remembering how Aiden had done the same. She glanced toward the bed, illuminated by a solitary lamp left burning on the bedside table. With a sigh, she realized she needed a moment to gain the wherewithal to prepare for slumber. She wondered what Aiden had been preparing for when he'd leaned against the door—not to ravage her perhaps. Her lips spread into the barest hint of a smile. She'd never before felt desired. It was an incredible—

"Did you have success at getting bedded?"

With a tiny screech, she jerked her gaze to the darkened corner where her brother sat, only his outstretched legs visible. She didn't hide her displeasure as she marched over to her vanity, set the mask on it, and began tugging off her gloves. "What are you doing in here?"

The Earl of Camberley slowly pushed himself to his feet. All of twenty-seven, he was not a towering man, and yet he had inherited their father's ability to appear intimidating. Although she had no doubt Aiden Trewlove would brush him away as though he were merely a pesky fly buzzing about. "Making sure you saw to your duty."

She suspected her brother had mourned her husband's passing more than anyone, because standing at the foot of the bed, watching as the Duke of Lushing drew his last breath, he'd looked over at her and said, "Pray tell me you are with child, lest we be ruined."

She couldn't tell him what he wished. For seven

years, in spite of her husband occasionally coming to her bed, she remained barren. Without a male heir, the title would become extinct and the entailed properties would pass to Her Majesty's Treasury. It seemed her husband and what few relations he'd possessed had not excelled at procreating or surviving long. Perhaps a man as virile as Mr. Trewlove might have better luck at giving her what she required.

Because her family, in spite of her brother's title, was as poor as dirt. And she had a very short time in which to get herself with child. She could still claim it as the duke's if it arrived ten months after his death. Babies sometimes arrived late. But after that . . .

And if it were a daughter, while the title would still become extinct, the girl would eventually inherit all the entailed properties because the terms of the entailment allowed it to go to a female if she had a direct bloodline to the first duke—which Selena would ensure the world believed she did.

What Selena was considering was deceitful and without honor, but she had need of the estates while the Crown did not. If Lushing had been content for everything to be handed over to the Treasury, he would never have married her, wouldn't have tried to get her with babe. He had worked hard to ensure his properties were the finest in all of England. Surely he wanted to see his legacy carried on. Where was the harm in the world believing the child had come from his loins?

She had always been a good and faithful wife. When the cold winds had blown across the moors and the snows had fallen and he had taken ill, she had nursed him hour upon hour, wiping the sweat from his brow, changing his nightshirt when it became damp, encouraging him to eat, reading to him until she was hoarse. She truly mourned the loss of him, riddled with guilt because she'd failed to give him the one thing he asked of her: an heir.

Sitting on the cushioned bench, she began pulling pins from her hair while glaring at her brother's reflection in the mirror. "Perhaps we'd all be better served if you'd attend to your duties as I'm well aware of mine."

"See that you are." He headed for the door.

"Winslow?"

He stopped but didn't look back at her. Their father had brought the family to ruin with his inability to make wise investments, his reckless spending and gambling, and his penchant for brandy. Lushing had money to burn but he'd been frugal—probably the reason he'd had so much squirreled away. While he'd been willing to help her family to a certain extent, it hadn't been enough to see them well situated.

The trustees of the entailment were presently limiting funds until it was known if she carried an heir. Apparently, they didn't want her absconding with what they didn't consider legally hers. "If anyone learns of this—"

"No one is going to learn of it," he said impatiently. "Only you and I know you are not presently with child. Only you and I know you will rectify that within the next week or so. As long as your lover doesn't realize your womb was empty when you came to him . . . and if he does suspect, it will be his word against ours. Who will give any credence to the ramblings of a commoner? You did go with a commoner, didn't you?"

She nodded. Unfortunately, she'd chosen a very smart and clever one.

"I do hope it wasn't too unpleasant for you. It may take more than once, you know."

"I'm well aware."

He suddenly appeared uncomfortable, the first time he'd seemed so since he'd cooked up this scheme. "Take strength from the fact that we're doing this for the girls."

The girls. Her three sisters. The twins, who were eighteen, and Alice, who was sixteen. She wanted them to have the choice she'd never had, wanted them to be able to marry for love.

She glanced down at her hands, surprised to find them knotted so tightly in her lap. "What if I'm barren?" The words were barely a whisper, but the fear had dogged her heels for some years now. Her husband had frequented her bed less often as their efforts failed to get her with child. The last few months, he'd not come to her at all.

"Mother wasn't. She gave birth to seven children."

Although two had died in infancy. They had come after Selena was born and before the twins, which was the reason so many years separated Selena from her sisters. "I'm not certain that a vibrant womb is handed down from one generation to the next."

"The fault could have rested with him. It's not as though his family tree is teeming with descendants, at least not on his father's side. Which is the reason you are now in a position to lose everything—or ensure that you hold on to it."

By passing another man's child off as Lushing's.

The deception didn't sit well with her, but their resources and recourses were so limited.

"Was the club as decadent as Torie claims?" She was taken aback by his abrupt change in topic and the way his eagerness to know the truth of the establishment and his hope of its titillating nature reverberated through his voice. Torie, his mistress, had told him of the place, having apparently visited while Winslow was away in the country.

He was the one who had suggested she go to the Elysium, but she hadn't told him upon whom precisely she'd set her eye. "More so. As a matter of fact, once our position is secured, I'll no doubt spend considerable time there."

"My dear sister, we are attempting to deceive the Crown. Should the truth come out, they'll have our heads. No. Once some blighter's seed takes root, you can't risk returning, can't risk anyone figuring things out. You'll retire to the country and live out your life a grieving widow, much as the Queen has done since the death of her dear Albert. Sleep well."

As though she'd be able to sleep at all. He immediately strode from the room, before she had time to pick up her hairbrush and throw it at him with all her might.

Despair and anger threatened to swamp her. It had always been left to her to save the family. First with marriage, and now through sin.

Not in the mood to deal with anyone else, she didn't send for her maid but simply saw to her own needs. She finished removing the pins, brushed out her hair, and braided it. With a great deal of effort, she managed to shed her clothing and slip into a soft flannel nightdress.

As she walked toward her bed, a profound sadness and loneliness struck her. She glanced over at the door that led into the duke's bedchamber. With a shuddering sigh, she opened it and stepped over the threshold into the room where her husband had always slept when they were in London.

On tiptoes, she crept toward the bed as though there would be hell to pay if she were caught sneaking about in this room. On the nights when her husband had not come to her bed, she'd never had the courage to slip into his, to come to him. She felt rather guilty that she'd gone in search of another man earlier tonight. The action had been out of character for her, and yet Aiden Trewlove had certainly given no hint that he'd been put off by it. Perhaps she should have gone to Lushing as well.

It was odd to be here now, but also soothing as she caught a wisp of his faint fragrance, lingering even though they'd not been back to the city since they'd attended the regatta in Cowes last August. Climbing onto the bed, she curled onto her side and brought up her knees.

Running her tongue over her lips, she could still taste Aiden Trewlove, dark, oak, smoky, whisky. She'd had no idea a man could taste so flavorful.

Why had Lushing never opened his mouth to her? Why had he never made her feel as though he wanted to devour her?

His kisses had always been so polite, so respectful, so gentlemanly. On their wedding night, he'd even whispered, "I'm sorry," in her ear before he worked his way into her. She'd always thought he was apologizing for the pain he knew their initial coupling would cause her. But now she was left to wonder if he'd harbored guilt because he'd known their passion would always be cool and reserved, their coming together a perfunctory thing, a duty, a task.

He'd commented often on her beauty. He'd never made her feel as though he didn't like her, wasn't fond of her. But neither had he ever gazed upon her with the hunger Aiden Trewlove had tonight.

Closing her eyes, she drifted off into slumber and did exactly as the club owner had predicted: she welcomed him into her dreams.

WITHIN THE ATTIC of his club, surrounded by numerous lamps because the solitary window provided insufficient light in the wee hours before dawn, amidst the chaos of clutter that soothed his soul, Aiden studied the face he'd sketched onto the canvas. It wasn't much of a face, really. Her jaw, her chin, and that luscious, luscious mouth that haunted him still. The flavor of it, the desperation of it, the way she'd explored his with equal abandon, as though it were all new, a mystery to be solved. Not his particular mouth but kissing in general. Surely her husband had not denied her that pleasure.

He'd lightly etched in her eyes, but the shape was wrong. He needed to see them without the mask because, unlike his other renderings, he yearned for this one to be a perfect reflection of her.

He always sketched out what he saw before painting the image in oils. Few knew he had this talent because he never signed his artwork, but always hidden away faintly, obscured by brighter colors, was the word *Ettie*. In honor of Ettie Trewlove, the woman who had taken him from his father's arms and given him reason to believe he had value.

He was passionate about creating items of beauty, scandalous though they might be as he seldom covered his subjects in clothing, preferring instead the flow of lines that comprised the naked human form. But even those were often shadowed, faded, or blurred leaving much to the viewer's imagination. He created illusions and allowed others to determine the reality. A woman waiting for her lover. A man haunted by unrequited love. Couples kissing, embracing, fornicating. One saw what one needed to see, what one felt inside. That was his talent, not so much the stroke of a brush, but bringing secrets out of the shadows, desire out of the darkness, allowing them to exist and flourish in the light.

The rap on the door would have angered him had it come five minutes earlier, before he'd put to canvas what his eyes had beheld and his fingers had caressed. If he cupped his hands just so until they threw shade over the lines, he could almost feel her face nestled within his palms and experience the softness of her skin, cared for no doubt with expensive creams or lotions, protected from the sun with an assortment of bonnets. A woman named Selena was one who should be spoiled.

The rap came again.

"Enter." When the door opened, he didn't turn his attention away from the etching because he could tell by the shift in the air that his brother Beast had walked in. For one so tall and broad, he was incredibly graceful, and it was as though space, the atmosphere, and everything around him bent to his will, accommodated his size and movements, without hesitation, the way one might quickly issue obedience to a king.

"That's an unusual rendering," Beast said, his voice deep but smooth, like fine whisky. "Or an odd way to etch someone. You're missing the middle portion of her face."

Setting his charcoal aside, Aiden crossed his arms and gave the sketch a critical appraisal. It wasn't yet what he wanted or needed it to be. "She wore a mask."

"One of the women who frequents here then."

"Frequent is too generous a term. She's been here only once." But he was hoping for more encounters, although after she had her bedding, she might not return—unless he gave her cause to want to, unless he ensured she found the fornicating an addiction she couldn't live without. He clapped his hands in order to turn his attention away from her and focus on his brother and the purpose of his visit. Beast seldom stopped by without a pressing reason. "Care for something to drink?" He walked over to a small table where a decanter of whisky sat at the ready.

"I wouldn't object to two fingers."

Aiden poured the amber liquid into the tumblers and passed one off to his brother. "So what brings you here?"

"Haven't seen much of you lately."

"I've been busy. I don't know how Mick does it with all the irons he has in the fire." The first of their group brought to Ettie Trewlove, Mick was considered the eldest. He was tearing down decrepit parts of London and building them anew, with so many projects going it was impossible to keep track—but his brother had become a wealthy man in the process, gaining the recognition and reputation he'd always longed for.

"He thrives on keeping busy and has an unquenchable need to succeed."

"I'd say that describes all of us."

Beast gave a nod to that, sipped his whisky. "Even Fancy."

Their baby sister, the only one of them born to their mum, was the result of an unscrupulous landlord taking payment in sexual favors when Ettie Trewlove had been short of funds for her weekly rent. Aiden and his brothers had been fourteen when Fancy came into the world and they'd discovered the price their mum was paying to keep a roof over their head. They might have been lads, but they'd been big and strong—and there had been four of them. When they'd finished giving the landlord a taste of their fists, breaking his jaw, he'd never again darkened their mum's door—or taken anything other than coins from another woman. They'd kept a close watch on him until he'd finally sold his properties to Mick.

"We're all gathering together this coming Thursday to help her get her shop ready for business," Beast continued. "We hoped you might make time in your schedule to join us."

Fancy would soon turn eighteen, and they all spoiled her rotten, Mick worst of all. She wanted to open a bookshop, so Mick had given her one of his recently built buildings for that purpose. "She could have asked me herself."

"I'm not sure Mum is keen on her coming to your house of sin."

"Better here where I can keep a watch over her than elsewhere. She's of an age where she's going to be curious. Mum can't possibly think she's not going to engage in a bit of naughtiness somewhere."

"Her shop will keep her too busy for that. Then next year, if Mick has his way, she'll have her Season and marry some lord."

"We all strive to keep Fancy innocent"—he thought of his duchess—"but eventually she'll rebel. God help us when she does. It's the quiet ones you've got to watch."

The quiet ones, the shy ones, the ones who hid beneath masks.

Chapter 5

$\mathcal{B}$y half past six in the morning, dressed in black bombazine up to her chin and down to her wrists, Selena made her way down the stairs and into the front parlor where additional chairs had been brought in to fill out the various sitting areas because the wake for Arthur James Sheffield, Duke of Lushing, would be held here throughout the day and into the evening. He'd passed away shortly after midnight on Friday at the estate. It wasn't until yesterday, Sunday, that they'd accompanied the casket to the train station for Lushing's final journey to London. Servants had lined the drive at the manor house to pay their final respects. Villagers had gathered along the edge of the road leading to the depot. The Duke of Lushing had been loved by many.

So she wasn't at all surprised now to see Viscount Kittridge occupying a chair near the gold satin-covered dais upon which the casket encasing the duke rested. It was a fanciful thing, Spanish mahogany inlaid with silver, bearing the ducal crest. Her husband had purchased it some time back, but when his fever was at its highest, he'd ordered it brought up to his bedchamber, so he could gaze upon his eternal home. She'd found it standing upright in the corner a morbid affair, as though it were waiting for him to get out of the bed, stroll over, and close himself up inside. Not that he'd have been uncomfortable there. The entire thing was lined with stuffing covered in satin. On the inside of the lid, the silk carried an embroidered crest, as though he expected to be able to view it from his position and take comfort in it. Like many of his friends, her late husband, bless him, had a macabre fascination with death.

The crinkling of her dress announced her arrival and the viscount rose to his feet. He appeared wan, with dark shadows beneath his eyes, and she did hope he wasn't on the verge of succumbing to the illness that had taken the duke.

"You're here early, Kit," she said quietly as she approached him.

He sighed heavily. "I wanted to pay my respects in peace, before the others begin arriving." Taking her black-gloved hand, he pressed a kiss to her knuckles, scrutinizing her as he did so. "How did you sleep?"

"Not so well," she admitted honestly, knowing he would attribute the blue half circles beneath her eyes to her mourning when in truth Aiden Trewlove had been responsible for her restlessness. He'd come to her in her dreams, his luscious mouth doing wicked things to hers, filling her with guilt because all her thoughts should be focused on her dear departed husband.

Kit offered his arm for support as she lowered herself into the chair, before taking the one next to her. "I can't believe he's gone."

Kit and Lushing had been the best of friends, hardly inseparable since their earliest days at Eton.

Kit had accompanied her and Lushing on many of their travels. She did have to give her husband credit for that: through her marriage to him she'd seen a good bit of the world. She placed her hand over Kit's, and he turned his up, threading their fingers together. "I fear the next two days will be trying."

He moved his head nearer to her. "Hence, my reason for coming early. He was much respected and liked among his peers. They shall all come to express their condolences."

The duke would remain in repose in the parlor until tomorrow morning when he would be paraded through the streets in grand style in a black hearse pulled by six black horses adorned in black ostrich feathers and laid to rest at Abingdon Park, the garden cemetery where he'd purchased two burial plots. Although she didn't think he'd expected to make use of his so soon. His final words to her seemed to relieve her of any obligation to use the one designated as hers: "Love is all that matters. Find someone deserving of yours."

As though he hadn't been. It hurt if she contemplated it too much.

Despite being only thirty-seven, he'd designed every aspect of the ceremony that would mark his departure from the world. Tomorrow's activities would not include her as she was too delicate for such a solemn and grief-filled occasion. The public was not to see her grieving. She was to stay in residence and do it privately.

"He had everything planned out, all the way down to his eulogy. Every Christmas Eve, he would pour himself a glass of brandy and rework his eulogy to better reflect his life at that moment. Who goes to such bother regarding how their death is to be handled when they are so young?" she asked.

"His three siblings never saw the age of twenty. On his father's side, the members were plagued with ill health and accidents, which is the reason he has no relations from that half of his family. He once told me he saw himself as a lone survivor. It gave him a rather grim outlook, I fear. He always felt the cold scepter of death lurking. On the other hand, he did tend to appreciate more than most each day he was given, tried to make the best of it."

"Was he faithful to me?"

Squeezing her eyes shut, she shook her head in order to erase the words spoken. But after the passion she'd experienced last night, she couldn't imagine Lushing not seeking elsewhere the same sort of fire that she'd been unable to stir to life within him. Opening her eyes, she gave Kit a bashful smile, rather certain her cheeks were aflame. "I don't know why I asked that. Please don't answer."

His blue eyes held sympathy and understanding. "He was involved with someone before you were married, but he had no relations with anyone other than you once your vows were exchanged."

"Did he love her? Why didn't he marry her?"

"It is not often that dukes are allowed to marry for love."

"Is she the reason he had a falling-out with his father?"

He hesitated for several heartbeats before finally nodding. "His father didn't approve of the choices Lushing's heart had made. I think his father would have disowned him if primogeniture and the terms of the entailment hadn't made it impossible for

Lushing *not* to inherit. His father was quite furious and unforgiving. Thank God for the law that protected his inheritance."

It was no secret that Lushing's deep and abiding friendship with Kit had helped him to survive those trying years when his father had cast him out. Even upon his deathbed, as he succumbed to the ravages of cancer, Lushing's father refused to allow his only remaining child entry into the residence in order to have a final farewell.

"I'm surprised he didn't rebel and marry her." If he had loved her enough to offend his father, why hadn't he taken her to wife?

"The relationship was complicated. It would not have served him well in the end to make it public."

She wondered if the lady had been married or perhaps a servant. Maybe someone uneducated who would not have fit in at all. Or a by-blow.

Kit gave her a warm smile. "Besides, you caught his fancy. You made him quite happy, Selena."

While the physical aspect of their relationship might have been lacking, she'd never doubted that Lushing had cared for her, and until last night had never doubted his devotion.

"And if this child you carry is a boy, he will be smiling down from heaven."

Her gut clenched, and her chest tightened. She'd needed to plant the seed of a possible heir early, so she'd decided to use him as her foil because he was so close to Lushing and people would take his word if he supported her claim regarding the child's paternity. "There could be other reasons my menses is delayed." It hadn't been late at all, had ended a mere five days ago.

"I shall pray you are late for the most joyous of reasons. Lushing had begun to fear the mumps had left him infertile."

Three years into their marriage, he'd confessed his worries to her. At nineteen, he'd contracted a rather severe case of the horrid disease that had caused swelling not only on either side of his jaw but in his testicles as well. He'd avoided looking at her when he'd shared what she realized was an incredibly personal and embarrassing situation for him. She'd feared the lack of ease between them when it came to the bedding had caused her womb to tighten up to such a degree that it wouldn't allow his seed to take root. "Please, don't mention my possible condition to anyone, not until more time has passed. I don't want to invite any bad luck," she told Kit now.

"All your secrets are safe with me."

He looked back toward the casket, and she couldn't help but wonder what secrets Lushing had shared with him. More than she'd ever be willing to share. She certainly wasn't going to tell him about Aiden Trewlove or her plans to return to the Elysium Club tonight. Only she wouldn't settle for a kiss in the wee hours of the morning, no matter that her knees were going soft simply with the thought of his mouth once more on hers. No, Aiden Trewlove would bed her, or she'd move on to someone more willing to act quickly.

Time was not on her side.

JUST AS HE had the night before, he spied her the moment she waltzed through the doorway. She wore the same gown of deep blue, no doubt purchased solely for her clandestine visits to his club, something she wouldn't wear on any other occasion lest one of the ladies in attendance recognize it and realize she'd been recalcitrant in observing her proper period of mourning. That possibility had occurred to him as he'd been sketching what he did know of her features. Her fear of discovery had little to do with the sinning and more to do with the timing of it. He'd never understood the requisite mourning periods, spelled out so succinctly in books on etiquette. Not that he'd ever admit to reading about the subject, but he'd always been fascinated by what was considered *proper* behavior. Not to mention, as a boy, a secretive part of him had wanted to be prepared if his father ever deemed to publicly acknowledge him. He hadn't wanted to embarrass his sire, even though his birth had managed to accomplish that, marking him as a child of shame.

So his widowed duchess was probably still in mourning. He'd wager tonight's take on his having the right of it. With a bit of asking around regarding which dukes had passed within the past two years, he could probably discern exactly who she was. Odd thing, though. He who always wanted to know everything about his clientele and was quite skilled at discovering things they didn't always know about themselves—family debts, by-blows, a distant uncle who liked to wear corsets, an aunt who had once posed in the nude for a famous artist, a sister who had turned to the church because of an affair—didn't want to ferret out her secrets. He wanted her to confess them all, whisper them in his ear as their bodies writhed over satin sheets.

He didn't make her wait for him tonight, even

though he knew his eagerness to be in her company gave her power over him. He'd find a way to offset it, to ensure he didn't become subservient to her desires, even as his for her were proving dangerous and reckless. While he flirted with the ladies who visited here, he never seduced them.

Her he wanted to seduce thoroughly and slowly, tormenting them both. For the life of him, he couldn't discern this need that seemed to override all common sense. Perhaps it was because she'd stated so bloody succinctly that she wanted to be bedded, and he feared once she was, she'd traipse out of his life as easily as she'd traipsed into it. He already knew that for him, one fuck wasn't going to be enough. No, he wanted a multitude of them, so many that they'd lose count, so many they'd still be going at it when they were wrinkled and silver-haired.

God help him. Not that many. He wasn't going to spend the remainder of his life shackled to her—or even an abundant number of years. He merely wanted more than one go with her, the exact number or amount of time to be determined at a later date.

As he neared, he could see no bump on the ring finger of her left hand. She'd not worn the symbol that proclaimed she belonged to another. Good. He was going to take a great deal of pleasure in peeling those gloves off her.

She didn't smile, didn't seem glad of his approach. Rather she looked like a deer that sensed the hunter's arrow aimed at it and believed it would remain notched as long as no movement disturbed the air. Yet still, she stood her ground, meeting and holding his gaze with a bit of defiance reflected in her eyes.

Ah, yes, his duchess was accustomed to bending others to her wishes. He had the odd sensation that, like a tree caught in a windstorm, he was bending as well—only he wouldn't realize the exact extent of his giving way until he was felled. Foolish thought there, as he was always aware of how much he was yielding and how much farther he would. It was the reason, until recently, he'd given his sire a large share of his earnings to save his brother from transportation to Australia for a crime he hadn't committed. He'd been willing to give much more than the earl had demanded for his favor, but then, when it came to his family, Aiden would give damn near anything required of him. Not that he went around boasting of that little flaw in himself.

When he reached her, he took her hand, pressed a kiss to it, never removing his gaze from hers. "Were your dreams as naughty as mine?"

She averted her eyes then, and he watched as a swath of dark pink swept over her décolletage, her throat, her chin, and he cursed the mask for preventing him from seeing her cheeks blush a rosy hue. He took pleasure from knowing she had dreamed about him. "Perhaps you'll tell me about them later."

Her eyes swung back to his. "I very much doubt it."

"I can be most persuasive when I set my mind to it."

"My reason for coming here has not changed. However, if you can't accommodate me—"

"Oh, I'll accommodate you, and when I'm done, you'll be ever so glad I did."

A hitch of her breath, a parting of those lush lips, another blush, a deeper pink than the first.

He tucked her hand into the crook of his elbow in a way that even to him seemed rather possessive. "Come. I want to share with you one of the rooms we didn't get to last night."

She didn't resist when he began to escort her along the outer rim of the gaming floor. He didn't go through its center because he didn't want any other lady snagging his attention or trying to divert him from his goal of seduction, especially as Selena had tossed down the gauntlet about accommodating her or she'd go elsewhere. Over his rotting corpse. He liked the challenge of her but was baffled by his reasoning for not simply tossing her on the bed, hiking up her skirts, and plowing the sweet furrow she was offering. He'd had women before who simply wanted a bit of the rough.

Perhaps that was all she wanted as well—to experience spreading her legs for someone beneath her. Why was he so deuced determined to ensure it wasn't the bedding she craved but *him*? Why was it not enough to simply have a frolic? Why did he want what they experienced to have some meaning for her, to be more than the scratch of an itch?

Damn her, damn him, but he didn't want her to be easy.

He took her to the ballroom, to the same door he'd opened for her the night before, up the same steps, into the same corridor, but past the room with the fainting couch to one at the end of the hallway. The footman posted outside it who, on an ordinary night, was to ensure any ladies within had all they required, had been told to gently tell any who wanted to make use of it that it was unavailable for entertainments this evening.

Once he spotted Aiden, he gave a curt nod, reached back, and opened the door. Aiden escorted her inside, the soft *snick* of the door closing behind them making the room seem far more intimate than it might otherwise.

"A billiards room?" she asked, clearly surprised, releasing her hold on him and wandering over to the green-baized carambole table.

He saw no point to answering the obvious. "Remove the mask."

With a sigh, she swung around. "I told you that I can't."

He strode over to her until they stood toe to toe. "Then I'll do it for you."

This time her sigh was long and drawn out as she no doubt fought to come up with a scathing retort. "You're so blasted annoying. That's not what I meant, and you know it."

"My man outside the room isn't going to let anyone come in. There's not a chance in hell that we'll be disturbed. I won't bed you if I can't see all of you."

"I'd have thought you'd be a man who'd enjoy the mystery of it. You could envision me to have an appearance most to your liking."

"Are you hideous then?"

"Would it matter to you if I were?"

"No." His answer came without hesitation, without falsehood. He was intrigued by her reasons, what she had revealed of herself so far. She could be a crone beneath that mask, and he wouldn't care. Well, he'd care a bit.

"Then why your obsession with my removing the mask?"

"Why your obsession with keeping it on?"

"It provides a shield, makes it easier to do what I ought not."

"That's the thing, sweetheart. You've already divulged that you're a widow. You're not being unfaithful to a husband. Not a single reason exists for you not to take pleasure where you can." He skimmed his fingers along her jaw, then down the nose of her mask. "I want to touch all of you. You can see the advantage to that, surely. Besides, I don't fancy feathers."

Blue ones adorned each side of the mask. He was tempted to count the seconds, but instead simply let them flow into eternity, ignored while he waited, while her eyes searched his face, her lips flattened. "Trust me," he finally said, surprised his voice rasped so rough and raw, as though he'd gone his entire life without a drop of water ever touching his tongue. He despised the desperation he heard there, hoped she didn't note it. He shouldn't care that she kept herself hidden from him. Other women did, had. A mask wasn't required for keeping oneself hidden.

She gave two quick nods, and she might as well have delivered two quick punches to his gut for the way it tightened, almost painfully. It wasn't so much that he was about to see exactly what she looked like. It was more about what her actions said regarding her feelings toward him. She wanted more than his cock, wanted to please him. Not as much as he wished to please her. He suspected that was impossible. But more could develop between them now. More than rutting.

Lifting his hands that vibrated with the barest

of trembles, he brought them around to the back of her head where the lacings secured the mask. Tugging on one dangling ribbon, he demolished the bow, then unraveled what remained and pulled the mask away.

Perfection greeted him, made it difficult to swallow. Her cheekbones were high, sharply cut, hollowed out, her nose a slender bridge that connected the blue of her eyes to the pink of her mouth. Unlike the blond of her thinly arched eyebrows, her eyelashes were thick and sooty, which made the blue stand out even more. Without the mask, everything was brighter, more vivid.

"You said you didn't marry for love. But you are too beautiful for your husband not to have loved you."

"Trust a man to equate beauty with love."

BEAUTY HAD ALWAYS been her currency, and for some reason, with him, she didn't want it to be, which was part of the reason she'd held fast to the mask for so long. But beneath it her face had grown dewy, and she'd become weary of it providing a barrier between them—in more ways than one. She hadn't wanted to discuss it anymore, had needed to move beyond it. And blast it, she'd wanted his fingers caressing her cheeks, caressing all of her.

This room had made her believe he wouldn't be fixated with her appearance, that he valued much more, truly understood women. Not that this chamber wasn't gorgeous, but it reflected a man's tastes, the sort of room a man would be comfortable in—and he'd given women access to a small corner of a man's world. Not with only the billiards table but the hunter-green walls, the masculinity of them.

One wall, the one she now neared at the far end of the room, was naught but shelves with books nestled tightly on most of them, the occasional figurine depicting a nude couple in one scandalous pose or another providing an interesting contrast. "Are these books just for show?"

"No. Those to the left of the midpoint I've read. Those to the right remain to be read."

She glanced over her shoulder at him. "You say that as though you intend to read them."

"I do."

She moved to the left, wanting to discern something about his taste. Biographies, mostly. Some books on travel.

"Scotch or brandy?" he asked.

"Brandy." She was in need of something to regain her equilibrium after unveiling herself. She heard the clatter of decanters and glasses being shifted around, had noted the well-appointed marble sideboard with its mahogany hutch when they'd come into the room. Several seating areas adorned the space, for those who might want to watch a game at play. The scent of cigars hovered on the air, and she imagined ladies sitting around, puffing on the horrid things, sipping scotch, lounging back in the plush chairs, legs crossed in a rarified exhibition of rebelliousness, acting as they imagined men did when they retreated to their male-dominated dominion after dinner.

He could have decorated the room in pink, with flounces on the curtains, with delicate flowers rather than the plain green fronds adorning the area. Instead Aiden Trewlove had given the ladies a room where they could feel equal to men. She could not help but imagine he would offer the same courtesy in the bedchamber.

Perhaps that was the real reason she'd removed the mask. Because she wanted to come to him as equally as possible, in a place where neither rank nor title mattered. He knew she was a duchess and yet he wasn't the least bit intimidated. Cared not one whit that fate had propelled her nearly to the ceiling of the social order while he was not even within shouting distance of it.

Speaking of ceilings, this one was painted with hunting scenes. Amid hounds, foxes, and forests, ladies wearing trousers and red jackets sat astride their mounts. Even in the décor, he gave women their due. He was a man of rare enlightenment.

She hadn't heard him approach, but suddenly a snifter appeared before her. Cradling it in one hand, she took a sip, relishing the burn as she trailed her finger along the spine of *On the Origin of Species.* "You seem to favor nonfiction."

"I like reading what I know to be true and real."

"Fiction can be both." She looked askance at him. "Or so my sister would argue. She forever has her nose buried in a book."

"You have a sister?"

She was rather pleased he'd chosen to question that particular portion of what she'd revealed, to take an interest in her family, even though she knew danger resided in his doing so. Yet none of the swains before her marriage had ever spoken of anything other than themselves or her possible role in their lives. "Three. Alice is the youngest. Sixteen.

She became a voracious reader after our parents died eight years ago. I rather think she was searching for an escape, and she found it in stories."

"How did they die? Your parents?"

"Being Good Samaritans. The cobbler in the village, a brute of a man, beat his wife. My father learned of it, went to pack her up, to bring her to . . ." To Camberley Glenn. But that was too much information to share. "To our estate. Mother went with him to reassure the woman, to let her know all would be well. Only it wasn't. The cobbler was in possession of a Tranter revolver—I don't know how he came to have it, but he shot my parents. Dead. Then his wife. Then he took his own life." Winslow had always been a weaponry enthusiast. Through him, she'd learned the Tranter's chamber held five bullets that could be fired in succession with the continual pulling of the trigger. The Crimean War as well as the war in America had resulted in the development of more effective firearms—if the number of people killed without reloading could be termed effective. "My father thought himself invincible, that his title girded him with armor. Only it didn't."

"I'm sorry." She heard true regret laced through his voice. "I've never had anyone close to me die. Death is making a nuisance of itself around you."

Her smile was a bit awkward, difficult to bring forth now that the memories were bombarding her. Alice had escaped into her books while Selena had bolted into marriage one year to the day after they died as her means of leaving the awfulness behind. Not that her route had been left entirely up to her—her siblings had needed her to make that sacrifice in order to ensure their world returned to being as right as possible. "So it seems. If you're a wise man, you'll keep our association short and to the point."

"I don't know that anyone has ever accused me of being wise as I tend to place more value in having fun. We'll play billiards, shall we? Get us back into a more jovial mood. I can teach you the basics."

"I'm not here to learn to play billiards. I'm here—"

"To be bedded. Yes, I know. You are of a singular purpose, aren't you?"

Because time was of the essence. "Mr. Trewlove—"

"I can ready you for bedding while I teach you to play." He leaned in, bringing the scent of fine scotch with him. "The thrusting of the stick to hit the ball isn't that different from other thrusting. Holding off just a bit can create an anticipation that will make what follows all the better. We'll play one game, keeping the scoring as simple as possible. Eight points. For the remainder of our night together, the loser will fulfill all of the winner's deepest desires."

The dare was delivered low, sultry, and filled with promises. He would win, he would command, and she would obey. Glancing over at the table, she imagined him spreading her out over it, how the green baize might prick her back. If he took her there, rather than being *bedded*, would she be *billiards tabled* or simply *billiarded*? "If I win, I can order you to do anything I wish?"

"Anything at all, sweetheart."

"All right, then, I'm up to the challenge of besting you."

But his sudden grin told her far too late that he had no intention of losing.

Leaning against the table where she was rather certain he would have her before the night was done, she sipped her brandy and watched as he shrugged out of his jacket, his back to her so she could enjoy the play of muscles across the broad expanse. The man was certainly a fine specimen.

He tossed the coat over the top of a stuffed chair, before facing her and rolling up the sleeves of his shirt to reveal dark hair covering forearms that looked as though they'd been carved from granite. She couldn't seem to take her eyes from the corded muscles that thinned as they flowed into his hands but left no doubt regarding the strength that resided there. She imagined them skimming over her flesh, closing around a breast, and kneading it until it fit perfectly within the curve of his palm, where his roughened skin would tease her nipple. Good Lord, but it had grown rather warm in here. Perhaps she should ask him to open a window, bring in some cool air.

"Come here," he said softly, not a command, but an enticement that had her body wanting to move toward him as though he'd attached strings to her limbs and she no longer had control over her movements.

Only she did maintain control, albeit in a weakened state. She'd never been so affected by any man. Why him? Because he was practiced at seduction, had mastered it in order to rule his empire and make a success of it. She would resist. A business-like coupling would serve. "The table is over here."

Holding up a hand, he crooked a finger, curled and straightened it, over and over. "Come along."

"You've not yet won. You can't order me about." Why was she being so stubborn when she desperately wanted to be nearer to him? Because she knew if she gave in once, she'd give in every time he asked something of her.

"Please."

Blast him for using the entreaty in such a way as to imply he would die if she didn't make her way to him as quickly as possible. So she did move, but she sauntered, taking her time, wondering if his limbs threatened to tremble in the same manner hers did. Why did he have such an effect on her?

When she was a mere few inches from him, she stopped and angled her head haughtily. "Yes?"

He gave her that grin that seemed to be such a part of him, and she could imagine him giving it to all his marks when he'd enticed them into playing his shell game. Taking the hand not holding the snifter, he began slowly, provocatively peeling off her glove, the tips of his fingers skimming along her flesh as it was revealed. "What are you doing?"

Silly question. She had eyes, hadn't she? Her skin was fluttering beneath his touch, wasn't it?

"You'll want a firm grip on the stick, and the silk will interfere with that. Better to have your skin in direct contact in order to maximize your control, to make the most of the thrust."

Was he referring to the cue stick or a more personal stick? Although as her gaze dropped to the fall of his trousers, she couldn't imagine any aspect of him as being so inconsequential as to be labeled a stick. She downed what remained of the brandy, nearly choking because it was too much too quick.

In fascination, she watched as the glove slid over her wrist, past her fingers, his lingering a moment as he turned her hand over and his thumb skimmed along the lines of her palm. He draped her glove over his coat, and it seemed so intimate, the coupling of their clothing.

Taking the snifter from her, he set it on a small table before returning his attention to her remaining gloved hand.

"I could do that." She sounded as though the brandy had gotten caught in her throat and she was strangling.

"But why should you when it brings me such pleasure? For you, it would simply be a chore. For me, it's an indulgence, to be able to reveal you bit by bit. No rush, no distraction. Just pure enjoyment."

His eyes, dark and smoldering, threatened to set her ablaze. She was beginning to think she might have misjudged, might be out of her element with him, might lose control of the situation. How could she effectively rebuff all the passion and fire he was stirring to life within her? How did she avoid the want and need that overtook all good sense? Or would it be worth it to fall just once into the abyss of frenzy?

He lowered his gaze, watching as more and more of her skin came into view, and she couldn't seem to stop herself from being entranced by his hands. Such capable hands that never faltered. She imagined the quickness it had taken for him to steal the pea away and hide it, then return it to its place as he lifted the cup. A direct contrast to the speed with which he worked now. Every subtle action could be seen, every tiny stroke felt. Nothing was by happenstance, all was deliberate. Her breasts grew heavy, as though they wanted to break free of the confines of her clothing in order to be touched as well.

Slowly, slowly, he slid the silk over her hand, off her fingers, his forefinger returning to provide support for her fingers as his thumb skimmed over the area where her wedding ring had been nestled the night before, had remained from the moment the duke had placed it on her hand at St. George's. But it wouldn't have been right to take Aiden Trewlove between her thighs while she wore something that tied her to Lushing. She hadn't realized it when she'd set out on her quest yesterday, but the club owner had brought that fact home, clearly and succinctly. She wouldn't cast Lushing from her heart or her memories, but she most certainly could not have him haunting her bed.

Aiden brought her hand up to his lips, placed a gentle kiss where the mark of her ring remained. Her eyes stung, and she very nearly hated him at that moment for being so understanding, for giving her such a kindness when she didn't deserve it.

Releasing his hold on her, he tossed her glove onto the first. "All right, then, let's get to the lesson."

Although she could not help but believe that one had already been given: Aiden Trewlove did not do things in half measures. When he was done with her, she was going to find herself well and truly bedded. The thought both exhilarated and terrified her.

Chapter 6

*C*hrist, removing her gloves had him so hard, Aiden was surprised he retained the ability to walk over to the wall and take a cue stick from the rack. He grabbed the chalk and began grinding it into the tip of the stick, which unfortunately had him thinking about grinding into her and did nothing to relieve his embarrassing circumstance.

"Select your ball," he said.

"The red."

Lifting his gaze to her helped reduce his swelling somewhat because she appeared so hopeful and innocent standing near the table with her hands clasped before her, so intent on learning the lesson he was to teach—only he didn't really want to teach her about billiards. He wanted to educate her on exactly what she wanted him to: bedding.

But tormenting them both was going to make it all so much sweeter in the end.

"Do you know nothing at all about the game?"

She blushed, and he was glad the mask was gone, so he could watch the swath of scarlet traverse slowly over her face. "We have a billiards room, of course, where the gentlemen retire whenever we have guests. The ladies aren't allowed in. The gents smoke their cigars and drink their scotch. I rather imagine they don't always discuss topics appropriate for a lady's ears."

"I'm sure they don't." Just as there were topics they'd not discussed. She spoke of her siblings, but not her children. She had children, surely. Providing an heir was the first order of business. It had taken his father two wives before he produced one. He imagined she'd have given her husband an heir within a year of exchanging vows. But for the remainder of the night, he wasn't going to ask about children or anyone else in her life because he wanted to create an atmosphere in which only the two of them existed. He tapped the end of the stick on the table, near where the three balls rested. "The red ball is the target. You need to select the white ball or the white ball with the dot."

"The dot."

"So that one is yours. The plain white one is mine. The system regarding the accumulation of points involves a series of additions and subtractions, but we're going to do away with that for tonight and play using simpler rules. You hit your ball in such a way that it bounces off the sides of the table and hits both remaining balls, in any order. Each time you hit both balls, you get a point and another go. If you hit one ball or neither ball, the turn comes to me." He placed the red ball near one end, the white balls near the other, then smacked his ball and set it sailing against one of the sides where it bounced off, raced to another side, hit it, rolled until it struck the red ball, carried on to *clack* against the white ball with the dot, and came to a halt a short distance away from it.

"You're very good," she said hesitantly.

"It's a matter of geometry. By figuring out where exactly to hit your ball, how hard to strike it, where it will hit the sides, you can plot its trajectory, determine its path."

"Which you no doubt learned by reading your books on *real* matters."

Her response pleased him, that she understood he wasn't a ninny. "I've always loved mathematics, numbers. It's one of the reasons I gravitated toward owning a gaming hell. I liked figuring the statistics, the odds."

"I daresay you have me at a disadvantage."

"I'll go easy on you. As long as you hit one of the balls, we'll let it count."

She jerked up her chin defiantly. "No, if we're going to play, we'll play fair. The same rules must apply to us both."

Which meant she was agreeing to do whatever he asked of her. Oh, the things he was going to do to her. He'd make her damned glad he'd won. He jerked his head to the side. "Come over here, and I'll show you how to position the cue, how to strike."

"The cue?"

He held it up. "The stick. It's a cue stick. Most people refer to it as a cue."

"And the thing you were rubbing it with?"

Rubbing. His body had finally calmed down, and he didn't need to think of her rubbing him. "Chalk. It helps to add some friction so when the leather at the tip of the cue strikes the ball, it's more likely not to go skidding off the ivory."

"I see. All right then." She came over to stand before him. He handed her the cue, explained how she was to hold it, bent her over slightly so her hand was resting on the table, and fought not to rub his crotch against her backside.

At some point, he would take her from behind, perhaps in this very room, while they played billiards naked.

With his arms around her, positioning her just so, he inhaled her fragrance of strawberries, the very fruit that he thought had inhabited her hair to give it the barest reddish tint when the light hit it at certain angles. He'd spent most of their journey to this room noting the different ways the light struck her hair, changed the shade of it. He wanted to remove all the pins that held the strands in place, gather them up in his hands, and bury his face in the silken tresses.

Instead he placed his lips against her neck where it curved into her delicate shoulder, took great satisfaction in the hitching of her breath. He had a feeling she'd be like kindling, easily set alight when he went about ravishing her completely. "Striking the ball here will send it on a path to the left." He guided her hands, moving the stick over. "Here, to the right." Another move of her hands and the cue. "Here, it will follow the path outlined by the cue."

Sliding the cue between her fingers, he imagined himself sliding within her. Taking a deep breath to clear his mind of everything other than the table, he envisioned the play, then guided her as together they struck her white dotted ball. It bounced off three sides before hitting the red ball, careening toward the other side—*bounce!*—and traveling across the green to *smack* against his ball.

He stepped back. "Easy. The balls remain where they are. Now you give it a go on your own."

He positioned himself to the side, so he could view her more easily. Her concentration was astounding, as though her task were a matter of life or death. She licked her upper lip before biting into the lower lush one. God help him, he'd be the one who was kindling when the time finally came.

She brought the cue back, pushed it forward—
Smack!

The ball rolled quickly toward the corner, bounced away to hit the opposite side, and rolled diagonally toward the other corner where it hit, bounded back, and came to rest a few inches from the red ball. Disappointment washed over her face. "May I try again?"

"If you like. We're not playing yet. Simply practicing."

The next strike hit the opposite side and rolled to a stop. She sighed. "I suppose it takes a good deal of practice to be as good as you are."

The third time was a charm, or part of one at least. She hit his white ball. She looked at him hopefully, her smile tentative. "Perhaps we should use your modified rules. If we did, I would have scored?"

"One point."

"And I'd get another turn? I wouldn't have to hand the cue over to you yet?"

"Correct. We'll go with the more flexible rules."

"You're incredibly kind and sporting. Are you going to allow me to go first?"

"There's a method for determining who goes first. It has to do with each of us hitting our balls, bouncing them off the far end, and the one—" He shook his head. This was all for fun. The wager didn't involve money or pride. "It doesn't matter. As my guest, you may go first."

"Thank you. May I alter *our* rules a bit?"

Leaning his hip against the side of the table, he crossed his arms over his chest. "What did you have in mind?"

"When one of us scores a point, he—or *she*—gets to ask the other a question, which must be answered truthfully or a forfeit must be paid."

"What will the forfeit be?"

Nibbling on that lower lip again. He could barely wait to do his own nibbling. "Whatever the point maker decides. I think it will add a level of excitement not to know what might be required."

Bless her. Fortune had smiled on her with the last hit, might again with a couple more shots, but once the cue came to him, he'd rack up eight points in a row. Eight questions. He could ask anything of her. He nodded. "Done."

She smiled brightly. "Very good. Will you set it up properly for us to begin?"

He placed the red ball at the opposite end, both whites at theirs.

Closing her eyes, she inhaled a deep breath, slowly released it. Opening her eyes, she bent over the table, holding the cue just as he'd instructed, her grip relaxed. Her eyes were focused with a predatory gleam in them.

She struck her ball, the *smack* echoing around the room, as it rapidly rolled toward its destination, bouncing off three walls before clacking against the red ball, and spinning off to send his white one upstream. With a triumphant smile, she placed the end of the cue on the floor, holding it as a knight might have held his liege lord's banner after claiming the castle. He couldn't blame her. She'd gotten incredibly lucky with that shot.

"That's a point for me, and a question for you. Tell me about your first time with a girl."

So that was the direction in which she wanted to take the inquiry. He was grateful she'd gotten an opportunity to ask such a brazen thing of him because he would return the favor when it was his turn. "That's not a question. That's a command."

"Fair enough. How old were you?"

"Sixteen."

Her eyes widening a bit, she gave a nod and moved around the corner to take up a position on that side of the table. She glanced down the length of the table one way, then the other. Two steps to the right. Lined up her shot—

Smack!

Bounce. Bounce. Bounce. *Clack* against the red ball. Bounce. *Clack* against his white one. A slow roll into stillness. Retrieving the chalk, she began dusting it over the end of her cue. "Did you love her?"

He was surprised to find himself having to answer another question. "No."

She arched a brow, indicating his answer had been insufficient, although it had been to the point.

"I like women. I enjoy them immensely. But I don't fall in love, which I should think you'd find reassuring. I won't be a clingy lover."

"You've *never* loved a woman?"

He grinned. "You haven't earned the right to ask

another question." He doubted she would. Her luck should be running out.

"True." She set aside the chalk, walked around the table until she was in front of him. "I need you to step aside."

"I think you could get a better shot from across the way."

Narrowing her eyes, she glanced over the table. "Possibly. But I like my chances here." With a pointed look, she jerked her chin to the side.

He situated himself at the head of the table, near the farthest corner from her so he could watch her more closely. She didn't hesitate. Another series of bounces and clacks.

"When was the last time you were with a woman?"

Damnation, how was she managing to set herself up so she was hitting both balls, fairly flawlessly, moving each into position so she could strike both again?

"Mr. Trewlove?" she prodded.

Right. The annoying question. How long had it been? Several weeks before his brother Finn had given him this property in late November. Since then he'd been too busy getting it ready and striving to build his clientele while continuing to manage the Cerberus Club. "At least six months. How long since you slept with a man?"

Had she been with anyone since her husband died?

She gave him a sad smile, a small pouting of her lips. "My observation skills are somewhat lacking, but I don't believe you've had a turn and earned a point yet, so you can't ask any questions."

She took three steps to the right, lined up her

shot, and delivered another scoring play. Her saucy grin nearly had him drawing her into his arms. "Do you pay for your pleasures?"

He stared at her, at the confidence rolling off her. Four perfect shots. What were the odds that a novice—

Understanding dawned—bitter and sweet. Not four. Seven. The practice shots had been designed to make him *believe* she was unfamiliar with the details of the game. To add to her ruse, she'd claimed the incorrect ball as hers and asked silly questions of him regarding the rules. He released a great bark of laughter. "You conniving minx. I do believe you duped me. You've played before."

SHE HAD ANTICIPATED that he might sulk or mope about, perhaps even get angry with her and refuse to play, but she'd wanted to gauge the type of man he truly was. For some reason it had been important as the moment of actually being intimate with him grew closer to becoming a reality, as the intensity with which he looked at her had seeded doubts as to whether she could truly go through with the venture. But of all the reactions she'd expected of him, laughter had never been considered. She rather wished he hadn't laughed. It was boisterous and joyous, reached deep down inside her and made her want to laugh when she hadn't in months, perhaps years. Not full laughter, not the sort that made her eyes water with tears. He grinned at her as though she'd suddenly been crowned queen, as though he quite enjoyed being made sport of. Or perhaps he enjoyed that she'd managed to pull one over on him.

"You have played before," he repeated.

"You haven't any points to ask questions," she reminded him, "but then you didn't really phrase it as a question, rather more as conversation, so yes, I have played. Many times. And I did mention we had a billiards room. You were forewarned."

"Where all the gents go without the ladies in attendance," he said in a falsetto voice that was more teasing than mocking and made her smile.

"When we had company. Otherwise, my husband, my sisters, and my brother played. I enjoy the challenge of controlling the ball." Especially when she felt herself losing control elsewhere. "Some men might have taken offense at my tricking them."

"I, on the other hand, applaud your cleverness. I was a swindler in my youth with my little peas. I appreciate a well-played dodge."

"Dodge?"

"That's what they call it on the streets, when you gain something by underhanded means or by lying."

"I never lied," she was quick to point out. "I simply omitted the truth of things." She waved the cue stick over the table. "Shall we continue?"

"By all means." He walked over to the wall, leaned against the space between two large heavily draped windows, and crossed one foot in front of the other and his arms over his chest, appearing relaxed and satisfied. "But know this, sweetheart. If you miss those balls, I will show no mercy. My questions will be designed to make you blush from your toes clear up to your hairline."

She didn't know what possessed her to think his inquiries would be more exciting than hers, tempting her to deliberately miss the next shot. "You still haven't answered the question about paying for your pleasures."

"I don't. The ladies flock to me."

She arched a brow. "Not for the past six months or so."

"No. I've been too busy managing my businesses, in particular making a go of this place."

"Once the Season is fully underway in the next few weeks, you'll no doubt see an increase in interest and profit." Since Parliament had opened in February, most of the nobility was already in Town and the Social Season would soon begin in earnest.

He nodded toward the table. "Let's see how long you can keep this streak going."

For hours. She'd often done so, used it as entertainment when she awoke in the middle of the night in her lonely bed and couldn't drift back off. It amused her to see how long she could go without a miss. So she set herself up for the next shot, took it, succeeded, and glanced over at him. "Do you know who your father is?"

"We're getting a little personal now." His tone was flat, carrying the tiniest hint of displeasure.

Still she scoffed. "Asking about your paramours wasn't?"

He studied her for a full minute before confessing, "Yes, I know who sired me."

Another successful turn. "Who is he?"

Slowly he shook his head. "Sorry, love. I'll have to take a forfeit here because as I told you last night, I never discuss him."

She rather thought she could understand that, how it must have hurt when he learned he'd been given away. "My apologies. I shouldn't have pried.

The question was unconscionable. What's your favorite color?"

A corner of his mouth hitched up. "Sweetheart, you can ask me anything you want, doesn't mean I'll answer or am offended by your curiosity. I'm actually quite touched you want to know more about me, are beginning to see me as more than just a cock. Bodes well for the bedding."

Not if her face was as red as the heat of it made her think it was. He tossed that word *cock* out so casually, the way most people might say *tree* or *butter* or *good morning*.

"Name the price for my forfeit," he insisted.

Placing the larger end of the cue on the floor so the stick stood vertically, she wrapped her hands around the narrowing portion, fearing she might need the support if he accepted the forfeit. "Remove your waistcoat and cravat."

His eyes darkening, falling on her with the weight of stone, daring her to look away or not to— she couldn't be sure—he shoved himself away from the wall and leisurely began unknotting his cravat as though he had the remainder of his life in which to accomplish that goal. The movement of his fingers was mesmerizing, and she imagined them unlacing the back of her gown, drawing it down over her shoulders with the same sensual flexing and unflexing of his hands. Her mouth was suddenly dry. When he was done, she would ask for more brandy, perhaps request the entire bottle. Or maybe he could direct her to a nearby lake where she could plunge herself into the icy depths before she went up in a conflagration of heated desire.

When the white linen was free of its mooring,

he unwound it from about his neck, pulled one
end of it until it completely surrendered its hold
on him so he was able to toss it onto another chair.
She watched it sail effortlessly through the air as
she might journey if he lifted her up and tossed her
onto a silk-covered mattress.

It somehow seemed incredibly intimate to see so
much more of his neck. She had an urge to trail her
mouth over the corded tendons there.

Then he went to work on the buttons of his waistcoat. Never before had she seen a man undress himself. Had never seen as much of a man as she saw
of Aiden Trewlove. Forearms and neck, sinew and
strength. He was turning her into a wanton, revealing just enough to make her want to uncover more.

When the waistcoat hung loose and parted, he
shrugged out of it in a masculine roll of his shoulders that made it difficult to draw in air. That bit
of clothing was also flung aside. With his gaze still
focused intently on her, he reached up and flicked
three buttons of his shirt through their holes, revealing the tantalizing hollow in the center of his
collarbone at the base of his throat. Her tongue
touched her upper lip when it desperately wanted
to taste his skin there.

He dropped back against the wall, crossed those
magnificent arms over that incredible chest, and produced a smile that was at once wicked and tempting.
"I wonder what forfeit I shall ask of you when the
time comes."

The time wasn't going to come, but she did wish
she was bold enough to purposely miss simply to
see where he might lead her. No doubt into a temp-

tation she'd never known. It did not bode well that her fingers had tightened around the cue to such an extent they'd gone numb. Releasing her hold, she shook out her hands, opening and closing them to get feeling back into them. Regaining her equilibrium, she stated succinctly, "Wonder all you like, but it will be for naught. I have no intention of making a miscalculation in my shots."

And she didn't.

"Do you know anything about your mother?" she asked.

"I assume you're not referring to my mum, Ettie Trewlove, but to the woman who gave birth to me." His tone didn't hold the bitterness it did when discussing his father, but she sensed a bit of sorrow, remorse, perhaps even regret. "I don't know anything about her. I assume she was his mistress, but that's only speculation on my part."

"I can't imagine how difficult it is not to know everything about your past."

"I accepted the circumstances of my birth long ago. Ettie Trewlove made them not matter."

"I'm glad." She didn't like thinking of him as a young lad, picked on or beaten because of a situation over which he had no control. Well aware that people were not always kind to those born in shame, she didn't want to consider that her plans would involve her child being labeled as such—or worse—if the truth were ever discovered.

Taking a deep breath, she moved into position for her final play. She glanced over at him. For the lack of tension in him, he could have been stretched out on clover beneath the shade of a mighty oak watching as the billowy clouds passed by. "You seem rather relaxed for a man on the verge of having to fulfill all my demands."

He lifted a shoulder in a careless shrug. "I'd always intended for you to win, but I'd expected to have to work at the losing."

She didn't know what to say to that, to know he'd gone into the game with the express purpose of doing as she commanded. There was a kindness to him, an unselfishness she'd not entirely expected. "I'm glad to have been a surprise."

"You are definitely that, sweetheart."

The endearment seemed to be more heartfelt, which gave her pause. She was here for a bedding, not an emotional entanglement. Best to get the game over with and move on to business. She lined up her final shot, took it, knew both exhilaration for winning and disappointment the game was at an end. She turned to find him merely studying her, simply waiting.

As difficult as it was, she managed to hold his gaze. "Final question: Do you want me?"

"More than I crave air." He pushed himself away from the wall, walked to the table until only the narrow expanse of green separated them, placed his palms flat on it, and leaned toward her. "You won the game. What is my lady's pleasure?"

"Exactly that. Pleasure me until I forget I'm a widow."

Chapter 7

$\mathcal{I}$t pleased him beyond measure that she hadn't asked him to bed her, although he suspected she thought her words were merely another version of the same thing. But he wanted to teach her differently, wanted to show her there was more to it than the rutting.

In his youth, he'd been content with the quick in and out. Then an older woman had shown him the joy to be found in taking one's time. He wanted to gift his duchess with that elation, as he was fairly certain she'd never had it. Not all men were well versed in the art of fucking. Many had an aversion to sins of the flesh, but the need for surcease drove them to it and they wanted to be done as quickly as possible, as though sinning for a short time might be overlooked while a lengthier transgression was certain to send one to the eternal flames of perdition. But if a man was destined to go to hell anyway, which children born of shame were, he might as well make the most of the journey.

He took his time walking around the table, watching as the rise and fall of her bosom increased in tempo as he neared, how her breaths became more shallow, her blinks less frequent. Taking the cue from her, he placed his fingers where hers had been, noted the slight dampness there, couldn't decide if the sign of her nervousness pleased or bothered him. He certainly didn't want her to be fearful of what was to come. He was tempted to throw it across the room like a large dart, but the clatter would destroy the mood he was striving to create.

So while tension and anticipation built within him, he casually ambled over to the rack and slipped the cue into place. When he turned around, it was to discover she hadn't moved, not even an inch. If she didn't appear to be on the verge of regretting her request to the point of possibly bolting, he might have taken a few more minutes to simply appreciate the beauty of her. Instead, he sauntered over, threaded his fingers through hers, and drew her over to one of the narrow ends of the table.

"You're going to do it here?" she asked, her voice a bit thready, breathless, higher pitched than usual.

Quirking up a corner of his mouth, he glanced around. "This is as good a place as any."

"Would a bed not be better?"

"Not for what I have in mind. Besides, the setting will make for a singular memory. I've little doubt you've had numerous encounters on a bed. I want to give you something different, something you've possibly never had before."

She swallowed, the delicate muscles of her throat working as she simultaneously nodded and licked her lips.

Placing his hands on either side of her waist, he lifted her and placed her gently on the table, hovering on its precipice, her legs dangling over the edge. With his gaze holding hers, he skimmed his hands over her hips, along her outer thighs—

Guided them over her thighs until they were nestled in the valley between her legs and then parted them with a quickness and distance that had her eyes widening, her nostrils flaring, her lips parting. He stepped between them, her knees on either side of his hips, latched on to her arse, and pulled her forward until that honeyed spot he intended to torment was pressed up against him so she knew how desperately he wanted to possess her.

A farther widening of her eyes, flaring of her nostrils, parting of her lips—and now added to that a clutching of the front of his shirt as though she feared dropping into the abyss. It was his hope she would dive into it, unfettered and free.

Slowly, because he wanted none of his time with her rushed, wanted to sear every aspect of her into his memories, he began easing the pins from her hair, tossing them toward the far end of the table so she could easily find them if she wished to gather them to secure her hair later—although if he were successful with his plans, the last thing she'd be thinking about was tidying up. He wanted her completely undone and dazed.

The long heavy strands broke free of the few moorings remaining and tumbled down around her shoulders, revealing more of the strawberry coloring that so fascinated him. With one hand he gathered up the abundant tresses, buried his nose in them, and inhaled deeply the fragrance of strawberries.

"Did you eat strawberries as a child?"

"Yes. And now. They are my favorite. Especially the plump ones. I like when I bite into them and the juice begins to escape my mouth and I have to dart out my tongue to catch it before it gets away."

He growled low. "You're killing me."

"Am I?" An innocence to her tone belied her earlier words.

Releasing his hold on her hair, aware of it falling around her like silken draperies stirred by the wind, he met her gaze. "You know you are."

"I've never been called a minx before. It seems I should do something to earn the title."

He skimmed his thumb over her chin, then followed a path from the center of the rounded curve up to her bottom lip. "One day I shall feed you an incredibly plump strawberry and lick away any juice that manages to escape."

"Promise?"

"Promise."

In spite of her position, he still had to dip his head to reach her lips, and he imagined he tasted strawberries rather than the brandy she'd sipped earlier. She wasn't as shy tonight—or as inexperienced. She welcomed the thrust of his tongue with eagerness, taking hers on a journey through his mouth that had him growing all the harder. Christ, she was a quick study, turning the tables on him, making him want to shove back her skirts and have his lower body imitating the motions of his tongue, plunging, withdrawing, rolling over velvet and silk.

Her sighs echoed around him, her moans seemed to inhabit his soul, created a symphony of pitches that put the very finest musicians to shame. Until he drew his last breath, he would be able to recall the little noises she made. There was a sweetness to them, but also the hint of discovery, as though he were expanding her world.

God, he hoped so. Arrogant bugger that he was, he wanted to give her what no one else ever had. He wanted his to be the name on her lips as she drifted into her final slumber. Selfish on his part, to wish for her a life that was never more exquisite than what he delivered. But only fair because already he knew that the women who followed after her would pale in comparison.

He didn't know why she was different from the others, why with her he was breaking all his own rules. Why he knew once with her would not be enough. Why he was determined to leave her wanting so he would have more than the once. Eventually she would grow weary of him—his siblings might have lucked out by falling for aristocrats who were willing to embrace them, but he knew that most of the nobility tired of playing in the muck after a time. She'd been honest with her purpose in coming here. His performance might cause her to return but her presence in his life was temporary. He understood that and intended to make the most of it.

Breaking off the kiss, he trailed his mouth along her chin, the ivory column of her throat, her collarbone, then a detour up to the sweet curve where her neck eased into her shoulder. There he lingered, suckling and soothing, while her head dropped back, her moan deepened into a groan, and her fingers tightened on his shirt, more fabric gathered within her grasp. Her skin was so silky and smooth, heated alabaster marble beneath his tongue. He could spend the entire night feasting on her inch by delicious inch.

But other inches were in need of his attention.

Pulling back, he took pleasure in her languid gaze. He'd seen the same expression in a thousand eyes—intoxication at its very finest before one toppled over the edge into obliterating drunkenness. But she would be saved from that fate as her lethargy was spurred by sensation not drink.

"Free my buttons," he ordered on a rasp of desire that nearly unmanned him.

SHE'D THOUGHT HE'D never ask, although considering the tight hold she had of his shirt, the manner in which her knuckles were turning white, she was surprised to find the cloth not yet shredded into pieces. His kiss hindered her ability to think, to reason. All she could do was feel—the softness of his lips, the roughness of his tongue, the gentle abrading of his short whiskers against her skin. She might be red and a bit chapped in the morning, but she didn't care. It all added to the incredible sensations pouring through her.

The way his gaze seemed to darken and smolder as he watched her only added depth—very much like an aria as it reached its crescendo.

She wasn't surprised to find her fingers shaking as they attacked his buttons. She was trembling all over, but it was in a most pleasant way. His patient, slow mannerisms didn't transfer to her. Instead she worked quickly, shoving each button through its hole, watching the material part to reveal a thin V of flesh, lightly sprinkled with hair that would tickle her fingers if she found the courage to skim them over it.

She'd freed only three buttons from their mooring when he stretched his arms up, grabbed the back of his shirt, and tugged it over his head, a wider expanse of skin coming into view to delight her as he tossed the shirt aside. By inches, it missed the chair where his other clothing had been relegated earlier.

Without thought, merely giving in to her instincts, she flattened her palms against his chest, so warm, so firm. She flicked a finger over one of his erect nipples. He groaned low, grabbed her hips, and pressed her more solidly against him. She'd been shocked the first time to feel the hard length of him, to know he was well and truly prepared to possess her. But it seemed now he was even more ready.

Then his mouth once again claimed hers, with fervent devotion. Each time she thought he'd given all he had to give, he gave more. She glided her hands up his chest, around his neck, up into his hair, relishing the feel of the thick strands curling around her fingers. Pressing her knees against his hips—feeling power in his accompanying growl— she wrapped her legs around him, bringing him ever nearer. In spite of the layers of silk and satin separating them, she could feel the strength and heat of him. He caused her to burn for him, to experience wild and incredible sensations she hadn't even known were available to her. He made her feel alive, as though lightning rather than blood coursed through her veins.

She became aware of his hands at her back, of those long, nimble fingers making short work of her lacings, causing her bodice to loosen and fall forward slightly. Leaning back, he dipped his gaze to his fingers as they slowly trailed along her skin at the edge of the fabric, easing the gown off her shoulders. The heat flaring in his eyes was an aphrodisiac in its intensity. She'd longed to have a man gaze on her just so, to see his want and need bared—raw and primal.

"Shouldn't we douse the lamps?" Her voice sounded small, as though it were enthralled by him and didn't want to be disturbed from the enjoyment he was delivering.

"No."

So simple, yet so profound an answer. As a delicious shudder rippled through her, she considered it a miracle that she continued to find the wherewithal to draw in breath. The appreciation for her washing over his features held her captive.

Her bodice slipped away, and the heat in his eyes burned hotter, his nostrils flaring, his breathing going shallow. Using the side of a single finger, the one that bore the scar, he traced the path of her chemise where it lay against her skin, his finger deliciously rough against the soft mounds of her bosom. "Your skin reminds me of silk, only softer."

Then his mouth followed the path his finger had forged, and everything within her went languid. If he weren't standing there, if her legs hadn't clamped more tightly around his hips, she might have slid off the table. Instead she closed her hands around his upper arms, clinging to him as her body fought a battle, needing both to implode and explode. She gazed at the top of his head, the brown locks feathered here and there with burnished amber. She was torn between sliding her hand beneath his chin and lifting that lovely mouth to hers and leaving it to continue on its journey.

He made the choice for her, doing neither, but separating himself from her just enough so he could untie her ribbons, unfasten a portion of her corset, and peel away the material to expose her breasts to the air, to the light, to his smoldering gaze. She was surprised the intensity of his focus didn't ignite her.

"Beautiful." The word came out on little more than an exhaled breath.

He cupped each one, and they filled his palms. He flicked his thumbs over her puckered nipples, much as she'd teased his with her finger. The sensations elicited were wonderful. When he lowered his head and closed his mouth over her areola, his tongue taunting, she cried out in pleasure and pain as the haven between her thighs tightened with needs, her entire body—head to toe—tightened with needs.

With his hands returning to her back, he braced her, bowing her slightly as though to offer up her breasts as a tantalizing feast—and, oh, how he feasted. With slow licks, hot kisses, and quick nibbles. A suckling here, a soothing there. No area was left bereft of his attentions.

Leaning back on one hand, she scraped the other through his hair, along his neck, over his shoulder. She'd never experienced such devotion, hadn't known such sensations existed. Always something had hovered, but she'd thought it was merely a wantonness. Perhaps he did these things to her because he wasn't a gentleman, wasn't of the nobility, was a commoner. If so, she now understood why women whispered about wanting a bit of the rough.

His groans and moans were animalistic in tone, uncivilized—and she was so grateful he wasn't of a tamed nature. That he ran free over her skin, that he dared to explore what had remained unchartered. She imagined when he was done, he'd be able to draw a map of her.

With a feral growl, he reclaimed her mouth, making it his, and she feared if she were to ever remarry, no husband would be able to satisfy her as he did. His kiss spoke volumes, made her feel as though he reached deep within her soul and touched her throughout. So absorbed was she by the conquering of his mouth over hers it took her a moment to realize he'd eased her down to the table. She'd only just become aware of the baize at her back when he began peppering kisses over her chin, her jaw, her throat, her breasts—

Then his hands were circling her ankles before gliding up her legs, shoving up her skirts until they were a pool of blue gathered at her waist. She gasped, having never been thus exposed.

He stilled, only his eyes moving as they came to hold hers. "Do you want me to stop?"

What she wanted had no bearing on the matter. It was all about what she needed. And she needed what he could provide.

Swallowing hard, she gingerly shook her head. "I want you to make me forget."

His grin was wicked, filled with promise. "When I'm done, you won't even recall your name."

He disappeared behind the pile of her skirts and petticoats. His fingers danced along her thighs, his palms spreading her legs farther apart, separating the slit in the crotch of her undergarments. She felt the stroke of one long finger journeying down, then up.

"So juicy." His voice was hoarse and rough. "As juicy as a plump strawberry."

And she had little doubt she was even juicier now.

Her knees came into view as he placed her feet against the cushions that surrounded the edge of the table. She had a strong desire to cross her legs even as she wanted to part them wider.

A cool breath stirred her curls. A leisurely lick nearly had her coming up off the table. Her hands clenched. She reached for him. His fingers folded over hers.

Another lick that journeyed up, going side to side like the lacings on her gown. A circle. Yearning for something, she thrust up her hips, so she was closer to that luscious mouth.

He chuckled low, darkly. "Do you even know what you want?"

"No." Her breathing was shallow, quick. "I'm scared I'll find it, terrified I won't."

"Don't be frightened. It won't hurt. And don't fight it, sweetheart. When it comes, let it engulf you."

She almost asked what the *it* was, but his mouth closed over the swollen sensitive bud, and she cried out from the pure bliss of it. She tightened her hold on his fingers as the sensations built with each suck, each swirl, each kiss. Everything within her called to him, to what he was offering. He was between her thighs, but it was as though he'd somehow managed to encompass all of her. No part of her was unaware of his touch.

Every nerve ending was shooting sparks. And

when she might have fought to contain it, she followed his advice and gave herself over to it, to the passion, the stirring, the sin. The wickedness of allowing this man to whom she was not married perform such an intimate service. To know the very heart of her womanhood and to take possession of it as though it belonged to him, as though it were his to do with as he pleased.

But of course it was. She'd granted him permission. She'd won the wager, named her prize. How was she to have known that in the end the price would be to give herself completely over to him?

Yet she knew no regrets. Knew naught but pleasure, as it spiraled unmercifully through her until she did forget her name, until she forgot everything, was aware of nothing other than the ecstasy that overtook her until it alone remained, filling her, spilling out of her, conquering her until it was everything and she was crying out in elation as though she'd ascended into heaven.

And then she burst into tears.

Chapter 8

$\mathscr{I}$t was as though everything had come to a head. The years of longing for passion—discovering it was more profound and exquisite than anything she'd ever imagined. The sorrow over losing Lushing—in spite of what he'd not given her, he'd gifted her with other things. The burden of seeing that her sisters were well situated when she hadn't the means to assure it without the dukedom behind her. The weight of striving to ensure that her brother's title and estate did not fall over the precipice into total ruin. Her own disappointment of not having a babe to cradle in her arms. The fear that the fault rested with her and not Lushing, that all this was an exercise in futility.

And her deception, her horrid deception, that if this man got her with child, she'd never tell him that he had a son—or daughter—because it was imperative the entire world believe the boy or girl was Lushing's. Otherwise the child was as doomed as she was.

"Shh, shh. It's all right, sweetheart," Aiden Trewlove crooned as he gathered her into his arms.

Don't be kind to me, she wanted to scream. *I don't deserve it.*

But she seemed incapable of forming words. All she could do was blubber as he carried her several feet, lowered himself into a chair, and cradled her on his lap, pulling her clothing down here and up there, returning to her a semblance of modesty.

And the tears fell all the harder.

A woman of her station did not cry with such undignified force. She didn't wrap her fingers around a man's nape and bury her face against his neck and shower him in tears while he gently stroked her back.

"Did your husband never give you that?"

How did she explain that what Aiden Trewlove delivered had completely undone her? The intimacy of it, the overwhelming ecstasy of it? Shaking her head, she sniffed, fought to regain control, to not recall how unimpassioned and staid her encounters with Lushing had been. Had he desired her at all?

Aiden's arms closed more tightly around her. "Is that the reason you came here? You were searching for passion?"

She couldn't confess her true reason for seeking him out, but neither did she want to give him false words. "I'm not certain I was truly aware of everything I was searching for. I've never experienced anything so wondrous, all consuming. Should it always be like this?"

"Not always. Some men are hesitant to engage fully in carnal pleasures with their wives. They . . . they're not comfortable with the more . . . animalistic aspects of our nature."

The tears slowed to a trickle, leaving her weary and exhausted. "It was rather raw . . . what I felt just now. I hadn't expected to feel so vulnerable." A horrible thought occurred to her. "You won't ever tell—"

"No. You're safe with me. Whatever passes between us remains between us."

She took a great shuddering breath. "I miss him." The words were out before she'd even realized what they would be. The tears spilled forward again. "He was kind."

"Last night you said you didn't marry for love, but that doesn't mean you didn't love him. Did you?"

She didn't hesitate to nod. "But it wasn't a passionate love, not the sort you read about in romantic novels."

"I don't read romantic novels."

She smiled, almost laughed at the tone of his voice, as though he'd been insulted. "I enjoy them immensely. But regardless, our love was not a deep and abiding thing. Perhaps that is the reason other aspects of our relationship lacked passion."

"You can have passion without love."

Aiden Trewlove had certainly proved that point a mere few minutes ago. But could one have romantic love without passion? She imagined how much more fulfilling what she'd experienced earlier would be if shared with someone she adored beyond all reason.

"It can't be easy being a young widow," he said softly, turning them away from talk of love.

"I don't imagine it's easy being an old one either. My life is a series of routines—not in a boring way. But he was part of them. I dress for dinner and go down to the library, and he's not there, tumbler in hand as he stares into the fire, to turn and smile at me. When I'm reading and run across a particularly well-written passage and look up to share, he's not sitting in the chair across from me, engrossed in his own novel. I seek him out a dozen times a day, only to recall he's no longer there. And it always hurts."

Straightening, she held his gaze. "I don't know how long it takes before it stops hurting."

SKIMMING HIS FINGERS along her cheek, threading them into her hair, Aiden wished to hell he could offer her reassurance that the pain would ease, but he knew nothing of permanent loss. Nor had he expected the night to take the turn it had. Of all the reactions he'd anticipated of her, uncontrollable tears had not been one of them.

He was a stranger to offering comfort, suspected he rather failed at it. Perhaps that was the reason he didn't search for words but merely took her mouth as gently as he was able. It caused a sharp needlelike pain in his chest to see her so unhappy, an ache he didn't particularly fancy. Rogue that he was, when it came to women, as much as he enjoyed them, he kept a barrier between them and his emotions.

He had little to offer a woman in the way of influence, prestige, and—if he were honest with himself—pride in him as a man to stand at her side. He was a gambling hell owner, a purveyor of vice. He hadn't yet attained the level of wealth that would cause people to overlook his questionable businesses or his sordid entry into the world, because until recently he'd given a good bit of his earnings to his maggot of a sire. But even if he had an abundance of coins, would it be fair to ask any woman to love him when the world would always view him as the bastard he was? That taint could never be washed away, and he wouldn't be responsible for bringing children into the world who would have to carry the burden of his shame.

So he wasn't particularly pleased with how much he'd come to care for this woman in such a short time, especially when she'd made it clear she wanted only one thing of him. He didn't like knowing that when he eventually succumbed to her wishes and gave it to her fully, he might never see her again.

For he would always remember the feel of her tears gathering on his neck, the warmth of her nestled within his arms, the taste of her on his tongue.

When he pulled back, she smiled at him, causing the ache in his chest to increase.

"You have a way of distracting me from my troubles." Gratitude was mirrored in her eyes.

"I'm at your service anytime you require distracting."

A small half laugh. A blush that turned her pale cheeks a rosy hue. It occurred to him to have the walls repainted that shade so he was always reminded of her.

For several long minutes, she merely held his gaze, and he held hers, as though words were no longer of any consequence. She looked away first. "I have to leave now."

He almost asked her to stay, to spend the remainder of the night in his bed. Not that he would do anything other than hold her. While he was desperate to possess her, he didn't think she was yet of a mind to be possessed by *him*. She wasn't yet thoroughly seduced.

So he untangled himself from around her and

assisted her in climbing out of his lap. After slipping into his shirt, he watched with fascination as she tidied her clothing. Then he laced her back up.

She didn't bother with her hair. Merely returned the mask to its place so she was once again safe from recognition. Still, he escorted her down the hallway to a private stairwell that led to the foyer, so she wouldn't have to traverse through the gaming floor. Retrieving her wrap from the girl at the counter there, he draped it around her shoulders and ushered her out into the night, to the carriage that waited for her.

When they reached it, she faced him. "I apologize for making such a spectacle of myself."

"No need for apologies, sweetheart. But I do hope you won't allow any discomfort you might be feeling regarding your tears to prevent you from returning."

Reaching up, she skimmed her fingers along his jaw that was shadowed with bristles now. He could hear the rasp of them over her skin. "Tomorrow."

He handed her up into the carriage and closed the door. As the vehicle rumbled down the street, he watched it go, wondering how he could possibly seduce her half as much as she'd seduced him.

WHEN SELENA REACHED her bedchamber door, she hesitated, not wanting to deal with Winslow tonight if he was lurking about like a miscreant in the shadows of her room. It was quite possible he might look at her and know what she'd been up to. In spite of her tears, she felt as though she still glowed from Aiden's ministrations, and she wanted to hold those sensations close, take them with her beneath the sheets.

She considered seeking another bed rather than her own—the residence contained at least thirty other chambers—but in the end decided she was in want of familiar surroundings. When she stepped into her quarters it was to discover that her brother was nowhere to be seen, but her three sisters were all scrunched up in her bed, the twins appearing to be asleep, while Alice was sitting up, pillows at her back, her nose buried in a book. Aiden immediately came to mind, and she wondered if sleep had come easily for him or if it eluded him and forced him to pull one of his many books from the shelves to occupy his mind, so he didn't think of her.

Silly girl, as though he gave any thought to her at all after she left. If he required distracting, plenty of women in his club would be only too glad to provide a diversion. She didn't want to acknowledge the spark of jealousy that thought ignited. While she had his attentions, she wanted him giving them to no one else. Perhaps that should have been the prize she sought—but oh, the one she'd claimed could not be measured.

Alice set her book in her lap and looked at Selena with grave concern etched over her features. "Where have you been? We've been worried silly."

"Yes, I can quite see that. Nudge those two awake so you can all scamper back to your rooms."

Without the nudging, Constance and Florence stirred, squinted at her, and pushed themselves into sitting positions. "You're back," they said in unison.

"So I am."

"Where were you?" Flo asked.

With the mask nestled in the folds of her skirt,

she wandered over to the vanity, where she discreetly set it behind an ornate trinket box Lushing had once given her, went to remove her gloves, and realized she'd never put them back on, had left them with Aiden. Fortunately, she wasn't lacking in coverings for her hands but would need to remember to fetch them tomorrow. As unobtrusively as possible, she barely lifted the lid on her smaller jewelry box, slid out her wedding ring, and returned it to its proper place on her finger. "I needed to get out for a while, to be alone, to find some measure of peace. What are you girls doing in here?"

"We couldn't sleep with a corpse in residence," Alice said. "It's morbid having the casket remaining in the front parlor."

"It's the way it's done, sweeting."

"I hear him creeping along the hallways," Connie said.

"You mustn't speak of dear Lushing in that manner." Selena sat on the stuffed bench covered in a tapestry of flowers. "Although, if he were a ghost, he wouldn't haunt you. He loved you all dearly, you know that."

"Let us sleep here with you," Alice said. "Like we did when we were younger, after Mother and Father met their untimely end."

Which was how Alice always referred to their passing, as though anyone ever attained a timely end. She couldn't help but believe her youngest sister had been most affected by their parents' tragic deaths. Standing, she drew her unbound hair over one shoulder. Her pins had remained behind as well. "Come undo my lacings, so I don't have to send for Bailey." Her lady's maid tended to be a bit taciturn when awakened.

Setting her book aside, Alice scrambled out of the bed, darted over, and began unlacing the gown, her fingers nimble, never straying from the task. "How ever did you get that mark there? It looks ghastly."

With her heart pounding, Selena leaned toward the mirror. At the far side of her neck where it curved into her shoulder was a small discolored patch resembling a bruise but not, where earlier a mouth had been suckling, a tongue soothing. She grew warm with the memories of how it had come to be. He'd branded her, at least temporarily for surely eventually it would fade. "It's nothing."

"Does it hurt? It appears painful."

It had been anything but. "No."

"How did you get it?" Flo asked, coming up on her knees on the bed as though that would give her a better view.

Selena had to tell them something or they'd keep on about it. "Bailey dropped the brush earlier when she was managing my hair. It struck me at an odd angle."

"You should let her go if she's that careless," Connie said.

"I'm not going to let Bailey go. It was an accident. Don't say anything to her about it. Don't say anything to anyone. As I said earlier, it's nothing." With the collar of her mourning attire up to her chin, no one would see it.

"Why are you wearing a ball gown anyway?" Connie asked, flopping down on her stomach, with her head at the foot of the bed, her chin resting in her hands.

"I grew weary of mourning black and no one was going to see me, so what did it matter what I wore?"

"My word, Selena. It's a bit early to grow weary of it when you'll be wearing it for *two* years." Connie pronounced the length of time as though it were a death sentence handed down by a magistrate. "Thank God, we have to mourn for only three months, although I shall be sad much longer than that because you're right. Lushing was jolly nice. He made me laugh."

"He made us all laugh," Flo said. "Where did you go, Selena?"

"Around. Honestly you girls are going to have to cease with the inquisition if you want to remain in my bed."

Once Selena was in her nightdress, Alice offered to plait her hair. Studying her sister's reflection in the mirror, she could see the seriousness with which she saw to the task, the way she gripped the brush as though fearing she'd lose control of it and cause another injury. Selena should have come up with a reason for the mark that didn't involve her maid but hadn't expected to face questions upon walking into her bedchamber.

"She's practicing for when she has to become a lady's maid." Flo sighed heavily. "We'll all have to go into service. None of us will make a good marriage now without Lushing about to ensure it. Winslow is useless in that regard."

"I'm going to become a wealthy widow's companion and travel the world," Connie said.

"No one is going into service and no one is becoming anyone's companion," Selena assured them. "You will all have fine marriages."

"How will you arrange that when almost everything goes to the Crown?"

"Don't worry yourselves over it for now." She was worrying enough for all of them. "All will be well." She needed to ensure it was. Alice was terrible at plaiting hair. The braid was far too loose with tendrils sticking out everywhere. "Thank you, darling. That's wonderful."

So many lies she'd given to her sisters tonight. She hated herself for them, but what choice did she have? They must never learn the truth; no one must ever learn the truth. The remainder of her life would be spent living a lie.

"All right, to bed now. Tomorrow is going to be a frightfully long day." Lushing would be laid to rest. She settled in with the twins on her left and Alice on her right. Her youngest sister doused the lamp, enclosing them in darkness.

"I miss him," Alice said quietly.

"I know, sweeting. As do I."

"We'll be spinsters before we have our first Season," Connie said.

"Stop worrying about your future," Alice said.

"Flo and I were to have our coming out. Now it'll be delayed because we can't very well gad about when Selena is in mourning. We need her to accompany us. Winslow would be wretched at ensuring we're seen. It's not fair."

"It's not as though Lushing died on purpose," Alice reminded her. "We're supposed to be comforting Selena."

"Being squished in my bed is very comforting," she assured them.

"Where will we live?" Flo asked.

"The day after the funeral, the solicitor will read the will. I'm sure Lushing has provided for us. And there is always a chance that things could turn out very different from what you're expecting."

"How?" The bed shifted, and she was fairly certain Connie had sat up with her question. "What are you talking about?"

"She could be with child," Flo answered. "And if it's a boy, it would be Lushing's heir and nothing would change at all. It won't matter when we have our Seasons. We'll still be associated with a great dynasty and men will flock around us."

She had the rather maudlin thought that men should flock around them for themselves. They were smart, clever, and witty. Each had her own talents and interests. Why should the title with which they were associated or the residences in which they resided make a difference as to how they were perceived?

Aiden Trewlove had begun life cast aside with not so much as a farthing handed to him—and yet he'd worked hard to make something of himself, something to be admired. He was kind and liked to have fun. And his laugh, dear God, his laugh could lift the foulest of moods. He was a bastard, no man's son, and yet still found it within him to laugh. And for a short time, he'd made her forget she was a widow. Then he had comforted her with more sincerity than she'd heard today from those who'd come to express their regrets and she suspected she'd hear from others on the morrow.

"Are you with child?" Alice whispered as though saying the words aloud would prevent them from being true.

"It's possible. Too soon to tell."

"Lushing would be pleased."

"Only if it's a boy," Connie said. "Society cares only about heirs."

"I care about girls," Selena said. "I care about all of you. I love you dearly."

And because she did, she'd do anything necessary to see them happy and well situated.

$\mathcal{W}$alking into the Mermaid and Unicorn was always a bit like coming home, and the atmosphere of
the tavern had everything to do with Aiden's sister
Gillie. She'd worked hard to make the place a sanctuary for those facing hardships or in need of respite after long hours of laborious work. The tables
ranged from the small square ones that seated four
to the lengthy ones that would accommodate more
than a dozen. Benches and chairs provided rest for
weary bodies, and when those weren't available an
elbow planted on the counter in front of the barrels
and taps sufficed to provide refuge, especially as
Gillie spent most of her time behind it, constantly
offering a willing ear to those who had troubles to
whine about or joys in need of celebrating.

The rush of people popping in for a pint and
a midday meal had passed so Aiden didn't have
to jostle through a crowd to make his way to the
polished wood that fairly gleamed his reflection.
One of Gillie's girls smiled and winked at him. If
he were an ordinary customer, she'd have greeted
him with "What's your pleasure, treasure?" But
since she was well aware of who he was, she knew

Gillie was already pouring his pint. It was waiting for him when he reached the bar.

"I haven't seen you about in a while." His sister studied him intensely in an effort to ensure all was right with him.

"The new business is keeping me occupied—more so than I'd expected."

"It's going well, then?"

"No complaints." He took a sip of his beer, relishing the flavor. "I'm in need of your finest bottle of wine. One that goes particularly well with strawberries." The fruit was going to cost him a fortune, because it wasn't yet in season so he'd have to find some that had been cultivated in a conservatory. He had plans for Selena tonight, having no doubt whatsoever she'd be returning to his arms once darkness descended.

"My finest is in the cellar at Coventry House." Her duke's London residence—now hers as well.

"What would it cost me to have you part with it?"

"What do you need it for?"

"A little seduction."

Placing her elbow on the counter, she cradled her chin in her hand. "Tell me about her."

"Why should I? You kept your duke a secret."

"Because of what I felt for him. It rather frightened me, I think. Have you strong feelings for this woman?"

"God no." Although the words mocked him as a lie. What he felt for Selena was beyond description. That it terrified him on one level didn't mean he was following Gillie's path and falling in love. He'd spent thirty-two years on this earth without stumbling onto that path. He wasn't about to take a detour toward it now. "She's fun is all."

"*Fun* is hardly deserving of my finest wine. An inexpensive vintage would work just as well."

"She's accustomed to luxurious things."

Straightening, she scrutinized him. Nearly as tall as her brothers, she intimidated a good many. "Nobility, then. One of the ladies you've met through your new club, I've no doubt. Don't let her use you, Aiden."

"How's she going to do that? There's nothing at all she could do to me that I wouldn't welcome."

"You're thinking with the lower half of your body. I'm talking about the upper part, your heart."

"My heart's safe. I have no intention of ever giving it into another's keeping."

"Intentions can sometimes go astray. I never intended to fall in love with a duke."

"Speaking of your duke, why isn't he about? He seldom leaves your side these days." She was swelling with his child, and Thorne hovered around her as though she were the first woman to ever give birth and was in need of constant protection. He was rather surprised Gillie allowed it, because she'd been independent her entire life.

"He had a funeral to attend. The Duke of Lushing, a man he greatly admired."

Aiden's gut clenched as though preparing for a blow. A duke being buried today. A secretive widow coming to his club. "Had he a wife, this Lushing fellow?"

Nodding, she grabbed a bit of flannel and began wiping the counter. "I'm given to understand they'd been married for some years."

"Shouldn't you have accompanied your husband?" If she had, then he could have acquired a description of the man's widow, might know for certain if she was the woman who'd fallen apart in his arms. Although he couldn't imagine the woman he knew coming to him before her husband was even placed in the ground.

"I've never met the duchess. I suspect she'd not be of a mood to make any new acquaintances. I certainly wouldn't want some stranger bearing witness to my grieving. Besides, I'm not yet accepted by the nobility so that would add a layer of awkwardness to the whole affair."

"Do you know how he died?"

She stilled, her gaze narrowing as she scrutinized him. "Why would you care?"

"Half my family is now ensconced in the nobility. My businesses, especially the newer one, cater to them. It just seems I should stay abreast of what's happening among them, and you've become an incredibly wonderful source."

Her shrug indicated she wasn't at all susceptible to his flattery. He had no idea how a duke had won her over because Gillie had never been one to flirt.

"He fell ill. Thornley was quite taken aback to hear of his passing because the duke was a rather young man, in good health. A couple of days ago his widow brought him to London because he wished to be laid to rest in a cemetery here."

Surely this duke was not Selena's duke. It was merely coincidence that his arrival in London so well matched her appearance at his club. Yet what better way to escape grief than to become lost in living?

"Have any other dukes passed in the past year or so?"

His sister studied him as though he was speaking in another language. "I'm certain some have, but until Thorne came into my life, I paid very little attention to the goings-on among the nobility. It wasn't as though I was moving about in their circles to know any of them or for their names to truly have any meaning for me. Thorne would no doubt know. Shall I ask him?"

"No, it's not important." Whether she was a day, a week, a month, a year, a century a widow, his interest in her wouldn't diminish. Although it appeared another billiards game was in order, only this time he'd be the one posing the questions.

"Do you still want the wine?" Gillie asked, breaking into his thoughts.

"If you don't mind." He could always put fine wine to good use.

"I'll write a missive to the butler and tell him which vintage to pour into a bottle for you."

"I'll paint you another unicorn for your tavern walls." They were decorated with his artwork, as were those of the lodgings above where she'd once lived.

With a joyous grin, she patted his shoulder. "Paint one for the nursery."

"I was going to do that anyway. Better yet, maybe I'll paint the entire wall with unicorns."

"I daresay, Aiden, there is a whimsical bent to you."

He winked at her. "Keep it between us."

With the rag she'd been using to wipe her counter, she teasingly slapped his arm. "Wait there while I go pen a missive for you to take with you to hand over to the butler."

While she walked off, he took a long, slow swallow of his beer, already envisioning how he would seduce Selena until she lowered all her defenses and became an open book, confessing all her secrets and all her sins.

SITTING IN THE front parlor, Selena found herself surrounded by the well-meaning ladies of the *ton* who looked at her with unbridled sympathy and sorrow as though she were on the verge of following her husband into the grave. She rather wished she'd insisted on attending the funeral. The somber affair that included morbid mutes in tall black silk hats had to be far jollier than being in the center of all these black-clad women who reminded her of ravens eyeing their prey. What they were awaiting were her tears, but she'd released them all the night before, sheltered within Aiden Trewlove's strong arms.

So in addition to her sadness, she was battling against incredible guilt because she'd drawn such comfort from another man's tenderness. Although she suspected Lushing would forgive her for that slight. After all, he'd never purposefully sought to make her unhappy. He would be appalled by all the mournful looks cast her way at that precise moment. He'd always been one who enjoyed life, looked for the fun to be had, celebrated each day as an opportunity for new adventures.

Even her sisters, sitting around her, seemed at a loss. Certainly one was to be reflective and portray sadness at a time such as this—and she was devastated Lushing had passed. But it seemed wrong somehow that the silence was deafening. She wanted to ask Constance to play a lively tune on the pianoforte or Florence to belt out a vivacious song to her heart's content. She wanted joy and happiness. She wanted to laugh. God help her, she wanted to hear Aiden Trewlove's laughter circling the room just as it had when he'd realized she did indeed know her way around a carom game.

Then off to her right, she heard a whisper of glee that had her heart expanding as she recalled how many times Lushing would whisper something untoward in her ear—

"Do you think Lady Lilith owns a mirror? That gown is a ghastly shade on her."

"I daresay Lord Hammersmith will be sneaking into Lady Margaret's bedchamber later if I'm reading the message of her fan correctly."

"I believe Lady Downing is pouring spirits into her punch and it's not even two of the afternoon yet."

So she strained to make out the conversation, to hear something she might share with Lushing when she visited his grave, something that would have brought a smile to his face in life.

". . . decadent. Gambling, drinking. I smoked a cigar in the billiards room."

Selena closed her eyes. The billiards room. She'd done a good bit worse than smoke a cigar. Although perhaps the girl was talking of another—

"Mr. Trewlove prowls through the rooms like a great predatory cat, so lithe and smooth, and then suddenly he's there, standing beside you, whispering something delicious in your ear."

"Like what?" Lady Carolyn asked sotto voce.

Your skin reminds me of silk, only softer.

"That I should only ever waltz as I'm far too graceful for anything else." This from Lady Georgiana, the smoker of cigars.

"You've waltzed with him?"

Oh yes, but not nearly enough.

"Well, no. He never dances with anyone. I suspect with his upbringing he doesn't know how."

Oh, he knows how.

"He waltzed with someone the other night," Lady Josephine piped up. "My word, the way he held her, the way he looked at her, the way he moved with her—it was enough to make my mouth water."

"Who was she?" Lady Carolyn had never been afraid to ask questions.

"I don't know. She was masked. That's the thing. If you're not comfortable being seen there, you can wear a mask. Really, Lady Carolyn, you simply must give it a go."

The girls' voices had increased in volume until Selena was fairly certain she wasn't the only one eavesdropping on the conversation. The twins had perked up considerably, their attention no doubt snagged. Even as she thought it was not the sort of establishment that she wanted her sisters to visit, she couldn't help but consider that it would be a nice escape for them. She could limit their exposure to the ballroom. Perhaps she would confide in them and take them with her, although her reasons for going were far more unsavory than theirs would be and she would have to slip away unnoticed without igniting their curiosity. Better to leave them at home.

"Honestly, girls," one of the matrons, Lady Marrow, chastised. "This is entirely inappropriate conversation for the occasion."

"I thought the place was myth," Lady Waverly, another matron, said.

"No, it exists, and it's absolutely marvelous," Lady Hortense exclaimed, her voice rife with excitement.

"It is an establishment owned by someone born in shame. It's not to be tolerated, and you shouldn't be associated with him," Lady Marrow stated sternly.

Selena caught sight of Lady Elverton sitting perfectly still and stiffly, her face an unreadable mask. Her father was a baron, although whispers abounded that she was not welcomed into his home. It was rumored she'd been the Earl of Elverton's mistress before his wife had wretchedly drowned in a boating mishap. Nearly thirty years had passed since the tragedy and her marriage to the earl, yet still she was barely accepted or tolerated by the *ton*, although it didn't seem to bother her overly much. Selena hadn't yet been born when the scandal had taken place, so she couldn't testify to the veracity of the rumors and wasn't certain whether they had faded or intensified over the years.

"He once told me I was pretty." Lady Cecily had the unfortunate distinction of having rather large teeth that her upper lip couldn't quite cover.

"He is a scoundrel of the first water," Lady Marrow insisted. "Of course, he is going to flirt and tell you what you wish to hear. He wants something from you."

What could he possibly want from Selena that she wasn't willing to give him? She'd practically thrown herself at him, and he had yet to catch her fully.

"But he's ever so nice," one of the younger ladies said.

"So is the devil when he's seeking to take your soul." One of Lady Marrow's brows shot up so high it nearly disappeared in her hair.

"Despite the rumors regarding the Trewloves' origins, they don't seem a bad lot," Selena said.

Gasps at her audacity pounded her. Or perhaps it was simply that no one had expected her to escape her grief long enough to speak.

"You are pretty, Lady Cecily. I suspect he merely wanted to compliment your looks, and nothing more."

The poor girl blushed and ducked her head. Yes, Selena could see Aiden Trewlove delivering a kindness in the form of a bit of flattery to a shy lady with hopeful eyes who probably went without much kindness or flattery bestowed upon her. She'd had three Seasons already and would soon be relegated to the shelf.

"You give him too much credit, Duchess." It seemed Lady Marrow would not be deterred from her opinion or prone to changing it. "As for the rumors, they are fact. They were born in sin, which makes them immoral."

Although it wasn't the first time she'd heard that argument, she had never truly embraced it. Nor had Lushing. He'd always believed in judging people based on their own merits. However now she had to wonder: If Aiden Trewlove fathered her babe, would the little one be immoral? Would the child be condemned to hell? Would Aiden's sins pass through him to become the sins of her child? "I've never quite understood that reasoning. The sin should rest with the parents, surely. The child is innocent of any wrongdoing."

"The loose morals are passed down through the blood. Sinners give birth to sinners. It is the very reason we have a hierarchy in the social order."

"I doubt anyone in this room is without sin," Lady Elverton said quietly, but her eyes still held a challenge. "Which would make the entire aristocracy immoral, would it not? If indeed we follow your logic, Lady Marrow, which I for one do not. I agree with the duchess. Regardless of the circumstances of their birth, babes are pure, without sin, without shame. They are innocence at its most basic. *Tabula rasa* I believe is how philosophers view it."

The elderly matron sniffed. "I disagree. The Bible is quite clear. The sins of the father are visited—"

"Are the sins of the father," Lady Elverton stated emphatically, and Selena wondered if she had indeed been the mistress of the earl and if she might have given him children before they were wed. If she had, where were they now?

Selena could fairly see steam escaping Lady Marrow's ears as she opened her mouth—

"Lushing had such a forgiving nature that I think he would agree with Lady Elverton," Selena said, feeling a need to defend those born on the wrong side of the blanket. "I daresay, should I be blessed with a child, I shall hope he inherits none of my sins."

"Your only sin is eating too many strawberries," Alice said cheerily, which might have received a chuckle or two under different circumstances—if all eyes hadn't dropped suddenly and swiftly to Selena's abdomen. While initially they may have been looking for evidence of her gluttony, the speculation mirrored in their eyes indicated their curiosity had abruptly careened into another direction: the possibility of her being with child. Of their own accord her hands spread out over her belly as though she did indeed have something in need of protection.

"Is it possible?" Lady Josephine whispered, confirming Selena's interpretation of their intense stares.

Before she could respond, Florence announced impatiently, "Anything is possible. My dear sister is in mourning, and you're all being frightfully inconsiderate with your inappropriate conversations."

"When you're out of mourning," Lady Cecily whispered, leaning toward her, "you really must visit the Elysium. The relaxation room is just the thing. I'll be more than happy to accompany you to spare you feeling awkward at the place."

"Thank you. I shall keep your offer in mind." But regretfully, once Aiden Trewlove fulfilled her need for him, she would never again cross the threshold into his establishment.

SHE'D FOUND THE oppressiveness in the front parlor unbearable, but then the men arrived once Lushing was laid to rest and the somberness became too much. It was an odd thing, but an overwhelming urge overcame her to dart out of the residence, race through the mews, and run as fast as her legs could churn to the Elysium—to Aiden Trewlove. To once again be in his arms, to have his whispered words of reassurance echoing in her ears. To feel safe, secure, and protected. To draw strength from him in order to face all the challenges that awaited her.

Instead she did the proper thing. When condolences had all been offered and received, when those gathered in the parlor finally wandered into the dining room where refreshments awaited them, she snuck out into the gardens and sat on a wrought-iron bench where roses would bloom in a couple of months. Lushing had so enjoyed his flowers. Envisioning him strolling among the spring blossoms brought her a measure of peace.

A peace that was disturbed by the harsh sound of boot heels on the stone bricks that comprised the path wending its way through the grounds. Glancing over she was disappointed to see the Earl of Elverton. Kit she would have welcomed. Even her brother, but she was not in the mood to deal with others of the nobility, hoped he would see he was intruding and reverse his course.

"Quite the crush indoors." He came to stand before her. He was equal in height to Aiden Trewlove, but his body was not nearly as toned, his indulgence in rich foods evident by the rounding of his stomach. Strange how she found herself comparing him to Aiden, and yet she feared in the future she would compare all men to him as he had a way of intruding on her thoughts at the oddest of times. The earl's hair was a faded brown speckled with silver, and she rather regretted she wouldn't see Aiden's hair turn snowy white. In spite of having walked the earth for nearly six decades, Elverton possessed the energy of a younger man. Although his features sagged a bit and were populated with wrinkles, he was still quite the handsome devil. She could readily understand why it was rumored he'd had a bevy of lovers in his youth. But comeliness did not justify infidelity.

"Yes. I was in search of a bit of quiet."

"I thought as much when I caught sight of you leaving."

Yet, still you followed, denying me the peace I sought.

He glanced around. "As I understand it, a good bit of your husband's holdings will go to the Treasury."

"Possibly."

He jerked his head back around so quickly to stare at her that she thought she might have heard the clack of his bones. "Are you with child then?"

"That's hardly an appropriate question at a time such as this, my lord."

"Quite right. Regardless, you are a young and beautiful woman. I doubt you fancy the notion of a life alone and without comfort."

Oh dear Lord. Was he honestly on the verge of making a pitch at this precise moment under these trying circumstances that she consider marrying his heir? Viscount Wyeth, at eight and twenty, was nearer to her age than Lushing had been and was quite the charmer—

"Perhaps you would not mind if I called upon you."

Had she been standing, she'd have staggered back by the forthrightness of his statement and its implication. "I beg your pardon?"

"You are the most gorgeous woman in all of England. It would be a shame for such beauty to be spent cloistered away."

She had a strong desire to smack him for focusing only on her prettiness, recalling how Aiden had thoroughly kissed her without knowing her precise appearance. Her words came out curt with disapproval. "I am in mourning."

"Two years is an ungodly amount of time to go without the comfort of a man. I can be most discreet."

"You're married," she pointed out succinctly, bristling with the knowledge that he would be so incredibly discourteous and disrespectful of his countess. Did he truly believe that Selena would think he would treat her any differently after a time?

"My wife and I have an understanding." He took the liberty of sitting on the bench beside her. She shot to her feet, unwilling to offer him any encouragement in his pursuit of her. He grinned. Something about that grin was familiar and yet not. "You are a widow, free of societal restraints."

"I'm not in the market to be your mistress."

"The role would be temporary—until your mourning period is done with. Then I would take you to wife."

"You have a wife," she reminded him again, horrified that he was engaging her in this ridiculous conversation.

"One who is aging, not as vivacious as she once was. I doubt she is long for this world."

Stunned, she floundered around for some retort. "She appears perfectly healthy to me, and I daresay I find her most vivacious." Especially when defending the innocence of babes born in sin.

"Looks can be deceiving." He rose to his full height, no doubt striving to intimidate. "I meant no offense. I simply wanted to assure you that if you allowed me to call on you, to offer you comfort during your hour of need, that my intentions would be honorable. If you do not deliver an heir after seven years of marriage, no lord in need of one will take you to wife. I am not in need of one."

Her mind was stuttering with his implication that she was doomed to spend the remainder of her life alone, unless she accepted his offer. She was well aware that her current course could be futile, that she might be unable to conceive—that the fault for Lushing's absence of an heir rested with her. Still, she wasn't quite ready to accept defeat, not when so much was at stake. She could do little more than stare at this smug man who had, intentionally or not, struck a blow to her confidence.

"Duchess?"

Glancing over, she was grateful to see the Duke of Thornley standing within the curve of the path, having just emerged from behind the hedgerows. Or at least she hoped he'd only just arrived. She wondered how much he might have heard. "I was in need of some fresh air."

Thornley looked from her to Elverton, back to her. "I can't say as I blame you. Lushing was beloved by a good many. Still I think even he would have been surprised by the number of mourners who turned out today." He ambled over to her, placing himself between her and the earl, effectively creating a barrier between them. "Elverton."

"Thornley. I was just offering my condolences to the duchess on her loss."

"I've no doubt she was comforted by your words. If you'll excuse us, I wish to do the same—in private."

"Of course." Elverton bowed his head toward her. "Should you need anything at all, I am at your service."

An offer she would ignore. Angling her chin haughtily, she met his gaze. "In case I don't get a chance, please relay to your countess how very much I appreciated her presence today."

He twisted his lips into an ironic smile, and once more she was hit with a sense of familiarity. Perhaps she'd seen a similar smile on Viscount Wyeth during one of the many times they'd danced. Finally, Elverton walked away, and the tension within her eased.

"Are you all right?" Thornley asked.

Looking up at him, she knew no propositions would be coming from this man. It was no secret how much he adored his wife. "As all right as any woman can be on the day her husband is placed in the ground."

"That was a rather thoughtless question on my part, although to be honest, I was referring to your encounter with Elverton. I know sometimes he can be a bit . . . uh—"

"Of an arse?"

He chuckled low. "Insensitive."

"He can be that." She decided to move the conversation away from the man who had unsettled her. "I'm sorry your duchess didn't come. I would have welcomed her."

"Gillie didn't feel the circumstances were ideal for making your acquaintance. But she does send her condolences."

"Are you happy with her, Thorne?"

"Happier than I have a right to be."

"I look forward to meeting her someday." Other duties had prevented her and Lushing from attending their wedding.

"I think you'll like her."

"I'm sure I will. I suppose you've come to know

her siblings well." Odd how she wanted him to reaffirm that her instincts regarding Aiden Trewlove were accurate, that in spite of his businesses, he was an honorable man. She knew her focus should be on Lushing this day, but he'd held a curiosity about the Trewloves, had even suggested she invite them to the ball they'd have hosted this Season. He'd been in favor of welcoming them into the aristocratic fold.

"It took them a while to accept me."

She released a huff of surprise. "I'd have thought it would have been the other way around."

"They are impressed with neither rank nor title. But there is a goodness to them that initially put me to shame. They look out for the poorest and weakest among us, looking for nothing in return. Lady Aslyn and Mick recently opened a home for unwed mothers, while Lady Lavinia and Finn are taking in orphans. My dear wife feeds the hungry."

"With your assistance."

He shook his head. "No, she was doing that long before I ever came along. I suspect Lushing would have supported all their various charitable works."

"I'm sure he would have. He had an extremely generous nature." She should stop there, and yet she seemed unable to do so. "There's another Trewlove who's recently opened . . . well, only ladies are supposed to know about it, and they were discussing it earlier, as inappropriate as that might be, but I imagine you know of it, being related by marriage."

He nodded. "A club where ladies can raise a little hell. Aiden owns that."

"Is it his intention to corrupt us all?"

He grinned. "You can never tell with Aiden."

"That's not very reassuring. Do you think women are unsafe with him?"

"He likes to have a jolly good time, but he'd never do it at another's expense. He won't take advantage of the ladies who come to his club, if that's your concern."

It was reassuring to hear voiced by another what she had already surmised. Not that she was going to confess to having gone there. "Some of the ladies sharing their experiences earlier are just so young. The older ladies were a bit appalled."

"I suspect there are few places in London where a young lady is safer."

"Perhaps my sisters and I will visit once we're out of mourning."

"It'll serve as a nice distraction. Now if you'll excuse me, I'm most anxious to return to my wife."

"Rumors are rife that she's with child."

Joy wreathed his face, and she regretted that Lushing had never had occasion to shine with such delight, to share in the elation of expectancy. "She is."

"I'm so happy for you, for you both."

"Thank you. May I escort you to the residence?"

"I suppose I've abandoned my guests long enough." She slipped her arm around the one he offered.

"It'll get easier," he assured her.

"One can only hope."

Chapter 10

*H*e knew the moment she walked in that something was amiss, even with the damn mask keeping her expression from him. He could see it in the set of her jaw, the dimpling of her chin. When he reached her, before he could even touch her, she shook her head.

"I shouldn't have come. I can't do this tonight, and yet I wanted to see you."

"What happened? Tell me what's wrong." Although he had his suspicions.

A quivering smile. "Would you come somewhere with me?"

"To the ends of the earth." His immediate response took him off guard. It was not delivered in a flirtatious manner, but because he meant the words. He would contemplate that unsettling thought later.

A little huff of breath that might have passed for a laugh in other circumstances escaped her lips. "Not nearly that far. My carriage is down the street, waiting."

"Then lead the way."

He escorted her through the grand foyer, out the door, and onto the bricked walkway. Even with a destination in mind, she ambled slowly, her heels barely making a sound while they traversed as though she hadn't the energy to lift her feet properly. She was saddened, melancholy, a woman quite possibly only a few days into her mourning period.

Either that or she was embarrassed and ashamed for falling apart in his arms the night before. But if that were the case, would she have returned?

When they neared the familiar black coach, the driver opened the door and she whispered something as he handed her up. Aiden resisted the urge to snap the man's fingers in two. He was merely doing his job, but Aiden didn't much like the notion of anyone touching her, which he knew was not at all rational. Following her inside, he settled on the seat opposite her, where he would remain until she indicated she wanted him beside her, holding her. Black curtains were drawn at the windows. A lit lamp inside provided him with the light by which to see her.

With a lurch the vehicle took off. Reaching up, she removed the mask and set it beside her on the seat. "No one is likely to see us where we are going."

"Where would that be?"

"A cemetery. I do hope you're not afraid of ghosts or hauntings."

"I fear very little, sweetheart." Not giving her what she required to be happy came to mind. "I'm going to take a wild guess here that you're the Duchess of Lushing and the sorrow I sense coming from you has to do with the duke being laid to rest today."

"How clever you are. Although I'm relieved that you figured it out because now you understand why it's imperative no one else learn I've been to

your club. I suppose you saw his obituary in the
Times."

"No, actually. I went to see my sister, who told
me her husband was spending the day engaged in
somber business."

"Of course. Thornley came to show his respect.
You should know that I'd have welcomed your sister into my home had she come, although I was not
at my best. I didn't expect it all to hit me so hard.
Lushing had always made it a point to be at my side
when guests arrived, to greet them and make them
feel welcome, and today I felt his absence keenly. It
struck me that he would never be there again. For
some reason tonight, I had an overwhelming urge
to go to the cemetery. Naturally, Kit would accompany me tomorrow—"

"Kit?" Another man who might need his fingers
broken.

Her smile was brief but soft. "Viscount Kittridge.
He and Lushing were close. He oversaw matters today, the procession to the church, the service, the
burial. Since women are discouraged from attending funerals—we are too delicate, you see—I sat in
the parlor while ladies tried to comfort me, mostly
by talking about your establishment."

It might have been inappropriate but still he
grinned. "All good, I hope."

"Oh yes. Apparently, the relaxation room is just
the thing. You've not shared that one with me."

"I'll put it on the list, although I suspect you'll
find it a trifle boring. Ladies lounge around while
men rub their feet or brush their hair or massage
their shoulders."

He didn't think she was really listening, as her

attention was concentrated on her knotted hands, and he suspected that if he removed her gloves, he'd find her knuckles had turned white.

"My attire is entirely inappropriate for visiting my dead husband, but I couldn't very well walk into your place in mourning black—it would have given me away. For some reason I can't explain, once I left the residence, I had an immediate need to go see Lushing and decided to disturb you and take you from your work." She rubbed her fingers over her forehead. "I don't know what I was thinking."

"You're grieving. I doubt you're thinking at all, but I'm glad you came to me tonight." More than he cared to admit.

"I don't know why I did. I knew only that I didn't wish to be alone and you provided such comfort last night."

He'd provided a good deal more than that, but now wasn't the time for reminding her or teasing her about it.

"It was selfish of me to impose on your kindness."

Although he'd not known her long, he'd managed to discern selfishness was a stranger to her. He'd known selfish women before. They wouldn't have pulled a dodge in order to ask questions of him; they'd have used the opportunity to speak of themselves or to have him slathering over them. Even succumbing to her wishes had proved to be no burden. "If I didn't want to be here, I'd have said no."

With a sigh, she looked toward the window, no doubt forgetting that the curtains prevented her from seeing the passing scenery. "I should have gone to the funeral. I think it would have helped put matters behind me. At the moment I feel untethered. I suspect you have a dim view of me now that you know I sought out pleasure so soon after falling into widowhood."

"People grieve in different ways."

Her gaze came back to him. "Have you had cause to grieve, then, Mr. Trewlove? You told me no one you held dear had ever died."

"There are all sorts of losses." When his brother Finn had been sent to prison, he'd felt as though the iron door had been shut on him as well. He'd mourned the loss of someone who had been a part of his days, his nights. But fury had tempered the grief, and he'd known he'd see Finn again. Her husband was now lost to her forever. "I've been spared the misery of death."

"You're fortunate. I'm all of twenty-five and have had far too much to mourn."

Her husband might not have brought her pleasure in bed, but it was obvious she'd cared for him.

The carriage rolled to a stop, and she appeared uncertain, even as she angled her chin in an attempt to put on a brave front. "We've arrived."

For the life of her, she couldn't explain why she'd gone to him, asked him to accompany her. She'd known only that she'd longed for his company, but not in the role of a lover—simply as a friend. A friend who laughed when she bested him. Knowing she would give away her identity no longer seemed to matter as she was relatively certain he'd have figured it out eventually. They conversed far more than she'd anticipated, but she found she rather liked it. And if she required naught but silence as they strolled through the cemetery, she knew he would sense her needs and provide only his presence.

If they'd been allowed to stroll within. But when they reached the gates, and he held the lamp he'd taken from inside the carriage aloft, she could do little more than stare in overwhelming disappointment at the padlock that held them securely closed. "I'd not considered that they'd lock it up for the night."

"To discourage graverobbers I suspect. If you can spare two hairpins, I'll unlock it for you."

"Are you also a thief, then?"

His grin, somewhat self-mocking, flashed in the night. "My brother was."

Glancing around, she realized if constables were wandering about, they might be arrested. No, they would not. Her position would see her needs indulged. Reaching up, she removed two pins and handed them to him.

"Hold this." He extended the lamp toward her, which she took without hesitation. He crouched, balancing on the balls of his feet, an extremely masculine pose. "Bring the light nearer, so I can see."

Again she followed his order, watched as he placed one hairpin between his teeth, securing it as he straightened it with his fingers, then did the same to the other. "So your brother thought you might need this skill at some point?"

He inserted the pins into a hole in the lock. "My siblings and I had an understanding—if one of us learned something, he or she would teach it to the others. Mick taught us all about the nobility, peerage, titles, rank, how to address the nobs, how to drink tea around them." His fingers stilled; he twisted around slightly, glanced up at her, and winked. "I could drink tea in your parlor with the Queen present, and she wouldn't know I'd begun my life in the gutter."

He returned his attention to his task. "As I told you, Gillie was about posh talk and knowing your liquors. Finn, the thief, was a young lad when he embarked on that career. Our mum got wind of it and took nearly an inch of flesh off his backside with her switch, so he became a horse slaughterer. He taught us about all the various equines. The different types, how to ride them, care for them. Then Beast . . . well." He looked back up at her and grinned. "You'd be surprised by the things I know."

A click echoed around them. He removed the lock, slipped it into his pocket, and pulled the chain through the bars on the gate, setting it aside. He pushed himself to his feet, tucked her pins inside his jacket, and she mourned the fact that they were ruined to such an extent he couldn't tuck them back into her hair, not that she wanted the pins so much as she wanted his fingers skimming over the strands. "You have another sister. I saw her at Lady Aslyn's wedding, although I didn't get a chance to speak with her."

"Fancy."

"What did she teach you?"

"That children are irritating little buggers. I was fourteen when she was born. Not a lot she could teach me by the time she was old enough to provide lessons." He took the lamp from her and offered his arm, which she gladly took. "Do you know where we're going?"

"Yes." Lushing brought her after he purchased the plots, so she would know where they would be laid to rest. "Once we enter, we turn right at the first pathway."

"He seems to have prepared for things. Did he know he was going to die?" he asked as he escorted her into the cemetery.

"No. He took a chill in the winter. It worsened into this horrible gurgling cough." Influenza morphing into pneumonia, the physician had told her. Until eventually he hadn't been able to draw in air.

"I'm surprised he's buried in a public cemetery rather than at his estate. There's a mausoleum there, surely."

A very ornate one of stone. "He preferred the gardens here at Abingdon Park. He was never particularly close to his father. My husband's mother died when he was around fifteen. He and his father had a terrible row shortly thereafter. As a result, his father forbid him to use his courtesy title, cut off his allowance, disowned him for all practical purposes, although he couldn't stop him from eventually inheriting. Lushing was the legal heir, and the law protected his inheritance. Thank goodness for Kittridge. His father had passed a few years earlier, so he'd already inherited the title and properties that placed him in a position to provide a haven for Lushing—or Arthur Sheffield, as he was known at the time—until the titles and properties passed on to him. Or so I was told. I was only a child when all this started. Lushing was twelve years my senior."

"I can't get a good look at things, but it seems peaceful here."

"It is. Like so many these days, Lushing was very much obsessed with the celebration of death. I find it all very morbid. This morning a photographer arrived to take a photo of Lushing laid out in the casket. Apparently, he'd arranged for it to be done some time back. I don't understand the need to have an image of him dead."

"For some, who can't afford photographers, it's the last, perhaps the only, chance for the family to have the deceased immortalized."

"Cost was not a factor for him. Nor was it the only chance. He was photographed many times. I don't fancy death mementos. Lord Kittridge asked if he could take some snippets of Lushing's hair to have a watch fob made. I know it's customary to use the hair for various pieces of jewelry, but I can't bring myself to be so adorned. This way." They turned down a path and followed it around a small pond, circled by willows, their branches hanging down like gossamer curtains. It was lovely during the day. At night it seemed more mystical. She could imagine sprites darting around. Tightening her hold on his arm, she relished the strength she found there.

On a puff of laughter, she said, "He'll no doubt roll over in his grave if he catches sight of the risqué clothing I'm wearing."

"On the contrary, I think he'd appreciate it."

She glanced over and up at him. He was such a reassuring presence. If any spirits decided to engage in some hauntings, he'd send them back to where they came from right quick. It was odd to feel so close to someone she'd known only a couple of days, but then, the intense intimacy they'd shared was no doubt responsible. How could a woman not draw comfort from a man who had feasted between her thighs? "Did you ever meet him? Did he come to your other club?"

"If he did, he didn't use his real name or title. Although I'm fairly good at ferreting out deception so I rather doubt it."

Swallowing became difficult as she wondered if he'd correctly ferret out her deception and motivations. If he discovered the truth, would he be angry or not care?

"Here we are," she said.

HE WATCHED AS she knelt at the foot of a mound of dirt covered in flowers.

"I had no tears for him today. I wept them all last night," she said quietly.

Crouching beside her, he draped his forearm over his thigh. He was in an odd place, not so much the cemetery as offering comfort. He'd always been about the laughs, the fun, the pleasure when it came to women. She was causing him to delve beneath the surface and he wasn't sure he liked it. Yet the alternative was not to be here for her, and he liked that notion even less. "I'd have thought he'd have a monstrous headstone."

"Oh he does. It's a huge angel carved from stone that will watch over him, us. The vicar said it would be best to wait a year before putting it in place. Apparently, it takes the ground a while to settle after it's been disturbed by a burial."

He didn't care about the ground, but something else had caught his attention. "Us, you said."

"Yes, he purchased the plot next to him, on his left so I'm buried near his heart."

"Not for a good long while yet, I should think."

She offered him a small smile. "I shall hope not."

The thought of losing her caused a tightness in his chest—

As though she were his to lose, an inner voice castigated him. She was only for jollies, until she tired of him or he tired of her. Yet here he was in one of the least fun places in the world, and he wasn't thinking about how he'd like to pleasure her again, but only how best to comfort her. He was grateful she'd wanted him to be with her as she made this little excursion. "How did you come to marry him?"

Her laugh was as wispy as the tendrils of fog that were beginning to gather. "I'd known of him, of course. But only by name and reputation—the black sheep of Sheffield Hall, the family estate. When I was seventeen, I was presented to the Queen so I might have my first Season."

"That seems rather young."

"With your refined speech and well-tailored clothing, it's easy to forget that you don't come from my world and might be unfamiliar with the details of it. There isn't a specific age requirement for being presented to the Queen. A girl need be merely viewed as mature and having reached a level of sophistication deemed sufficient by her parents. I have a friend who was presented at fourteen." She hesitated before continuing. "In my case, my father was most anxious to see me married because his financial situation was dire. He was struggling to maintain the estate and feared if I didn't marry soon, he'd have to sell the small property he'd set aside as my dowry. He made it quite clear that I needed to set my sights on someone who had the means to be generous. My cause was aided by the fact that the gossip rags referred to me as the most beautiful debutante of the Season."

Her focus on the grave, all he could see were the shadows of her profile. "That's the reason you weren't happy when I complimented your beauty."

Slowly she turned her head and her gaze came to rest on him. "I am more than my features, but when I was seventeen, they were all that mattered. As fate would have it, Arthur Sheffield's father had died two years before, and now he was well ensconced as the Duke of Lushing and had decided that it was long past the time that he took a wife. At twenty-nine, handsome and wealthy, he was declared the catch of the Season. Within minutes of arriving at my first ball, the hostess, the Duchess of Ainsley, brought him over for an introduction. He claimed my first waltz. Halfway through he confessed that he'd done it as a lark because he found it humorous that we were considered *catches* and thought our dancing together would cause tongues to wag. He also confessed to liking me very much and being surprised by it. He didn't take anyone else out on the floor that night. So, naturally tongues *did* wag."

He didn't want to consider that once her mourning period was over, she would be attending other balls, dancing with other men, having another lord confessing that he liked her very much. "And you were smitten."

"That's rather a strong word for what I felt. I liked

him well enough. He was kind and had a lovely smile. The following morning, he sent flowers. The next afternoon he took me for a ride through the park in his barouche. Soon after that my father had a word with him. Very soon after that, Lushing asked for my hand in marriage."

"And you accepted."

"I told him I needed to think about it. The Season had been underway for such a short time. It was only May. So much attention was being bestowed upon me by other lords that I was wearing out two pairs of slippers at every ball. I was having a grand time. I knew a good bit of the attention would end once a betrothal was announced. My father was furious. He packed up us girls and returned us to the country estate. I think he intended it as a sort of punishment, to take me away from all the fun, to make me rethink my answer, to remind me that the Season was not a game but had a purpose to it: to see me wed. Two weeks later he and Mother were dead."

He clearly heard the guilt she harbored reflected in her voice. "Their deaths were not your fault."

"If I'd said yes to Lushing, we'd have stayed in the city."

"But now you needed the wealthy duke more than ever."

"He arrived at the estate without my sending for him. My brother had stayed in London. I sent word to him about what had happened, so I suppose he told others before he returned home. Hours after he arrived, there was Lushing. Winslow was only nineteen, completely unprepared to take on the mantle of the earldom. Lushing saw to everything without being asked. He made all the funeral arrangements, spoke with the solicitor, the vicar, and the undertaker. I'd given him cause to doubt my devotion, yet he became my rock. My fondness for him grew. I told him if he was willing to wait until my mourning period was over, I would marry him. He waited. The following May, one year to the day after my parents died, we were wed."

"It sounds as though he was a good bloke."

Another tiny laugh from her. "I don't know if Lushing has ever been referred to as a 'bloke' but yes, there was much goodness in him." She turned her attention back to the grave. "He certainly deserved better than a wife who would go to your club three nights after he passed. I don't know what I was thinking, what possessed me to do such a thing."

He was ever so glad she had, and didn't want her regretting her decision or avoiding the club in the future. "Who is there for you at night?"

"My sisters. Lushing didn't object to their living with us. His residences were so much more organized, and I was quite skilled at managing them. It's what I'd been trained to do. Winslow, as a bachelor, is rubbish at caring for the girls. He was especially so when he was only twenty. I like having them about, but they retire by nine, and then the house becomes so quiet."

"So you came to the Elysium in search of comfort as much as anything." Not just the sex as she'd initially indicated.

"You might have the right of it. While for Lushing and myself the act itself was never . . . might have been lacking, afterward provided me with some of my favorite memories. He would simply hold me, and we would speak in low voices about nonsensical matters: dreams we'd held as children, disappointments, moments that filled us with happiness. We'd recount our favorite aspects of journeys we'd taken, and we'd plan where we'd go next. He wouldn't stay long. Half an hour or so. But I always felt we shared more intimacy during those minutes than at any other time. I was always bereft when he left, but never found the courage to ask him to stay. Marriage is an odd thing, Mr. Trewlove."

"Based on what you've revealed, I don't think he would have found fault with you seeking solace away from the residence."

"I hope you're right. I never wanted him to find me disappointing." She glanced up, sighed. "I pray he's at peace."

"Is there a reason he shouldn't be?"

She shook her head slowly, wistfully. "As you deduced, he was a good man, well liked. The residence was packed with mourners this afternoon. Yet all I wanted was to be alone."

"Shall I walk away for a bit?"

Shifting slightly, she faced him. "No. Why is it that I draw such comfort from you, a man I've known for only a couple of days, and found little with those I've known for ages?"

"Perhaps because we have no history to muddy the waters."

"It's more than that. I can't explain it. From the first moment I spied you, it was as though something within me recognized a kindred spirit." Her laugh was brief but mocking, slicing into the air that was beginning to gray with fog. "Yet, we couldn't be more different."

He didn't put much stock in fanciful things like love at first sight but had to admit he was drawn to her, had been from the moment he'd spotted her entering his establishment, without even knowing precisely what she looked like or who she was. Reaching out, he stroked his finger along the length of her face before cupping her chin. He couldn't deny something burned between them, but she had the right of it. They were far too different for anything to come of it, other than a jolly good time.

"The fog is thickening. We can't have you getting damp, catching a chill."

"No, of course not. Thank you for coming with me."

"I'm available anytime you need me." The words were out before he considered the implication of them. Yet, he also realized they held truth, for now anyway. Until they parted ways, for surely a parting would come. His businesses were not the sort in which a wife would take pride or children would boast. Why the bloody hell were thoughts of family rushing through his head? Two of his brothers might have chosen marriage, but it was not for him. Too confining in its demands that one act in a respectable manner.

Impatient with himself and the path his thoughts traveled, he pushed himself to his feet and then gently brought her up from her kneeling position. With the lantern in one hand, he placed the other on the small of her back and began guiding her out of a place that he'd at first found peaceful and now found unsettling. Death had a way of making a person think about life, about the manner in which one applied himself to the hours that he was granted breath. He was not now going to begin wishing a different road stretched out before him. As much as he hated to admit it, he was his father's son, had always been so. At his core, his needs ruled.

IN THE CARRIAGE, he sat beside her, his hand wrapped protectively around hers as it rested on his thigh. Such an intimate positioning, yet Selena hadn't objected when he'd placed it there. Nor had she protested when he informed her driver that he was to deliver her to the residence and Aiden would make his own way back to his club after he'd seen her safely inside. He knew who she was. What did it matter that he discovered where she lived? He could ask around and learn where the Duke of Lushing resided when in London. She was rather certain Aiden understood boundaries existed for them, and he would not cross over them to call upon her at her residence. Their association was to be limited to the night shadows, their encounters to be initiated by her appearing at his club. She didn't need to spell that out—and if she discovered she did, then she most certainly would.

She needed to remain in charge of this relationship—except for the moments when he was in control and bringing her pleasure.

She drew comfort from his silence, from his not having a need to fill the confines with the deepness of his voice. He could convey so much with a mere touch, with little more than his presence. In spite of the manner in which he'd shattered her world the night before, he'd effectively pieced it all back together tonight.

"Why gambling hells?" she eventually asked. "I know you enjoy numbers and figuring odds, but surely more thought than that went into the businesses you decided to open."

"There is a good deal of wealth to be made in vice. And it can be made quickly. I wanted to put myself in a position where my achievements were impressive enough that I could lord them over my sire."

She was surprised he'd mentioned his father after claiming to never speak of him, but then, it seemed a night for sharing revelations. "He knows of your successes?"

"I make sure he does. I want him to be aware that I am a man to be reckoned with. Within my world I have more power than he has within his."

"Who is he?" she asked, hoping this time he might tell her. It would be nice to know the bloodline her child would inherit, if she were to get pregnant.

"A lord of no consequence. I shouldn't have mentioned him."

"Was it difficult growing up in your world?"

"I had my brothers and Gillie. We always stuck together and stood up for each other. And my mum was wicked with a broom. If anyone came after us, she'd go after them. No one wanted to have to fend off Ettie Trewlove and her broom."

Smiling at that, she wished she'd known him as a boy.

When they arrived at the residence, she wasn't at all surprised when Aiden leaped out of the vehicle and then reached back to hand her down. Nor was she surprised when he escorted her up the steps to the massive arched doorway. He took the key she'd removed from her reticule and used it to unlock the door, shoving it open slightly before handing the brass back to her. She considered inviting him in, but how would she explain his presence to her sisters should they come upon them or her brother if he wasn't at his residence but was instead lurking about in hers?

So instead she merely turned to him. "Thank you for accompanying me tonight. Have my driver take you back to the club."

"I could do with a walk."

"It's a good distance away."

"I'll run across a hansom somewhere. Don't worry yourself over it. Will you come to the club tomorrow?"

She was grateful for the darkness that prevented him from seeing the blush she was fairly certain was creeping over her cheeks, if their sudden warmth were any indication of what was transpiring. "My mood will be much improved."

"I'll improve it even more. I had something special planned for this evening, but it'll keep." He tucked his forefinger beneath her chin, stroked his thumb over her lips. "Until tomorrow."

Before she could respond, he was striding away. She'd been certain he was going to kiss her, had wanted him to. How was it that he always left her yearning for more even as he somehow managed to leave her satisfied?

" . . . *t*he property in Hertfordshire has been designated as your dower residence and as such will be placed in your name and become your property, although it may not be sold or passed on to another until your death. The exception, naturally, is that should you marry, it would go to your husband. In addition, your late husband created a trust for you that is to be overseen by Lord Kittridge. The yield in interest will be two thousand pounds per annum."

Dazed by Lushing's generosity, Selena stared at Mr. Beckwith, Lushing's solicitor, as he sat incredibly still behind the duke's desk in the library, having just read what he understood to be the most crucial part of her late husband's will. He was no doubt waiting for a burst of grateful tears from her or—

"Why Kittridge and not me?" her brother blurted petulantly. "Why must he oversee this trust?"

Winslow, she, Kittridge, and her sisters were seated in front of the desk as though in a classroom. Glancing at her, Kit did little more than arch one eyebrow. He knew why, just as she did. The viscount was not in need of funds; her brother was. Her husband had feared Winslow might use her allotment to line his own pockets, whereas he had always given Kit his complete trust. How often had the two men stayed up late into the night talking, laughing, enjoying each other's company? How often, when faced with a decision, had Lushing mused, "I'll have to get Kit's opinion on that"? How often had she been disappointed that he'd valued his friend's opinion over hers? Not that it was unusual for one man to place more faith in another man's judgment rather than in a woman's. Still, it had sometimes hurt that her views were not more often sought.

"Because it is what Lushing thought best," she said calmly, not really in the mood to have to deal with salvaging his pride.

"It's not very much," he stated sourly.

It was a princely sum, but it would not allow her to set aside dowries for her sisters or help Winslow get his crumbling estate back up to snuff. "Is there anything else of import, Mr. Beckwith?"

"Yes, Your Grace." He gazed down at the will and read, "'To Lord Kittridge, who has always remained the firmest of friends, I leave my thoroughbreds and hounds.'"

Reaching over, she patted Kit's arm. "He knew you would care for them as he did. They couldn't be in better hands."

"We could have sold them," Winslow muttered.

"Which is the reason he left them to Kit," she snapped. "He wanted to ensure they went to someone who would appreciate them."

"Not to worry," Kit said. "Your mare will remain with you. He did not mean for me to have her."

Lushing had gifted her with the white Arabian

shortly after they'd wed, and she adored the beast. "Thank you." She gave her attention back to the solicitor. "Anything else, sir?"

"As you are no doubt aware, the terms of the entailment have not changed since they were agreed to centuries ago. The properties—other than the dower property—and all incomes, thereof, are to be inherited by a male of the body lawfully begotten. Should none exist, they could be settled on a female lawfully born who can trace her bloodline back to the first duke. Unfortunately, the Sheffields were a cursed lot, prone to bleeding disorders, which resulted in early deaths for many. Accidents or illness led to the demise of the others. The family history of births and deaths is well documented, and all evidence indicates your husband was the last of the line. In the absence of an heir or heiress, the entailed properties will go to Her Majesty's Treasury, and the Crown will determine how they are to be dispensed. We can make an appeal for them to be given to you, but to be quite honest"—he sighed heavily—"based upon the extensive nature of the duke's holdings, I believe it highly unlikely we would see a favorable outcome since you are not of his blood and were married for such a short span of time in the grand scheme of things."

"Lushing held the same opinion." He had talked of making additional arrangements for her but had never gotten around to it, no doubt believing he had more time.

"Because the detailed records prove the absence of an heir, I suspect the title will be deemed extinct. However, you will retain your title as Duchess of

Lushing. All that said, I don't wish to be indelicate, Your Grace, but is there any chance an heir might appear within the next few months?"

In her head, she did quick calculations. While the two thousand pounds was generous and would see her alone in good stead, if she were to divide her yearly income between herself and the girls—she sighed. Five hundred pounds per annum each was hardly a suitable dowry and would be an insufficient amount for maintaining her own property, servants, horses, and carriages. Nothing would remain to assist Winslow. The reality was that more drastic measures were called for.

She could sense breaths being held, tension becoming palpable as they all awaited her answer. Her lie. The words that would haunt her to the grave. "There is, sir."

"Then I shall so inform the Crown and the College of Arms."

"ALTHOUGH YOU HESITATED before answering Beckwith's inquiry regarding the possibility of an heir, you seemed a bit more confident in your condition than you were two days ago when we spoke about the possibility of you being with child," Kit said as they strolled through the garden, her arm nestled within the crook of his.

"I didn't want to give him cause to doubt"—to question the legitimacy of the child being Lushing's—"but my hopes could still fail to come to fruition. I've had occasions before where I thought I was with child, only to be disappointed, so I shall wait before making any formal announcement."

"Beckwith is known for his discretion. And I for my optimism. It would be grand indeed to have a little Arthur running around."

Her stomach roiled. If anyone were capable of detecting that the child did not favor her late husband, it would be Kit.

"He would have made a remarkable father," Kit continued. "Much more loving than his own. So I shall continue to pray fervently that you are with child. It would be a shame to have Sheffield Hall go on the market."

"If I am incorrect in the assessment of my condition, perhaps you could purchase it."

He gave a short laugh. "It will go for an exorbitant amount that is beyond the reach of my coffers." Glancing over at her, he smiled. "You've been set up rather nicely."

"Lushing was incredibly generous." But her father had only set aside a dowry for one daughter, and it had been a modest one at that. A small cottage on a bit of land that brought in no income and would now serve as her dower house. He'd thought he'd had plenty of time to get his financial affairs in order with the help of the man she would marry and provide proper dowries for his other daughters. Under Winslow's hand, Camberley was not even matching the income it had brought in when her father managed it. Tenants were moving to the cities to work in factories, crops from abroad were cheaper than what was grown at home. Even Lushing had lamented his fall in income.

"How are you holding up?" Kit asked.

"As well as can be expected, I suppose. I miss him dearly."

"As do I."

She touched the black armband he wore. "I want to thank you for handling all the funeral affairs."

"It was my privilege to do so."

"The photograph that the photographer took yesterday morning of Lushing in his casket . . . I don't want to remember him like that. Would you like to have it?"

"If you don't mind."

"Not at all. It would be a great relief to be honest. I know it was important to him to have it taken, and I don't think he would have been disappointed that it went to you." She squeezed his arm. "I miss you as well, you know. You joined us for dinner so often. Please don't be a stranger."

"When we've both grieved a bit more, I shall plague you with visits."

She smiled softly. "I look forward to it."

"How long are you going to stay in London?"

That all depended on Aiden Trewlove. "A few more weeks, I should think."

"If you've no objection, I'll go to the estates and retrieve the hounds. But I'll leave the horses, shall I? At least until we know the fate of the estates."

"That would be lovely. The twins so enjoy riding, and the girls will be staying with me until everything is settled."

"I do hope I'm not speaking out of turn here, but you are a young woman, Selena, and two years is a devil of a long time. While Lushing was fascinated by the rituals surrounding death, he didn't approve of lengthy mourning periods. He wouldn't fault you if you didn't strictly observe them."

She wanted to take comfort from his words, but

she suspected what she was doing was not what Lushing had in mind when it came to not strictly observing a mourning period.

"I DEMAND YOU forbid my daughter from entering this . . . this house of sin."

It wasn't the first time a mother had come to him to handle what she apparently couldn't, but he did wish this one hadn't stormed into his office near the hour that Selena would be arriving on his gaming floor—if the timing of her past appearances was any indication.

"Lady Fontaine, I assure you there is nothing a lady can do here that she cannot do elsewhere. At least here, I provide a safe environment for her explorations."

"Her explorations? Sir, it is *your* explorations with which I find fault."

"I do not involve myself with my clientele." To do so would result in fathers arriving with shotguns in hand, waving special licenses. Instead he had mothers with heaving bosoms, lips set in a firm line, and cheeks of high color ignited by their wrath sitting before him.

Reaching into her reticule, she pulled out a small leather-bound book and slammed it on the desk. "I submit proof to the contrary. Her journal in which she has catalogued your flirtation."

"Handed that to you, did she?"

The woman's shoulders quivered with her indignation, even as she averted her gaze while answering. "No. I found it in a drawer amongst her unmentionables."

And yet, they were mentioned. "What precisely have I done that offends your sensibilities?"

She snatched up the book and opened it to a page marked with a purple ribbon. "'Tonight A. T. complimented my eyes. The blue reminds him of the sky as the sun bids farewell to day.' Such poppycock."

The words were a bit too flowery to have been delivered by him. No doubt he'd merely told her she had pretty eyes. But everyone was entitled to their fantasies. This girl wrote hers in a journal. Aiden painted his on canvas. Leaning back in his chair, he propped his elbow on his chair, his chin in his hand. "Why? Why is it poppycock?"

"She is a plain girl, Mr. Trewlove. You fill her with hope."

"Why shouldn't she have hope?"

"Few gentlemen danced with her last Season. The balls will start up in earnest soon, and once again she will be a wallflower, and it will hurt all the more because within these walls you are making her forget what she is."

"Or perhaps it won't hurt as much because within these walls she can dance to her heart's content."

"And gamble. And drink." She shook the journal at him. "She has smoked a cheroot!"

"Have you?"

"Most certainly not."

"Would you like to?"

Her eyes bulged, her mouth opened and closed several times as though she were a fish tossed onto a riverbank. "Most certainly not."

Those words came with less conviction this time around. He leaned forward, clasped his hands on his desk, feeling the minutes ticking by, fearful he was going to miss Selena's arrival. "What say you to this, Lady Fontaine? I will have one of my gents give you a tour and if you see something to which you heartily object, I'll forbid entry to your daughter in the future."

Reaching behind him, he pulled on a sash. A handsome young man soon appeared in the doorway. "Richard, give Lady Fontaine a tour. Be sure to stop in the relaxation room. I think she would benefit from having her feet rubbed."

"By a strange man?" she asked indignantly.

Standing, ready to head down to the gaming floor, he winked at her. "Trust me. You'll be ever so glad you did."

Chapter 12

*I*t was madness, his counting of the hours, minutes, seconds since he'd last seen her, the way his attention kept wandering to the doorway through which she should emerge at any time, the tension building within him as the hour neared ten. He knew where she resided. Perhaps he'd go to her. If for no other reason than to reassure himself that she was well—as well as she could be under the circumstances—to see her, to say something that might make her smile. To lift her burden just a tad. To let her know that he cared—

He brought that thought to a grinding halt as though he'd smacked into a brick wall. He didn't *care* for her. She was a customer he wished to please, to ensure she returned and spent her coins here, even though she had yet to leave any at his tables. He wished he had a proper residence to which he could take her, but he kept rooms here. It was convenient. He worked long hours, late into the night, rising early in the morning. Hours were filled looking over his ledgers, striving to determine how he could increase business. He was of a single purpose: to make himself as wealthy as possible. No, not wealthy—successful. He wanted respect, wanted the circumstances of his birth to no longer matter.

Yes, the ladies here gave him shy looks, smiled at him, and spoke with him, but it was because they were seeking a sort of rebelliousness. And how better to do that than by flirting with a bastard? But only within these walls. Beyond them, they would snub him, cut him, ignore him. Turn their backs on him. He would not be invited into their parlors or ballrooms. He would not be allowed to dine at their tables. He would not be welcomed at *hers*.

She would keep him to the shadows of her life. While on the one hand it grated, on the other he was desperate enough to have her however she stipulated. He understood the terms of their relationship—it was based on the physical only. She wished to be bedded. He wished to bed her.

Beyond that he gave no further thought.

Still when he caught sight of her gliding through the doorway, he envisioned her doing so without the mask, walking into a library where he read, into a dining room where he ate, into a parlor where he lounged, into a bedchamber where he slept, into every room in a grand manor where he resided. He imagined her on his arm striding into shops and taverns and theaters. Strolling through parks. Riding in his barouche. Not that he presently owned one, but no matter what he envisioned himself doing, he imagined her there. Madness indeed.

He made short work of reaching her, aware of the pleasure coursing through him as she bestowed upon him a warm smile. No sadness tonight. No distractions. No unexpected journeys elsewhere. She was here to stay.

Taking her hand, he led her back into the foyer and down a narrow hallway to a set of stairs and didn't hesitate to head up them.

"Where are we going?" she asked.

"Someplace more private."

At the top, he escorted her along a short corridor that on one side was open to the gaming floor. When he reached a door at the corner, he shoved it open and ushered her inside, closing out the world beyond. With his back against the hard wood, he watched as she reached up, undid the lacings on her mask, and removed it. It dangled between her fingers as she wandered around the room, taking in her surroundings. The sofa, the chairs before the fireplace, the low tables, the flames flickering on various candles spread sparingly around the room.

She stopped at the round white linen-covered table near the window where Gillie's finest wine had already been poured, breathing, awaiting Selena's arrival. Assorted cheeses and bread were also there. Along with—

"Strawberries." Glancing over her shoulder, she gave him a gentle smile, one wreathed with pleasure. "They must have cost you a fortune."

"You're worth it."

Slowly, she turned. "Is this the relaxation room?"

"No."

She meandered to an open doorway and peered inside. Grew still, and he knew she recognized a bedchamber when she saw one, especially as this one contained a larger than normal four-poster bed. "Is this where the gents with red buttons bring ladies?"

"No."

She faced him, a thousand questions reflected in her eyes, or perhaps it was merely the flames from all the candles. He crossed over to her, touched his fingers to her soft cheek. "These are my lodgings. I've never brought a woman here." For some reason, he thought it important she know that.

"Why me?"

Because she was different, because she touched him in ways no other woman ever had. Because he wanted to walk in here and inhale her fragrance, wanted to sit in a chair and bring forth memories of her within these walls, wanted to lie in his bed and recall how it had felt to have her beneath him there. "Because you asked to be bedded, and I want you to have more than that. I intend to seduce you."

"With strawberries and wine?"

"For starters."

She wound her arms around his neck, pressed her body up against his, and he went immediately hard. She undid him so easily, and he wanted to have the same effect on her.

"You seduced me from the beginning, Aiden Trewlove, until all I think about, all I dream about is you." Her voice was low, throaty, sensual.

Lifting up on her toes, she planted her mouth on his and he was lost. He cursed her for being the seducer, cursed himself for falling, then cast all his plans onto the wind. For what did it matter when they were of a like mind, when they each craved the other?

And he did crave her, as he'd never yearned for anything in his life. It was not her beauty but her spirit that drew him. Her adventuresome nature that had her searching for what she'd never acquired after the bonds that held her to an oath had been severed. She'd not hesitated to come after what she wanted. She'd rebelled against a mourning period that would have held her in seclusion. Her strength was apparent.

But it was tempered by her caring and concern, her depth of grief for a kind husband who had left her unsatisfied. Tonight Aiden would satisfy her in every way possible. He would take her, possess her, claim her until she thought of no one other than him, until she was convinced that only in his arms would she ever find complete satisfaction, acceptance, fulfillment.

When he was done, she would leave, but would do so with the knowledge that she would return.

At long last he would be hers. Completely. Absolutely. Totally. It was the only thought racing through her mind as he deepened the kiss, thoroughly exploring her mouth as though he'd not done so before. He tasted rich and dark, dangerous. Whisky, perhaps. Or brandy. She imagined him lounging in a chair before the fire, slowly sipping and savoring the amber liquid, preparing for when he would do the same of her.

The stroke of his tongue over hers was leisurely, yet meticulous. He left no aspect of her mouth wanting. His capable hands closed over her bottom, squeezed the cheeks there, pushed her up against him, and the hard ridge of his desire pressed against her belly. Evidence of his own need for her inflamed her passions. He wanted her, yearned for her. This would not be a cold, mindless coupling. It was not about business. It would not be about results. There was a purpose to it beyond anything she'd ever envisioned. It would be about need, the need to possess, the need to share bodies, sensations, pleasure.

How she had longed to be wanted like this, to know with certainty that she was desired. He wanted to please her. The strawberries told her that. The fact he'd not taken her immediately that first night told her more. Their coming together was not the result of animalistic needs requiring satisfaction, no matter how feral his growls or how demanding his hands. It would not be rutting at its most basic. No, there was caring here. A need to satisfy the heart and soul as well as the body. She'd never felt more treasured.

And that was a danger. To her emotions, to her goals, to her fragile heart.

She should put a stop to things immediately, before it was too late. But she wanted what he was offering. She wanted his kiss that turned her knees to jam. She wanted the taste of him, the warmth of him, the feel of him, the scent of him penetrating every aspect of her being. She wanted him, the man. No other would suffice. He was what she craved.

He trailed his hot, moist lips along her throat. "Lena." The rasp was that of a man calling for salvation.

"No one calls me that."

"All the more reason I should."

He had the right of it there. Everything about their encounter would be unique to him. No memory he gave her would ever be usurped by another.

She pressed her mouth to the silky underside of his jaw where his whiskers were the softest. No pet name seemed adequate for him. *Sweetheart* and *darling* were not powerful enough for what he did to her, for the way he made her tremble inside and out. Only one word worked for him, captured his strong and formidable presence. "Aiden."

His growl was long and low, a rumbling in his chest that vibrated against her breasts. He swept her up in his arms and carried her into the bedchamber where the massive bed awaited them.

HE'D NEVER WANTED anything in his life as much as he wanted her—all of her, every aspect of her. His name on her lips was an aphrodisiac he'd never experienced. Others had spoken his name, but no other utterance had sounded as breathless, as sweet. A benediction.

He'd wanted her to desire him. How was he to have known his desire for her would eclipse any longing he'd ever experienced? She was a witch, a vixen, a lady knocking on the door to his heart. He was so tempted to answer, to invite her in, but he understood that what was happening between them was not grounded in reality—it was part and parcel of the fantasy world he'd created. She was not a duchess of the realm and he was not the bastard son of an earl. Within these walls, they were not at opposite ends of the social hierarchy. Within his private chambers, they were all that existed and soon they would be supplanted by pleasure.

While he was anxious to see her completely nude, he took his time divesting her of her clothing, making the removal of each item as sensual as possible. He was succeeding if the glaze in her eyes was any indication. He skimmed his fingers slowly over every inch of skin revealed. When her breasts were freed, he felt as though they were old friends returning to visit. He cupped them in his palms, plumped them up, offered them to his mouth for feasting. He kissed, licked, suckled, first one and then the other.

Moaning softly, she wrapped her fingers around his upper arms and dropped her head back, exposing the long column of her throat. God, how could he resist that? So he nibbled and nipped, relishing the way her fingers tightened their hold.

Then he returned to the task at hand, shoving her loosened gown and petticoats down over her hips so she could step out of them. Quickly he rid her of the remainder of her undergarments, leaving her stockings for last. Balancing on the balls of his feet, he rolled the delicate silk past her knee, down her calf, over her ankle, teasing her flesh with feather-like strokes of his fingertips as he went. Her hands folded over his shoulders as he eased the stocking over her heel, her arch, her toes. He rubbed her foot, lifted it for a kiss, before giving his attention to the other stocking. When it had joined the first, he lifted his gaze to her, taking in the wonderful, slender, long length of her. "Spread your legs for me, sweetheart."

Even though the light in this room was naught but candles flickering, he saw her eyes darken, smoldering with the knowledge of what he would offer.

"I want your clothes removed."

"Let me pleasure you first."

Slowly she shook her head. "My passions are certain to be heightened by the sight of you."

He couldn't refuse so earnest a request. Still, he leaned in and pressed a kiss to the heart of her sex and whispered a fervent promise, "Soon."

Straightening, he stood before her, holding out his arms in supplication. "I'm all yours."

She took a small step forward before helping him out of his jacket. Then her fingers ran the length of his waistcoat, pushing buttons free, her movements not as smooth or sure as his had been.

"Have you ever removed a man's clothing before?"

Her fingers stilled, and she lifted her gaze to his. "No. My husband always came to me already in his nightshirt. Am I doing it incorrectly?"

With one hand, he cradled her cheek. "No, sweetheart. When it comes to lovemaking, nothing is incorrect as long as it's what we both want."

Placing her hand over his, she held it in place as she turned her face into his palm and pressed a kiss there. "Everything with you is a new experience, Aiden."

The knowledge both delighted and saddened him. He never wanted her to have done without, but at the same time, he knew what he delivered would not pale in comparison to another's. "Finish the chore. Much is still awaiting you."

She gave him a saucy, but shy smile. "It's no chore."

He shrugged off the waistcoat. As she went to work unknotting his neck cloth, he touched all the soft areas of her that were within easy reach, skimming his fingers over the silk of her skin. With the neck cloth gone, she began freeing the buttons on his shirt, but his impatience was beginning to make itself known. He loosened his cuffs and as soon as she finished with the buttons, he dragged his shirt over his head and tossed it aside. He dropped onto the bed and tugged off his boots and stockings. Then he stood and waited, watched as she licked her lips.

"I've never actually seen . . . we were very proper in our bedding."

"You are going to find I am very improper." He dropped his hand to the fall of his trousers, slid it down to the base, brought it back up. Again. Again. Saw her swallow.

Tentatively her fingers neared his. He moved his aside. The length of her hand, from fingertips to wrist, landed against the fall of his trousers, against the bulge housed there. His groan was an entreaty that she answered with a long slow stroke. Down. Up. Then she was loosening buttons, parting cloth, and his cock sprang free.

"My goodness. It's larger than I thought."

"Men come in different sizes." He shoved down his trousers, stepped out of them, and tossed them aside.

"Still, it didn't feel so big through the cloth." Kneeling before him, she skimmed her bare fingers over the length of him.

"Christ, Lena." Her touch deprived him of breath.

"So silky. So hot."

While she explored, he removed the pins from her hair until the heavy strands cascaded around her shoulders, over his cock. Pure bliss.

Dropping her head back, she captured and held his gaze. "I want you inside me."

The words were nearly his undoing, almost had him spilling his seed then and there. He'd never ached with such need.

Bringing her to her feet, he clasped her to him and tumbled them both onto the bed.

THEY WERE A tangle of limbs, and it felt wonderful. The front of her, every inch, was touching his skin. Flesh against flesh, heated and dewy. Taking her mouth, plundering, he rolled her onto her back, wedging himself between her thighs, his thick cock pressing against her cleft.

It seemed wicked to use that word—*cock*—but she didn't think any other would do him justice, would adequately describe that portion of him that would soon be entering her. Never before had she looked so forward to the joining.

But it seemed he was not yet done denying her, tormenting her, because he pushed himself down until he could take one of her nipples in his mouth. His tongue laved the little pearl, causing delicious sensations to swarm through her. Then he suckled gently, before taking his lips on a tour about her breast, kissing the underside, the sides, the top. So much attention given to the one while his hand tenderly kneaded the other.

He reversed his attentions, giving his mouth to the other breast, while his fingers toyed with the one now coated in dew. She loved the feel of his rough palms skimming over her flesh with purpose. He'd touched much of her before, but not all of her, and now every aspect was laid bare before him and was his for the taking.

And he took.

With his mouth, his hands, his lips, his tongue. He scooted down farther and treated her to the same ministrations he'd given her when she'd been splayed out on the billiards table. Where the intimacy of it had shocked her before, now she embraced it with full fervor, tilting her hips to give him easier access, welcoming his throaty moan of approval.

She clutched his shoulders as her thighs began to tremble with want, with need. So close, so close. She thrashed her head from side to side, pressed her feet to his calves, loving the feel of his silky hair against her soles. But then there was no aspect to him that she didn't love.

Combing her fingers through his hair, she knotted them in the strands, tugged until he lifted his head to meet her gaze. "I want you inside me, part of me, when I come undone."

With a low growl, he raised himself up and rolled off her. Sitting on the edge of the bed, he opened a drawer in the small table beside the bed, pulled something out, and used it to cover his cock.

"What are you doing?"

"Putting on a sheath." He came back to her and nuzzled her neck. "It'll stop my seed from spilling into you without my having to leave you first."

She tried to make sense of his words, but he began doing deliciously wicked things with his fingers, stroking her cleft as his thumb pressed against her swollen nubbin while circling it. Once more the sensations took precedence, claimed her full attention, had her writhing with need.

He shifted until he was once again resting between her thighs. Taking hold of himself, he rubbed against her with the head of his penis, over and over, and she was frantically aware of how wet she'd become. Stilling at her opening, he claimed her mouth and slowly eased his way into her, stretching her, filling her, before plunging deep.

A shudder of pleasure swept through her. "Oh God."

She dug her fingers into his backside, holding

him as she absorbed the wonder of it all. She was not a virgin, and yet what she felt at that moment was nearly foreign to her. Apparently not all mating was the same. Or perhaps it was because he had caused her to want him so desperately. He made her nerve endings sing, her skin more sensitive to the touch. He'd prepared her as she'd never before been prepared.

He had not taken her because of duty. And he made her forget that it was duty that had driven her to him.

As he began to move against her, leaving her only to quickly thrust back into her, she focused on him, on them, seeking only the pleasure he could provide. She skimmed her hands along his back, taking note of the way his muscles bunched and flexed with his movements. When he rose above her, captured her gaze, and undulated his hips with more force, more speed, more urgency, she fell into the smoldering darkness of his eyes, held on to him with arms, hands, thighs, and allowed ecstasy to conquer, to reign.

When she fell apart in his arms, she welcomed the bliss, knowing he had the power to put her back together.

When he threw back his head, his jaw clenched, as passion overcame him, she held him tightly, absorbing the spasms that rocked him.

And nearly wept for the joy of the joining.

Chapter 13

"*O*pen your mouth."

With her bare back against his chest and the water lapping around them with his movements, Selena didn't hesitate to do as he bade. Taking a bite of the strawberry he placed against her lips, she laughed as the juice dribbled down her chin. With his thumb, he turned her head toward him and licked her clean before delivering a kiss that very nearly caused steam to rise from the tub.

After they'd made love, he'd called for a bath to be prepared. With sheets draped around her, she'd sat in a chair in the corner, facing the wall, nearly completely hidden from the servants who brought up the bathwater. Once they left, he shoved a small table against the large copper tub and brought in the offerings that had been laid out on the linen-covered table in the front room.

Reaching for the wine, she took a sip and considered her feelings at the moment. She most certainly could not claim disappointment, as she'd never felt more replete and had never before experienced such intense pleasure, but she was a bit frustrated to discover that Aiden was not going to give her what she needed as easily as she'd hoped. "I was quite taken aback when you . . . sheathed yourself. I wasn't aware men did that."

His fingers lazily trailed up and down her arm, sending delicious tingles through her. "No reason for your husband to do so. He'd want to get you with child."

"Do you always don a sheath when you make love?"

"Always."

"Even when you were sixteen?"

"Mmm. When we were around fifteen, our mum sat all of us boys down and explained the methods we could use so as not to get a girl knapped."

She was unfamiliar with the term. "Knapped?"

"Pregnant."

She took another sip of wine, finding it difficult to believe she was actually having this conversation. She'd never discussed the facets of sex with anyone, not even her mother. "Are there other methods?"

She felt his shrug against her back, then his lips on the nape of her neck. "A man can withdraw right before he spills his seed. However he needs to be quick and he needs not to forget. But sometimes, oftentimes, he's not thinking at all except about how good it all feels."

Twisting around slightly, she looked at him, certain her cheeks were flaming red. "Your mother explained all that to you?"

"She raised bastards. She said abstinence was best but wasn't fool enough to think we'd choose that route, so she wanted to make sure we didn't dip our wick and come to regret it. If we got a girl with child, we'd be marrying her."

"Even at fifteen?"

"The age of consent is twelve. Mum believed if we were old enough to fuck, we were old enough to marry. Not that she used those exact words, but she got her message across."

"So you've never been . . . inside . . . a woman without wearing a sheath?"

Her hair was piled on top of her head. He brushed some stray strands away from her cheek. "Never."

Turning back around, she settled against him. "I can't fathom it."

"I didn't want to marry a girl just because I got her with babe. Nor do I want any bastards."

She squeezed her eyes shut as her stomach clenched. But if he got her with child, it wouldn't be labeled a bastard. Surely that would bring him some comfort were he to ever learn of her deception. *Deception.* She hated the word, the need for it. Unclenching her eyes, she watched the flames on the hearth writhing as she had been a short time ago.

"Open."

As she obeyed his command, she placed her hand over his, held it in place, taking not only his offering of a bit of cheese between her lips but also his forefinger, suckling, and taking great satisfaction in his low groan and the jump of his penis against her bottom. Removing his finger from her mouth, she chewed the tart cheese and scraped her nail over the scar that ran the length of his forefinger and beyond to the back of his hand. "How did you come to have this?"

"Got into a brawl with a fellow who had a knife." He began dotting her nape with kisses.

"How old were you?"

"Fourteen." His mouth lingered until it seemed he was painting kisses over her.

"You don't strike me as someone who gets into fights without a reason."

A low grunt that could have served as agreement.

The marred flesh was a ghastly ugly thing and yet the story of its existence called to her. "Why did you challenge him?"

The kisses were growing ever more slower, ever more purposeful. She had no doubt they would soon be leaving the bath for the bed. "Aiden."

His mouth was near her ear now. "He called my mum a whore."

In his voice, she heard the pain from his youth, the embarrassment he might have suffered. "Is that what everyone thought of the woman who gave birth to you?"

"He was referring to Ettie Trewlove."

Her heart tightened with the realization that for this man, only one woman was his mother—the good soul who had taken him in.

Pressing his finger against her lips, she glided her tongue over the scar. "Did you give the lad a sound thrashing?"

"I did. His nose never did straighten, remained a bit crooked pointing off to the side."

"You protect what's yours."

He moved that scarred finger up and skimmed it along her chin, before using it to turn her face back slightly so he could hold her gaze. "Always."

She couldn't help but believe that he considered her his, believed her worthy of his protection. Only she wasn't. She was with him for a purpose, a purpose that would ensure she remain with him only a short while.

Twisting about in the tub, she took his mouth with all the fervor she could muster. He touched her in ways she'd not foreseen—not with his hands, although he certainly did that, but with his soul, his heart, his very being. She'd not anticipated that of a man known for sin. Had expected him to be of loose morals and character, caring for nothing save his own pleasures. But he was nothing of the sort. Goodness had taken up residence within him, and she wanted to ensure he regretted not a minute that he spent with her.

Leaning back, she cupped his dark whiskered jaw with one hand. The bristles were heavier, thicker now, and she considered offering to shave him, but she rather enjoyed the unkempt rugged look of him. "As a man, you have control over everything in your life. I've had very little control in mine, almost none at all." Shifting, causing the water to lap around them, she straddled his hips. "I want to have complete and absolute control over you."

His hands bracketed her waist, his fingers flexed, his eyes darkened. "I am yours to do with as you please. What would you have of me?"

"I would have you bound to the bed. I would have you at my mercy."

IT WAS A wonder he didn't immediately embarrass himself and spill his seed at her softly spoken words, edged with a desire that turned her blue eyes cerulean. He could deny her nothing, especially a request that had his heart galloping like a runaway stallion and threatening to burst through his chest.

He still might embarrass himself. He'd never been so hard in anticipation of what was to come.

Using his neck cloths, she secured his wrists and ankles to the four bedposts, leaving him spread-eagled over the satin sheets he'd purchased earlier in the day for her enjoyment. He'd never been in such a vulnerable position, couldn't imagine placing himself thus with anyone other than her. He trusted her. Completely. It was a rather odd moment to come to that realization, especially as they'd known each other such a short while, but he didn't think the heart measured depth of feeling using a timepiece.

Not that he loved her, but he did care for her—immensely. Probably more so than was wise for a man in his position. He was not the sort a woman could walk proudly alongside. Until her, it had never mattered. He wished it still didn't.

But the ability to rationally argue any philosophical questions regarding his life left him as she sauntered around the bed, her heated gaze fixed on his. He made to reach for her, the linen wrapped around his wrist halting his movement, reminding him that he could do little except wait for her to have her way with him.

The mattress dipped as she climbed onto it, never averting her eyes from his. God, but she was beautiful in her confidence that she could undo him. And she would. He knew that as surely as he knew that when she was done with him, he was going to reverse the tables, and have her bound and sprawled for his enjoyment. And hers.

Strange how they seemed connected, how the more he gave to her, the more he gained for himself.

Slowly, she trailed her fingers along his side, from the strip of cloth binding his ankle, along his calf, up his thigh, over his hip, up to his rib—

He gave a little jerk.

She looked as though he'd just handed her the Koh-i-Noor diamond. "You're ticklish."

"A bit."

Leaning down, she pressed her open mouth, hot and dewy, against his lowest rib. He closed his eyes as the warmth seeped into him. "Only to fingers."

Lifting her head, she arched a brow and ran her tongue over her lips. "I'll keep that in mind."

Straddling his stomach, she eased up, bringing those luscious breasts nearer. Again, he reached, testing the limits of his tether. "Perhaps you could give one hand the freedom to touch you."

Her smile was that of a saucy minx. "No."

Lowering herself, she rubbed her breasts over his chest before bringing one to his mouth. "You may lick."

He did so without hesitating, circling the pink areola with his tongue, before flicking at it. She dropped her head back, moaned.

"You're killing me," he rasped.

Her look was sultry, that of a woman relishing her power. "I've not even begun."

Pushing herself down until her knees were resting between his, she sat back on her heels and wrapped her fingers around his straining cock. "I'm amazed by the silkiness of it. I can't decide if it feels like satin or velvet."

She kissed the head. He jerked.

"Ticklish?"

"No."

"You like that, then."

"Yes."

Then she did what he'd done with her breast and circled her tongue over him. He groaned low, deep.

"Do you like that?" Her tone was rife with innocence.

"God, yes."

"And this?"

She took him in her mouth and he very nearly came off the bed, might have if he hadn't been secured to it. How he longed to tangle his fingers in her hair, grip the sheets. She was all heat and slow strokes that drove him wild. He loved the feel of her closing her lips around him and sucking. "Oh, you wicked vixen."

He was fairly certain she smiled before continuing to torment him. "Lena, I'm on the edge here, on the verge of giving you a little surprise if you continue."

Pure enjoyment and satisfaction wreathed her face. "Nothing about you is little, Aiden."

She palmed him and stroked the length of him. "Tell me again. You've never been inside a woman without a sheath?"

"Never."

Up and down, her hand pumped him. "Do you ever think about what it might feel like?"

He knew how a woman felt around his fingers, but around his cock—

"I imagine it."

"Are you ever tempted?"

With her, he'd been tempted from the first. "Yes."

He hated how the word sounded like an entreaty, a begging.

She swung her leg over him, straddling his hips, rose up onto her knees. "It's the only way I've thought about it, dreamed about it, imagined it. You with no barrier between us."

He shook his head. "I won't risk—"

"Just a taste, just for a minute."

Taking hold of him, she positioned him at her opening. His body reacted instinctively, straining toward the heat of her tunnel. "You'll have to leave me before I spill—"

"I know. But I'm in control now, and this is what I want. You inside me, slick skin against slick skin."

His body was so tense with need, with the eroticism of her sultry voice, her come-hither eyes watching him that he barely felt his nod, such a small thing, giving her permission. Slowly, tormentingly, she slid down, enveloping him in the sweltering velvet. Down, down, down. Until he filled her to the hilt.

"Christ, you feel bloody good. Hot, wet, silky. And tight. So damn tight." He'd felt it with the sheath, but without it, miraculously, she seemed even more snug.

"I love the sensation of you, with naught separating us." She lifted up, slid back down.

His growl was that of a man in torment.

With her head resting back, she began undulating her body, riding him. Bound as he was, his movements were limited, but he pumped into her as much as he was able, matching his movements to hers. He yearned to dig his fingers into her hips, thrusting faster, deeper, with more urgency. "Untie me."

"Not yet." Her voice seemed to come from a far-off place where fantasy reigned.

She guided her hands over his chest, splaying her fingers over his lower ribs, bracing herself. Her tempo increased. Mewling whimpers escaped her lips. Her back bowed, her breasts pushed upward as her cry of release echoed around them.

Her climax came swift and hard, her muscles clenching his cock before throbbing around him. The sensations were sublime, more detailed than he'd ever experienced. They added to his own pleasure, his own torture as he fought to hold himself in check until she came back into herself.

Her breathing was shallow, harsh, her smile pure satisfaction, her eyes aglow. Licking her lips, holding his gaze now, she began rocking against him in earnest, faster, harder, taking him deeper, deeper. Pleasure cascaded through him. He tugged on the bindings, needing to hold her. It was all too much as ecstasy built, shooting through him, building to nearly unbearable intensity.

"Leave me, Lena. Now," he ground out through clenched teeth.

Instead she rode him with single-minded purpose as though her life depended on it. As though his did.

"I'm close to bursting. Leave."

She shook her head, increasing the tempo, pistoning harder, faster.

He was on the cusp, hovering at the edge of the abyss. "For God's sake, Lena, I beg of you—"

Then she was no longer encasing him, had left him completely. Knowing she was safe, he immediately gave in to his needs, his body jerking, spasming as his orgasm overtook him.

In the farthest recesses of his mind, he was

vaguely aware of a sob. Opening his eyes, he watched as she scampered off the bed, another sob escaping. "Lena? What's wrong, sweetheart?"

"I'm sorry. I couldn't, I can't." She began snatching up her clothes. "It's just . . . it's not fair."

"Couldn't what? Lena, what the devil is going on here?"

"Forgive me."

"Untie me."

Without looking back at him, clutching her clothing, she dashed into the front room.

"Lena!" He tugged on the bindings. They held fast. He heard the rustle of silk and satin as though she was dressing herself. "Lena, get back here and free me!"

More rustling, followed by hurried footsteps and the slamming of the door. "Lena!"

But all he heard was the silence of her having left him.

Chapter 14

$\mathcal{S}$itting in the library, before a hearth as empty as her womb, she sipped the brandy, wondering if she'd ever known such desolation and despair, such shame and disappointment in herself. When it came right down to it, she'd been unable to go through with her plans to take his seed into her body, because he'd been so adamant that he had no desire to bring a child into the world. She hadn't even been aware ways to avoid impregnating a woman existed. Why, then, were there so many bastards? Why were so many children orphans? Why didn't all men take precautions?

Even knowing his child would not have been labeled a bastard, that he—or she—would have been considered the legitimate issue of the Duke of Lushing, she'd not been able to place her own wants and needs above Aiden's. She'd felt the tension in him increasing as passion gave rise to mindless lust, as his body sought surcease, as he went beyond the boundaries where he could stop. Because she had continued to ride him, determined to force his capitulation, the spilling of his seed—not into a sheath but into her. She'd felt powerful, in control, until the only thing that mattered was gaining what she wanted.

"For God's sake, Lena, I beg of you—"

Then those words ground out through his clenched teeth had bombarded her soul, reached into her heart. She couldn't imagine this man had ever before begged anything of anyone. And yet he begged of her. As his growl had echoed around her, his body had stiffened, and when she'd known his seed would be pouring forth, she'd not been able to stay.

In the end, she'd not been able to stay at all—not on top of him, not in his bed, not in his rooms. She'd heard the confusion in his voice as he called out to her, and she'd been unable to face him.

From the moment he'd first approached her at the club, he'd asked nothing of her. He'd charmed her and given her all she'd demanded. And then he'd requested something of her, and she'd not been able to deny him.

The rawness of his entreaty had shamed her; her actions had mortified her. Not only because she'd been willing to steal something so precious from Aiden, but because she'd been planning to pass another's child off as Lushing's. She'd been willing to betray two men who had never done her any harm, and in so doing she'd have betrayed herself.

As the guilt had bombarded her, all she'd wanted was to escape from Aiden and herself. But there was no escaping herself, her failure to protect those she loved. There would be no heir. She might be the Duchess of Lushing, but she would have no husband with a revered title to stand beside her, no great dynasty to provide power and influence. She had failed to produce an heir after seven years. No young titled gentleman in need of a son would risk taking her to wife. She would fade into obscurity. She deserved no less.

What a fool she'd been to agree to Winslow's plan.

Finishing off the brandy, taking comfort in the lethargy it brought her, she set aside her snifter and shoved herself to her feet. The room tilted, righted itself. Her face felt immobile from the salt of the tears she'd wept, tears that had long since dried, leaving only their remnants. Because of her failings, a title would be declared extinct. And the ruination of her family would be her legacy.

Slowly she made her way from the library into the hallway, following a path she knew by heart. She would become an old maid, living alone in the dower house. She would do what she could to see her sisters well married, but without dowries, it was unlikely they would find happiness.

Trudging up the stairs, she felt as though she were striving to ascend an impossibly high mountain of rugged terrain. She couldn't recall how much brandy she'd sipped or how long she'd sat in the library wallowing in despair. An hour? Two?

She could barely think, put her thoughts in order, but she would find a way to see her sisters married well. "Tomorrow," she whispered. "I'll worry about it all tomorrow."

For now a keen sadness and sense of loss made her want to cry out. Never again would she see Aiden Trewlove, taste his kiss, grow warm from his smile, have her heart soar as his laughter circled her, be brought to her knees by his gentle caresses. Never again would she share confidences without fear of judgment.

Opening the door to her bedchamber, she welcomed the shadows emerging from the corners, the lone lamp on the bedside table burning too low to effectively hold them at bay. Then she noticed the toes of a pair of shining boots near the chair in the corner. Her brother, damn him. She was not in the mood to deal with him tonight. "Winslow—"

"You left me bound to the bloody bedposts!"

Her heart fairly jumped into her throat, her lungs froze. Not Winslow. Not Winslow at all. She watched in horror as a darker shadow slowly rose from the chair, tall and broad and menacing. When he stepped into the light, she knew she'd never seen such rage.

"You left me bound to the bloody bedposts!" he repeated, as though perhaps she hadn't heard him the first time.

"Lower your voice. My sisters are down the hallway." It wouldn't do at all for them to discover this man in her bedchamber. She closed the door, locked it, leaned against it for support as though it could save her from his wrath.

"Do you think I give a bloody damn? You just left me there. With no explanation, with no way to free myself."

His appearance had chased off her lethargy. Her heart was beating so rapidly, it had no doubt pounded the effects of the brandy into submission. "Yet, you managed it. I knew you were a man of resource."

"Only because trouble downstairs required my assistance. How do you think it looked to my gaming boss to see me naked and trussed up like a Christmas goose?"

"How did you get in here?" she asked, unwilling

to address his question, the mortification he must have felt.

"I'm a man who can pick locks, sweetheart. Do you really think you can find any place where you'll be safe from me?" He took a long stride toward her. "Why, Lena, why were you crying? Why did you run off?"

It was so much harder to face him when he used her name rather than an endearment. So much more difficult when his first concern was her sobs and not her abandonment. Shaking her head, she felt the tears threatening once more.

"Why?" he asked again, but this time his voice reflected no hint of anger, only true concern.

Taking a deep breath, she met and held his gaze. "Because you take such precautions not to have children. And I need desperately to get with child."

HER WORDS BLUDGEONED him. He'd been correct from the beginning. All she desired of him was his cock. No, that wasn't quite true. She wanted his seed.

She was a widow, a very recent widow. He'd never asked if she had children; she'd never spoken of them. He didn't ask now, but merely stated fact, as her reasons crystallized. "You didn't give your husband an heir."

Slowly, she shook her head, finally unplastered herself from the door, walked to the sitting area, and lowered herself into a chair near the fireplace. Against his better judgment, he dropped into the one opposite hers. He preferred standing when fury had ahold of him, but his anger was abating.

Damn her for that, for making him care about her troubles. "Surely the next in line will ensure you are provided for."

"Lushing was the last. He had no surviving brothers or male cousins, distant or otherwise, to take his place. His titles will be declared extinct. His entailed properties will go to Her Majesty's Treasury. I inherited a dower house, and he set up a trust. The interest will see me in good stead but it's not enough." She shook her head. "It's not the money. It's the prestige, the influence. My sisters have not yet had their Seasons. I want them to make good matches but without the dukedom"—she spread her arms—"I am naught. I have no power."

"I suspect you have more than you think."

With sadness etched over her features, she stared at her clasped hands.

"What of your brother? The responsibility of seeing to their welfare falls to him, surely."

She lifted her gaze to his, her somberness tightening his heart, which irritated him. That he should allow her to affect him at all after what she'd done. He'd rubbed his wrists raw striving to get out of the bindings, had nearly wrenched his shoulder from its socket in his contortions to free himself. If not for his gaming manager knocking on his door and his yelling for the man to come in, Aiden might still be writhing about, feeling helpless and humiliated.

"The Earl of Camberley. Unfortunately, my father left the estate in shambles. It is not a particularly respected title. All my siblings are dependent on my position. And it is greatly diminished unless I become the mother of the next duke."

"That was the reason you came to the club to be bedded."

Her cheeks turning a soft pink hue, she nodded. "I thought if I could get with child within the month, before my next menses, I could pass it off as Lushing's. It might arrive a tad late, but sometimes children do. Or perhaps I could find a way to make it come early. If I give birth to a son, all would remain as it was."

"And if you bring a daughter into the world?"

"While the title will still go into extinction, the terms outlined in the entailment would allow her to inherit all Lushing's assets and properties. Property is power. Lushing taught me that. She would grow up to become an independent woman of means. In addition, by showing I was not barren, my marriage prospects would increase and perhaps I could land another duke."

He hated her plan, every aspect of it. Her willingness to do anything to get with child. "So if I hadn't intercepted you that first night, you'd have gone with one of the gents with the red buttons."

"No. It was always you I wanted."

He was torn between feeling flattered and feeling the fool. "Why me?"

"I saw you at Lady Aslyn's wedding. I thought you pleasing to the eye. And I liked your smile."

"You haven't very high standards."

A corner of her mouth twitched, and he cursed himself for wanting to see her smile fully. "Rumors are that your father is nobility, so I thought at least my child would have noble blood in his veins, even if he wasn't Lushing's. But then I came to like you—

immensely—and it seemed wrong to take what you had no desire to give."

"Why not just ask me?"

"The fewer people who know, the better a secret is kept."

"You didn't trust me."

"To be quite honest, Mr. Trewlove, I was ashamed of the circumstances that brought me to your establishment."

"We've fucked, sweetheart." She flinched as though he'd struck her. He might have taken pity on her if his shoulder wasn't still aching and his wrists weren't bothering him. "I know the taste of that pink valley between your thighs. I don't think we need to be so formal."

"Must you be so crude? It makes you most unattractive."

He should apologize. He knew it. His mother would take a switch to his backside if she ever learned of the manner in which he'd spoken to the lady. But his pride was a beastly thing, and her reasons for wanting him had bruised it considerably so the words of apology clogged his throat, refusing to be uttered.

He shoved himself out of the chair, strode to the fireplace, and stared into the cold, empty hearth. In spite of his upbringing, the kindness of his mum, it was in his veins to be crude, unkind, selfish. "Elverton."

The word came out hard, bitter, leaving a vile taste on his tongue.

"I suppose I could accept his offer to rescue me," she said quietly. "How did you even know of it?"

He jerked his head around to glare at her. Over

his dead body would she take anything from the man who had sired him. "He made you an offer?"

Her laughter was harsh, filled with loathing. "Yesterday morning, in the garden, following the funeral. Initially, I thought he was proposing I wed his son, but then it became clear he was referring to himself as a potential suitor."

"He has a wife."

"So I pointed out to him, but he didn't seem to think that was a cause for concern. He hinted she might not be around much longer. Made me wonder if perhaps she was ill."

He wouldn't put it past his sire to find a way to dispose of his countess. "Do you fancy him?"

Her look of abject horror brought him a measure of peace. "Absolutely not. He is more than twice my age."

"He has the influence you seek."

She sighed, the sound echoing her despair. "And he does not require an heir, which he reassured me was to the benefit of my barren womb."

Had his father truly been so grotesque as to make his proposition in such an unflattering manner? "He sired me."

Her eyes widened slightly, her lips parted. She blinked, stared at him, blinked again. Angled her head. Squinted. Finally her face relaxed. "I can see it now. In the cut of your square jaw, the patrician sharpness of your nose, the depth of your brow. It's your eyes that threw me off. They're not as harsh as his—which they no doubt should be as you've had a much harder life."

Because of his heritage, because of the legacy his vile father had handed down to him, which was no legacy at all, just being allocated to the rubbish heap, he had a strong urge to strike something. He'd never felt so tainted, so cursed by his origins. "If I were to get you with child, it would be his blood coursing through the babe."

She smiled wistfully. "No, it would be yours."

Not much liking the way her words called to his pride, he gave his attention back to the hearth. Was he seriously considering striving to give her what she desired? Then what was he to do? Watch her walk out of his life? He'd always known his time with her would be brief. Would two or three more weeks of passion and a jolly good time be enough to last him a lifetime?

"Your son would be a duke," she said with a measure of guilt coupled with an urging he understand all she was offering him. "He would hold within his hands what most men can only dream of and never attain: land, wealth, power. None of Lushing's properties are in a state of disrepair. His ducal estate is the envy of other lords. Your son would walk those hallowed halls. He would attend the finest of schools, receive the best education. He would want for nothing. He would be ranked above your father, seated ahead of him at tables. You relish the fact that you have more power in your world than your father has in his. In your father's world, your son would hold more power. What an incredible dodge that would be to pull off, wouldn't it? The idea must appeal to the swindler in you, surely."

My son would be a duke. He could never offer any son he claimed that prestige, that influence. But hidden in shadows, with a series of clandestine trysts, with secrets held close, he could give the fruit of his loins a dukedom. Power, authority. His boy, when grown, would sit in the House of Lords. While he could never publicly boast about his child, while he'd be relegated to being an observer in his son's life, deep down he'd know he was responsible for all his son would acquire and accomplish. His son would outrank the Earl of Elverton. But even that, Aiden wouldn't be able to toss in the old goat's face.

Crossing his arms over his chest, he turned and faced her. "You don't think people will question the lad not looking like your deceased husband?"

"Lushing's eyes were brown, as was his hair. While the similarities between you may end there, years from now people are not going to recall precisely what Lushing looked like. I doubt anyone will gaze closely at his portraits in order to make a comparison. Besides, I suspect not every family of the *ton* is completely pure of blood. And he will have the duke's name to protect him."

"I cannot guarantee you a male."

"As I mentioned, my giving birth to a daughter is not completely without advantages."

He would be giving Selena the means to marry another man of influence—because his wasn't enough. "So you're proposing I plant the seed and walk away."

Her gaze held his, although he could see the struggle in the tightening of her features. "Not necessarily. We could continue to see each other, remain lovers, discreetly of course. You might be able to see your son—or daughter—on occasion, but it would be imperative that the child never learn that you're the father. I wouldn't want to burden him, or her, with our deception."

Discreet. Burden. Deception. Those words slammed into him as though they were delivered with a cudgel. Even as he understood the truth of them, the necessity of keeping their relationship to the shadows.

"I'm not ashamed to be seen with you, but we have to protect the child at all cost," she continued into his silence.

Yet in the incredibly short time they'd been together, she'd never actually been seen with him, at least not without the mask. No one, other than her driver, knew she'd been with him, and he wasn't even certain her driver knew who he was.

"Perhaps I could offer you a bit more in return." Her tone was hesitant, no doubt because he still held his silence.

He narrowed his eyes. She eased up to the edge of her chair.

"My dower property. I couldn't give it to you outright, but I could bequeath it to you, so it becomes yours upon my death."

He barked out a bitter laugh. "So now I am to become your whore?"

The horror etched over her face took the edge off his anger. "No, no. I didn't mean it like that. But all you're getting out of our arrangement is me in your bed—which I am not arrogant enough to believe is of much value—and a bit of time spent with your child. I'm trying to make it worth your while, worth what you might sacrifice."

"If I die before you?"

"It would go to your heirs."

"And if my only heir is your child? I never

planned to marry, Duchess. I never planned to have children."

Now she looked to be the one bludgeoned. "Why wouldn't you?"

"Because I know what I am, where I came from."

She rose to her feet and joined him at the fireplace, her bare hand coming to rest against his shadowed jaw, and it took everything within him not to place his over it and hold it steady as he planted a kiss in the center of her palm. But if he touched her, he'd lose his ability to reason, to consider all the consequences as rationally as possible. He'd want to carry her to that bed and finish what they'd begun earlier.

"As impossible as it seems, I feel as though I've known you my entire life. Such goodness resides in you, Aiden Trewlove." She smiled slightly. "Yes, you're a bit of a scamp and quite the flirt, but you are nothing at all like your father. You've brought me more comfort in my sorrow than anyone else I know. I would love your child all the more for reminding me of you."

"And if I decline your offer to be allowed to pour my seed into you?"

She angled up her chin, and he could see the determination in the set of her jaw, as well as the displeasure at his choice of words. "I'd be forced to look elsewhere for a willing partner."

His damn sire, the scapegrace, had already indicated his keenness to have her in his bed. Would she go to him? Her desperation implied she might. He couldn't bear the thought of the Earl of Elverton touching her. But neither did he fancy giving in to the whims of a duchess who was merely interested in his cock and what it could deliver—a child who would never know the truth of his parentage. He felt as though his soul was being scraped raw. How could he still want this woman after learning her true reason for coming to him?

Stepping away from her before he did something foolish like admitting he'd take her on any terms she dictated for whatever length of time she ordained, he took a deep breath and walked over to her secretary. After locating a piece of foolscap, he dipped the golden nib—of course a duchess would have a golden nib—of the pen into the inkwell and scrawled out an address. Turning, he faced her. "My sister has a bookshop. Tomorrow we'll be helping her to ready it for opening, placing books on shelves and such. Bring your sisters there at two so I can judge if they're worth the price of my soul." Or as he feared more likely—the cost to his heart.

"We're in mourning."

"Wear black. Surely, even when mourning, one can be excused for doing good deeds."

"My sisters don't know of my plans, what I'm striving to achieve."

"No reason for them to learn of it. You can tell them Lady Aslyn invited you to give you a bit of respite from the boredom of bereavement."

The sadness reflected in her eyes almost had him going to her and offering to give her everything she desired. She nodded. "Shouldn't I bring my brother as well, so you can measure his worth?"

A sharp bite to her words. She apparently didn't like him setting out terms, but his pride was salvaged a trifle because she hadn't immediately told him to go to hell, because she wasn't seeking another to plant his seed within her. "I know the Earl of Camberley. He plays at my tables. Odd that. How he can find the coins to pursue his own pleasures while his sister is forced to set out on a path that will lead her into hell."

"You've made it an enjoyable journey thus far, Mr. Trewlove."

With her compliment she was striving to appease him, perhaps regain her own honor. With her formal addressing of him, she was striving to put distance between them, to remind him of his place.

"My brother is a young man, with wild oats still in need of sowing," she added.

"How old were you when you took on the mantle of responsibility for your siblings and married?"

"Much younger than him," she admitted. "Is he in debt to you?"

He merely gave an inconsequential shrug. "Not as much as *you'll* be if we go through with this."

Heading for the door, he pointed toward the secretary and tossed back over his shoulder, "Tomorrow. At the stroke of two be there."

Chapter 15

*T*here were certain sights that a man should never see. His sire's hairy, flabby bare arse quivering as he pounded into a woman who stared at the canopy while she released a small moan with the regularity of a ticking clock was one of them. He'd expected to find the Earl of Elverton asleep this time of night and had been looking forward to disturbing his slumber.

The woman—too young to be the current countess—shifted her gaze to the side, caught sight of Aiden, and released a bloodcurdling scream as she fought frantically to rid herself of the toad weighing her down.

"Bloody hell!" the earl roared before glancing in the same direction as his mistress. In an ungainly manner, he extricated himself from the lass who scrambled to the far side of the bed, snatching up the covers in an effort to protect her modesty.

Aiden was aware of the patter of light footsteps coming down the hallway, and then a slender woman whose head reached his shoulder edged around him.

"What's happened?"

Based on the intricate embroidery in her satin

dressing gown, and her lack of surprise at the tab-
leau before her, he assumed she was the current
Countess of Elverton. In his youth, he'd seen her
from afar on a couple of occasions when curiosity
regarding his sire had him following the old goat
around. Seeing her so clearly now, he mused that
she'd been a beauty in her day, her porcelain com-
plexion still radiant in spite of the late hour. Her
brown hair gathered in a long braid was streaked
with wisps of red and silver.

Breathing heavily, sitting on the edge of the bed,
not demonstrating the same modesty as his mistress, the earl waved his hand in the air as though
shooing away a swarm of flies. "My bastard. What
the devil are you doing here?"

"I need a word."

"Come see me in the morning."

"Now."

His sire narrowed brown eyes that mirrored
Aiden's in shade, and his square jaw tightened with
his irritation, but still he gave a nod. "I'll meet you
in the library shortly."

"I'll escort you," his countess said, quickly turning on her heel and heading into the hallway.

With one parting glare that promised retribution if the old man reneged on his words, Aiden
closed the door and joined the earl's wife. "It doesn't
bother you that he cares so little for you that he
brings his doxy here?"

She lifted one finely arched dark brow in a knowing way. "She keeps him out of my bed. Why would
I object to that, I ask you?"

He couldn't argue with her reasoning when
he'd often hoped that his mother's time with the

whoremonger had been brief. "I know my way to the library."

She gave him a lofty once-over and a serene smile. "I've no doubt. Still, it would make me an inhospitable hostess not to accompany you, Mr. Trewlove."

Without waiting for him, she began walking elegantly toward the stairs. He hurried to catch up. "You know who I am." It was a statement, not a question.

"Several years back, as I recall, you arrived at a late hour and informed the butler who greeted you—I shall never forget the words—'I'm Aiden Trewlove, the earl's bastard, and I'll have a word with him.' I think you quite frightened the poor fellow. I was standing on the stairs"—which she now descended—"unnoticed, as you were singular in your purpose that evening. To be honest, I was quite shocked as well by your arrival."

"You were unaware he had bastards?"

She held her tongue until she finished her descent, stopped, and faced him. "Oh no, Mr. Trewlove. I knew he had bastards. I gave birth to three of them, but he took them from me within minutes of their birth. He considered children born on the wrong side of the blanket to be an inconvenience. Your arrival gave me hope that he had kept his promise to see them loved and well cared for. This way."

He tried to study her more closely to determine if he could see any of himself in her, but she turned on her heel, once more leaving him to catch up. Could she possibly be his mother? Or maybe Finn's?

"You were his mistress before you were his wife." Again, a statement not a question.

"How clever you are, Mr. Trewlove."

"Did you have boys?"

"I did." Opening a door, she crossed the threshold into the library. "As I recall from your last visit, the earl neglected to offer you anything to drink so I don't know your preference." She glanced at him over her shoulder, a bit of teasing mirrored in her brown eyes. "I listened at the door. What may I pour you?"

"Scotch."

Watching the efficiency with which she opened the decanter and poured the amber liquid into a tumbler, he imagined she'd done so for his sire a hundred times. She held the glass out to him, and he wondered if that hand had ever stroked his brow, if her arms had ever cradled him. Would she even know if he was her son? Shouldn't some connection exist between them, so when he looked at her, he'd feel deep in his bones *this is the woman who birthed me*?

Taking her offering, he swallowed a good bit before asking, "Do you know what became of your boys?"

"Well, one is presently a viscount. I suppose in some manner he is your brother as well. I wonder if you would go to such lengths to save him as you did Finn."

She truly had eavesdropped, not that he'd doubted her. Not that she'd have had to be at the door to hear what passed between Aiden and his sire. Much of what they'd had to say to each other had been shouted.

"He visited a few months back," she continued as she walked over to the desk and leaned against it. "Broke your father's arm—"

"He's not my father."

Her eyes widened at that; no doubt she was taken by surprise by his vehemence.

"I'm his bastard, I won't deny that. But he is not my father. A father does not abandon"—but if he got Selena with child he'd be doing exactly that—"his child. He's my vile sire, the blackguard who planted the seed, but he is no more to than that."

She held his gaze firmly, not flinching, not looking away during the battering of his harsh words, and he wondered if she was imagining the bastards that she'd brought into the world tossing the same words at her. "He can be quite charming when he sets his mind to it, especially when he was younger, more handsome, more virile. I actually loved him for a time." She lowered her eyes to her satin slippers, the toes peering out from beneath her dressing gown. "Tell me, Mr. Trewlove"—she lifted her eyes, locked them on to his—"do you know when you were delivered to the baby farmer?"

So she was wondering the same thing he was. "The scapegrace dropped me into Ettie Trewlove's arms on the twenty-sixth of February in the year of our Lord eighteen hundred and forty." With his pronouncement, her expression changed not one whit. He might as well have said the dawn of time. He wasn't quite certain what he thought of this woman who had let the earl take children from her and then deemed herself in love with him enough to marry him.

"Is that date significant to you?" he prodded, the

words tart and impatient. He wanted to see something from her other than cool reserve.

She sighed. "I fear not. Which is probably just as well. I suspect you hate the woman who allowed you to be taken from her."

"I don't know how I feel about her. Why would you marry a man who gave away your children?"

"I was seventeen, enjoying my first Season, when I caught Elverton's fancy. I knew he was married, but I didn't care. I loved him, and he promised to take care of me. So I became his mistress. My father, a baron, disowned me. I never held his actions against him, because I fully understood that I was a sinner, but his casting me aside did limit my options. A fallen woman with no skills. I couldn't risk angering my keeper by insisting I be allowed to keep the babes. Perhaps your mother shared the same fate, Mr. Trewlove. For the most part, women have very little power. We do what we must to survive or to ensure the survival of those we love. Seldom are the choices easily made nor are they generally pleasant."

He thought of Selena, the choice she was making, how he despised it. Yet she would soldier on, putting the needs of others before her own.

"When his wife died tragically in a boating mishap," she continued, "I was all of twenty-one, still had my looks. And he knew I was fertile. I could provide him with the heir his wife had failed to. While it does not speak well of me, I did still love him and thought my sacrifices had earned me the right to be at his side, and to finally have access to everything—his household, his money, respectability. So I moved off Mistress Row—our informal name for the area because quite a few of the town houses on the street served as lodgings for the mistresses of lords—to a grand residence in Mayfair. And now I live every day with the memory of the weaknesses of my youth."

"I'm not sitting in judgment of you," he felt compelled to say. He knew the world was a harsh place for women. He and his brothers had come to the aid of many through the years.

"That makes you the only one in London."

The echo of footsteps had the countess straightening away from the desk. "Your host arrives." Her smile was self-mocking. "I shan't listen at the keyhole this time. Good night, Mr. Trewlove."

She began walking toward the door.

"My brother Finn."

Stopping, she glanced back.

"He was brought to Ettie Trewlove on April eighth of the same year. Perhaps—"

She shook her head. "No, he is not one of my sons."

The earl burst into the room, staggered to a stop. "Good God, Frances, what are you doing here?"

"Entertaining your guest."

"Will you see to Polly? Her nerves are still rattled."

"I'll take her some warm milk."

Aiden wanted to shout at her to kick the doxy out, felt rather grateful that he'd grown up with far different examples—but then his mum wasn't all innocence and goodness either. She'd done things of which she wasn't proud in order to survive. The countess was correct. Women had a rougher go of it than men.

As he lumbered over to the sideboard housing decanters, Elverton didn't deem to acknowledge Aiden, but then Aiden hadn't expected he would. The earl followed the same routine he had when Aiden had first called on him years earlier. He poured himself a scotch, stalked to the desk, dropped into his chair, and glared. "What do you want?"

"I want nothing. I'm here to make a demand. Stay clear of the Duchess of Lushing."

Elverton barked out a laugh. "You do not make demands of me, boy."

Aiden tossed back the scotch, then hurled the glass into the hearth where it shattered into shards. The earl jumped, which brought him a great deal of satisfaction. "She is not for you."

"Think she's for you, do you? She'd not give you the time of day. How do you even know her?" Holding up a hand, he snapped his fingers. "Your club. No, that can't be. She's in mourning, observing it quite strictly. Unless she went before Lushing died."

"Don't worry yourself over it. Just stay away from her or you'll find yourself with more broken bones."

"You've got nothing to offer her. Not respectability, not a place in Society. She's the daughter of an earl, has been the wife of a duke, for God's sake. Do you really believe she would allow herself to be seen with you?"

No, she'd fuck him but not walk beside him. And that grated, not that he'd give Elverton the satisfaction of seeing how his words had hit the mark. Aiden marched over to the desk, flattened his hands on it, and leaned toward the arrogant sod. "Stay. Away. From. Her."

His sire tapped a finger against his glass. "For seventy-five percent of your profits."

He'd given him sixty percent to save Finn, but

he'd been younger then, all of twenty-three, not as confident, not as sure of himself. Then Finn had visited the earl a few months back and put an end to the arrangement. "Heed my warning or see yourself ruined."

Turning on his heel, he strode with purpose for the door.

"You are nothing!" his sire yelled after him.

He fought not to let the words take root, but it was a challenge. He'd believed he had something special with Selena. He thought she'd cared for him. But she wanted to use him, just as the earl had used whoever Aiden's mother had been. When it came to the heart, no one had power.

THE EARL OF Camberley liked playing cards at the Cerberus Club. Nothing about it was fancy. The dark smoke-filled rooms were a reflection of London's underworld, and within these walls, commoners mixed with the lesser lords, second sons, third, and fourth. Those with pockets that held little save lint. Those no longer welcomed at White's or allowed through the doors of other proper gentlemen's clubs.

The language was rough, the laughter loud, the liquor cheap. Gin mostly. But he was not in a position to complain. He was able to get credit extended to him here, while he wasn't at other places. And in a few more hands, he was going to have to ask for more credit. His luck was atrocious this evening.

Although it could very well be day by now. No windows allowed for the viewing of the passage of time, and he was always surprised when he looked at his watch to see how many hours had passed. He was reaching into his waistcoat pocket to retrieve his timepiece when everyone around him went quiet. Glancing up, he saw Aiden Trewlove, the club's owner, standing there. It wasn't often that he made an appearance. He was too busy managing his new club, the club Selena was now frequenting, the club that would provide their salvation.

"Camberley."

He didn't much like being singled out, especially when he heard no respect in the club owner's tone. He was determined to match it. "Trewlove."

"What say you and I play a game, just the two of us?"

Before Camberley could provide an answer, the lads with whom he'd been playing shoved back their chairs and went in search of other tables. Trewlove dropped into a vacated chair and began gathering up the scattered cards. "You don't seem to be having much luck tonight."

"I've had better."

"Not often. You're an atrocious player."

"I shouldn't think you'd complain about that. It puts money in your coffers."

Trewlove's grin was more predatory than friendly. He began shuffling the cards with a skill and swiftness that was unnerving. In his hands, the cards merely whispered as they fell into place. "Do you know what you owe on your marker here?"

"Twelve thousand pounds."

"We're going to play a game of War. Your vowels will be the bet. Double or nothing. If I win, you'll owe me twenty-four thousand. If you win, your debt to me is cleared."

Camberley's heart began racing as though it were a thoroughbred on a racetrack. Never before had he wagered so much in a single go. Everything within him screamed for him to decline, get up, and go home now. Instead, he nodded.

Trewlove fanned the cards out over the table. "We're playing a simplified version. You select a card, I select a card. The higher card wins."

Swallowing hard, Camberley placed the tip of a finger on a card—

No, not that one. He touched another, then another. Twelve thousand pounds at stake. If he lost, he had no means with which to see his debt cleared. Ah, but if he won . . .

Using only his fingertip, he snagged a card and dragged it toward him. Slowly, he lifted the edge of the card. Eight of clubs. Damn.

Trewlove didn't hesitate. He simply snatched up the very last card, the one that had been on the bottom of the stack. He nodded toward Camberley.

Striving to look as haughty as possible, to give the impression he wasn't afraid his world was about to crumble around him, he tossed down his card, faceup.

Trewlove flicked his card in such a way that it did a little somersault in the air before landing on the earl's card. Two of hearts.

Camberley laughed. "I won! I owe you nothing."

"You're a fortunate man, Lord Camberley. You leave here free of debt. Make the most of it. Don't come back."

"How is it that you have the means to visit gaming hells?"

Camberley had always known Selena was a formidable force to be reckoned with when the situation warranted the rising of her temper, but he'd always thought himself immune to her anger. He was the only boy among a sea of girls. He was the heir, now the earl.

But he'd returned to his residence at nearly four in the morning only to be informed by his butler that Selena had arrived two hours earlier and was awaiting him in the library. Apparently, she'd spent the time stewing. He'd never known her to be so agitated. "I managed to get my credit extended."

She folded her arms across her stomach, and he wondered if it was to stop herself from yanking out his hair. "Do you not think any extended credit would be better served being applied to bringing your estate up to snuff?"

"A man needs his distractions."

She took a menacing step forward, and he leaped back, not much liking the mutinous fire burning in her eyes. "I'd like distractions as well, Winslow, but they are not to be had at present. I thought we were of a like mind, in agreement that we needed to get matters put to right as quickly as possible—for the girls' sakes."

"You're going to get yourself with child—"

"And if it doesn't happen?"

"If you apply yourself fervently—"

Her eyes narrowing to the point they could slice open a man stilled his words. "You will cease your gambling. You will divest yourself of your mistress. You will no longer be viewed as a wastrel but will dedicate yourself to bringing honor and respect back to the title and estates. Not only for the girls' sakes but for your own. As things stand now, what sort of wife do you think you would procure?"

He didn't want a wife. He wanted his mistress. He loved her. But he held his tongue because he doubted Selena would welcome the news. "I am too young to wed."

"No, Winslow, you are not. Nor are you too young to prove yourself worthy of your place in Society. You will pull back your shoulders and march forward as I've been required to do. Or you shall find yourself in a very unpleasant spot, indeed."

He jerked up his chin. "Are you threatening me?"

"I am saying I will no longer carry you. I will help where I can, naturally, but only if I see you are making an equal effort. Represent yourself as any respectable lord who found himself to be a pauper would and marry yourself a wealthy heiress. And make no further visits to the Cerberus Club."

He flung himself into a chair. "I have no choice in that particular matter. Aiden Trewlove, the bastard—"

"Don't call him that."

He stared at her. "Why should you care what I call him?"

"Aiden has worked extremely hard to better himself, has earned his success—"

"Aiden?" Suspicions, unwanted and chilling, dawned. "How did you even know I frequented the Cerberus?"

If her hair had been unbound, it would have swirled around her with the force with which she jerked up her chin. "I've heard rumors."

"No, you haven't." Slowly he came to his feet. "Pray tell me that you are not consorting with Aiden Trewlove, that he is not the one who will be getting you with child."

"What difference does it make?"

"He is a man to be reckoned with, a man who will not take lightly being made a fool of. Three of his siblings have married into the nobility. Eventually they will be skirting the edges of Society, and he will be right there with them. Should he ever catch sight of your son, should he realize—"

"I can handle him."

"Do you know what he did tonight? He came to his club and challenged me to a game. Just the two of us. He wagered my debt to him. Twelve thousand pounds—"

"Twelve thousand pounds? Are you mad? That is my income for six years! That money could have been put to much better use than card play."

"You're missing the point. He wagered it as though it was nothing. We each drew a card. The one with the higher card won. I won, Selena. He canceled my debt, then forbid me to ever return. He was angry at me for winning."

To his surprise, her face softened as she shook her head. "I don't think that's the reason he warned you against going to his club."

"Of course it is. That's the sort of man he is. No one crosses him. No one. He will not take kindly to your using him."

"I am well aware of that fact."

"You were supposed to choose some lowly commoner who there was no chance in hell you'd ever see again. What were you thinking to select a man whose family is the talk of all of London? That's hardly being discreet."

"I liked his smile."

"Selena—"

"Don't worry yourself so, Winslow. My secret will be safe with him." She made to move past him, stopped, and turned back to him, her brow deeply furrowed. "Where is the statue of Atlas that resided in that far corner?"

He'd sold it. The few coins it had brought allowed him to keep his mistress happy with baubles. "I rearranged a few of the knickknacks."

He watched as she slowly gazed around the room, knew each time she noted the absence of a treasure.

"You're selling things," she said quietly.

"Here and there," he admitted.

She faced him. "The statue was Father's favorite."

"He's not here to enjoy it, is he? It serves us better elsewhere."

"I gather this is not the only room that is not as it once was."

"Nothing about our life is as it once was. I'm sorry, Selena, that I have been negligent in my responsibilities. I will step up and do my part."

"That's all I ask."

He did hope she'd ask at a more reasonable hour in the future.

Chapter 16

The following afternoon, as the coach rumbled through the streets, Selena decided she didn't care if she were castigated for behaving in a manner unbecoming of a woman so early into her widowhood. The girls' delight at a distraction from their mourning was worth any glares of disapproval she might have to endure.

"I don't recall Lady Aslyn calling on you the day of the funeral," Connie said, sitting on the bench across from her with Flo.

"Her husband is not yet fully accepted by the nobility," Selena told her. "She would not attend without him, but she did send me a rather nice missive, expressing her condolences."

"And that's when she invited us to join her today in this worthy endeavor?"

"Yes." No. Her letter had expressed only her sorrow over Lushing's passing. She did hope Aiden informed Lady Aslyn that she was to have issued an invitation to Selena and her sisters. Otherwise matters could become quite awkward.

"I'm not quite convinced we should be on an outing," Flo said, her brow deeply furrowed.

"We shall be engaged in a good deed, helping a

young lady earn her way in the world. Even while mourning, one is forgiven for partaking in good deeds."

"Is one?" Flo asked.

"Yes, of course." She did not need her sister pushing back on this.

"I think it's exciting," Alice said, from her place beside Selena. "Think of all the books we'll get to touch as we put them on the shelves. We'll be building a bookshop."

"We're not supposed to experience any sort of excitement while in mourning," Flo said. "It's the reason I'm questioning it. We're all smiling a bit too much."

"I like to believe that Lushing would approve." Selena gave her glove a tug, finding it easier to look at the leather than her sister's inquisitive stare. "He enjoyed seeing us happy. He would not like for us to be unduly sad."

"Mother, on the other hand, is probably rolling over in her grave." Flo pursed her lips together in disapproval, before whispering harshly, "The Trewloves are all . . . *bastards*."

"It's not a disease, Flo," Selena responded tartly. "It's not going to rub off on you."

"But to associate with them is scandalous. It could hurt our marriage prospects."

The whole point was to improve their marriage prospects, although she couldn't explain that to them. But before she could think of an appropriate response to put her sister's mind at rest, Alice piped up. "It's not their fault. Should we blame people for things that aren't their fault?"

"I agree with Alice," Connie said. "To a point.

I'm thinking of it as research. I've never spoken to a lesser being before."

"They're not lesser," Selena snapped, taking no pleasure in her sisters' wide, round eyes landing on her with the full weight of their surprise.

"Have you spoken with one of them?" Flo asked cautiously.

"I attended one of their weddings, did I not?" Not that she'd spoken to any of them there as she'd not attended the breakfast following, but it was best to let her sisters draw their own conclusions. They had not attended, having not yet had their coming outs.

"What are they like?" Alice asked innocently.

"They're people." Selena turned her attention to the scenery beyond the window. "With dreams and ambitions. They"—*make me laugh, bring me pleasure, make me forget my sorrows when I'm in Aiden's presence*—"want what we all want: to be loved, to be happy, to have shelter, food, and clothing. I think it is quite commendable that they are seeking to improve their lot in life through business. Mick Trewlove has his building empire. Finn Trewlove has his horse farm where he and his wife, Lady Lavinia, take in orphans. Their sister Gillie, who married the Duke of Thornley, has her tavern. And now this other sister will have a bookshop."

"Then there is the Trewlove with the house of sin for ladies," Connie said. "To be honest, I was quite intrigued by the place after hearing the ladies carrying on about it the day of the funeral. Have you been there, Selena?"

"I'm in mourning." Not a lie, but not an answer either.

"When you are not, will you go there?"

"Perhaps we all will." Everything depended on the state of her relationship with Aiden.

"You know an awfully lot about them," Flo said.

"They are on everyone's tongue. Please do be on your best behavior." Selena needed Aiden to find them worthy. "You don't want to embarrass Lady Aslyn when she was kind enough to offer us a reprieve from the maudlin for a while. Simply think of it as an afternoon of good works."

She caught sight of the Trewlove Hotel first, grand and majestic, dominating the street, the neighborhood. Lushing had planned for them to spend a night in one of the well-appointed rooms upon their return to London for the Season. His appearance there would have done much to ensure other noble families visited. He'd always been humble regarding his influence but had used it where he could to the betterment of others. From afar, he'd admired Mick Trewlove for his efforts in improving areas of London. "Where others see decay, he sees the potential for brilliance," Lushing had once told her. "We shall offer our support and hasten his acceptance among the *ton*." He was wont to accept those others did not.

Then she spotted the man leaning against the lamppost across the street from the hotel and all thoughts of Lushing fled her mind. The coach came to a halt, and before the footman could climb down and see to his duties, Aiden was opening the door and extending his hand to her. Even as she placed her palm against his, she feared her sisters could hear the wild pounding of her heart. He helped her disembark and then immediately reached back to assist each of the girls.

Once they were all standing on the bricked walkway outside the Fancy Book Emporium—the letters stenciled elaborately and with a flourish in gold on one of the windows—Selena said, "Mr. Trewlove, it was so thoughtful of Lady Aslyn to invite us. Allow me the honor of introducing my sisters." Even as she knew she should be introducing him to them. He was turning her life inside out, and to be honest, she didn't care.

"Lady Constance and Lady Florence."

He bowed his head slightly. "Ladies, it's my pleasure."

"You wouldn't know it to look at them, but they are twins."

"Like my brother Finn and myself." He winked. "Although we were born six weeks apart."

"Your mother held one of you in her womb for six weeks?" Flo asked.

He grinned. "No. We have different mothers."

"Then you're not twins."

"I suppose not in the classical sense, no."

It wasn't going to serve her well if Flo continued to argue with him. "And this is Lady Alice," she interrupted, striving to steer them back to important matters.

His smile for Alice was devastating in its tenderness, its kindness, as though he recognized that the losses in their lives were hardest on her because of her young age. "The lover of books."

Alice's eyes widened, and her jaw dropped. "How did you know that?"

"I no doubt mentioned it when I met Mr. Trewlove at Lady Aslyn's wedding." Her lie came so easily and swiftly that it was a bit unsettling.

"Do you like books?" Alice asked.

"I adore them," he said. "As does my sister Fancy—which is the reason she's surrounding herself with them. Come along, ladies. Let's put you all to work."

He ushered them to the door and opened it. Alice fairly skipped into the building. Flo and Connie entered with a bit more decorum, but Selena could sense the anticipation thrumming through them. Selena, however, fearing the afternoon was designated for disaster, stopped beside him. "Does Lady Aslyn know I've told them she issued the invitation?"

"Everyone knows what they need to know."

"Did you tell them . . . *everything*?"

"It's not their business, sweetheart."

"They had questions, surely."

He tucked a bare knuckle beneath her chin, tilted her face up slightly. "They know I met you at my club. They know I'm intrigued. They know how to hold their tongues. You and your sisters were simply in need of a distraction, and I thought to provide it. You're safe with us, Selena."

No, she wasn't. Whenever he was near, she was in danger of losing her heart.

He'd spoken true. He hadn't needed to tell his family much in order to obtain their cooperation. They knew he'd met her at his club—although he hadn't told them how recently they'd met, leaving them to assume their paths had crossed before she became a widow. He'd admitted she intrigued him. He'd explained that he wanted to give her and her sisters a respite from their grieving.

So he wasn't surprised when he escorted Selena inside to find his family surrounding the younger ladies and welcoming them into the fold. It helped, of course, that they were already acquainted with Mick's wife—Lady Aslyn—as well as Finn's wife, Lady Lavinia. It was also clear they knew the Duke of Thornley—Gillie's husband—as he was a well-placed, influential duke, probably on par with Selena's late husband. As Thorne took control of the situation, introducing Fancy, Mick, Finn, and Beast, Lady Aslyn broke free of the gathering, strolled over, and took Selena's hand.

"I was most sorry to hear of Lushing's passing. You have my deepest condolences."

"Your kind letter was much appreciated."

"I should have been there in person to offer what comfort I could, but . . ." Her voice trailed off as she seemed rather uncomfortable with where her words were leading.

"We're not the most accepting lot," Selena said with a gentle smile that tightened his gut. Why did she have to be so gracious?

Aslyn laughed lightly. "No, we're not. Come, I'll introduce you to everyone."

Just like that she took Selena under her wing, which was something Aiden wanted to provide for her: shelter and comfort. But he would be relegated to doing it all in shadows, hidden away. His father had hidden him away, still took no pleasure in his existence. It seemed no matter how much success he attained, it was never enough to make him respectable.

"Ye kissed her yet, guv?"

Aiden glanced down at the little urchin who had for some years lived in Gillie's tavern, but now resided at the horse farm with Finn. The lad had probably seen eight years or so, although they weren't certain. They knew only that he was an orphan, like so many. "A gentleman never tells, Robin."

"But ye ain't a gentleman. Ye be a scoundrel. That's what Mum says."

Mum. Lavinia. The boy had taken quickly to having a family. "She doesn't know everything."

Robin's expression turned mutinous, no doubt because he believed Aiden had insulted the woman he considered to be his mother, and Aiden expected the lad to come at him with fists flying. "Although on that particular matter she is correct. I am a scoundrel."

"And a lazy one at that," Fancy said as she neared, a bright smile wreathing her face with joy. She placed her hand on top of Robin's head. "Why don't you help the duke place books on the shelves? He's working in the animal section."

With a smart salute, the lad dashed off.

"The animal section?" Aiden asked.

"If you'd joined us in our little circle a moment ago, you'd have learned that I have divided the shop into sections according to the types of books to be found there." She waved a foolscap with some sort of layout and markings in front of his nose. She would be eight and ten in a few months, but already had a good head on her shoulders for business, no doubt having learned quite a bit from her older siblings. Mick had sent her to a posh finishing school to prepare for her introduction into Society. His desire to see Fancy well situated among the nobility had been one of his motivations for achieving the success he had. "Upstairs is a sitting room. You'll find some boxes marked with an *S*. If you'll haul them up and assist the duchess in arranging them on the shelves—"

"Which duchess?" There was Selena, of course, but his sister Gillie was also a duchess, not that she was yet comfortable with that title.

Fancy smirked. "The one you're interested in, naturally. I thought you might appreciate having a task that wouldn't have everyone watching you. She seems rather nice. I like her sisters."

He didn't think there was a soul in the entire world Fancy wouldn't like. She had a rather innocent view of life, but then he and his siblings had ensured she'd been protected from all the harshness they'd faced. "You're a conniving little minx."

"Thank you."

"That wasn't a compliment."

"You're a bit of a grouse. Do you love her?"

What he felt for her defied description, but he wasn't fool enough to give away his heart no matter how forcefully she was tugging on it. "You've too much of the romantic in you, Fancy. Now show me where these boxes are."

She took him to a storage room, but after she left him, he didn't immediately see to the task set before him. Rather he wanted to take a measure of Selena's sisters. So he wandered through the maze of bookcases he imagined his sister would take comfort from when they were lined with all the volumes she'd amassed. Peering around the edge of one of the cases, he was surprised to find the twins working diligently together, Florence on her knees, sitting back on her heels, pulling a book from a box and handing it up to Constance, who placed it on the shelf.

"This could become our life," Florence said on a wispy sigh. "Laboring all day."

"It's not going to come to that," Constance assured her. "Although I rather like feeling useful. Sometimes it seems we are expected to be mere ornaments."

Florence extended her body up until her bottom was no longer on the floor, yet she remained on her knees. "Why do you think we're really here?" Her voice was a low, conspiratorial whisper.

Constance appeared dumbstruck. "Well, to be helpful."

"Did you see the way he looked at her? Aiden Trewlove? Mark my words. The invitation came from him, not Lady Aslyn."

"But Selena barely knows him."

"So she would have us think. But why was he waiting?"

"To be hospitable."

"Fire lit in his eyes when he saw her. He'd keep her warm on a winter day."

"All gentlemen perk up when they see her. They are all enthralled by her beauty."

"Her cheeks were as red as apples. Have you ever known her to blush? I think perhaps he has piqued her interest."

Constance laughed lightly. "My word, Flo. I do believe you are seeing things that aren't there, because you are bored, because our Season has been delayed. But if you are correct, I won't fault her. I know she adored Lushing, but I don't think there was ever any great passion between them. A woman should have passion, at least once in her life. I suspect that is why Aiden Trewlove's sinful parlor will thrive."

"Are you thinking of going?"

Constance lifted a shoulder. "I'm curious. Aren't you?"

Turning away, knowing he'd eavesdropped enough on a private conversation, he decided to restrict entry into his establishment to those of a more mature age. He didn't need young ladies making stupid mistakes. On the other hand, was it his responsibility if others didn't keep a close watch on them? Although even when mothers did and approached him about denying their daughters access to his club, they often changed their mind with a bit of pampering. Lady Fontaine certainly had. He'd received a missive from her that afternoon stating that both she and her daughter would be returning in the near future. The foot rub had done the trick—but then, it always did.

He located Alice in a back corner, sitting on the floor, her skirts fanned out around her, an open book in her lap. "It'll take you forever if you read each book before you put it in its place."

Jerking her head up as she snapped the book closed, she looked at him through large innocent eyes, her cheeks turning a burnished pink. "I hadn't had a chance to read this one yet. It came out too late for me to receive it as a gift for Christmas."

Crouching before her, he noted the title. *Through the Looking-Glass.* "Perhaps Fancy will allow you to purchase it today, even though her shop's not yet open. You could be her first customer."

Slowly, she shook her head. "It's an extravagance, and I can't ask it of Selena. Her coins are precious of late." Her blush deepened. "I probably shouldn't have revealed that. It's terribly crass to talk of money."

"It'll be our secret." Although he was impressed with her sacrifice. While his family was now teeming with nobs, his opinion of nobles as a whole was not favorable. He viewed them in light of the pennies they could add to his coffers, not the ones absent from theirs.

"You're nice."

He winked at her. "That should remain our secret as well."

She giggled, and damn if he didn't understand why Selena wanted to ensure her sisters made good marriages. He'd known too many women who had been abused or lived harsh lives, women who aged before their time, worn out by the burdens that life had given them to bear. It was the reason they'd supported Gillie when she wanted to open her tavern, and now Fancy with her bookshop. They all wanted Fancy to marry well, but if no man was wise enough to ask for her hand, she'd have her business to see her through, and her siblings each had the means to ensure she never did without. Alice couldn't rely on her brother in the same manner, in spite of his title.

"Excuse me, sir."

Glancing back, Aiden stepped aside as Mick's secretary, carrying a cumbersome box, edged past him.

"Lady Alice," the young man said, his face turning a bright red that almost matched the shade of his hair. "Miss Trewlove thought the volumes in this box were best suited to this portion of the shop."

"Thank you, Mr. Tittlefitz."

He set down the box, stepped back, and didn't seem to know what to do next. He cleared his throat.

"She also thought I should assist you. I can place books on the higher shelves if you like."

"That would be lovely, thank you."

With a shake of his head, wondering if his younger sister was striving to play matchmaker, Aiden went to retrieve his own boxes. Or box, as the one Beast pointed to in the storage room was incredibly heavy. Still, he hefted it onto his shoulder and headed through the shop and up the stairs to what Fancy had designated as the reading room. From a previous afternoon spent assisting her, he knew clusters of small sitting areas were arranged throughout the space, and bookcases lined each side of the fireplace and stretched out along one wall. The rooms on the floor above would serve as her lodgings, which meant another afternoon of hauling things— furniture and personal belongings—up. Not that he was complaining. His mum had taught him that family did for family and did so without grumbling.

All thoughts of being inconvenienced drifted away when he crossed the threshold and caught sight of Selena standing by the window, gazing out on the street below, with the afternoon sunlight washing over her. He didn't much like her widow's weeds, the way they reminded him she'd had a recent loss. She was buttoned up to her chin, down to her wrists. He imagined the pleasure it would bring him to set all the buttons free. Even knowing she intended to use him, he couldn't seem to not want her. He set down the box in the middle of the room. "You're not working nearly as diligently as your sisters."

With a smile softening her face, she glanced over at him. "I was just watching people going on with their lives. It's an odd thing, how one's life can seem all out of kilter, and yet the world carries on as though nothing is amiss."

Joining her, he crossed his arms over his chest and leaned a shoulder against the window's edge. "I'm sure there are people down below whose world is equally awry."

"But you wouldn't know it to watch them. I'm discovering that you can't look at someone and know the trials they face. We all wear masks. They just aren't as visible as the ones worn at your club."

"You seem of a maudlin mood."

"I lied to my sisters. I'm keeping secrets from them. They might not appreciate this outing so much if they knew the true purpose behind it."

"I like them."

She gave a curt laugh. "Do you? That was a rather quick assessment."

"The twins gossip. Alice reads. They're not complaining about the tasks set before them. They have dreams. They aren't that different from Fancy."

"Did you think they would be?"

He wasn't quite certain what he'd expected. He wished he'd known Selena when she was their ages. How innocent might she have been? How had the burdens of caring for her family weighed on her? Finn had been a lad when he'd fallen in love with the woman who eventually became his wife. At the time Aiden had thought his brother a fool but now could see the advantage of knowing a person, of watching as circumstances slowly shaped the girl into the woman she would become. "If you have a son"—*if I give you a boy*—"what exactly would he inherit other than a title?"

Pursing her lips, she turned her attention once more to the traffic on the cobblestoned street, the people rushing along the bricked pathways. "The ducal estate—Sheffield Hall—as well as two earldoms."

"He'd have three titles?"

"Yes."

Three estates, three titles. He could never offer that to any other children he might have, if he had children. "Where is this Sheffield Hall?"

"Kent."

"You can reach it in a day?"

"A few hours by coach."

Possibly faster by railway, although that mode of transport put her at risk of being seen with him. Now he was the one staring at people going on about their lives. He'd always preferred the shadows, but damn if he didn't want to walk with her in the sunlight, to not be a dark secret she would forever have to keep hidden away. But a dukedom and two earldoms were more than he would ever hold, and he wanted his children to have more than he could ever possibly attain. With a curt nod, he turned away from the window. "We'd best get to work here."

She touched his arm. He stilled and glanced back at her.

"You've closed the doors of your gaming hell to Winslow—Lord Camberley. And you canceled his debt to you."

"I didn't cancel it. We wagered it. He won."

Her expression was one of skepticism. "I should think a man skilled at sleight of hand when it comes to peas would be equally accomplished when it comes to manipulating cards."

"What a cynic you are." Although he had indeed known precisely where to find the two of hearts because he'd placed it on the bottom before he'd ever begun shuffling and had known how to keep it there. He'd wanted to ease at least one burden off her shoulders, although he couldn't guarantee Camberley wouldn't gamble elsewhere. "I'm actually surprised he confessed all that to you."

"I was waiting in his residence when he arrived home. I've forbidden him to gamble in the future or spend any more time not tending to his duties."

He certainly admired her tenacity in seeing after her sisters' welfare. "How did he take that?"

"Not well, but he understands the import of it. He doesn't have a very high opinion of you."

"Few men who owe me money do."

"And women who owe you? Should they fear you?"

"If you don't know the answer to that question, then you shouldn't make any bargains with me." Crouching, he opened the box, grabbed a book, and held it out to her.

Horror swept over her lovely features as she knelt beside him, took the book, set it aside, and closed her fingers lightly around his wrist. "You really did chaff your skin."

The rough-hewn abrasion circled just above his hand. He regretted not tugging the sleeves of his shirt or jacket down before offering her the book. He'd not liked one bit how vulnerable he'd felt lying on his bed, unable to free himself. Although now he couldn't help but contemplate that she was equally bound, her bonds simply invisible. "Did you think I'd lied?"

"No, but I didn't realize it was this bad."

"It'll heal."

"I fear it will leave behind scars, constant re-minders of what I did to you." Lifting his arm to her mouth, she placed the gentlest of kisses against the still red and raw flesh. His gut tightened into an annoying knot. He didn't want to soften toward her, needed to remain distant so he could view what their relationship might become as a business ar-rangement, one of convenience that would elevate the fruit of his loins into the upper echelons of Society. But from the moment he'd spied her, he'd strayed onto paths he'd never before traveled, taken actions he'd known would lead to no good outcome. Yet, here he was once again, dangling himself in front of her, giving her leave to do with him as she would. "Damn you. How is it that you have man-aged to bewitch me?"

Cradling her cheek with one hand, plowing his fingers into her hair, he brought her in and took her mouth like the greedy bastard he was, relishing the taste and warmth of her, how easily she surrendered and shifted until it was more than their lips touch-ing, until her body was nestled within the curve of his. His plan to make a rational, informed decision regarding whether he would once again have her was mocking him. He had so little resistance where she was concerned. It was sheer and utter madness, the ease with which she controlled him.

With great care, as though she were spun glass and easily shattered, never taking his mouth from hers, he lowered her to the Aubusson carpet that dominated this particular sitting area. With a lift-ing of her skirts, an unfastening of his trousers, he could claim her here, now. Recklessly. With no sheath about to offer her protection, before he fully decided if he would take the risk of bringing a child into the world. Her sighs and moans inflamed his desires. The manner in which she writhed beneath him as though she were desperate to have him closer fueled his body's needs, leaving them wanting, wanting of her and the hot, velvety slickness that had encased him the night before, that had driven him nearly mad. He'd wanted to stay buried in her, to pour his seed into her, as much as he'd wanted to leave and spare her the possibility of giving birth to his progeny. But it was what she wanted, and he imagined her swelling with his babe.

Bracketing her face between his hands, he deepened the kiss, his tongue imitating the primal motions his cock longed to make, thrusting, parrying. Why did she have to taste so damn good? Why did it have to feel as though her hands belonged on his back, stroking, caressing, urging him ever closer? Why—

A loud clearing of a throat had him jerking his head up to glare at Beast, who stood just inside the doorway, holding a box. Selena gave a little mewl of distress, clutched his shirt, and buried her face against his chest. While being caught in such an intimate position was embarrassing for a woman, he couldn't help but wonder if being caught with him specifically added to her shame.

"Fancy's bringing the sisters up to see the reading salon." Beast's voice was quiet, even, gave no hint that he was surprised by what he'd witnessed. But then his brother had always had a knack for seeing things as they were, had never been one to judge.

"I thought she wanted them filling the shelves downstairs." It's what they'd been doing when he'd left them.

Beast shrugged, walked in, and set down the box. "She decided they needed a break from their labors."

After tapping Selena's hand gently to get her to release her hold, Aiden shoved himself to his feet, reached down, and assisted her up. She began frantically patting her hair. He took her hands, stilled her actions. "You look fine." Except for the red blossoming over her cheeks, indicating her mortification. "Beast is skilled at holding secrets and forgetting things he sees."

She gave Beast a furtive glance. "Thank you for the warning."

Not that they'd needed it. Aiden could hear the feminine voices coming up the stairs, although he was no doubt being quite optimistic to believe he'd have taken note of them when he'd been so lost in Selena.

The girls crossed the threshold with Fancy in the lead. "The reading salon," she announced with affection and a spreading of her arms, before scowling at Aiden. "You've not made much progress."

"The duchess and I were discussing how best to arrange the books."

She narrowed her eyes as though suspecting another matter entirely might have been the reason for his delay in getting to work. Then she carried on with her purpose, once more spreading her arms to encompass the entirety of the sitting areas. "In here, people may read to their hearts' content."

"After they've purchased the books," he pointed out.

"No. It'll be like a lending library except I won't charge a subscription fee."

"Fancy, you're running a business here. You can't simply give things away. The books you are allowing them to read cost money."

"I'm not a dolt, Aiden. I'm aware of how business works."

"So you want to make a profit."

"Neither am I greedy. A modest profit will suffice. Besides I intend to take donations in order to maintain the reading salon."

He shifted his gaze to Beast, who quirked one corner of his mouth. None of this was news to his brother, which immediately made Aiden suspicious. He'd not had much time for the family of late, and he had a feeling it was about to cost him. He turned his attention back to his sister. "From whom will you be gathering these donations? Your siblings?"

"For a start. Then others with a charitable bent. Like the duchess, for example."

He sighed. The duchess couldn't afford to be charitable—not unless he gave her a child. Although he wasn't about to share any of that with Fancy.

"We're also going to teach people how to read," she continued. "A couple of nights a week, we'll hold lessons. As you're well aware, a good many of the poorer among us lack education."

It was one of the things his mum had insisted upon: her children would attend the free ragged schools.

While it was only for half a day, until they reached the age of eleven, she'd never allowed them to miss a day—even when they were ill. She'd wanted to give them whatever advantages she could. "*We?*"

"Mr. Tittlefitz and I at first. Perhaps you'll even teach a class."

"I run my businesses at night."

"Then I'll schedule a class in the afternoon. We can discuss it later. At the moment, I want to give the ladies here a tour of the area and gather their opinions on how I might improve it. Ladies, if you'll follow me?" She began leading them around the room, explaining how she thought one sitting area would appeal to men, another to ladies, yet another to a mother with her children.

"You won't say no to her, will you?" Selena's question sounded more like a statement.

He faced her. "She has a way of wrapping us around her finger."

"And you'll fund her free library."

He sighed, striving to sound irritated. He didn't need her to know how easily he could be won over. "I suspect we all will."

"Families do for each other."

He knew what she was saying, what she was explaining with so few words. Just as he would do everything within his power to ensure Fancy was happy, that she had all she wanted, desired, and needed, so Selena would do whatever was necessary to safeguard her sisters and assist them in bringing about their dreams.

Chapter 17

After her sisters and the others returned downstairs, she and Aiden worked in silence, placing the books on the shelves on opposite sides of the fireplace, as though he knew that if they were in easy reach of each other, they would come together again, as though they no longer had a choice, as though their bodies, now familiar to each other's, had become magnetized and would always seek to rejoin.

Selena had been fascinated watching his interaction with his sister, the easy camaraderie between them, realizing that his irritated tone was feigned, understanding that his sister realized it as well. Fancy would have her bookshop, where people who could afford to do so made purchases, and her reading salon, where people of lesser means could lose themselves in the pages between the covers, where those who might have never known the magic books offered would learn to read and in so doing might better their lives.

Selena had taken her affluence for granted until her parents died, and she'd discovered it had all been false. Even though she had the privilege of being able to read, it had never occurred to her to work because people of her status did not lower themselves to such degrading activities. And yet from the moment she'd crossed the threshold into the shop, she'd been caught up in the excitement of a young woman on the verge of managing her own business. Fancy could do with it as she wished, decorate it as she pleased. She determined how the rooms would be arranged, how the books would line the shelves. So much power. So much risk. Yet Selena suspected the risk added to the excitement because when one had so much to lose, achieving success would be all the sweeter.

"A penny for your thoughts."

She nearly leaped out of her skin, only then noticing Aiden leaning against her side of the fireplace, his arms crossed over his chest. Why did he always have to appear so masculine, yet so rough? Why was her first thought upon seeing him always how much she longed to wrap her arms around his neck, lift up on her toes, and kiss him? "I was striving to recall if I'd read this book."

"Liar."

She laughed lightly, wondering if she'd ever be able to keep a secret from him, wondering if she'd ever want to. Her relationship with him, in spite of its initial deceptions, was the most honest one she'd ever experienced. "You've found me out. I was thinking how marvelous it is for your sister to have this opportunity. How brave she is to go forth not knowing the outcome. She could fail."

"She could succeed."

"Precisely. Is everyone in your family always so optimistic?"

"Life seldom rewards the faint of heart."

She shook her head. "I wish I had your sister's courage."

"You came to my club, to me. You married a man you didn't love in order to protect your family. Hardly the acts of a coward."

"I did them out of fear."

"It is not courageous if there is no fear."

She was scared now, scared of the deception she wanted to perpetrate, scared of the guilt she harbored regarding the unfairness to Lushing, scared she might lose Aiden. "What do you fear?"

"Too many things to count."

"I'm not certain I believe that."

Reaching out, he skimmed his knuckles along her cheek. "I fear disappointing you."

"By not giving me what I need?" Had he made his decision? Had he not found her sisters worthy of his seed? Did he not consider her worthy?

"Apologies for interrupting again."

This time neither of them were startled by Beast's voice. They didn't jerk, didn't back away, didn't try to hide. Aiden merely turned his head to look at his brother, a dark brow winging up in query.

"Mum has supper ready. We're heading over now."

Those words caused Selena to start. "Oh. My sisters and I should be on our way then."

"You're invited," Aiden said.

She shook her head. "We couldn't possibly impose."

"No imposition. She was counting on you being there and prepared more than enough food. We're supping in the hotel dining room across the way."

Panic threaded itself through her. "We can't eat there. We can't be seen in public."

"The room has been closed off for our private gathering. We'll enter through the back. No one will see you."

"We can't possibly—"

"My mum went to a lot of trouble."

"Well, she shouldn't have. Our agreement was to help in the shop, not dine with your family."

"I need more time to observe your sisters."

Backing away from him, she wanted to pound the shelves, noted that his brother was nowhere to be seen, had no doubt gone down the stairs to prepare for going over to the hotel or perhaps he'd noted the tension and realized a private discourse was needed. "You should have been observing them all afternoon instead of being up here with me."

She should have thought of that earlier, should have insisted he not assist her. Only she enjoyed his presence so much. Still it had resulted in his not being able to make an assessment.

"Watching them place books on shelves hardly tells me what I need to know. What are you afraid of, Selena?"

That she might come to like him more than she already did, that seeing him with his family might make her reconsider her stupid plan.

Again, he touched his knuckles to her cheek. "It's only dinner."

With him, nothing was ever *only* anything. Still, she disliked leaving knowing his mother had gone to such trouble. Besides she was curious about the woman. Ettie Trewlove had not been in the shop, so she had yet to meet her. She wondered what sort of woman would provide a home for bastards when many considered them not worthy of breath. While her own son would be considered legitimate under the law, in truth his status would mirror his father's, because she would not be married to his sire.

She nodded. "If you can ensure we will not be seen."

An edge of triumph made its way into the smile he bestowed upon her. "I am nothing if not a planner."

Taking her elbow, he escorted her down the stairs and into the main portion of the shop. Her sisters were hovering near the door, looking somewhat concerned and uncertain. Fancy seemed not to know what to do with her guests either.

"We're dining with them?" Connie asked as soon as she clapped eyes on Selena.

"Yes. They kindly issued an invitation and I thought we should accept."

"We're in mourning." The words were whispered in the same tone one might use to announce one wasn't fully clothed.

"I've been assured we won't be seen, and it's not as though it will be a formal dinner with a great many guests."

"But we're not dressed for dinner."

"What you're wearing is fine," Aiden announced with authority. "We never dress formally for dinner. Come along."

It was difficult to argue with a man who was ushering her and her sisters out the door before all his words had reached their ears. She wasn't accustomed to his impatience, feared he might view Connie's argumentative nature in a bad light and might decide she wasn't worth his trouble. "It'll be lovely," she assured her sisters, glancing back to see Fancy locking up her shop.

How marvelous it must feel to have such inde-
pendence, to actually own something of value that
simultaneously added to one's personal worth and
esteem. She was suddenly struck with the realization that she didn't really *own* anything. Oh, she had
her clothes and a few pieces of jewelry, but a home,
coaches, horses—she had use of them, but they
weren't hers. Even the dower house was not hers to
sell, merely to use.

In silence, they crossed the street. Aiden led them
down an alleyway and into some gardens that she
thought would soon be bursting with spring colors
as it was evident that they were well maintained.
Several benches where one could rest lined different pathways. She would have liked to explore
the area, but he escorted them to a door—the staff
entry—opened it, and shepherded them inside.

Her sisters' eyes were wide as they traversed
through the kitchens, and it occurred to her that they
may have never before visited kitchens. Certainly
they'd been trained to manage a household and
staff, but had they ever seen servants at their labors?
Doubtful, because in retrospect, she had to admit
that she met with the housekeeper to discuss matters
but had never actually visited her below stairs.

People carried on with their work, which most
certainly would not have happened if they realized a duchess was walking in their midst. But the
Trewloves had no airs about them. Aiden and his
sister greeted those they passed, made a few inquiries regarding health and families, and continued
on barely breaking their stride. They were comfortable here within their brother's dominion, and she
suspected they were each equally at home within

their siblings' businesses. She recalled Aiden telling her how they all shared everything they learned, all they knew. Each worked to lift the others, and in so doing lifted themselves. Seeing all of this firsthand, she could not help but believe that he could equate what she was doing for her family with measures he'd taken regarding his own siblings. It gave her hope that tonight she would return to the Elysium Club and continue in her efforts, with him being a willing partner in her desire to get with child.

He shoved open a door that servants used to enter the dining room, and she led her sisters through it. A long table with a white tablecloth had been set up on the far side of the grandiose area, away from the door and the wall of windows that looked out into the foyer. She was rather certain the door was locked, but even so a footman stood at attention on the other side of it, no doubt to explain to people that the room had been reserved for private use this evening. The draperies at the windows that faced the street were closed, cocooning them in, creating a rather intimate feel for a gathering of so many.

All the people she'd met earlier and the ones she'd known from before were chatting near the table. Fancy walked toward the group, greeting an older woman who broke away from the others. Her hair was a combination of salt-and-pepper strands pulled back into a simple knot. She was small of stature, well-rounded but not in a plump sort of way. Selena decided hugging her would be very much like wrapping her arms around a soft pillow: comforting.

Which was exactly what Aiden did when the woman was close enough. He bent slightly and embraced her, and something within Selena's chest tightened with his show of affection. She was accustomed to men holding themselves erect, perfect posture, bowing, sometimes taking a hand, pressing a kiss to knuckles—not welcoming a woman with arms coming around her in a gesture of familiarity that appeared so natural it had to have been done a thousand times. She couldn't recall ever having seen Winslow hug their mother thus. But it was obvious Mrs. Trewlove greeted her children as though she was truly glad to see them.

She stepped out of Aiden's embrace. With his arm resting lightly on her shoulders, he steered his mother toward Selena and her sisters, and she realized that this—not working in the bookshop—was the test he'd devised for her sisters. How they received his mother was how he would judge their character and their worth.

Tears stung her eyes with the understanding that the woman who had raised him meant so much to him. He was a man who encouraged sin, who trafficked in vice, who by all accounts was a scoundrel, but he loved his mother, loved his family. And if her sisters were the least bit insulting, all would be lost. But just as she'd had confidence when they'd played billiards, she had equal confidence in her sisters' kindness and knew she would win here as well.

"Mum, I'd like you to meet Selena Sheffield, Duchess of Lushing."

Proper etiquette dictated that a commoner should be introduced to the noble, but Selena had already dispensed with exhibiting well-bred manners when she'd introduced Aiden to her sisters earlier. Besides, she understood that within this room, there might be titles, but there were no ranks. No doubt at the table, she would find a muddled arrangement of the seating. No orderly procession to the dining area, no chairs assigned based on where one was positioned in the social order. With his introduction, Aiden was making a point: he didn't give a fig about *Debrett's* or *Burke's Peerage*; no one rated a place above the saintly woman who had taken him in and raised him as her own. Ah, yes, this was the gauntlet her sisters must pass. *Pay attention, girls.*

She curtsied, not as deeply as she would to the Queen, but still with a show of deference. "Mrs. Trewlove, I'm honored to make your acquaintance. It was so kind of you to invite us to dine with your family. Allow me the honor of presenting my sisters. Ladies Constance, Florence, and Alice."

Connie and Flo bobbed respectful curtsies. Alice's dipping, a bit more enthusiastic, was accompanied with an endearing smile. "A pleasure, Mrs. Trewlove."

Selena noted the approval in Aiden's eyes, the triumph within the dark depths, and felt as though his win was hers. Had he felt the same when she'd bested him at billiards? Had he been as glad that she'd won then as she was that he'd won now? Strange, how she never wanted to see him defeated.

"It was kind of you to help Fancy with her bookshop," Mrs. Trewlove said. "Now come along and eat before the food gets cold." Turning on her heel, she headed for the table, which seemed to be a signal to everyone else because they scattered, claiming seats—just as Selena had surmised they would—in no particular order.

"Ladies." Aiden's voice held a warmth that reached out and wrapped around her.

Once everyone was settled, she found herself sitting beside Lady Aslyn. Her husband had taken his seat at one end of the long table, his mother at the far end. Her sisters sat beside Selena, youngest to oldest. Aiden was across from her. His other two brothers were seated near his mother. Wives sat beside husbands. Mr. Tittlefitz was in attendance, as was the young boy, Robin.

Assorted platters and bowls lined the table. Mick Trewlove stood and began slicing into a rather hefty-looking roast. "Pass your plates!"

"Are there no servants?" Connie whispered.

"Might as well learn how it's done when there aren't, as we might be without soon enough," Flo responded, equally low but still Selena heard her.

It was interesting to watch the china dishes make their way around the table, empty when they were handed to Mick, filled with strips of beef when he passed them on. Once all the plates were resting in front of their proper person, people began reaching for bowls, adding potatoes, peas, and carrots to their meal before handing the pottery off to the next person.

"Bread!" Finn called out.

Aiden plucked a muffin from a wicker basket and tossed it down the length of the table. Finn snatched it from the air.

"Boys," Ettie Trewlove chided. "We have company. Mind your manners."

Selena imagined the woman had spent a good part of her life telling her boys to mind their manners.

Obviously when she spoke, they obeyed because the bread basket made its way around the table.

A footman went about pouring the wine. Selena noted that Gillie, the Duchess of Thornley, already heavy with child, gave a quick shake of her head when the footman offered her the Bordeaux. The gossips tittered that she'd been pregnant when the duke married her, but the deep devotion mirrored in his eyes whenever he looked at his wife told Selena that he hadn't married her because of her condition, but simply because he loved her so fiercely.

Lady Aslyn sipped tentatively at her wine, and Selena thought she, too, might be in the family way, as her husband was particularly solicitous toward her as though of a sudden she was fragile when Selena knew her to be of firmer stuff. Like Selena, she'd lost both her parents in one fell swoop—a railway accident—although at a much younger age. They'd found comfort in lamenting their losses. Aslyn had become the ward of the wealthy and powerful Duke of Hedley—who very much resembled her husband. It was rumored that Mick Trewlove was the noble's bastard, although Selena couldn't envision the duke being unfaithful to his duchess.

Lady Lavinia did indulge in the fine wine, a sign she might not yet be with child, but then she hadn't been married very long. Based upon the way her husband, Finn, continually reached out to touch her hand, caress her arm, tuck a stray strand of hair behind her ear, Selena was rather certain Lavinia would soon find herself increasing. It was obvious the man adored her, and she him.

These married couples all reflected the sort of devotion she'd hoped to inspire when she married.

Beast smiled indulgently at Fancy, and Selena realized with dawning awareness that his expression of brotherly affection very much mirrored the way Lushing had looked at her. Perhaps the reason he'd apologized when he first came to her bed was because his feelings toward her were more brotherly than husbandly.

She'd not truly understood the intimacy of the act, how it could bind two people. She certainly understood that now as she looked across the table at Aiden, noting the way he watched her as though he were striving to memorize the sight of her dining with his family because it would be a one-time occurrence.

The conversations ebbed and flowed around her, voices louder than she was accustomed to hearing during a meal. When someone laughed, an echo of "What's so funny?" reverberated through the room, and a story was retold so all could join in on the mirth: an overly drunk patron at the tavern who had decided to shed his clothing, a woman who had locked her husband out of their hotel room because she didn't like the way he smiled at the maids. Then there were the somber tales of discarded children taken in by Lady Lavinia, the articles she wrote describing the women she met who were shamed for giving in to their passions, who brought her their babes because she would see them well cared for. Selena listened to these women discussing matters that were normally the domain of men, was ever conscious that they lived in a world apart from hers. Two had once resided in it with her, but she couldn't recall ever seeing them looking so satisfied, so happy. They'd found love and fulfillment, but then neither had siblings for whom they were responsible. They'd been able to put their own wants and needs first. Selena couldn't imagine being so free.

When the dinner was finished, it appeared that people were going to lounge around and visit a bit more. But darkness had fallen, and Selena had grown weary of the test. Surely by now, Aiden had made his assessment of her sisters. She made their excuses, thanked Aiden's mother for the lovely meal, wished Fancy success with her business, said her goodbyes to the others, and was grateful when Aiden began leading them back the way they'd come. Through the hotel and across the street. Then around to the back of the corner bookshop, where her coach waited. The footman leaning against it straightened and opened the door, assisting her sisters into the conveyance.

Selena stopped a short distance away in order to have a private word with her escort. Distant light from the streetlamps cast his face in shadows, making it impossible to read his features, to know his decision. She certainly didn't want to ask outright. "I shall come to the club later, shall I?"

"I want to visit the ducal estate. I want to see what my son would inherit."

Not the response she'd expected, and she couldn't prevent her heart from kicking against her ribs or her eyes widening slightly. "We are in a bit of a rush here. To make my claim believable, I must be with child before my next menses and I am already more than a week gone from the ending of my last one."

"Then we'd best not delay. Have your coach at the club at dawn."

She squeezed her eyes shut. Why was he being so stubborn, so doggedly determined to make this difficult? Why was she? She could find a willing gentleman elsewhere, one of his red-badged fellows. Only she didn't want someone else. She wanted to see his features etched into those of her child, be it a girl or a boy. With a sigh, she opened her eyes. "It is one of the grandest estates in all of England."

"All the more reason it'll hold sway over my decision."

Why can't you simply do it for me? she wanted to ask. But they'd only known each other a handful of days. Why should he feel any allegiance or commitment to her? "Dawn," she stated flatly.

She turned to the coach, surprised to find him nudging the footman aside and handing her up into the vehicle.

"Thank you, ladies, for helping my sister and for the kindness you showed my mother. I wish you the best."

He slammed the door closed as though he had no intention of ever seeing any of them again, as though their business was completed, but she'd heard in his voice genuine gratitude, and if she were a wagering woman, she'd wager that her sisters had passed the test. Now if only the estate would.

"I HOPE YOU know what you're doing."

As Finn came to stand beside him, Aiden didn't bother to turn around, but merely crossed his arms over his chest and watched as the carriage disappeared in the distance. "Odd warning from a man who married the daughter of an earl."

"Lavinia has no interest in moving about within the upper echelons of Society. I have the impression the same can't be said of your duchess."

No, the same couldn't be said of her. Everything Selena was doing was to ensure her place among that Society, to guarantee she maintained power and influence within it. "She's not my duchess."

"I'm not blind, Aiden. I saw the way you looked at her."

"You might not be blind, but you're obviously in need of spectacles."

Finn chuckled low. "Just watch yourself, brother. A broken heart never fully mends. It will always have cracks."

He didn't doubt Finn's words because he knew his brother was an expert when it came to shattered hearts. "Is it hard, Finn?" he asked somberly. "Is it hard not telling your daughter you're her father?"

Finn had only recently learned he had a daughter. "One of the hardest things I've ever done, but it helps that the couple raising her are good people and don't object to my spending time with her. As a matter of fact, of late, I've been helping her build a cottage in a tree. She's an adventurous one, my little sprite."

In Finn's voice, Aiden heard all the love he held for the child, and he fully understood it. He himself had met the adorable little girl. All the family had spent time in her company because Finn didn't have to keep her a secret. He had only to protect her from the knowledge he was her father until she was older and able to fully understand all the circumstances surrounding her birth. But Aiden wouldn't have that luxury. His child, should he have one by Selena, would have to remain a secret, even from those he loved and trusted. And he could never admit to being the father—not under any circumstances. They might design a scenario where he could spend time with the lad or lass, but it wouldn't be as open as Finn's relationship with his daughter. Finn's child wasn't being raised among the aristocracy. Aiden's would be and that made his being in the child's life in a believable way all the more difficult.

ONCE SELENA AND her sisters arrived home, in the foyer, they all handed their cloaks and hats to the butler.

"Girls, I need a moment of your time in the library," Selena announced. Preceding them into the room, she went straightway to the sideboard and poured herself a sherry for fortitude. Turning, she smiled at her sisters, who all wore identical furrows in their brows. "Please sit."

She indicated a nearby sitting area with two small sofas and one plush chair. Taking the chair, she waited while they settled themselves on the sofas. "I need to go to Sheffield Hall in the morning to see to some business."

Connie looked at Flo and Alice, then met Selena's gaze. "We'll go with you."

"I need you all to remain here. People are still stopping by to offer their condolences, and I would like you to represent me in my short absence. I'll return tomorrow evening." All Aiden had to do was catch a glimpse of the estate, the manor house, and he would be impressed with the grandness of what his son would inherit.

Flo angled her head in thought. "Why do you have to go?"

"A matter's been brought to my attention that requires my presence." She hated lying to them, but it was preferable to the truth.

"What matter?"

"It has to do with the estate."

"In what manner?"

"I'm not exactly certain, which is the reason I have to go." She shot to her feet, paced three steps away before returning. "Please, just know that it's crucial to your futures."

"I don't understand—"

She interrupted Flo. "You don't need to. Simply trust me. And do as I ask. Remain here, and if anyone should inquire regarding my absence, explain that I had to tend to business at Sheffield Hall."

"Yes, all right."

"Thank you." She returned to the chair, tried to think of what else she might say to reassure them, was grateful when the butler strode in, carrying a package wrapped in brown paper.

"I'm sorry to interrupt, Your Grace, but this was just delivered for Lady Alice."

"For me?" The look of surprise on Alice's face was a bit comical, but then she had no swain to send her little gifts and it was unusual for something to be delivered this time of night. She took the proffered package, and the butler made his exit.

"What is it?" Connie asked.

"Well, I don't know." Alice glanced over at Selena. "Shall I open it?"

"Yes, of course."

After pulling the string, granting the bow its freedom, she folded back the paper and gasped as a book came into view. A note rested on top. She smiled. "It's from Mr. Aiden Trewlove."

"What does it say?" Connie asked impatiently.

Alice handed it to Selena.

> *The best escapes are found within the pages of a book. Enjoy your journey* Through the Looking-Glass.
>
> —*Your ever-faithful servant,*
> *Aiden Trewlove*

"He caught me reading it at the shop," Alice confessed. "But it wouldn't be appropriate for me to keep it, would it?"

Oh, Alice had certainly passed the test, and for some unaccountable reason his gifting her with the book made Selena's eyes burn. "Under the circumstances, I think it's entirely appropriate. Write a letter to thank him and give it to me before you retire. I'll post it tomorrow on my way to Sheffield Hall."

"He might be a commoner," Alice said, "but I don't believe he is common."

No, Selena thought, he wasn't common at all.

Chapter 18

*T*he following dawn, Selena wasn't at all surprised to see Aiden standing by a lamppost outside his club. The coach had barely slowed when he opened the door, hopped in, and pounded the ceiling before settling in across from her. The vehicle carried on, the horses barely breaking stride.

And the confines suddenly seemed far too small. His presence enveloped the space, his scent of bay rum wafted around her. She had a strong urge to invite him to sit beside her, to have the warmth of his body seep into her on this chilly morning. Although to be honest, she wouldn't object to his warmth seeping into her on a sultry afternoon. It was somewhat torturous to have him so near and yet so far away. She finally found the wherewithal to greet him properly. "Good morning."

"You smell differently in the morning."

He couldn't have unsettled her more if he'd leaned in and kissed her. Words failed her.

"You carry the scent of sleep." His voice was low, raw, as though he were imagining awakening with her in his arms and sniffing every inch of her skin.

"Perhaps you'll experience it before I awaken if we move forward with the plans." She was rather proud of that volley, could sense him going very still across from her.

"If I don't agree to strive to get you with child—it doesn't mean we can't become involved."

She'd spent a good deal of last night, when she couldn't sleep, ruminating on that possibility, to simply lose herself in him, surrounded by him. To escape with him would be far more rewarding than the pages of any book. But that was a selfish desire, want. She had such a short time in which to gain what she needed. "I fear, Mr. Trewlove, you have the wrong of it there. If you cannot give me what I require, I will have to go elsewhere."

Although she couldn't imagine taking another man between her thighs. Even now she wanted Aiden with a need that was frightening. Rather than remain on that path of thought, she decided to alter the direction of their conversation. "It was very kind of you to send the book to Alice."

The sky was lightening, and she more easily saw his shrug, as though his gift had been nothing at all. Reaching into her reticule, she removed the sealed letter that Alice had given her and held it out to him. "Alice sends her appreciation."

He took the missive and tucked it into a pocket inside the left breast of his jacket.

"I take it she passed your test."

With a deep sigh, he stretched out his long legs, so his booted feet rested on either side of hers. "I like your sisters."

It was a simple statement, but it held a great deal of warmth and approval. "I like yours as well. And your brothers. The little bit I saw of them."

"Fancy had them working their backsides off."

"She has a great deal of ambition, your sister."

"We all do." He glanced out the window. "Nothing was handed to us, nothing has come easily."

She wondered if he were contemplating how easily he might hand his son a dukedom. Or his daughter properties and marriage into the nobility. He was the result of a man who seemed to plant his seed hither and yon with no regard for the consequences. Aiden, on the other hand, accepted responsibility for all his actions. She didn't think his adopted mother would have accepted less of her children.

"The cook prepared us a light repast. Bread, cheese, boiled eggs." She would have tapped the wicker basket on the floor in the corner if it wouldn't have meant tangling her skirts in his leg, having it between her calves, conjuring up images of other aspects of him between her knees.

"I've eaten, thank you. Would you like me to hand the basket up to you?"

She shook her head. "No, I'm not hungry." She'd eaten as well, worried that with his nearness her stomach might have knotted until she couldn't digest properly. What if he wasn't impressed with Sheffield Hall?

They were leaving London proper now, the buildings becoming sparser, more distance separating them. The sun was rising ever higher. It appeared spring might be well on its way to making itself known.

"Fancy is your mother's daughter, born to her, unlike the rest of you, who were not." The resemblance between mother and daughter was striking.

His eyes slid away from the view to land on her with the full weight of his attention. "Yes."

"So when you were first brought to her, she was married. You had both a father and a mother."

He crossed his arms over his chest. "No, she was already a widow. She took in bastards as a means for supporting herself. But it's not a lucrative practice if you allow the children to live. Their upkeep is costly, much more than the few coins placed in your palm when you take them."

The practice of farming out children born out of wedlock so the mother could remain as untainted as possible was becoming more widely known. Selena had read several articles written by Lady Lavinia exposing the horrors of what she'd discovered in her quest to rescue children from those who would do them harm. "Your mother was not married when Fancy was born?"

"Just spit it out, Selena. Fancy is a bastard, like all of us. And before you travel a path and view my mum as immoral, know that Fancy was the result of our mum doing what she had to do to ensure our survival. When she didn't have coins for the landlord, he took payment in other ways. Fancy was an unintended consequence." His gaze bore into her. "So I understand your desperation."

He was liking her situation to his mother's? They were nothing alike. But the argument fell short because they were indeed very similar: she was willingly going to take a man within her body in order to ensure the best lives possible for her siblings. His mother had been doing it for the children she'd adopted. "I was not sitting in judgment of her."

"Weren't you?"

She refrained from nodding, shamed by the realization that she had been. That she had judged the woman a sinner, that she herself would be as harshly judged if anyone realized what she had done. "You told me once that you were fourteen when Fancy was born. I can't imagine things went well for the landlord once you and your brothers realized how he was exacting payment."

His grin was wolfish, predatory, lethal. "It doesn't go well for any man we discover has taken advantage of a woman."

She wasn't surprised. She'd noted the protective bent of his nature, perhaps had even unconsciously sought to take advantage of it. Instinctively she knew if he got her with child, he would keep a watch over his offspring to ensure no harm would ever come to him or her—even if he did it from a distance. The guilt gnawed at her because if they managed to work out a way for him to participate in the child's life publicly, he would never be able to acknowledge him or her. She was being exceedingly unfair to Aiden. She'd assumed a great majority of men would not care. She'd loved her own father, but he had given her very little attention. It seemed matters were always calling to him, although at the moment she thought if he'd truly been seeing to his estates as she'd always assumed, his death would not have left it in shambles.

"There is a goodness to you that I'd not expected. People assume those born in sin are destined to sin."

"I've done my fair share of sinning." He said it as though he took great pride in his misbehavior, but if not for it, they wouldn't be here now. It was one of the reasons she'd chosen him. That and the way he appealed to her on a more primal level.

He hadn't worn gloves. She wondered if he even owned a pair. Although she thought it would be a shame to cover those bare hands that rested on his thighs. Hands with roughened palms that titillated her when they skimmed over her flesh. Capable hands. Strong yet amazingly gentle. Perhaps she should give up her quest for a child and simply take him as a lover. Never to marry but to live out the remainder of her life blissfully in his arms.

The sun was suddenly far too bright, fairly filling the conveyance with warmth, threatening to broil her on the spot. She needed to distract herself from thoughts of what his hands could do to her, of how tempting it was to invite him over to her side of the carriage and let him have his way with her. As though he followed the direction of her thoughts, his hands clamped his thighs, the muscles and tendons bulging, and she wondered if another aspect of him bulged as well. "Have you traveled beyond London before?"

His eyes slowly closed, opened, and his penetrating stare through half-lowered lids told her that he knew precisely what she was about. Why was she not surprised? They were far too attuned with each other, especially now that he knew all her secrets.

"When I was younger, I would save my coins until I could afford a trip on the railway, just to see what lay beyond what I knew."

"You've a curious nature."

A long nod that affirmed her conclusion. "I once thought of running off to sea. I wanted to explore more of the world. I was in search of a place where life was better than what I knew, and then I realized that I had it within me to create the better."

"And is your life better?"

"I want for naught."

"You want for nothing at all?"

"What should I want for, Lena?" His voice was low, sultry, hinted at stolen kisses and pilfered minutes and thieved touches.

Me. The solitary word was a lonesome wail within her heart and soul. She wanted him to want her with a need that matched hers for him, with a hunger that didn't care about consequences and wouldn't allow him to sit so calmly opposite her but would drive him to cross over and take her within his arms, claim her mouth, her body, her senses. But she had too much pride to confess to that.

She wanted him to bed her not because her sisters were worthy or the estate would bring his child riches, but because he would cease to breathe if he did not. Instead, she squeezed her gloved hands together in her lap. "Sleep, I should think."

The hysteria edging her voice caused her to inwardly flinch, and the awkward laugh that followed didn't help matters. "Knowing how you keep watch over your establishment into the wee hours, I can't imagine you retired at a reasonable hour and you had to arise so frightfully early. Please don't feel a need to entertain me"—she did wish all the various ways he might entertain her physically hadn't rushed through her mind in a kaleidoscope of images—"during the journey. Rest for a bit. I'll awaken you when we near."

"I am a bit weary." He crossed his arms over his

chest, settled back more fully against the squabs, and closed his eyes.

His legs relaxed more, stretched a bit farther, until she was fully imprisoned within them. Not that she had any desire to go anywhere. Soon he was snoring lightly, and she imagined herself with a child who had brown hair, feathery streaks here and there burnished to a faint, pleasing red. Long, thick, sooty lashes that rested on sharp cheekbones. She wanted to reach across and press a kiss to the underside of that strong jaw, wanted to snuggle against him and find her own slumber.

Instead she merely watched him sleep, wishing she could make his claim. *I want for naught.*

But she couldn't because it was dawning on her as brightly as the sun now hovering over them that she wanted what she couldn't have: him walking proudly beside her for all the world to see. But she couldn't risk any doubt regarding her child's parentage, would not risk him or her growing up as the subject of whispers.

Perhaps they could keep their relationship clandestine until they knew how much the child favored him. And if he favored him not at all, maybe in a few years, once she was out of mourning, once enough time had passed so no suspicions surfaced—

But if the child favored him, they wouldn't be able to risk people seeing them together. She would not allow her child to doubt his parentage. The sins were hers. She wouldn't pass them on to her child, would not risk his having to defend his birthright. Or his mother. Would he end up in a brawl, slashed by a knife, because someone called her a whore?

They would have to be secretive about his time

with the child, his time with her. For the sake of their little one, whom they would need to protect from the truth at all costs.

HE DREAMED OF removing her black-veiled hat and tossing it out the window, so shadows could no longer lurk over her face and keep her true feelings hidden from him. Of unclasping her pelisse and giving freedom to every button on her traveling frock. Of taking her on the well-padded cushions, holding her close afterward, and yelling up to the driver to never bring the carriage to a halt. To simply spend eternity traveling about within these confines where no one was present to judge them, where Society held no sway, where they were hidden away from censure, where his time with her wasn't measured in hours but in years.

It was her hand nudging his knee that woke him. Opening his eyes to her tender smile was bittersweet. Why should he care if he gave her a child? He knew she would love it, would see that it had every advantage. Its status would be elevated, far above his.

But even knowing all this, he couldn't get past the notion that he would be aping his father, creating a child only to cast it aside, to not be part and parcel of its life. In truth, not having his sire involved in his upbringing had been a blessing, but the man's blatant disregard for his offspring, his foisting them off on others, still had a way of making Aiden feel worthless. His existence had been a mere inconvenience. He didn't want his child to ever harbor the same sentiment, to believe he'd not been wanted.

So it was imperative the child never discover the truth of his origins, and yet Aiden was well aware that long-buried secrets had a way of being uncovered. His mum's garden proved that. Within it, she had laid to rest the first two children brought to her. Mick's discovery of an unmarked grave when he was eight had led to them all learning that she hadn't given birth to them but that they had been handed over to her because others had not wanted them. Fear of others discovering what she had done kept her tethered to her shambles of a residence when they all wanted to move her into something more luxurious. Yes, secrets had a way of haunting their holders.

Noting that she'd stirred him awake, she straightened. "We'll be arriving soon. You might want to move over here in order to catch the view at its most impressive."

She scooted nearer to the window, giving him ample room to settle in beside her. The strawberries that had been a faint whiff on the air now wrapped in earnest around him, and he was tempted to lean in and nibble on her neck, outline the shell of her ear with his tongue, nip at her lobe. Resisting her was testing the limits of his endurance when it came to the Duchess of Lushing. Never before had he found it so difficult not to succumb to his desires. Insisting on making this journey had been foolish because it kept them in such close proximity, made him begin reordering his priorities. Perhaps he was being overly stubborn to take such care to never plant his seed. His father certainly hadn't cared. Perhaps that was the reason Aiden did.

As the carriage turned onto a narrower road, he rolled into her, buffeting his chest against her shoulder. He could have sworn she very nearly turned into him because he felt the subtle shift in her body, as though it recognized where it belonged, nestled up against him.

She stiffened, straightened, moved nearer to the wall of the coach. He was tempted to taunt her, tease her, skim his knuckles along her cheek, convince her with strategized touches to give herself over to him without his capitulation to her terms. To be content to have him, even if it meant no offspring.

"You can see it as easily if you lean the other way and look out the window nearer to you." Her voice was flat, and he suspected she'd meant for the words to come out as tart as a lemon. Instead they held a bit of regret.

"I prefer this view because even if it does not impress me, what I see out of the corner of my eye is most pleasing."

She gave a curt laugh. "Aiden, you are such a flirt. Please don't try to charm me. I wish I could make you understand how serious this matter is."

"I understand its seriousness, Lena. I wouldn't be here, otherwise. I wouldn't be going to the bother of determining all the costs involved in the decision."

Her gaze shifted over to him, and he saw both humor and self-deprecation mingling there. "Who would have thought a gambling hell owner, a man who lured others into sin, would possess such a moral center?"

Before her, he wasn't certain he had. She made him question all that he knew about himself. He might have carried the conversation further, but his attention was snagged by the edge of a large pond coming into view. Perfect in its oblong shape, he wondered if it had been created by man rather than God. Beautiful swans graced it. Yew hedges, occasionally broken up by a stone bench, bordered the pond. He imagined Selena sitting there, watching as the wind rippled the water.

The pond came to an end, as elaborate landscaping took over, more hedges creating various shapes—circles and half crescents—that led to the back of an enormous stone angel, wings spread wide, as though it had been sent from the heavens for the precise purpose of protecting what lay before it: the manor house, Sheffield Hall.

It was huge, majestic, grander than anything he'd seen in London, other than Buckingham Palace perhaps. He thought the golden bricks might actually contain gold, the way they glittered in the sunlight. The roofline was crenelated, the structure a mixture of residence and castle, displaying its fortification, hinting at its need to ward off invaders. "How many dukes have there been?"

"Your son would be the twelfth."

Generations of families had lived, worked, and fought for this bit of England. A long history, possibly from the time of the Conqueror. Perhaps before. Years steeped in tradition and service to the Crown.

The drive circled around in front. Without slowing, the horses followed the curve. Reaching up, he banged on the ceiling, grateful to feel the vehicle slowing.

"What are you doing?"

Ridiculous question, but still he answered. "Stopping. I want to have a look around."

"But you can see the stateliness of it from here."

He didn't much like the horror reflected in her face, the realization she was embarrassed to be seen with him, that she truly wanted nothing more from him than his seed. If he were a wise man, a not-so-proud man, he would again bang his fist to catch the driver's attention, to signal that they should carry on. And when he exited the conveyance in front of his club, he would give her his answer: no. And never set eyes upon her again.

But stretched out before him, over acres and acres of green, was an opportunity to give the fruit of his loins something magnificent, profound. Something that no matter how diligently he worked, he'd never acquire. "I want to see all of it, the details of it."

"How will I explain your presence?"

"A friend, a distant cousin, the Queen's man come to check on the estate. I'm sure you can think of something."

The carriage rolled to a stop. He opened the door and leaped out before a footman could see to the task. One had been riding atop with the driver. Another, liveried in purple, exited the residence at a fast but stately clip, followed by a fit, older bloke in black. The butler no doubt.

Reaching back, Aiden extended his hand to Selena, grateful when her fingers landed on his. She stepped down and straightened her shoulders.

"Your Grace, we weren't expecting your return so soon," the older chap said.

"It came about unexpectedly and is to be a short visit. Mr. Trewlove, here, is to assess the estate for the Crown. Have Cook prepare us a light luncheon, something simple. We'll enjoy it on the terrace in an hour. Mr. Trewlove, if you'll be so good as to follow me?"

She wasn't happy with him, he heard it in the tone of her voice, but he didn't care. His son would make memories here, and Aiden was likely to have no part in them. He needed to have an idea of everything those moments might encompass. Would his son swim in the pond, be chased by swans, look out over the parapets?

She marched toward the manor, and he followed, greedily taking in everything he could: the arched windows and doorway, the red roof, the tower in the corner that buttressed up against two wings of the building, seemingly joining them. The place was nearly medieval in design, but also showed signs of modernization. It had been well cared for, no doubt because, as he'd already learned, the duke had been a man of immense wealth, but he suspected a good bit of his assets had been tied up in the estate. It had to cost a fortune to keep it maintained. He was beginning to understand why she would risk so much to hold on to this. He imagined the hunting parties and the gatherings of nobility. Hell, royalty probably visited on occasion.

She crossed over the threshold, and immediately her footsteps echoed through the great chamber as her booted feet landed on marble. Tapestries hung from on high. At more reasonable heights were portraits of men, women, and children—sometimes alone, sometimes with others, sometimes with a horse or dog. All arrogant, all self-possessed, all understanding it was their right by birth to look down on others. A portrait of his son might possibly join these. Would people gaze at it and see an imposter? Would the lad instinctually feel out of place, sense he didn't belong? Or would he embrace a heritage that was not rightfully his, carry on the sort of legacy that had been denied his true sire?

Aiden couldn't ignore the irony of the situation. Because he himself had not been recognized by an earl, his son could very well become a duke. Bittersweet retribution toward the blasted nobility who judged so harshly was threaded through the plan. He'd been denied a birthright but had the power to give his son another's. The temptation to take was stronger than he'd have liked.

"And I thought Mick's hotel was fancy. I've never seen the like such as this."

"There is a good deal more." Her voice was low, soft, as though it was forbidden to disturb the quiet of the place. "Come along."

The massive residence was a warren of hallways, parlors, sitting rooms, stairways. Every bit of space was bold, larger than life, as though giants had once resided within these walls. Her portrait hung above a fireplace in a blue room, her gown a darker hue that contrasted with the draperies and furnishings. It was as tall as she was, had been painted true to her form. She was young, a lass really, but she held herself as though she carried a great weight on those narrow shoulders. "When did you have the portrait done?"

"A few months after we were married. I had barely turned eighteen."

In the portrait, her eyes held no laughter, little joy. They belonged to a woman who had married out of love—to protect her family—but not for love. He knew she would do so again, would do whatever was necessary to see her sisters happy. The artist had captured her temerity in the firm set of her mouth, the angle of her chin, the square set of her shoulders. She stood there, a warrior prepared to do battle. She might as well have been wearing a suit of armor, a sword raised high in defiance. She would sacrifice herself on the battlefield of happiness for those she loved.

SITTING ON THE terrace, looking out over the elaborate gardens, she knew Aiden was impressed with all he'd seen. How could he not be?

She had heard of the splendor of Sheffield Hall but had not seen it until after she was married. It had overwhelmed her to realize she had become mistress of all that lay before her.

Nibbling on a small square of cucumber sandwich, she peered over at her guest who had spoken very little as she'd taken him through the assortment of rooms. She'd pointed out the duke's bedchamber and given him leave to peer inside. She had not invited him into her chamber beside it, although it seemed as they passed it that a stillness came over him, even as they carried on. He had spent a great deal more time than she would have expected in the nursery, and she wondered if he'd been envisioning his son lying in the bassinet with its lacy canopy. Every aspect of the residence was elaborate, screamed wealth. No expense had been spared by previous dukes to display their power.

"After luncheon, we'll take a stroll through the gardens, shall we? Twelve acres that represented Lushing's pride and joy. He did love his gardens."

"He did the work himself?"

She laughed lightly at the absurdity of any noble toiling in the soil, getting dirt beneath his nails. "Oh no. But he designed them, then hired others to bring to life what he'd envisioned. Some areas are extremely calming, others invigorating."

Ahead of them was a fountain, Poseidon leaping from it, his trident in hand. The babbling water always brought her a sense of peace. She finished off her sandwich. "Is it what you expected?"

"More so."

"Does it hold sway over you?"

He shifted his gaze over to her. "It's impressive. And it certainly calls to my greedier instincts. Don't you feel guilty about what you're planning? It's theft, sweetheart."

"I can't afford the luxury of guilt at the moment. It is not the *things* that I want. It is the prestige, the position. We once had two hundred guests visit. Every bedchamber occupied. Tents were erected on the lawn for those who didn't warrant a bed within the residence. I planned the guest list and the itinerary. The Prince of Wales took several suites of rooms. I was terrified I would get something wrong. But I handled it all with aplomb, never let on that I was trembling in my slippers, because that was what was expected of me. We've had foreign dignitaries in residence. I was ever the gracious hostess here, at the other estates, in London. They say that nobles do not work. Well, I worked. Not backbreaking labor but soul-crushing endeavors that often prevented me from eating or sleeping because of worry that whatever I did would be found lacking. And because I wanted Lushing to be proud, proud he'd taken me to wife."

"I can't imagine that he wasn't."

"He certainly never made me feel as though he wasn't. Still, in the end I didn't give him the one thing he required: an heir."

"That responsibility could have rested with him."

"People always view it as the fault of the woman. I can't help but believe, however, that his vanity would find solace in my giving birth to a child presumed to be his heir, so his manhood would not be doubted." She glanced back toward the lush gardens that were presently a sea of white. In a couple of months, they would be blue, then red in the height of summer. The flowers had been chosen based on when they bloomed so the blossoms became a rolling tide of colors that changed with the seasons. "Because while the woman is held accountable, whispers about the man do emerge. He was undeserving of any sort of ill gossip. He was incredibly kind, sometimes I think too kind for this world. And remarkably tolerant of those not of his class. I think he'd have liked you and you him."

After taking a small sip of her white wine, she settled back against the chair. "So what say you? A leisurely stroll through the gardens and then we'll away back to London?"

"We'll be staying the night."

She shot up quickly. "I beg your pardon?"

He gave her a laconic look beneath half-lowered lids. "I've not finished seeing all I wish to see. I want to view the stables, ride out over the land, visit the village—"

"But you can simply look about you and see how majestic everything is. I don't understand why seeing *every little thing* is so important to you."

"Because if I decide in your favor, and fortune smiles on you and gives you a boy, I may never actually see my son playing here. All my memories of him will be what I create in my imagination. His riding a hobbyhorse. Sitting on your lap in the library while you read him a story. You expect me to be like my father, to plant the seed and be done with it, to never give my child another thought. I don't know if I have it within me not to wonder. I think you'll be a marvelous mother, but even that, I may never witness."

The earnestness of his answer made her ashamed that she was even asking of him what she was. "As we discussed before, we'll find a way for you to spend some time with him."

"Stolen moments here and there. But so many lost to me. And I will never be able to acknowledge him as my son—not even to my family. Lena, I'm striving to ensure that if I embark on this deception with you, that I do so with no regrets. For once begun, there will be no going back."

She turned her attention to the blooms that the gardener managed to coax into opening even during the chilliest of winters, but now spring was emerging. White for innocence and yet she'd fallen far from any sainted position. Was she being unfair to this man, unfair to Lushing? "I won't be able to accompany you. It wouldn't do for the villagers to see the recently widowed duchess out and about. And we wouldn't want, years from now, someone remembering and remarking on your visit to Sheffield Hall." It was risky enough for the servants to know he was here, but they adored her, and it was unlikely they would see anything sinister in his presence.

"I'll be most discreet."

So against her better judgment, she took him to the stables and ordered that the duke's stallion be readied. Lushing had loved his animals, and she was rather certain he would approve of his horse being given the run of the grounds and beyond. While she knew the stable lads were taking him for a daily canter, she had little doubt the beast would find it a treat to be ridden by one who she instinctually knew would give the horse his lead while remaining in command. She was not at all surprised to see how well Aiden sat a horse. Nor was she surprised by the pang in her heart as she watched him gallop away, knowing a day might soon arrive when his leaving would herald his never returning to her.

He'd galloped over the verdant green, taking the cool country air deep within his lungs, until he reached the edge of England and could stare out over the glorious blue sea. No soot, no stink, no grime to make a man always feel in need of a bath. Although he knew that wasn't true of the entire area. He understood that when he stopped in at the local pub where miners took a pint, along with farmers and laborers. He wondered if the duke had owned mines, if he'd gone down into them to encourage the men. For some reason, he suspected he had. He wondered if those trips had weakened his lungs, had contributed to his succumbing to influenza.

He didn't bother to engage with anyone, merely observed and eavesdropped, tried to get a sense of how the nobility in the area were regarded. It seemed the duke and his duchess were greatly admired, and the locals voiced a worry or two regarding how their lives might change if the duchess didn't produce an heir "right quick." He found it inconceivable that a child's birth should affect so many.

But he also decided Lena was no doubt correct: he'd have liked the duke.

From the village, he traveled at a more sedate pace. After delivering the horse to the stables, he strode back to the manor, not much liking the gladness that swept through him when Lena emerged, having obviously been on the watch for his return. He didn't want to contemplate how very much he would like to have her greet him anytime he returned from anywhere.

"Did you see all you needed to see?"

He nodded as he came to stand before her. How difficult it was not to take her in his arms and lower his mouth to hers, but it wouldn't do at all for the servants to see anything untoward pass between them. He wanted to reach out and press the crease between her brows until it disappeared. "It's impressive. Gorgeous really. So much space. I think after a while, however, I'd become a bit antsy."

"Lushing liked the openness of it, but he had few fond memories of the place. His father was most strict when he was growing up. Then they had their falling-out, and it was years before he was able to return here."

"Disappointing a father was certainly nothing I ever had to worry over."

"Was it difficult growing up without a father?"

Slowly he shook his head. "My mum was a strong woman, like you. She was all I needed."

Her eyes softened, her cheeks pinkened. "Even when you're a bit put out with me, you still manage to flirt with your little compliments."

"I'm not flirting if what I say is true."

Her lips twitched. "More flirtation, but never mind. I feared you might not arrive in time. I want to show you something." With her left hand, she grabbed her right, and he wondered if she'd been on the verge of taking his and had to remind herself it would not do.

He followed her inside, through a maze of hallways until eventually they came to the area where the tower loomed. The curved wall and spiral staircase told him where they were. Without stopping, she began ascending the stairs, giving him a lovely view of her backside as he trailed up behind her. At the top, she opened a door and led him out onto the crenelated walkway. When she had traversed half of it, she turned to face him, her features wreathed with a solemn joy.

"This was always my favorite part of Sheffield Hall." She nodded away from the roofline behind them.

When he looked out, he couldn't stop his breath from hitching at the sight of the angel gilded in late afternoon sunlight, giving the impression the wings weren't spread to signify its protection of the manor but instead to declare, "Behold all that is glorious and beautiful!"

Within the carriage or from his perch atop the horse, he'd seen the green and the hedgerows and the trees. He'd seen the land stretching out before him. He'd caught bits of acreage here and there and thought he could assemble all of it into a whole. But from up here, the massive estate spread out in all its glory as the waning sun bathed it in cooling twilight.

Perhaps it was because no servants were about or the waist-high height of the wall provided some protection from prying eyes, but without taking her gaze from the marvel before them, she threaded her fingers through his and squeezed. *I love it here*, she might as well have announced. *See what I see and love it as well. I'll bring your son up here and share this sight with him.*

And he imagined her doing just that. Being kind and loving and introducing her child to a world that far eclipsed anything he could offer. It was unfair, to look from on high and to see unfolding before him all that his child would possess.

All it required of him were a few nights of being lost in mad, passionate lovemaking—not a hardship at all—

And then walking away, never, ever, to look back.

Because he'd come to realize what she had yet to understand: a life lived in shadows was no life at all.

Chapter 19

*D*inner was decidedly more formal than luncheon. They took it in what she described as the small dining room, which meant the table sat only about a dozen people. She'd offered to let him borrow the duke's dinner attire, but he wasn't about to don anything that would remind her of her late husband, although he suspected being in residence did that well enough.

Conversation was stilted, sparse as though they both had other more pressing matters occupying their minds. Now and then, her lips moved as though she was contemplating the wisdom of forming the question and he knew precisely what it would be: *Have you decided?*

If she did dare ask it, he didn't know if he'd voice the word out loud or merely shake his head. Because he didn't bloody well know what the answer was.

When the ordeal of dinner was thankfully over, they walked out into the hallway, feet dragging, like mourners headed for the crypt. In a cavernous room where stairs led up to bedchambers, she stopped and faced him. Her lips parted—

"I don't know yet," he said quietly.

With a sigh that held both patience and under-standing, she nodded. "I believe I shall retire. It's been a long, taxing day, and we'll depart early in the morning. Sleep well."

He doubted he'd sleep at all, especially as now he was wandering through the manor like a wraith, a glass of excellent scotch in hand. Gillie would approve as it went down smoothly, filling him with a lethargic warmth.

Everywhere he looked, he saw history. The fading of the tapestries indicated they had existed for centuries, but he was rather certain they weren't a recent purchase. No, they had been handed down through generations. Throughout the residence, armor was displayed. Whether it was a full suit worn by a knight or merely the breastplate, shiny but dented, a brass plaque indicated to which duke it had belonged. Some plaques went even further and identified battles in which it had been tested. If he gave Lena a son, the lad would take pride in this heritage, would believe it his own. He'd never know the truth regarding from whence he truly came.

It seemed both deceitful and protective at the same time.

What did it matter what one believed of one's past? It was what one did with the present that was of import.

Aiden had always embraced what was to his benefit. But he'd been insulted when Lena had offered him her property in exchange for his *services*. He didn't want payment. He wanted her. And he could have her—as long as no one knew.

She had shown him what he would give his child, and damn her for making him see how grand it all would be. The additional benefit was knowing he'd be pulling the wool over the eyes of the Society that shunned him. And what was in it for him? Satisfaction, a bit of retribution, and more nights of being nestled between Lena's thighs.

And to do the one thing he'd sworn to never do: be responsible for bringing a bastard into the world.

Even though the child wouldn't be viewed as such, it went against his core principle.

Finishing off his scotch, he left the glass on a table in a hallway, certain a servant would find it. The place gleamed to such an extent, he imagined they had an army of servants, not that he'd seen many other than the butler and a couple of footmen. The rest were hidden away because it wouldn't do for the lord and lady of the manor to see them going about their labors, to know exactly what was required to keep the place sparkling like sunlight.

He located the stairs that led to the bedchambers. They were wide enough to accommodate a coach traveling up them. At the top, the landing split into two hallways. He took the one to the left, strolled the length of it to his room at the end. He closed his hand around the knob, pressed his forehead to the polished wood.

He thought of her waiting in her bedchamber, waiting for him, waiting for his decision. He remembered the way she had watched the sunset, the estate stretched out before them. She'd gazed upon it with appreciation—not the greed that had been mirrored in his eyes. She wanted none of this for herself. She needed it in order to ensure those she loved had the best that life had to offer.

He was not one of the people she loved or she wouldn't ask of him what she had. She should have taken his rejection and moved on to another. The fact that she hadn't hinted that perhaps she did have a small care for him or perhaps he had succeeded in his original plan and caused her to at least desire him, to want him in her bed.

She was brave, courageous, kind, unselfish. She placed the needs of others before her own. She moved him in ways no one else ever had.

He'd never planned to marry, to have children, to fall in love. He wasn't in love now. He was fairly certain of it. But damn her for stirring something within him that made it impossible not to at least try to give her what she wanted. Damn her for managing to worm her way into his very being so when it came time to walk away, it would be like tearing a hole in his very soul. And he knew eventually he would have to walk away in order to protect the child, to protect Lena.

His common sense and pride insisted that he end things now.

But his heart, that part of him that had never served any other purpose than to pump blood through his veins, his heart had him turning on his heel, heading back down the hallway, opening the door to her bedchamber, and striding over the threshold.

HE CAME TO her.

He looked like a man suffering the torments of hell, but he'd come to her.

She was standing at the window in her nightdress, counting the minutes until midnight because she had decided that if he didn't come to her by the witching hour, she would go to him, not to pressure, not to ask of him what he had no desire to give, but simply because she wanted another night within his arms.

He stopped in the middle of the room, on the lush Aubusson carpet. His jacket, waistcoat, and neck cloth were gone, and she imagined he'd been wandering the halls in only his shirt, trousers, and boots.

Slowly she gave freedom to her buttons, noting the way his eyes tracked the path of her fingers. When the last one was free of its mooring, she eased the soft linen off her left shoulder, then her right, and gave a little wiggle, sending the cotton on its journey to the floor. Although he'd seen her bared before, still she heard the hitch of his breath, as though he'd been waiting the entire length of his life for this moment.

Her steps were silent, her toes sinking into the thick weave of the carpet, as she glided over to him. "I'm glad you came to me. If you hadn't, I'd have come to you." Reaching up, she cupped his shadowed jaw, not at all bothered that he was in need of a shave, having refused earlier to use Lushing's razor. "I want you in my bed tonight."

"I haven't any sheaths."

So he had decided against spilling his seed into her. She was surprised the disappointment was less than she'd expected. But then she respected the thought he'd given his decision, that he struggled with his obligation to do what was right, that he didn't see her as simply a woman to be plowed. Because she'd come to see him as more than a possible sire for her child. She desired this man, craved the feel of him between her thighs. Admired all that he was. He who had been born with nothing had risen above it all and achieved success. He who had been unfairly treated did not blame others for his circumstances. He took responsibility for himself, his actions. And it was that devotion that would see him not giving her the child she sought.

But she found no fault with it. Instead it made her love him just a little bit more.

And she did love him. She wasn't certain when the realization came upon her. But she wouldn't burden him with that truth because there was no future for them. She did not have the freedom that Lady Aslyn or Lady Lavinia had to marry without considering Societal rank or privilege. They did not have siblings dependent upon them. She could not risk being shunned by Society. A direct cut to her would have ramifications for her sisters.

She glided her hand down to his shirt and flicked the first secured button through its opening. "You can leave me, spill your seed elsewhere. You once told me that I warranted a scandalous and thorough seduction. Consider me thoroughly seduced."

His feral growl was in direct contrast to the gentleness with which he claimed her mouth. Even as she fell into the wonder of it, of how each kiss was unlike any other, she continued on with her task of freeing his buttons.

Breaking away from her, he glided his hand down her arm until he could lace his fingers with hers. Then he began pulling her from the room. "Not here. I don't want to take you in a bed where another had you, where other memories reside."

She dug in her heels. "Let me get my wrap."

He gave her a teasing, provocative smile. "Who's going to see?"

When he tugged, she didn't resist, but followed him into the hallway, a small nervous giggle escaping. She covered her mouth. Never before had she wandered about nude outside of her own chambers. It was at once decadent and titillating, wicked. Breaking free of his hold, she dashed toward the corner room that the servants had prepared for him. She heard the echo of his quickening steps as he rushed after her. Darting into his chamber, she came to an abrupt halt and swung around to face him.

With purpose mirrored in his gaze, he slammed the door shut. Quickly he dragged his shirt over his head before divesting himself of his boots and the remainder of his clothing in smooth, practiced moves that had Selena's mouth going dry. She'd seen him in the buff before. Still it was a pleasure to see him so again. And she thought if she lived to be a hundred, she'd never tire of the sight, even as a spark of reality reminded her that tonight would no doubt be the last time ever. Tomorrow they would return to London only to part ways: he to his scandalous gaming hells and she to search for another accomplice in her quest to deceive the Crown.

Presently, though, she didn't want to consider options or speculate as to whom she might approach. She wanted only to be focused on her remaining hours with this man who caused her to experience emotions that were new to her, who brought forth her passions with the ease one pulled a book off a shelf, who had shown her she was a creature of wants, needs, and desires when it came to the flesh.

Although perhaps it was not as general as all

that. Perhaps it was more specific. All her needs were related to him, for certainly she'd never looked upon another man and thought, *I shall die if I do not have him.*

It was *his* touch she craved, *his* body melding with hers, *his* hands stroking, *his* mouth devouring.

She held her ground as he prowled toward her, his movements sensual and predatory, just as they'd been that first night when she'd seen him at the club. When he reached her, she lifted her arms to welcome him. With an undulation of her fingers moving across his scalp, she tangled them in the strands of his hair as she flattened her breasts against his broad chest and welcomed his mouth returning to hers with an urgency that spoke volumes regarding his own desires. She was the object of them, the focus.

They weren't engaged in a simple mating between two individuals, but a mating between Aiden Trewlove and Selena Sheffield. The individuals mattered. It was his eyes of dark brown into which she wanted to gaze. His coarsened palms she relished skimming over her skin. His groans that were music to her ears. His roughened voice growling her name over and over like a benediction that caused her heart to pump more madly, joy to spiral out from her core until it encompassed the entirety of the world.

Even if that world at present was small, only them, ensconced in a bedchamber in which she'd never before slept.

Oh, how wise he was to insist they come to a room that held no memories. None of their stolen moments here would be intruded upon. Through the years as she took them out to savor them, they would mix with no other remembrances, would forever remain their own, pristine and untouched by anything that had come before.

She was barely aware of his backing her up until her knees hit the mattress. Lifting her as though she weighed nothing at all, he tossed her onto the velveteen duvet and followed her down, covering her body with his as he once again plundered her mouth.

His flavor was rich and dark, oaky. Scotch had recently passed his lips, and she wondered if the remnants on his tongue were responsible for the drunkenness she was experiencing or if it was merely his nearness that made her dizzy and breathless. He was the finest of liquors, and she feared she'd never have enough of him. That she would always long for another taste, another sip, another joining.

He trailed his wicked mouth over every inch of her as though he were memorizing the words in a book so if the tome were no longer available to be held in his hands, he could still find pleasure in recalling every sentence that made up the story. A lick here, a nip there, a stroke of his velvety tongue where her skin was its silkiest.

Everything within her tightened, everything reached for him, for this man who could stir her to life so easily. She felt no embarrassment as her moans and gasps echoed around them. Instead she reveled in the sounds, in how he managed to make her feel comfortable enough to release them. Within his arms, she felt as though she could reveal her true self: wanton and lustful.

After spreading her legs wide, he placed his hands

beneath her bottom, tilted her slightly, and plunged deep and sure. Her cry of pleasure erupted unheeded. It was so marvelous to have him within her once again. Only one night had passed without their bodies joined and yet it had seemed an eternity.

Resting on his elbows, he threaded his fingers through hers, held her hands in place on either side of her head on the pillow. A pang of regret lanced her because she understood the reasons behind his actions. He feared she would dig her fingers into his buttocks and hold him in place when he was desperate to leave her and spill his seed elsewhere.

"I won't take what you don't wish to give," she whispered.

His eyes were dark, penetrating. Lowering his head, he kissed her thoroughly before rising up over her, holding her gaze, and sliding out of her, only to glide back in. Over and over, slowly, languidly. His fingers clutching hers.

He increased the tempo. She watched his hair flap against his brow, dew begin coating his chest, his nostrils flaring as his breathing became harsher. Her body responded in kind, meeting his thrusts, gyrating as she took him deep, so deep she felt as though he had pierced her soul. Sensations began to build, rolling up from her toes. She squeezed her thighs against his hips, striving to contain the pleasure, not yet ready for it to have its way with her, for him to leave her.

They moved in tandem, giving and taking, eliciting gratification from the other. As though he knew precisely what she needed, his movements became more frenzied, harder, more purposeful, until ecstasy took hold and burst through her. She cried out his name, bowed her back, pressed her head more deeply into the pillow. As much as she fought against it, she couldn't stop herself from closing her eyes as sublime bliss overtook her. It felt as though her nerve endings had become stars shooting through the heavens.

He continued to pump into her until she was well and truly spent. Opening her eyes, she met and held his gaze. His jaw was clenched, his muscles taut and rigid. Her name was a growl on his lips as he bucked against her, his body a series of spasms, his head thrown back.

His fingers loosened their hold on hers and he closed his arms around her, burying his face in the curve of her neck.

Tears stung her eyes as she realized he hadn't left her, hadn't spilled his seed elsewhere. She wrapped herself around him as much as she was able and held on tight.

As HE WATCHED her fall into the abyss of physical release, he realized he could deny her nothing she wanted. And so when he should have left, he stayed, doing what he'd never before done: poured his seed into a womb.

He had expected to feel a measure of regret, but it was not to be found. Nothing, it seemed, mattered more than she did, more than her happiness. He'd been playing at a game, striving to justify not giving her the only thing she asked of him. Just like the billiards game they'd played, the odds were stacked against him winning. Not because she was coy or clever or knew how to manipulate him.

But because she hadn't pushed. She'd given him

time. She'd accepted his qualms and allowed him to come to his own conclusions. In the end, they weren't what he'd expected.

He who had never loved before loved at last, and it was the most rewarding, the most terrifying thing he'd ever known.

He'd almost voiced the words *I love you* out loud, but had known that doing so would only make things more difficult when the time for parting came. Because they would have to part. Eventually she would realize that.

Or perhaps he hadn't voiced the words because he feared discovering her feelings for him weren't equal to his for her. Not that it mattered. Which was a recent and surprising discovery.

Years ago, when Finn had fallen in love with the daughter of an earl, Aiden had called him a fool. Only now did he truly understand that his brother had been given no choice in the matter. The heart did as it wanted, loved who it would love. And seemed to have a penchant for choosing those who provided the most difficult of challenges. But then if love were easy, poets would hardly be heralded for putting into words what most found indescribable.

He pressed a kiss to the spot where her neck met her shoulder, where a love bite was fading. He'd sought to brand her that night. What a fool he'd been not to realize how she had the power to permanently brand him. His heart was hers. Would remain so. He'd never give it to another. That he knew with certainty.

Lifting his head, he captured her gaze, frowned. "Why the tears?"

Her eyes were glistening with them. He watched as one rolled along her cheek.

She gave him a tremulous smile. "I don't know. Silly, isn't it?"

With his fingers, he brushed the damp strands of her hair away from her face. "Nothing about you has ever struck me as silly."

"I suppose I just didn't expect—"

Gently, he placed a finger against her lips. He didn't want to discuss how he'd arrived at his decision or what it meant for their future—separately or together. "A gift horse and all that."

He'd expected her to laugh. Instead she appeared somewhat bewildered and sad. Still, she nodded.

He rolled off her, taking solace that she rolled right along with him until her head was nestled in the curve of his shoulder, her leg resting across his hips, her thigh nudging against his flaccid cock that immediately perked up. Not to the extent it was ready for another go, but it was definitely hoping to be in short order. Her fingers trailed lazily along his breastbone.

"What do you like best about the estate?" she asked.

"You." He was aware of the movement of her head as she tilted it up to look at him. He glanced down. "My favorite part is that you're here."

Her cheeks blossomed into a pink that mirrored the shade of the sky just before the sun disappeared behind the horizon, coating everything in a blanket of darkness. As long as he lived, he'd never forget the sight of that sunset or the feel of her hand nestled in his.

She kissed his shoulder before settling back into its curve. "You make me wish things were different, that I had no responsibilities, that—" She scoffed, laughed. "I was going to say that I wished I was a shopgirl, but we'd have never met if I were."

"I go into shops sometimes."

"But what are the odds that you'd go into mine?"

"My businesses are built on the premise that the odds always favor the house but that does not mean that the house always wins. Even if the odds are one in a hundred, someone has to be that one. Those are the dreamers, the ones who believe they could be that *one*. The realists are more practical, know they probably aren't."

"I'd have not thought you would be so whimsical."

"Normally I'm not. But I've known men to bet their last shilling and walk out with their pockets stuffed with their winnings. So if you were a shopgirl, we might still have met." But she wouldn't have needed him and wouldn't have sought him out.

"I'm afraid my parents' deaths ensured I became more of a realist. I don't like to take chances that things will work out. I need to know they will. I could never start a business, risk failure."

"That is what makes the success so sweet—to know you might have failed, but you didn't."

Pushing herself upright, she straddled his hips and his cock came to full attention. "I doubt you've ever questioned your ability to succeed. I can't say the same. I'm afraid I'll fail now, that I'm barren."

"You're not a failure if you don't conceive. You told me that you wanted people to see that you were more than your beauty. Lena, you're more than your womb."

Sitting, he claimed her mouth even as he lifted her up, brought her down, and filled her heated tunnel with the long, hard length of him, determined to give her all she longed for. He now understood that love made one reckless. And he embraced the knowledge as he embraced her, with all that was within him.

Chapter 20

They journeyed back to London in the carriage in silence, but it was a comfortable quiet. Sitting across from Selena, Aiden wore a small satisfied smile that no doubt matched the one on her face.

She fought against folding her hands over her belly and holding close what might already be growing there. After seven long years, the odds were against her. She knew this. Yet still she held out hope, hope he'd given to her when he'd spoken about odds. Even when they were low, it still meant there was a chance. While the realist in her revolted, the dreamer she'd long ago been peered out as though from a lengthy sleep and refused to retreat.

Being with him was like running barefoot over clover, wild with abandon. It was joyous. She would find a way to keep him in her life while protecting their child.

"Why have you grown sad?"

His voice brought her from her reverie, and she wondered if anyone else in the world would ever know her as well as he did.

"I'm not sad."

"What are the other estates like?"

"Smaller, but no less opulent. The Dukes of Lushing took their responsibilities quite seriously. Ensuring their estates were the envy of all was seen as a duty, a requirement of the position." She glanced out the window. "Commoners resent the nobility their place in Society, but it comes with sacrifice."

"All positions in Society come with sacrifice."

She glanced over at him. "True enough, I suppose. Have you ever visited your father's estate?"

He shook his head. "I have as little to do with him as possible. Speaking of him, has he made an appearance on your doorstep since his atrocious proposal?"

"Not as far as I know, although I've not been at home that much. You're keeping me rather busy."

"You will let me know if he does."

His voice contained something dark and foreboding. "What will you do if he does?"

"Pay him another visit."

She felt her eyes widen with her alarm. "You paid him a visit? When? Why?"

"A couple of nights ago. Because he's not to bother you."

She was more than slightly distressed. "He knows about us?"

He shifted on his seat. "Whatever he may think he knows, he won't tell anyone. There is little he fears more than he fears the wrath of the Trewlove brothers."

"What if he guesses? What if he seeks to—"

Leaning across, he took her hand, putting a stop to her words. "Lena, I may not be publicly involved in your life or that of the child, but I will be like that great statue on the front lawn, ever watchful from afar. No harm will ever come to the child. No one will ever question his parentage." Reaching up, he skimmed his knuckles along her cheek. "I'm very good at keeping to the shadows."

While she took immense comfort from his words, she couldn't help but wonder how difficult, how *painful*, it might be for him to be hovering at the edge of his child's life. "It will not be easy for you."

"It is the price I pay. Willingly."

For you was not said, but he might as well have etched the words on her heart because she felt them all the same.

She had struggled mightily to make her decision to live the remainder of her life without honor. She regretted that her actions would have such a profound effect on his life as well. Perhaps years from now when the child was grown, had made a life for himself, Selena would return to the Elysium Club and find true happiness with the owner. By then who would care? Who would be suspicious? The odds were against that happening, and yet it gave her something to hold on to.

He settled back. The satisfied smile was gone. Now she saw longing—not hunger, not desire—but a pining for something that could never be: quiet conversations before a fire, long walks in the park. A public acknowledgment that they meant something to each other.

She barely noted that they'd reached London, not until the carriage came to a halt outside the club. He made a move toward the door that had not yet been opened.

"I'll meet you here tonight, shall I?" She could barely stand the thought of a night without him.

He paused and looked back at her, his smile soft,

his eyes filled with a satisfaction that came from knowing he meant something to her. "Midnight. Fewer ladies about then, fewer tasks that require my attention."

Then he was gone, leaping from the carriage, striding into the club, disappearing from her sight.

THEY HAD LEFT Sheffield Hall early enough that she arrived home shortly before noon. She noted a black horse secured to a post out front and assumed it was Winslow or Kittridge come to call. She was hoping for Kit as she wanted to indulge in a short nap before addressing any concerns that Winslow might bring with him regarding his estate and lack of funds. She really needed to find someone to take him in hand and help him adjust to his duties, because Lushing's passing had left him in a boat with no oar or rudder. As she darted up the steps, it occurred to her that the Duke of Thornley might be just the ticket, an excellent example to follow. While she knew him fairly well, it wasn't well enough to impose but perhaps Aiden could make the suggestion to Thornley. It would be lovely to have one fewer sibling to worry over.

She opened the door, crossed the threshold, and came to a stop as though she'd slammed into a brick wall. Not Kit or Winslow.

Her butler dipped his head slightly. "Your Grace, I was just explaining to Lord Elverton that you were not in residence."

"Yet here you are," Elverton said, his smile a bit too bright. Aiden had not inherited the shape of his mouth from his father.

"I've only just returned from Sheffield Hall and

am quite weary. How might I be of service, my lord?"

"I was hoping for a few minutes of your time, perhaps a spot of tea."

She wondered if his presence indicated he gave no credence to whatever threat his son had made or if he was marking his defiance of it. "If you'll give me a moment to right myself, I'll join you in the parlor. Wiggins, see that tea is brought in."

Making her way to the stairs, she was grateful he'd caught her after traveling, when she wore black, rather than after a night at the club when she was decked out in blue. In her rooms, she removed her hat, washed her face, tidied her hair, and fortified herself for a social call she had little doubt would turn out to be beyond the pale. He'd already offered his condolences. What more was there for him to say?

She returned downstairs to find him standing at the fireplace, looking down into the empty hearth. Nothing in his stance reminded her of his son. It wasn't because Elverton wasn't as fit, that the years had brought a roundness to his shoulders and belly. It was simply that he was not in possession of the magnetic presence that encompassed his by-blow. Aiden quite simply commanded the room, took control of it the moment he strode into it. His father might yield power through his position, but Aiden yielded it through his very existence. He didn't need a title to mark his place in the world. He'd accomplished it all through his own merit. He was what the earl would never be: his own man.

Strip away Elverton's title and he would be nothing more than a wisp of smoke with no substance. Aiden was all substance, caring and loyal, and *real*. Honest. He didn't put on airs. She'd always known precisely where she stood with him.

As Elverton turned and gave her a small smile that caused the hair on her arms to rise, she realized she could not say the same of the earl. She didn't trust the upturn of his lips or the glint in his eyes. She settled into a plush chair near the tea service that had already been brought in and began pouring the dark brew into the delicate china cup that sported small pink roses. The earl dropped onto the nearby settee, which put a comfortable distance between them. She finished preparing his tea, handed it off to him, saw to her own brew, took a sip, and settled back.

The silence stretching out between them wasn't nearly as comfortable or natural as that between her and Aiden. "I'm fairly certain you didn't come here for my tea."

Setting aside his cup, he leaned forward. "I wondered if you'd given our previous conversation any thought."

Another sip of her tea, a placement of the cup on the saucer so it made not a sound. "Indeed. I've given all the condolences I've received great thought. They bring me a good deal of comfort in these trying times."

Something like impatience flashed in his eyes. "I was referring to other matters we discussed."

"I don't recall much of a discussion."

He shifted his backside over the brocade cushion. "You are a young woman with needs. Many needs from what I understand. I have heard Lushing left you a rather modest trust. It will not see you acquiring all you deserve."

She wondered where he'd gathered that information. Certainly not from Mr. Beckwith. She doubted very much that it had come from Kittridge. Possibly one of her sisters, in innocence, had spouted to a friend and from there it had made the rounds. Or perhaps Winslow had let it slip at one of his clubs when he was in his cups. "I am content with the accommodations my husband made for me."

"A woman as beautiful as you deserves more than contentment. I want to ensure that as a potential future husband I am not dismissed out of hand." He scooted up to the edge of his seat. "I would like to take advantage of this time while you are in mourning to forge a friendship—a deep and abiding friendship—with you."

"I fear, my lord, that I will be too busy seeing that my sisters are properly situated to have time to spend building friendships."

"I can see them well married."

Her breath caught, and she froze, the teacup suddenly feeling as though it weighed as much as an elephant. Before it began to rattle in her hand, disclosing her shock at his words, she set it aside. He was not making that offer out of the goodness of his heart. He was doing it in exchange for *her*. "My lord—"

"It is not an idle boast. I have influence and prestige, which I will put at your disposal. Their mourning period will be at an end shortly after the Season gets underway. I shall see all three married to lords of the highest caliber. This is not a claim your brother can make or see through as he is too young, too green. But my word carries weight. I can start planting the seeds now and we shall see them bloom by Season's end."

"That's quite a generous offer, my lord. I am, however, befuddled regarding why you would care so much about their well-being."

"It is yours I care about. Once they are situated, once I have proved my devotion to you, once your initial mourning period has ended in a year, we may wed."

Although a widow went into half mourning after a year, it was not unheard of for her to marry at that time. Still, she was likely to suffer the indignity of being thought promiscuous. Not that the Earl of Elverton cared about that, apparently. "There is still the matter of your present wife, my lord."

"As I mentioned, she has not been well of late."

It turned her stomach knowing he was already on the hunt for her replacement. "To be quite honest, Lord Elverton, I find your offer not only grievously vulgar but insulting to your wife as well." She rose to her feet. "I decline. Please see yourself out."

With her head held high and her shoulders back, she headed for the door.

"I can see that they have no offers at all." The low menacing threat stopped her in her tracks.

Slowly she turned and impaled with her eyes this vile blackguard, and she found herself grateful he'd had no part in Aiden's upbringing. "I fear, my lord, that you have underestimated my influence. While I may no longer have a duke at my side, I am still the Duchess of Lushing and I am fully capable of seeing to the needs of my family. I warn you, sir, that you do not want to incur my wrath."

With that, she quit the room.

FROM THE MOMENT she'd left Elverton's presence, she'd debated whether to tell Aiden of his father's visit, but finally decided against mentioning it, fearing only ill would come of his learning of the earl's further pursuit of her. Certainly she had made her position clear. She had no interest in the man, would not entertain the notion of having him in her life in any intimate capacity, whether as a mistress or a wife.

It was a challenge to reconcile the odious behavior of the Earl of Elverton against the goodness that was his son. If there was an argument to be made against children born out of wedlock being the carriers of their parents' immoral behavior, surely Aiden and his father served as the perfect example to exemplify John Locke's theory that at birth a babe's mind was a blank slate. Other than the shade of his eyes, his jaw, his brow, Aiden in no way resembled his father. He was all that was good.

Even if he owned a den of iniquity, a den she entered with a great deal of anticipation. After handing her wrap off to the young woman at the front counter, she wandered into the gaming area and spotted Aiden immediately. In spite of there being other gents in the room, he stood out as though he alone occupied the entire space. It wasn't his height or breadth that gave him an advantage, but his very presence that spoke volumes, reflected a man of both confidence and daring.

He was speaking with a younger man, but as though her appearance carried weight as well, he glanced over, and she could see the slow lift of one corner of his mouth. With a nod, he patted the younger man's shoulder before beginning to make his way to her, never breaking his stride in spite of acknowledging the ladies here and there, even bending over to whisper something to one of them. Jealousy was a sharp spear, but she deflected it before it could do any damage. She had little doubt he would be whispering a great deal more in her ear later, words far more delicious than what he might have shared with one of his customers.

Then he was before her, threading his fingers through hers, leading her away from the doorway, back into the foyer, and down the darkened, secluded hallway. Not a word spoken. A man on a mission. To claim her, and she couldn't help but wonder if their coupling would be as perfunctory as what she'd experienced in her marriage. Now that he had thoroughly seduced her, would he see no further need of making her mad with desire?

Up the stairs they went. When they reached the top, however, he pulled her in a direction they'd never before traveled.

"Where are we going?"

"I want to share something with you."

She almost quipped that he could share it with her right then and there, against the wall, and she'd not find fault with him, but didn't want their encounters to revolve only around the bedding. "The relaxation room?"

He chuckled low. "Not tonight."

Another corridor, another set of stairs, then another, narrower with more creaks and moans. He opened a door. "Wait here."

She stepped into the doorway while he went farther into the room with a solitary window, faint moonlight or streetlamps spilling in to reveal what appeared to be a rather cluttered attic. The hiss of a match strike, the flaring of a flame, the lighting of a lamp, and her suspicions were confirmed, but the clutter, dear God, the clutter was magnificent.

Cautiously she walked to an easel where the canvas revealed the profile of a woman—her but not her—her hair pinned up, her shoulders seemingly bared. Everything about the painting was muted, muted by sorrow, blurred so it was impossible to be certain he had used her as the model and yet it could be no one else. She was surprised no tears rained down the cheek. "The night we went to the cemetery."

"Yes."

She glanced over her shoulder at him, not certain she'd ever known him to look so tense, as though he were awaiting her judgment and feared her pronouncement would lead him to the gallows. "You did this?"

A single nod.

Her gaze circled the room. "All of these?"

"Yes."

She wandered over to the wall where a dozen portraits hung and one, the one nearest to the door, snagged her attention. It revealed only eyes and a heart-shaped chin, again all muted. It could have represented anyone and while it was not revealed, she imaged a mask hiding what had not been painted.

Another portrayed a woman with the look of a warrior about her, holding a cue stick, the portrait beginning with the upper swells of her breasts. "I see you don't bother with clothing."

"I never had much luck with that. The lines of the human form come more naturally to me."

She thought of the paintings in the billiards room, on the walls in other rooms. All sensual, all nudes but muddled in a way that never really gave away the identity of the person. "Do you paint everyone you've bedded?"

"I paint those who intrigue me."

She glanced over her shoulder, meeting and holding his gaze. "Have you bedded all these ladies?"

"Only a couple."

"Did the others pose for you?"

"I paint from memory."

Moving farther into the confined area she realized he'd lied about clothing being a challenge for him, because there was a portrait of a boy decked out in finery, a beaver hat and walking stick in hand, an arrogant grin on his darling face. "This is Robin, the lad who helped out at the bookshop."

"He lived with Gillie before moving in with Finn. She won't admit it, but I think she misses him. I thought to give that to her."

He had a good heart, a caring heart that caused her own to tighten painfully in her chest. A time would come when he would create portraits of his own children. "You're quite talented."

She wandered back over to him, pressed her palm against his cheek. "Will you be hanging me in one of the salons downstairs?"

"No. They're only for me. But I wanted you to

know about them. I don't know why, but it seemed important somehow. Perhaps because in the past few days you've been forced to bare your secrets and soul to me. It seemed only fair that I bare some of my soul to you."

"How much simpler all this would be if you weren't so complicated." Rising up on her toes, she claimed his mouth as though it was her right to do so, although at the moment she readily believed it was. With their bodies, they'd made their vows, sealed their fates when they'd come together the night before.

Was it only last night that she'd decided she wanted him regardless of his decision, that she wanted no conditions, no terms when it came to their relationship? She wouldn't have gone to another. She wanted him, only Aiden, as long as he'd have her.

His arms closing securely around her, followed by his low groan, heightened her own pleasure, and she moaned in response.

He walked her backward, reached out, and slammed the door shut. Suddenly she found herself pressed against the pine, his hands gathering up her skirts while her fingers made their way to the fall of his trousers.

Then he was inside her, pumping away, growling with the intensity of his thrusts. His hand skimmed along her thigh and he brought her leg up until it circled his waist, and he plunged deeper still.

"I love the way you feel," he rasped, dragging his mouth along her throat. "So hot, so tight, so wet."

"I love the way you fill me, so large, so thick, so heavy."

His rough laughter only added to the spiraling sensations building within her, propelling her toward the pinnacle of release. When she reached it and screamed his name in a manner that rather sounded like a benediction, she imagined all the ladies in the paintings looking on blushed or perhaps turned red with envy. He undid her in ways she'd never imagined a person could be undone.

And she knew in her heart that no one else would ever touch her as he did, no one would ever follow him into her heart.

"You've spoiled me."

Although he'd spoken the words low, almost muffled by his mouth being pressed to the nape of her neck, they still disturbed the silence that had settled in around them after they'd had another rousing coming together—this time in his bed.

He hadn't planned to take her in the attic like a savage unable to control his urges, but then she'd looked at him with wonder and something he couldn't quite identify. It was the way Gillie looked at Thornley, Aslyn at Mick, Lavinia at Finn. He might have labeled it love, but it was not what she wanted of him, not what he wanted of her. Love would be bad for business, curtail his ability to flirt with the ladies, to make each one feel special.

He'd already begun getting a few icy glares, a few speculative looks. While the ladies came here to lavish themselves in vices, they also enjoyed his attentions, teasing though they were. He couldn't risk upsetting those who were putting coins in his coffers.

"In what way?" she asked lethargically, as though his taking of her—rough, fast, and hard—had left her too spent to even form words.

He didn't know why he'd said what he had. She spoiled him in ways he didn't want to admit. Their bodies fit together like the perfect interlocking pieces of a puzzle. They communicated without words, knowing what the other needed, wanted, desired. He'd never spoken as honestly with any other woman—save his mother and sisters—as he spoke with her. He could tell her anything, wanted to tell her everything. It was the reason he'd shared his paintings. He only displayed a few; no one except his family knew they were his. Some were far too personal, had come from the depths of his soul. Sharing them made him feel vulnerable— but he hadn't had that feeling with her. How could he when she'd had him at his most vulnerable: tied to a bed? He'd trusted her then, even if it had been poor timing on his part. He trusted her now. Still, he couldn't confess all that, couldn't allow her to know what an important part of his life she'd become. Because a time could come when she wouldn't be a part of it at all, when she would grow weary of doing so much in public alone and would be in want of a man who could be seen by her side. "I shall resent wearing a sheath when I'm with other ladies in the future."

Within his arms, with her back to his chest, she went completely still. He wasn't even certain she drew breath. "I will never be with another man."

He squeezed his eyes shut. Her response was not what he expected. He tightened his hold on her, wanted to encourage her to find someone else, another duke, because he couldn't bear the thought of her living out her years in loneliness. "You're too young to never again marry."

"Lushing said the same thing as he grew weaker. He encouraged me to find someone else, to remarry. But if I become someone else's wife, I'll no longer be able to come to you."

He couldn't imagine her being content to spend the next half century sharing only stolen moments with him. Eventually the world would again open up to her once she was out of mourning. She would be flirted with and courted. Marriage proposals would come her way. How long before one appealed to her? Another man would then have influence over his child. He didn't want to consider that. Turning her over, he offered a self-deprecating smile. "Perhaps we should avoid speculating about our futures."

Her eyes were limpid pools as she nodded. "We should concentrate on the present. Make the most of it."

Pulling her onto him until she was straddling his hips, he intended to do just that, make the most of every minute, hour, day that she was with him. As she took him within her, he fought not to think of the future because it would be a lonely abyss without her.

IT WAS NEARLY dawn before she prepared to take her leave. Their short time at Sheffield Hall had spoiled her, and she'd wanted a few hours of sleeping within the circle of his arms, inhaling his purely masculine smell laced with the scent of their lovemaking. And she loved watching him donning his clothes to begin the day almost as much as she enjoyed watching him take them off.

He didn't bother to take a razor to his face, perhaps because of the early hour, so thick dark whiskers shadowed his jaw. "I like the beard."

He rubbed the stubble, and she heard the rasp of the bristles against his palms, knew the sensation they caused, having felt them against the soft skin at her throat and breasts when he'd tucked her beneath him upon first awakening and made love to her.

That was how she thought of it, what he did to her. It was as though he gave more to her than just his seed, that he gifted her with portions of himself, parts she was arrogant enough to believe he'd given to no other. Being with him was more profound, more fulfilling, more satisfying than she'd ever dreamed it would be. It was more than the way he made her body thrum with pleasure. It was the manner in which he made her soul glow.

"Maybe I'll keep it." He opened a drawer of a small wooden box that rested atop his bureau. He held out a key to her. "For you."

She took it, closing her fingers around something that seemed significant. "Why?"

"So we can be a little more discreet and my customers don't get the notion that I've taken a lover. When you arrive, just come on up. I'll have Angie send one of the footmen to let me know you're here, and I'll join you when I can."

He'd told her that he'd never brought another woman here, so instinctually she knew she was the first to whom he'd given unfettered access to his lodgings. Closing her fingers tightly around the brass, she was reluctant to part with it, to put it safely in her reticule. She wanted to place it on a chain and keep it nestled between her breasts, close to her heart. Quite suddenly she wished she had a gift for him, something of equal value. "Thank you for striving to protect my reputation."

A corner of his mouth hitched up. "It's better for business if I'm seen as unfettered."

"Oh? Have I fettered you, then?" She made her voice light and airy when in fact she was profoundly touched by his dedication to her.

"You know you have." Snaking his arm around her, he pulled her up against him and blanketed her mouth with his, kissing her deeply and thoroughly, as though needing to prove that she was equally fettered to him.

Only she feared she was more so. That she and her heart would remain bound to him until the end of time.

Chapter 21

*T*oo many days later to count, Selena languidly stretched in her bed. Glancing over, she imagined how glorious it would be to be greeted by the sight of Aiden each morning, to see him unshaven, unkempt, his hair sticking out in all directions, his slow smile just before he reached for her and tucked her beneath his powerful body. She doubted very much that he would adhere to the nobility's practice of the husband and wife sleeping in separate bedchambers. No, he would hold her as she slept, his body warming her, his hand cradling her breast, just as he'd done at Sheffield Hall.

That night seemed so long ago now because so many nights had followed, nights when she'd gone to him. She'd thought of asking him to come to her, but it would not do at all for her sisters to discover him visiting, which they no doubt would because she and Aiden lost in the throes of passion was not a quiet thing. She kept expecting their joining to shift into a staid and boring routine. But beneath his hands she turned to kindling, beneath his body she became enflamed.

When the knock sounded, she pushed herself upright and settled back against the pillows.

Early in her marriage, she'd gotten into the habit of taking her breakfast in bed because that was the manner in which a proper duchess began her day. Although at present, she was anything except a proper duchess. Still, as Bailey walked in carrying a tray laden with dishes, Selena fought to give the appearance of one.

Bailey set the tray over Selena's lap, went about fluffing up the pillows behind her, then wandered over to the windows and threw open the draperies with a dramatic flourish, as she liked nothing more than letting in the day.

Selena lifted a lid to reveal buttered eggs, their aroma causing her stomach to grow a bit queasy. Deciding she wasn't in the mood for them, she covered them back up. Toast and jam appealed.

"Let Wiggins know that I'll need the carriage at half one. My sisters and I will be going out this afternoon for a charitable endeavor." Fancy's shop would be opening this evening with a grand party. They couldn't attend that, naturally, but Fancy had invited them to a private celebration with her family before the main event. It was unlikely they'd be seen by anyone they knew—other than Trewlove family members, of course.

With her brow furrowed and her hands clasped in front of her, her maid came to stand at the foot of the bed. "I don't know that they'll be up to it, Your Grace. The girls are having their monthly unwellness."

Selena went still, so still, it was a wonder she continued to draw in breath. As incredible as it seemed, she and her sisters had always been on the same schedule when it came to the curse. They

were like well-tuned clockwork, a vicious head-
ache coming upon them before the painful cramps
arrived. They always spent the first day or so abed,
bemoaning God's punishment upon them. "When
did their menses begin?"

"Yesterday afternoon."

"All three of them?"

"Yes, ma'am. As always. I prepared some rags
for you, though mayhap you won't be needin'
them?"

The last two words were spoken in a high pitch
as though her maid feared that even a hint of her
possibly carrying the heir would prevent it from being true. Although her servant knew when her last
menses had ended, still the innocent woman held
out hope that even though his health had been fail-
ing, the duke had managed to rise to the challenge
and do his duty one last time. It was that absurd
belief that Selena had planned to exploit if she managed to get herself with child.

The possibility now loomed and yet—

She could think of a hundred reasons why her
sisters were presently suffering and she wasn't.
The stress of becoming a widow, of mourning, had
blocked her flow. She wasn't spending as much time
with her sisters, and so they'd fallen out of their
rhythm. She was so occupied, fairly obsessed with
her time with Aiden, that she'd somehow conveyed
to her body that it should do nothing to prevent her
from seeing him every night—and that included
any hint of a monthly bleeding.

Or she could be with child.

His child. Aiden's.

She closed her eyes, fought back tears for everything it would mean. The joy that his babe might be growing inside her. Dark-haired, dark-eyed. Strong-jawed. Tiny hands and feet that would grow into larger ones.

Sadness because Aiden wouldn't be with her when the child was born. That his moments with his progeny would be short and infrequent.

As her body began swelling, she would have to stop going to the club. She couldn't risk being seen there in her condition. If some of his customers were hinting that they thought he'd taken a mistress, it wouldn't do at all for them to realize that mistress was pregnant. Even if they weren't sure it was her, if it caused the tiniest of speculations—she couldn't risk their association being discovered.

They would have to make other accommodations.

The price of what they'd done suddenly seemed far too high. When she had set out on this mission, she hadn't expected to fall in love.

SHE ARRIVED AT the bookshop without her sisters. She'd considered sending a missive with their regrets, but in the end, she wanted to see the shop all put together, wanted to see Aiden in a setting other than a bedchamber.

After much thought, she decided she couldn't be certain she was with child. She would give it another week, perhaps two, before calling upon her physician to solicit his opinion on the matter. Then she would decide her course of action.

For now it was enough to see him waiting for her outside the shop, the sight of him always bringing her a kick of joy, joy that increased as he opened the door and closed his fingers around hers, assisting her out of the carriage. How many times had he handed her up or down? Not nearly enough.

"Is something amiss? You seem a bit pale."

"I'm perfectly fine. My sisters are unwell, however. They send their regrets."

Concern narrowed his eyes. "Is it contagious?"

"No. They'll be right as rain in a day or so. Can we take a stroll through your sister's shop now?"

"By all means." He tucked her hand within the crook of his elbow. The familiarity of it after such a short time was astounding.

But then everything about their relationship seemed to have happened at breakneck speed, as though they'd been sitting astride a runaway horse. Never had so many varying emotions pummeled her as they did now. A mixture of joy and sadness, a need to hoard away memories.

Inside the shop, she took comfort from the musty aroma emanating from the books stacked neatly on the beautifully carved bookcases.

Fancy hurried over to her, curtsied. "Your Grace, I'm so glad you were able to come by for a peek." She glanced past Selena, her delicate brow furrowing. "Your sisters—"

"Are indisposed. They send their apologies, but as their mourning period is not as long as mine, I'm certain they'll pay a visit at the appropriate time."

"I look forward to welcoming them. We already have the punch set up if you'd like some. Mick has asked his hotel chef to prepare us some tea cakes, but they won't be here for a while yet."

"I'd actually just like to wander about."

Aiden strolled with her as she wended her way among the bookcases, touching a spine here and there, imagining all the various worlds into which a person could escape. Eventually they made their way upstairs. Flowers had been added to the sitting areas, making them appear cozier. All the shelves on either side of the fireplace were crammed with books, but it was what hung above the mantel-piece that snagged her attention, and like someone caught in a trance, she floated toward it, captivated. The painting depicted a young woman lounging on a settee, reading a book, a stack of tomes scattered on the floor about her. While her face was muted and soft, the lady was obviously Fancy. "You created this, capturing Fancy's love of reading."

He didn't answer. He didn't need to. She recognized his handiwork, the care that went into it, the love he delivered with every brushstroke. "I think you could make a fortune as an artist."

"Its value comes from the pleasure it brings me."

And that it brought others.

To her left, near a window, was the nook Fancy had designed as an area for children to read. On the wall were other paintings, smaller ones, seemingly arranged haphazardly. As she neared, she laughed at the sight of a cat, dog, hedgehog, dormouse, unicorn, and mermaid reading, each in their own little world, their own individual frames. He had told her he painted from memory, but it was also obvious he had quite the vivid imagination. "You created these as well. Who'd have thought Aiden Trewlove had a bit of whimsy to him?"

Turning, she smiled, touched to see his cheeks darkening with the heat of embarrassment. "Is that the reason you don't sign them? So people won't realize you possess a tender heart?"

"I don't do them for the acclaim, so I don't see any need to put my name to them. They're just a bit of fun."

But they were so much more. Just as he was.

"They're going to delight the children." And she couldn't help but wonder if he would create flights of fancy for his own offspring—and stopped herself from going further and contemplating what the woman who gave them to him would be like. If they continued to see each other, she couldn't give him any more children. They would have to return to using the sheaths. But eventually, he might want a real family that he didn't have to hide away.

He merely shrugged. "Walls weren't meant to be bare. I painted some pictures for Gillie's pub."

"Mermaids and unicorns?"

He grinned. "Of course. So I couldn't very well not paint something for Fancy." He stepped nearer, trailed his finger along her chin. "I should paint something for you. What would you like?"

A portrait of you. A miniature. Something she could put in a locket and keep near her heart. "I don't know. I'll have to think on it."

"I'm glad you came this afternoon. I enjoy seeing you away from the club."

It made their being together seem of a greater purpose.

"I wish I could do more with you," he said quietly.

"Widows aren't allowed to give out or accept invitations, not for a year. It wouldn't do for us to be seen gadding about."

He moved nearer, his legs brushing against her skirts, his hand folding around her neck, his fingers skimming along her spine at her nape. "I've been trying to think of someplace I could take you."

"Like the theater? Have you ever been to a play?"

"Once. When I was younger, about twelve, we all saved up and took our mum to a play on Drury Lane. I enjoyed it, but not enough to spend my coins on it again. At least not then. I could take you to a penny gaff. It's unlikely any nobs would be there."

"But we can't guarantee some young lord isn't up to some mischief."

"No." He lowered his lips to the underside of her jaw, and with a sigh, she dropped her head back. "There was a time I could have taken you to Gillie's pub but now that she's married to a duke, lords are always dropping by."

"A pity."

"I can't take you on a stroll through a park. It seems all I can do is take you to bed." Regret and sorrow laced his voice.

Guilt pricked her conscience because she couldn't offer him more.

Chapter 22

$\mathscr{A}$ little over two weeks later, Aiden strode into his private chambers and saw Lena gazing out the window, a subdued excitement vibrating off her. They had settled into a routine: she'd let herself into his lodgings and a footman would discreetly alert Aiden to her arrival. Shortly thereafter, he would join her here. Sometimes they'd have dinner and share stories from their day or he'd tell her about changes he was planning for the club or she'd share the gossip an occasional visitor brought her.

He wanted to expand their world beyond these chambers, but he was very much aware that even if her mourning period didn't dictate their seclusion, her disgrace at being seen consorting with him would.

Three of his siblings had landed themselves noble spouses, but none of them had families dependent upon them maintaining a reputation above reproach. None of them had sisters whose future well-being and prospects for a good marriage could be destroyed because of their choices. None of them had stared at the possibility of losing so very much.

As he neared, she turned away from the window

and gave him a tremulous smile, tears welling. "I'm with child."

Having been with her every night with no impediments to their lovemaking surfacing, he wasn't taken by surprise, didn't ask if she was certain. Still her words slammed into him with the force of a hard punch to his solar plexus, making it impossible to draw in air, and without thought, he dropped his gaze and flattened his palm against her belly as though he'd be able to feel movement, could connect with the babe that was growing inside her, had probably been doing so for close to a month already. It was difficult to believe she'd been in his life for not much longer than that when each night spent with her seemed unlike any that had come before.

She placed her hand over his. "I've suspected for a couple of weeks now but was afraid to get too hopeful. The physician confirmed it this afternoon. I'd always feared I was barren. That it was my fault Lushing had no heir." A sob escaped and she pressed her fingers to her mouth. "I'm so happy."

He drew her into his arms, held her near, wondered if she could hear the thudding of his heart as joy spiraled through him. The elation was unexpected, but he found he wanted to shout from the rooftops that this remarkable woman would be bringing his child into the world. And yet the world must never know. And just like that, the bubble of gladness burst as reality demanded acknowledgment.

"Then why the tears?" He was pleased his voice came out strong and clear, in spite of the knot in his throat that was threatening to strangle him.

This bairn would secure Lena's place among the aristocracy, would ensure she could see her sisters well situated. She would raise the child at Sheffield Hall. Aiden could never give her so fine a residence, an estate, no matter how full his coffers.

"Women weep when they're happy."

"Have you told anyone?"

"No, not yet." Leaning back, she held his gaze. "I wanted to share the news with you first. But I will have to make an announcement very soon to lessen any doubt that this babe is Lushing's."

He'd gone into this scheme knowing the terms, and yet it was more difficult than he'd expected to relinquish his fatherhood, to be reminded that this child would never know the true circumstances of how he'd come to be. He'd never know that he'd been conceived in love and sacrifice.

Breaking away from him, she returned to the window and gazed out. "This child will gain so much. We will hold on to everything. My sisters will benefit." She faced him. "Our place in Society is assured. They will marry well. But they'll never know how much they owe to you. And that I regret."

"I didn't do it for their damn gratitude."

"Why did you do it?"

Because I love you. Because you asked it of me. He shrugged. "I appreciate a well-executed dodge. For the estates this child will inherit, and if it's a boy for the titles as well. And it certainly wasn't a hardship to have you in my bed. But I've served my purpose. It's time for our association to come to an end."

Her brow wrinkled as though she could sense that he was distancing himself, building a wall around his heart. He hadn't expected it to go up so quickly.

But he'd come to understand that they could not continue as they had been: living in a narrow world that only encompassed the two of them, keeping to the shadows. While he thrived in them, it was no life for her. She deserved nights at the theater, waltzing in glittering ballrooms, drives through the park with a man beside her who brought her pride. Not one who catered in sin.

He finally understood why Finn had risked so much for Lavinia, had dared to love a girl who could bring him naught but heartache. For as bitter as the pain was, there was a sweetness to it as well in knowing that he was capable of such depth of emotion. Yet he knew he would never feel for another what he felt for Lena. And because of how much she meant to him, he knew he had to let her go now, before she was swelling with a bairn he could never publicly acknowledge. Each passing night would only make it more difficult to do what must be done for the good of all: walk out of her life.

"No." She cradled his jaw. "We agreed to continue to see each other."

"Are you going to march down the stairs without wearing a mask? Are you going to stroll through the gaming floor at my side with your features on display for all to see?"

"Well, no, of course not. I'm not even two months a widow yet. I can't have people thinking I turned to you within days of my husband's death. But perhaps in two or three years—"

Always there would be a dishonesty to their public relationship, a hiding of the truth. Always he would need to protect her and his child from gossipmongers. Holding her hand against his jaw, he turned his face into it and pressed a kiss against the palm that had caressed him so lovingly and would never do so again. "It's been fun, sweetheart, but we both knew it was only for a short time, and that added to the thrill. From experience I know boredom is a mere short distance away. You were fooling yourself if you thought otherwise."

"You can't mean that." Jerking her hand out from beneath his, she appeared stricken, and he wondered if he could locate someone to flay his back before dawn, even as he knew turning her away unmercifully was the kindest thing he could do.

"I'll want to see the child, of course. In secret." Always in secret because they couldn't risk anyone noting any similarities in appearance between the twelfth Duke of Lushing and a man who owned a gaming hell and a notorious club that catered to women's fantasies. "We'll work out the details later. Send word when you've given birth." He was amazed by how cool he was able to keep his tone when everything inside him was being shredded into useless bits.

Fire burned in her eyes. He preferred the fire to the sorrow, knew she would find the strength to move forward. It was one of the reasons he loved her. She would not be cowed or deterred. "It seems I misjudged you, Aiden Trewlove."

"More's the pity. I'll walk you to your carriage."

"Don't bother. I can see myself out."

Her strides were filled with purpose, her arms swinging with her righteous anger.

"Lena?"

She stopped but didn't look back at him, and he admired her restraint, her fury. "Find a man who loves you."

"I thought I had."

She jerked open the door and gave a startled yelp. His floor boss was standing there, his fist raised as though he were in the process of knocking.

"What the devil is it, Toombs?" Aiden barked.

"There's a woman to see you, sir. I escorted her to your office. She's waiting for you there."

Lena swung around and skewered him with her gaze as though his man had just delivered evidence of his unfaithfulness to her. "Have her return in the morning. I'll see her then."

He wasn't in the mood for a meeting with some high-bred woman wanting her daughter escorted out should the young chit visit.

"She says she's your mother."

Alarm spread through him. His mum never came here, didn't completely approve of the place. He was charging through the doorway before Lena continued her journey through it. "Escort the lady out," he told Toombs as he edged past him.

"I don't need—"

But Lena's words trailed away as he rapidly put more distance between them. Something was wrong, terribly wrong. His mum wouldn't be here otherwise. A dozen scenarios went through his mind, all involving his siblings and a dire accident.

He rushed into the room and staggered to a stop. It wasn't his mum. It was Lady Elverton, sitting in a chair near his desk. Her face was pale and clammy. She seemed to be trembling. An awful stench was on the air, and he noticed the bin he normally kept behind his desk was resting near her feet. "Lady Elverton, are you ill?"

"My apologies, but it appears something at dinner did not agree with me. I began to feel unwell on the journey here, but it seems to have arrived with full force."

He neared and gently wrapped his hand around her upper arm. "Allow me to assist you to your coach. We can talk another time."

She clutched his hand, tugging until he lowered himself. "I can no longer live with the guilt. Please forgive me." Reaching up with a shaking hand, she touched his cheek. "You *are* my son."

IT SEEMED TO be a night destined to bring punches to his gut that threatened to bring him to his knees. He was a man skilled at transferring images to canvas, attentive to the smallest of details. He'd noticed similarities between them before but had discounted his findings as those of a man who longed to know the truth about his past and was willing to see things that didn't exist. But if he imposed his features over hers, the shape of the eyes, the sharp cut of the cheeks—

Still he couldn't bring himself to believe it. "At our last meeting, you implied you were not."

"Shame held me silent." Her eyes flooded with tears. "I let him take you. I—oh God. Have mercy." With a little cry, she clutched at her belly, doubled over, grabbed the bin, and retched, leaving him to feel helpless, with little to do other than stroke her back until the heaving subsided.

He handed her his handkerchief as she again

muttered apologies for which he had no patience. "You're unwell."

Scooping her up into his arms, surprised by how feathery light she was, he strode from the room as she sagged against him. "Send for a physician!" he bellowed. The hallway was open to the gaming floor and he had no doubt someone who worked for him would jump to the order.

He barged into his rooms—grateful to see Lena pacing in front of the fire, her brow deeply furrowed as she rubbed her hands. He hated the relief that swept through him, the manner in which her mere presence so steadied his nerves, made him believe all would be well.

"Is that Lady Elverton?"

"It is." He carried her through to his bedchamber and laid the countess down gently on the bed.

"I understood Toombs to say it was your mother waiting for you."

"She claims to be my mother."

When he looked up, it was to see astonishment clearly etched on Lena's face as her gaze whipped between him and the countess several times as though she were cataloguing features.

"She's dreadfully ill. I've sent for the physician. Can you assist me in making her comfortable?"

"Yes, of course."

While he removed the countess's shoes, Lena loosened buttons in order to loosen stays.

"I'm so sorry," the countess muttered over and over. "The salmon must have been bad."

"Don't be troubled, my lady," he told her. "The doctor will be here shortly."

"I didn't want him to take you."

After bringing a blanket over to her, he settled at her side and clasped her hand. "You're not to worry yourself over it."

"He told me you would be well cared for."

"I was. Ettie Trewlove was a marvel of a mum."

"Please don't hate me."

"I would never." His father, yes. This woman, no.

He was aware of Lena pouring water from the pitcher into the bowl at the washstand. Soon after, she came over, eased down onto the bed, and began wiping the woman's brow.

"Your Grace, I'd not expected to see you here."

"Perhaps you'd be so kind as not to mention my presence to anyone."

"I'm never one to gossip. I am, however, utterly embarrassed to put you to such bother."

"My lady, it's my privilege to tend to you. I'm only sorry you're feeling so poorly."

With a little cry, the countess rolled onto her side, brought her knees up, and pressed a hand to her belly. "I may retch again."

Aiden grabbed a bin and brought it over. "Do what you must. I'm going to fetch some milk. We'll see if that will help to settle your stomach."

He was quick about popping down to the kitchens to grab a pitcher of milk and a glass. When he returned to his rooms, he was alarmed to see her looking frailer, paler. It didn't help matters that Lena appeared more worried.

Sitting on the edge of the bed, he slid his arm beneath her slender shoulders and lifted her slightly, holding the glass against her lips. "Here, my lady, drink this."

With a grimace, she slowly sipped.

"That's it. Just a little at a time." He cooed with encouragement, praising her further.

After she drank a good bit and shook her head, he set the glass aside and eased her back down to the pillows. With her cloth, Lena wiped gently at the countess's mouth.

Moaning softly, Lady Elverton closed her eyes. "Will you tell me of your childhood, Mr. Trewlove?"

If she was looking to be absolved of guilt, he very much doubted she wanted to hear the truth of that, the many nights he went to bed with his gut gnawing at his spine for want of food, how callused and rough his soles became for want of shoes, how often he shivered until he feared his teeth would loosen for want of coal or a proper-fitting and less frayed jacket. "Under the circumstances, I should think you could call me Aiden."

Her mouth curled up slightly. "Luke. I thought of you as Luke. The first was Matthew. Then Mark. Luke. John. Johnny. I was able to keep Johnny, Viscount Wyeth, because I was Elverton's wife by then." The words came slowly, a breath taken between each one.

He squeezed her hand. "Save your strength, my lady, and rest easy. We'll talk later."

"I need to make things right with you. I don't know how much longer I have."

"The earl told me you were unwell," Selena said softly. "Do you know what ails you?"

"A husband who wishes to be rid of me. He favors young and beautiful women. The years have taken their toll on me and my looks have faded." Her eyelids struggled to lift as though she found them heavy as irons. Slowly she turned her gaze toward Lena. "Take care, Duchess. He'll have his eye on you."

SELENA HAD NEVER known her bones to feel so cold as she stood before the fireplace in the front parlor, striving to find some warmth in the dancing flames, while Dr. Graves, who had arrived only a short time ago, was examining the countess. Aiden sat in a nearby chair, his forearms pressed to his thighs, his head bent.

"Why didn't you leave?" he asked somberly.

As harsh as his earlier words had been, as much as they'd bludgeoned her heart, she found that she couldn't dismiss him easily, couldn't simply walk out of his life as though he meant nothing at all to her. She suspected in the future, on rare occasions, she would come to the club, simply to catch a glimpse of him. She would look forward to sharing whatever time he spent with his child. Although she'd never been comfortable with the scheme Winslow had cooked up, she hadn't fully understood the extent of its costs, hadn't realized what Aiden would come to mean to her. "The way you rushed out of here, I feared trouble was afoot. I remained in case you had need of me."

He raised his eyes to her. "Thank you for helping me with her."

"I'll just stay until the doctor is finished examining her, in case there's more I can do."

He merely nodded.

"Do you know why she came to see you?"

"I met her the night I told Elverton to steer clear of you. She lied then about being my mother. I suppose the truth of things began to weigh heavily upon her. She needed to ease her guilt."

"I can see the resemblance . . . in your eyes, the sleekness of your nose. Elverton's is rather broader."

"I thought I'd noticed similarities before, but I blamed it on my imagination and my wish she was my mother—that at long last I knew who had brought me into the world."

Her heart ached for him. "I didn't realize you yearned to know who your mother was."

He lifted a shoulder, dropped it, seemed to clutch his hands more tightly. "I think every motherless child hungers to know the tale of his origins. It's just easier to claim not to, to pretend it doesn't matter."

Which made it even more important that the babe growing within her never doubt its origins. Perhaps Aiden was correct that they should part ways. How much longer could she refrain from letting the love she felt him shine through in her eyes for all the world to see? Was it fair to ask him to wait for her for a few years, to then pretend they'd only just met?

"How do you feel knowing Viscount Wyeth is your brother?"

"I always knew he was my brother through Elverton." He studied his clasped hands. "It's an odd thing to know that we share the same mother as well."

His voice had hesitated at *mother,* and she wondered if it would have been easier to learn all this when he was younger—or to have not learned any of it at all. Would Selena's son look for similarities in Lushing's portraits? Would he hate her if he ever learned the truth regarding his existence?

Wandering over to the sideboard, she splashed some whisky into a glass and handed it off to Aiden.

He tossed back a good portion of it. "Thank you."

Kneeling before him, she placed her hands on his wrists as he did little more than clasp the glass. "Even though we are not going to continue to see each other, I want you to know—I *need* you to know—that if you are ever in want of solace or anything at all, you can come to me and I'll be there for you."

"But only in the shadows." His eyes contained enough sorrow to bring tears to hers. "Even when we arrange for me to spend time with my child— it'll have to be in such a way that no one sees us. I'm beginning to think it might be best if I simply observe from afar."

"I want you to have the opportunity to know your son—or daughter."

"And when he or she grows older, wiser, more aware of the world and begins to wonder why I have such a keen interest—"

"Because you're my friend."

He shook his head. "I wanted you so badly that I may have ignored all the possible ramifications of our actions."

She could hear in his tone the falsehood of his earlier words. He hadn't grown weary of her. "You've come to mean a great deal to me."

"For what it's worth, I won't ever forget you. But for any of us to have any semblance of a normal life—"

"I think she was poisoned," Graves announced as he came to stand before them.

As he rose to his feet, Aiden brought Selena to hers. "What do we do for her?" he asked.

"I think you've already done it by giving her

milk. I'm glad you didn't wait for my arrival." It had taken him more than an hour to get to them.

"How does milk help?" Aiden asked.

Graves cupped his elbow with one hand in order to support his arm while he rubbed his chin. "I'm not quite certain of the particulars, but it seems to neutralize the arsenic if it's not already completely digested and in the blood."

"Arsenic? What? She had a mishap applying her face creams or powders?"

Selena could see that raging fury was rushing through Aiden as his eyes burned.

"She said she was feeling perfectly well until tonight, and as this came on quite suddenly, I suspect it was placed in her food or drink during dinner," Graves said.

"By whom?" Aiden demanded.

"That's the question, isn't it?"

"The Earl of Elverton," Selena said quietly. "He came to see me recently, propositioning me again. I assured him I wouldn't become his mistress."

"Why didn't you tell me?" Aiden asked.

"Because I didn't want you confronting him, earning his ire. He's a powerful man, and I thought I'd put an end to it. But now I have to wonder if I merely gave him cause to strive to make a place for me as his wife. To show that he could."

Aiden met the doctor's gaze. "Is there a way to prove he poisoned her?"

"In a household such as his, even if we could locate the food laced with poison, with so many servants about, he'd point the finger elsewhere."

"Then I'll deal with him."

"That tone indicates a man who will do something

foolish that will see him ending his life on the gallows. Talk with Chief Inspector Swindler at Scotland Yard. He may have some ideas."

"What if we could get him to confess?" Selena asked.

Aiden narrowed his eyes. "And how would we do that?"

"If my suspicions are correct, and he did this as a way to win me over, if I were to invite him over for tea, perhaps he would feel a need to share the lengths he will go to in order to have me."

"No. I want you nowhere near the bastard."

"I wouldn't be alone. You and the chief inspector would be on hand, hidden away somewhere, listening, as it would be important that an officer of the law hear his words."

"No."

"Aiden—"

"For two reasons, Lena. First, the risk to you is far too great. He could very well run mad when he discovers you—we—duped him and harm you. And second, if he is found guilty of committing a crime for which he would hang—and trust me, I would not at all mind seeing him hang—I believe there is a chance the Crown would take his title and properties, which would leave his heir with nothing."

Her eyes softened. "And you won't do that to your brother, even though you don't know him."

Aiden gave a brisk nod. "Finn and I will deal with him, and he will rue the day we were ever born."

SHE HAD NO reason to stay, and yet Selena couldn't bring herself to leave. If she hadn't fallen in love with Aiden before, she would have done so tonight as she watched the gentleness with which he tended his mother, wiping her brow, ensuring she drank more milk. Told her pleasant tales from his childhood about a dog he'd once had, his love of mincemeat pies, the books he enjoyed reading.

Selena sat in a nearby chair, knowing he was painting a pretty picture of his life for this woman so she would harbor no guilt for not having raised him herself.

"My brothers and I were always getting up to some mischief, Gillie usually tagging along behind us. Mum managed to keep a roof over our heads, food in our bellies, and clothes on our backs. Shoes were sometimes an issue, but I never minded going barefoot. I liked all the different textures my feet would encounter, and I could run faster without the weight." His eyes met and held Selena's, and she remembered how insistent he'd been about removing her shoes that first night. She wondered if he'd ever frolicked barefoot in clover. She wished they'd had an opportunity to go on a picnic near a river.

"You loved the woman who took you in," the countess said weakly.

"I still do. The way she cared for us, you'd have not thought she hadn't given birth to us."

"I wanted that for you. After we married, I asked him if he would bring my children back to me, but he couldn't remember where he'd taken you all. There were other mistresses you see, other babes. I always made excuses for him. He was a man of strong needs and urges. He had such vitality. How could one woman satisfy him?"

"You told me you loved him."

"I did . . . when I had a young heart. Then he

broke it too many times. It is naught now but cracks and fissures into which regret takes root."

Selena wondered if a time would come when she would regret the bargains she'd made, the deception she would perpetrate. Already she was feeling a tiny crack in her heart because Aiden would not be in her life.

"You're not going back to him," Aiden said quietly. "You'll stay here until you're strong enough and then I'll find accommodations for you elsewhere."

"I need to let Johnny know."

"I will handle the matter. Don't worry yourself. Try to sleep."

"You're such a good boy."

But Selena knew he was an exceptionally good man.

When the countess finally drifted off, Aiden looked across the way at Selena and jerked his head to the side. She followed him into the front parlor.

"You need to be getting home," he said quietly. "Dawn will be arriving soon."

"I don't understand how Elverton can be so callous, so vile. If your mother hadn't come here, she might have died. And who would have been the wiser regarding the circumstances behind her death?"

"She's with me now. And I will keep her safe."

She didn't doubt his words or his ability to do just that. "When are you going to confront Elverton?"

"Tonight. I'll keep the countess here until that matter is done."

"When all this is behind you, perhaps we can discuss our future."

"We don't have a future, Lena. We never did."

"I can't just cast you aside."

"You are too vibrant a woman to live your public life alone and without escort."

"Perhaps there's another way."

He shook his head. "You need to leave."

"Will you at least give me one last kiss?"

She shouldn't have asked but as he joined his mouth to hers, she was ever so glad she had. It was bittersweet to know it was the last and to know it would never be enough.

When he drew back, she gave him a soft smile, then turned on her heel and walked out of his life and into the one she had thought she wanted.

Chapter 23

*T*he Earl of Elverton poured himself a scotch, dropped into a chair in his library, and brooded. Late last night, while he'd been at his club, his wife had called for a carriage. The vehicle and driver had yet to return. No one seemed to know where his countess had gone.

All day and into evening, he considered his dilemma. Was it better to sound the alarm and have people searching for her or to wait until someone came to inform him that she was dead? Because she would die, was probably already staring sightlessly into oblivion. Perhaps she'd expired in the carriage and the driver was too terrified to return her to the residence. Or she'd passed elsewhere and had yet to be found.

He would be shocked, of course, horrified, bereaved.

He wanted Polly, to become lost in her, but it would not do to be caught plowing into her when news came regarding the demise of his countess. His time would be better spent planning his lies, his disbelief, his sorrow. There was a small chance she still lived. If she returned to the residence . . . well, more direct measures might be called for because he was determined, one way or another, that Selena Sheffield, Duchess of Lushing, would become his wife within the year.

AIDEN HAD GONE to Finn's farm and explained the situation to him, knowing his brother wouldn't hesitate to saddle a horse and accompany him to Elverton's residence. They didn't bother to knock on the door, but simply strode in and demanded the butler tell them where they'd find the earl. Dismissing him, not waiting for an introduction, they marched down the hallway and into the library, where the toad who had sired them sat in a chair by the fireplace, glass in hand, sipping an amber liquid.

He released an impatient gust of air. "I rid myself of you bastards so I wouldn't be bothered with you. You're making a nuisance of yourselves."

"Was your countess making a nuisance of herself?" Aiden asked. "Is that the reason you poisoned her?"

The earl went so still it was impossible to tell if he even breathed. "I did no such thing. Is she dead, then?"

Aiden lunged forward, grabbed the armrests, and caged in the vile excuse for a man. "She came to me. I nursed her through the night. But Dr. William Graves confirms she was given arsenic, probably during dinner."

"It must have been a servant. I'll let go the lot of them."

Grabbing his lapels, Aiden jerked him out of the

chair with such force that his glass went flying before crashing to the floor. "I know it was you."

The old man shoved himself free. "You can't prove it. You can't prove anything."

"We're well aware of that, but that doesn't mean we can't see justice done."

"Touch me again, and I'll have you arrested. It is against the law to strike a lord."

"Think you we care about your threats? She is my mother."

"Who asked me to rid her of you so she could continue to live in luxury."

That wasn't what she'd told Aiden. He'd been taken from her. He placed more value on her words.

"That damned Trewlove woman was supposed to kill you both. I should ask her for recompense."

Aiden's fist struck fast and hard, square in the middle of his sire's face, sending the man reeling back and landing with a hard thud on the floor.

Finn was there, slipping his arms beneath the man's shoulders, helping him to his feet. Once the lord was steady, Finn rapidly locked the earl's arms behind him and held him in place.

"What the devil—"

Aiden sank his balled hand into the pudgy gut. The sound of flesh pounding into flesh and the grunt were both satisfying to his ears. "Your wife is under our protection now."

Another strike. Another *oof!* "She won't be returning to you."

He would set her up in a room at Mick's hotel until he could work out other accommodations. Shrugging out of his jacket, he tossed it onto the desk and rolled his shoulders.

"You have no right," the earl yelled, his face blotchy and red.

"We protect what is ours." Aiden didn't restrain himself as he delivered another solid blow.

The earl's legs buckled, but Finn clenched his jaw and continued to keep him upright.

"I'll see you both hanged!"

"We'll see you dead first." He didn't plan to kill the man, but he was going to leave him hurting. He pummeled him three times, taking satisfaction in the grunt and groans. Stepping back, he nodded at Finn, who immediately released his hold. The earl dropped to the floor like a sack of potatoes tossed into the cupboard. His face was blotchy red with anger, his eyes bulging with hatred, his breathing labored as though even the air sought to avoid being in his presence.

Aiden crouched in front of him. "You'll stay away from the Duchess of Lushing. You'll stay away from your wife. As a matter of fact, I believe you're going to steer clear of all your mistresses as well. We're going to keep a close watch on you and won't hesitate to visit you again to make our position clear."

"You bast—bast—ba . . ." His mouth went slack and one side of his face seemed to melt as it drooped and he made murmurs of distress.

Finn knelt beside Aiden. "What the devil is wrong with him?"

The blows might have rendered him immobile for a time, but this reaction was more than that. With his gaze distant and his eyes glazed over, it didn't seem the earl was with them any longer, but he certainly wasn't dead.

"Could it be apoplexy?" Aiden asked.

"It's possible, I suppose. If so, I shall take no pity on him."

"Neither will I. He's brought far worse hell to others."

GRAVES HAD ARRIVED and gone to the earl's bed-chamber to examine him. Aiden had gone to the club to inform the countess of what had transpired, and she'd returned with him to the manor. Aiden and Finn sat with her in the front parlor, awaiting the physician's diagnosis.

The slamming of the front door echoed through the residence, and they all came to their feet as a young man rushed into the parlor. Aiden didn't need an introduction to know he was Viscount Wyeth. He saw himself reflected in the man's brown hair, dark eyes, and strong jaw.

"Mother." He had his arms around the countess before the word was completely uttered. "I left my club as soon as I received your missive about Father. How does he fair?"

Aiden knew a pang of unjustified envy at the evidence of their close relationship. She wasn't his mother. His mum was Ettie Trewlove. Yet, he couldn't help but believe that he would have found her arms as welcoming as he did his mum's.

"Dr. Graves is with him now. We hope to hear shortly."

Wyeth leaned back and studied her. "You don't look too chipper yourself."

"I've been a bit under the weather, but I'm all right now."

"Your father tried to poison her," Aiden told him.

"My God!" Wyeth appeared horrified and incensed as he studied his mother more intently. "Is this true?"

"I fear so, although I have no proof. I was poisoned, yes. Dr. Graves can attest to that fact, but I can't prove your father was the culprit. I'd be dead now if not for Aiden."

"Aiden?"

"Your brother," the countess said softly, looking toward him.

Wyeth's gaze landed on him so hard that Aiden was surprised he didn't hear a thud. The man's eyes traveled the length of him, his curiosity obvious. "One of my father's bastards that I've heard rumors about?"

"And one of mine as well." The countess's voice was quiet, but Aiden heard no shame mirrored in it. She was merely stating fact.

Her legitimate son's gaze swung back to her, a corner of his mouth hiking up laconically. "So those rumors are also true."

Aiden doubted the man saw him as a threat in any way because children born out of wedlock were not allowed to inherit, even if the parents eventually married. Only those born *within* the union of a marriage had any rights, so Wyeth would still inherit his father's titles and properties.

She nodded. "Allow me to introduce Mr. Aiden Trewlove."

"Trewlove. That's a name that seems to be on everyone's lips these days. I don't know whether to be delighted to make your acquaintance or appalled."

"Appalled is probably the safer way to go," Finn assured him, drawing Wyeth's attention.

"Another bastard, I assume, as I see Father's likeness in you as well," the young lordling said. He looked at his mother. "Also yours?"

She shook her head.

"Finn was born about six weeks after I was," Aiden said.

"Your father always did have strong appetites." The countess had some color in her cheeks now, perhaps because she'd spoken of something so intimate. "It was unusual for him to be satisfied with . . . one . . . lady." Her voice had gone faint as she went pale and began to sway.

Both Aiden and Wyeth reached her at the same time, assisting her onto the settee.

"My apologies. It seems I'm not as recovered as I thought."

"Here." Finn held out a glass of water he'd retrieved from a table that housed several decanters.

Taking it from him, Aiden wrapped his mother's fingers around it. "You need to drink this, get some fluids into you. Dr. Graves's orders."

"Yours as well it seems. Your mother raised you boys well." Following his command, she slowly sipped.

Sitting beside her, Wyeth took her free hand. His concern was evident in his eyes and the gentleness with which he treated her. "Why didn't you come to me when you realized what Father had done to you?"

"I didn't realize, not at first. I simply thought I'd eaten something that had gone bad. I went to Aiden's club to speak with him, to confess he was my son . . . only I worsened, and he saw to me."

"Well, you're not staying here. You'll come to my

residence where you'll be safe." He shook his head, his jaw taut. "I suppose he sought to rid himself of you because someone younger, equally beautiful caught his fancy. The Duchess of Lushing, perhaps. I saw him follow her out into the garden on the day the duke was laid to rest. I wanted to give him the benefit of the doubt—that he sought to console her. But I would not be at all surprised to discover he'd propositioned her. I should have gone after him."

"He's not your responsibility, sweetheart. Although I suspect you are correct when it comes to the duchess. I, too, saw him follow her into the garden. And before that I saw the lust in his eyes when he looked at her."

Aiden had a strong urge to go up to the bedchamber and give his sire another solid thrashing, only this time he might not stop until the man ceased to draw breath. He'd known the earl had approached Lena, but hearing it all again only served to rekindle his anger.

"I've been expecting him to do something for some time." The countess looked up at Aiden. "Another reason I didn't object to that tart he brings here. My amenability ensured I drew breath a while longer. For some time I've suspected he disposed of his first wife to make room for me."

"Bastard," his two illegitimate sons growled, at the same moment his heir proclaimed, "Rotter."

Wyeth shoved himself to his feet and began to pace, clearly agitated, his fists clenched. "We'll have to find a way to deal with Father. I haven't it within me to kill him." With a nod, he came to a halt and faced them. "But I could see that he is committed to an asylum. He is obviously not well and is a danger. I will not allow my mother to be put at further risk."

"If what Finn and I witnessed regarding his apoplectic fit is any indication," Aiden said, "I don't think he's going to be capable of creating much havoc in the future."

"So how is it that you two happen to be here?" Wyeth asked, returning to his mother's side.

After settling into a chair, Aiden explained the entire story, including the beating he'd given the old man.

"I wish I'd been here with you to deliver a few blows of my own. I've lived my entire life ashamed to be called his son. He flaunts his mistresses, spends a fortune keeping them in residences, clothes, and baubles. Disposes of the children they bring into the world."

"*Dispose* is a rather harsh term," the countess said. "He finds loving homes for them. Aiden and Finn here are proof of that."

Wyeth glanced over at Aiden, and he could see the battle the young man was facing. Did he hide the truth from this woman he loved?

"No, Mother. I fear they are the exception. When he is in his cups, he gets rather loud, likes to hear the sound of his voice, wants others to hear it as well. On occasion, I've heard him advise others on how to rid themselves of their by-blows so as never to be inconvenienced by them again."

"But he promised me."

"Perhaps he made an exception for you."

But Aiden could tell from Wyeth's tone that he didn't think exceptions were made. How fortunate he and Finn were to have been given over to Ettie Trewlove.

"I always imagined his heir had a charmed life," Finn said.

Wyeth snorted. "When he gave me attention, which was rare, it was usually to find fault or to reiterate how I was falling short of his expectations. He was the better cricket player, the better yachtsman, the more skilled horseman. The better shot. It was as though we were always in competition. And when I did best him, he would get angry and somehow find fault with my achievement. It got to the point where I no longer cared if I pleased him."

Footsteps sounded, increasing in volume as someone descended the stairs. With a somberness hovering around him, Graves walked into the parlor. The men stood while Lady Elverton remained seated. Aiden wasn't certain what message Graves communicated to Wyeth, but the young man moved aside, and Graves joined the countess on the sofa, taking her hand. "As we feared, Lord Elverton has suffered apoplexy. Quite severely. A good bit of his body has gone numb. He seems to have lost his ability to speak. I fear, dear lady, that he is presently bedridden, and I do not hold out much hope that situation will change."

With very little expression revealed, the countess nodded sagely, as though she'd expected his dire words. "How long? How long will he suffer?"

"It's difficult to tell. It could be as short as a few hours or as long as several years."

As unkind as it was, Aiden hoped for years. He wanted the man to have nothing else to do but ponder his actions and live with the unhappiness he'd brought others.

"Is there no treatment?" Wyeth asked.

Graves shifted his attention over to the viscount. "I fear not, my lord. You could hire a nurse to see to him, move his limbs about so the muscles don't atrophy on the off chance he gains the ability to use them again."

"No," the countess said. "We'll have no need to hire a nurse. He is my husband and I shall tend to him. His valet can handle the unpleasant tasks such as washing him up and keeping him tidy. I'll increase his salary."

"Extreme patience is required to attend to the needs of an invalid," the doctor told her kindly.

"Tending to any of my husband's needs has always required significant patience."

"Lady Elverton—"

She patted his hand gently. "Do not worry yourself, Doctor. I won't slip arsenic into his food. I will do naught to hasten his demise."

He nodded. "How are you feeling, my lady?"

Her smile was gentle and kind. Aiden imagined she might have looked at him that way when he was a lad and got into a scrape—had he been allowed to remain in her life. "Weary. But I have my sons to look after me. We shall persevere in the face of this tragedy."

Two things struck Aiden. That she didn't view this turn of events as a tragedy at all. And that she was referencing him as her son.

Graves must have concluded to whom she was referring or perhaps she'd confessed to him while he was tending her, but in either case he shifted his gaze between Wyeth and Aiden before rising to his feet. "Then I leave you in their care. Send for me if you have a need."

She rose gracefully to her feet. "Thank you, Doctor. Johnny, will you be good enough to see him out?"

"I can see myself out. Thank you, my lady." He gave a brisk nod. "Gentlemen."

Then he strode from the room. No one moved until the front door made a hushed *thunk* as it was closed, no doubt as a result of the physician's effort not to disturb them further.

Without a word, Lord Wyeth went to the decanters and poured his mother a sherry. Then he offered Aiden and Finn each a glass of scotch. "Make yourselves comfortable, gentlemen."

They seated themselves while Wyeth took a glass of scotch for himself before dropping down into a chair with a gust of a sigh. "Well, that's that, then."

"You'll need to take over all your father's duties," the countess said.

Wyeth lifted a slender shoulder. "That won't be much of a bother. I've been taking on more responsibilities of late anyway." He studied Aiden. "Are you the bastard who was paying my father a princely sum each month?"

Most people spat the term *bastard* as though it left a foul taste in their mouths, but Wyeth wove a semblance of respect around it as though it reflected a badge of honor.

"Until Finn here visited him a few months back and put an end to it."

He nodded with what appeared to be admiration at Finn. "Are you, then, the bastard who broke his arm?"

"I am."

"Did he cry out?"

"Screamed like a baby."

The viscount grinned. "I imagine he did." He brought his attention back to Aiden. "How did he manage to extort you?"

"Finn was arrested for stealing a horse he didn't steal. They were going to transport him to Australia. I knew the earl had influence. So I asked for his help, wrongly believing he would care that his blood was being sent halfway around the world. He'd only do it if I paid him a portion of the earnings from my gambling establishment."

"So Finn went free for a fee."

"No," Finn said curtly. "I wasn't transported but I served five years in prison."

Wyeth scoffed. "Naturally. Our father is not known for going beyond the bare minimum—"

"He's not our *father*," Aiden said.

The viscount's scrutiny was long and assessing, but Aiden never averted his gaze. Rather he met it head-on with an assessment of his own. He saw very little in this man's mannerisms reminiscent of the earl's, found his concern, loyalty, and devotion for his mother to be redeeming qualities.

"No, I suppose he's not." Wyeth tossed back his scotch. "Be grateful for that. Your records regarding how much you gave him are probably far more accurate than his regarding how much he took from you. Send me the figures and I'll see that every farthing is returned to you."

Aiden exchanged a surprised glance with Finn before looking over at . . . his mother. He supposed he could refer to her as that without feeling guilty about not reserving that particular affiliation for his mum. The countess seemed rather relaxed, with a small smile playing over her lips as though she was enjoying watching the exchange. "I was under the impression that the earl's financial situation is a . . . challenge."

His brother—his full brother—grinned. "His is. Mine is not. Whenever he and I would get into a row regarding the near empty coffers, he would give me a portion of your payment in an effort to bring me to heel, so I would learn how difficult it is to manage money. In addition, to punish my defiance, he placed the running of the estate into my hands so I would see how far the coins would *not* go. He, however, taking very little interest in my affairs, remained unaware that some friends and I are very keen on investing. And we're quite good at it."

The last was said very simply. A fact. Not a boasting. And Aiden realized he could come to like this fellow very much indeed.

Lord Wyeth leaned earnestly toward him. "You should not have been required to pay him to see to his duty regarding his *son*. I have lived my life with the rumors that he has over a dozen bastards. That he spread them around London as one might manure. He is not a man who commands respect among his peers, which made me all the more determined to be one who does. I believe in paying my debts. I would not be living as comfortably now as I do if not for what you paid him. To be honest I should have sought you out some time ago, but I wasn't quite certain you'd welcome the one he kept."

"You had no choice in that. None of us had any choice. But I would say we all made the best of our circumstances." He came to his feet. "Now that we know you'll be safe, countess, Finn and I are going to take our leave."

"I'm glad you all were finally able to meet," she said. "I hope something lasting can develop between you."

Aiden grinned at the viscount. "Our sister Gillie owns a tavern, the Mermaid and Unicorn. You'll have to join us there for a drink sometime."

"I'd like that very much."

He turned his attention back to the woman who'd given birth to him. "If you find yourself in need of anything at all, send word to me."

"Perhaps you'll join me for dinner sometime."

"I won't be a stranger. I promise you that. I'll stop by tomorrow to see how you're doing."

"I keep hoping I'll find a list of where Elverton took all the children, but I fear for him once they were out of sight, they were out of mind. But I know from experience that they never left their mother's hearts."

"I LIKE OUR brother," Finn said.

They were sitting at a back table at the Mermaid and Unicorn, downing their pints as though tomorrow all beer and ale would be banned from Britain. They'd gone up to see Elverton before leaving. Aiden had expected to feel some sort of satisfaction at seeing the earl so helpless with his sagging features. Instead, he'd merely felt sad that such a vile excuse for a human being had ever existed.

"I don't know how he managed to turn out halfway decent. I do know I'm glad the bugger didn't keep me."

Finn grinned. "The rotter."

Aiden laughed. God, it felt good to laugh. "Right. The rotter."

"Our brother might be in need of a bit of corrupting."

"And you, as the irritatingly happily married man, are just the one to do it."

"Point made. Those days are behind me."

They both sipped in silence for a while.

"Your blows didn't cause his apoplexy," Finn finally said.

"No, but our presence did. His face was red with fury and hatred. He despised us."

"We were a reminder of his sins."

"I don't think he cared anything about sinning. I think he just didn't want to be bothered by us. We were an inconvenience."

"I'm glad he gave us away and never publicly acknowledged us. He's despicable. I wouldn't want to be associated with him." He took a swallow of his beer. "Your mother, though—she seemed decent enough."

"Made mistakes in her youth, though."

"Didn't we all?"

"I'm sorry the countess didn't know who your mother might be."

"I never cared about my origins as much as you and Mick." He finished off his pint, slammed it on the table. "I'm going to order another. Care to join me?"

Aiden glanced around. "No, I have something I need to do."

"Say hello to her for me."

He narrowed his eyes. "You're bloody irritating, you know that?"

Finn had the audacity to grin. "That's what brothers are for."

LADY ELVERTON SAT on the edge of the bed and tenderly skimmed her fingers along her husband's cheek, remembering how she had once loved him enough to disobey her father, to dishonor her family. How she'd allowed him to take her first three sons from her. He'd never had much patience with children, and she suspected if he hadn't needed an heir, he might have been content with his first wife, barren though she'd been. "Blink once for yes."

He blinked.

"Twice for no."

Blink. Blink.

"Do you know who I am?"

Blink.

She cradled the jaw she had once peppered in kisses—when she was younger, more svelte, when he found her attractive. Before he'd begun bringing other women, other mistresses, into his bed within this chamber, knowing she could hear them through the wall, screaming out his name. He required that benediction. His name on their tongue at the moment of their release. She'd granted him the same favor a thousand times, even when the ultimate pleasure had eluded her. "The three bastards I placed in your arms, the ones you would not allow me to keep, they were your blood. You do know that, don't you?"

Blink.

Leaning down, she placed a kiss on his forehead, one on his temple, the last near the shell of his ear. "The heir I gave you . . . was not."

It was a lie, of course, but it would torment him, occupy his thoughts as he lay there with an active mind but an inactive body. With a self-satisfied smile, she rose from the bed and looked down on him.

Blink. Blink. Blink.

A strangling, gurgling sound in his throat.

"Careful now, darling," she warned calmly. "You don't want to have another apoplectic fit, surely."

Lovingly, she brought up the covers, tucked them in around him. "Now if you will be so good as to excuse my rudeness, I must leave you as my lover awaits."

Then ignoring his warbling of distress, she strolled from the room, her head held high, feeling her strength returning in full force. In her bedchamber, she took *Sense and Sensibility* from her night table, curled up in a chair, and turned to the page marked with a blue ribbon. Over the years, she'd had dozens of lovers, all found within the pages of novels. Her favorite was Colonel Brandon, and it was he who would keep her company this night.

But in the future, who knew? Perhaps she'd take on a real lover. Here, within this bedchamber, where her husband could hear her cries of pleasure. Ah, yes, she would torment him as he'd tormented her.

She would even visit Aiden's club, enjoy all the vices he offered. No longer would she live in fear of displeasing her husband, of displeasing any man. She would seek and find the happiness and joy that had eluded her for a good portion of her life.

SELENA WASN'T SURPRISED when the door to her bedchamber quietly opened a little after midnight and Aiden wandered in, closing and locking it behind him. Setting aside the book she'd been reading, she was grateful that he'd come to her, had hoped he would.

Confronting his father—his sire—had to have created an emotional turmoil within him.

Tossing off the covers, she slipped out of the bed, meeting him halfway, closing her arms around him as his circled her, holding her near. His sigh was long, drawn out, and she could feel the tension easing out of him.

"I have whisky," she whispered. She'd brought up a bottle and a glass, just in case he came to her.

"All I need is you."

His words humbling her, her heart squeezed as tightly as her eyes. Lifting her mouth to him, she waited as he lowered his to hers. No fire, no passion, only want and intense need. She could comfort him now as she'd wanted to from the moment Lady Elverton had revealed who she was. In spite of Aiden telling Selena that things were over between them, she did not have it within her to ever turn him away. Their discussion last night had escalated beyond her control, and in spite of harsh words uttered, still she'd known he could come to her. Still she'd been willing to welcome him.

Not releasing her hold on him, she guided them backward until her bottom hit the mattress. Easing away slightly, she cradled his beloved face between her hands, seeing in his countenance all three of his parents. The Earl and Countess of Elverton were responsible for the hills, valleys, and dips, the strong jaw, the sharp nose, the lush mouth, the shade of his eyes. But Ettie Trewlove had shaped the soul those eyes reflected, the smile that came so easily, the laugh that had first sung to her own soul. The physical features were nothing without the light that shone within him. Yes, there was a darkness to it, but it wasn't powerful enough to put out the flame, only to reshape it and make him more complicated and faceted.

Lowering her hands, she slid them beneath his jacket and shoved it over his shoulders, down his arms until it fell to the floor. His cravat went next, followed by his waistcoat. He didn't move, only aided her in the divesting of his clothing. She wondered if he was in shock from what had happened with his father or if he was uncertain regarding how she might welcome him.

When he was nude before her, she unbuttoned her nightdress and shimmied out of it before taking his hand, climbing onto the bed, and urging him to follow.

Only one night had passed without their coming together, and already it had begun to feel an eternity. As his body covered hers, her moan was low, appreciative, grateful. The feel of him was everything.

His taking of her was slow and sensual, his kisses and touches alighting upon every inch of her skin as though he was memorizing every hollow, every ridge. As though he were well aware that this time would be the last, and he wanted it unrushed, wanted it emblazoned on his soul to carry with him as one might a well-worn miniature portrait. To be looked upon and savored.

And she returned the favor, touching all she

could reach, pressing her mouth to his throat and shoulders, scraping her fingers over his back, skimming her soles along his calves.

When he plunged deeply, she was more than ready. Rising up, hovering over her, holding her gaze, he moved languorously in and out, as though they had the entire night, as though he didn't need to sneak out before the servants were up and moving about.

So much needed to be said. So much needed to be held in.

Lifting herself up, she licked at the hollow of his throat where dew gathered, took satisfaction in his low growl. Lowering herself, she wrapped her arms and legs around him, tightening her hold, pumping her hips in rhythm with his, as sensations built and everything within her cried out for him.

She thought she could contain the fire forming inside her, but when it broke free and engulfed her, he blanketed her mouth with his, capturing her scream as she absorbed his groan, their bodies stiffening and jerking in tandem as pleasure conquered them both.

REPLETE AND EXHAUSTED, he lay on his back with Selena nestled against his side, her finger drawing lazy circles on his chest. He shouldn't have come, but he'd been unable to stay away.

He'd needed her as the earth needed the sun and the night sky needed the stars.

He remembered a time when sharing a pint with Finn would have been enough, would have put him in the right frame of mind to carry on, but tonight he'd required more. He'd required her.

Gently she picked up his hand where it rested on his abdomen and brought it to her lips. "Your knuckles are bruising. You hit Elverton."

"Several times."

"Is he going to leave your mother be?"

"He doesn't have a choice. He had an apoplectic fit. Finn says it wasn't my fault, that it was his anger, not my fist, that caused it."

Rising up on an elbow, she brushed the hair from his brow. "How bad?"

"He can't move, can't speak. I almost told him that you were carrying my child, that my son would be a duke. But I realized I no longer cared what he thought. I always hoped if I achieved enough, perhaps he'd recognize me publicly. But there is no value to be found in having his regard."

She eased over until her thigh was nestled between his legs and half her body covered a portion of his. "You're nothing like him, you know. You're a much better man. More honest, more real, more caring."

But he had no title, no prestige. Being associated with a Trewlove did not elevate one's status in Society. Even Gillie, who had married a duke, was not yet accepted by the nobs. If Lena wanted her sisters to marry nobility, Aiden was not the one to see that happen.

Reaching down, he flattened his palm over her belly. "Have you felt him?"

She placed her hand over his. "It's too soon."

He was disappointed not to have the opportunity to feel his child wiggling around, and that disappointment surprised him. He'd never given any thought to having a child because he'd taken so many precautions not to have one. Now he rather liked the idea of his growing within her.

"Aiden, we don't have to stop seeing each other right away."

"It's best, Lena, if we call it quits now. I shouldn't have come here tonight." Easing her off him, he shoved himself to a sitting position and dropped his legs over the side of the bed.

She splayed her fingers over his back. "I'm glad you did."

He wanted to roll over and take her again, which was the reason he needed to leave. Because he would always want to take her again. Would always want one more word with her. Would always want to hold her one last time. Would always long for another kiss.

Snatching up his clothes, he began to get dressed. "Will you send word after he's born?"

"You don't think our paths will cross before then?"

Keeping his back to her, he didn't need to see her to know sadness was reflected in her eyes, because he heard it in her tone. "I don't see how they would."

"I could open a shop—"

"Don't, Lena." He did look back at her then, this incredible woman who had stolen his heart. "It'll only get harder if we continue to see each other."

"It's hard now, Aiden. When I agreed to this stupid plan Winslow concocted, I always thought I could just walk away. I wasn't supposed to fall in love with you."

He slammed his eyes closed as those five words— *fall in love with you*—words no other woman had ever bestowed on him, washed over him, through

him, around him. How powerful they were. How
humbling. How breathtaking.

If he gave them back to her, if he told her how
much she meant to him, they would be lost. Forever.
Irrevocably. Lost.

He was her secret. That made him easier to love.
How much more difficult would it be with Society's
censure surrounding them?

He opened his eyes. "Words easy to utter within
the safe confines of the shadows. My businesses
succeed because I know what people want to do in
secret. A duchess can have a bit of the rough with
no one the wiser. A bastard can have a duchess.
What can seem wonderful in the dark can have dire
consequences in the light. You deserve better than
a life hidden away from even those you care about."
Such as her sisters.

When his clothes were set to right, he reached out
and cupped her chin, pressed his thumb to her lush
lips. She hadn't bothered to cover herself but just sat
there like a nymph tempting the gods, and it took
all his inner strength not to glide his hand over her
silky skin. "Goodbye, sweetheart."

While everything within him urged him to stay,
he strode from the room leaving nothing behind except his heart.

Chapter 24

$\mathcal{S}$elena sat on a wrought-iron bench in the garden, watching as Connie and Flo played a game of croquet, their squeals and laughter floating around them. Beside her, Alice was reading *Through the Looking-Glass*.

A week had passed since she'd seen Aiden, a week in which loneliness had been a constant companion, in spite of her sisters' presence. She slept with her arms folded around the pillow that carried his scent, but the fragrance was fading with each breath she inhaled. A time would come when the only aspect of him that remained in her life was the child presently growing in her belly. She would forever be grateful for that gift. Still, she missed Aiden with an ache that hurt her chest.

She glanced over at Alice. "I'd have thought you'd have finished reading that book by now."

With a Cheshire cat–like smile, Alice lifted her head and looked at her. "Oh I have. I'm simply reading it again. Would you like to borrow it?"

She'd already experienced the character Alice's adventure of stepping into a world so very different from her own. Slowly, she shook her head. "No, thank you."

Alice's brow furrowed slightly. "It's odd but you

seem sadder of late, sadder than you were when Lushing first passed away."

"I suppose it's just the reality hitting home."

"The reality that you're not with child?"

She had yet to tell her sisters, to tell anyone, of her condition. Once she did, once she credited this child with being Lushing's—

Why was it so hard to move forward, to carry through with the plans? She wished she could talk with Lushing, although he would no doubt suggest they get Kit's opinion on the matter. Perhaps she should speak with him. Surely, he would know if Lushing would hate her for the deception. "I'm not yet certain of my state."

Alice closed her book. "Have you had your menses since Lushing passed?"

"It could be melancholy preventing it." Only it wasn't.

"Perhaps you should visit a physician."

Her sister's voice was laced with true concern. Selena should put an end to her worry, to all their worries, by telling them a babe was on the way. But the words simply knotted in her throat, would not spill forth. Although when Winslow had visited several nights ago and asked if she were with child, she hadn't denied it, had simply asked him to hold his tongue for a while longer.

"Why? The sooner word spreads, the more likely people will believe it's Lushing's," he'd told her.

So she couldn't be sure he wasn't already whispering about her condition around Town. Which was no doubt the best way for it to be spread: in whispers. No woman would be indelicate enough to blurt out she was with child.

"I'll visit one next week," she told Alice now. "After that, perhaps we'll return to Sheffield Hall." No point in staying in London where her sisters would be aware of all the social events they were missing out on.

Alice scooted up to the edge of her chair. "We need to do something to brighten your day. Let's go to Fancy's bookshop. I've been dying to see it now that it's open."

"Sweeting, I'm still in mourning."

"We all are. It's the reason we're dressed like crows, but it's doubtful we'll run into anyone we know there, and we can make it a somber excursion. We'll only look at books that deal with death or war or murder."

Alice's enthusiasm made her smile, although Selena had no desire to read books about murder since she'd nearly witnessed one firsthand. Although she wasn't presently involved in the social scene, she did occasionally get a visitor. It seemed there were no rumors going about regarding the Earl of Elverton's attempt to poison his wife. Her visitors did mention his unfortunate turn in health and the dedication of the countess in caring for him. One lady had admitted to seeing her waltzing at the Elysium. Selena was happy for the countess, hoped the gents at the club spoiled her with their attention. "I suppose a tranquil outing isn't uncalled for."

Alice popped up out of her seat. "I'll let the others know."

While she dashed off to tell Connie and Flo, Selena went upstairs to retrieve her veiled bonnet. Yes, getting out of here would do her some good.

After pinning her hat in place, she picked up her

reticule, surprised by the weight of it. Then she remembered the key to Aiden's chambers was still in her possession. She was torn between giving it back to him and placing it in her jewelry box to be looked at occasionally, a reminder of a time in her life during which she'd been remarkably happy.

But it was not hers to keep. While she could package it up and have it sent to him, she decided she wanted to deliver it personally, along with a small gift. After lying to her sisters once more by telling them she'd suddenly come down with a megrim and sending them on their way without her, she headed out to the shops.

THAT EVENING AFTER the girls were abed, she donned her blue gown and mask, finding comfort in the familiarity of it. A peace that had been elusive settled over her as the coach carried her to the Elysium Club. Her nerves had been frayed that first night, until she'd seen him, and then it had rather felt as though her heart had come home.

A silly thought, but then with him, she'd always felt truly revealed and understood—even when she'd held secrets from him. And when those had been uncovered, still he hadn't turned her away. She wasn't certain anyone had ever accepted her as he did, foibles and all.

When the carriage came to a stop in front of the club and the driver handed her down, she instructed him to wait where he was because she wouldn't be but a minute.

Then she strolled into the foyer, striving not to remember how her heart would always give a small hitch of anticipation at the prospect of seeing him whenever she walked through the door. She stopped at the counter where normally she handed her wrap off to Angie. "Don't send word to him that I'm here."

Angie blinked with confusion, her brow furrowing. "As you wish."

Selena made her way to the stairs, climbing them for what would be the very last time. Her body didn't seem to know what her mind realized because it began growing warm as though heated by a sensual flush. Yearning swept through her. The desire she'd always longed for was now a burden, but still she regretted not a single touch, not a single moment that had taught her about the fire that could truly burn between a man and a woman.

At the top of the stairs, she skirted the edge of the hallway until she reached his rooms. Removing the key from her reticule, she unlocked the door and crossed over the threshold, inhaling deeply the fragrance of Aiden, allowing it to fill her lungs, to penetrate her blood, to inhabit her once more.

A solitary lit lamp on the table near the window, the table that had once been covered in white linen and displayed strawberries, held enough shadows at bay that she was able to walk into his bedchamber. The bed was neatly made, and she had a strong urge to muss it up, to see it in disarray as it had been so many times in the past.

Carefully on a pillow, she placed the package containing the fine leather gloves she'd purchased that afternoon. On top of that she laid his key. They would greet Aiden when he was ready to lay down his head, which no doubt wouldn't be for several more hours.

That task done, she had no reason to stay. Still she lingered, glancing around and memorizing what she already knew by heart: the bureau where she had retrieved his neck cloths in order to bind him, the drawer of the night table where he housed the sheaths he kept on hand to protect women from an unwanted pregnancy, the chair where she had sat and watched him nurse his mother back to health. Everything in his life served a purpose. No clutter, no fanciful knickknacks. Nothing to remind him of her, except for the paintings he stored in the attic.

She debated whether she should take the gloves with her, but in the end left them where they lay.

Exiting the room, heading for the door, she glanced over at the fireplace and paused. She hadn't given it any notice when she'd first walked in, her focus on delivering her gift and the key.

With her heart hammering, she went to the table, picked up the lamp, and lifted it higher, throwing its glow over the gilt-framed painting hanging over the mantel. Slowly she approached, her chest tightening with each step.

In the distant background, the slight blur giving it a mystical feel, was Sheffield Hall. On the path leading up to it, the main focus of the piece, was a woman and a man, each holding a hand of the small boy walking between them. The man was fainter than the other two, as though he wasn't there, didn't truly belong.

While only their backs and a narrow profile of each of their faces as they gazed down on the boy were visible, she recognized herself and Aiden. In a world that for them would never exist. Tears flooded her eyes.

He had told her he painted from memory. At the bookshop, she'd seen that, in addition, he painted using his vivid imagination. Now, she understood that he also painted his dreams.

And his dream was the same as hers.

THE AIR SHIFTED as though more space was required for the arrival of a formidable presence. A collective intake of breath hissed through the room.

But neither of those things told Aiden she was here. Even though his back was to the doorway and he'd been giving his attention to a countess who was having a difficult time calculating the sum of the cards in her hand, he knew who had strolled into the room. He felt her as though she'd reached out and skimmed her fingers along his spine.

Straightening, turning, he saw he had the right of it, and every cell in his body rejoiced at the sight of her. So beautiful, so stunning, so—

Unmasked.

It had taken him a moment to realize she had entered his dominion without shielding her face and now was striding through it—

No, not *through*. Toward. Toward him.

Her blue eyes were aflame with purpose. That lovely mouth of hers was tilted up slightly at the corners. Her steps were measured, graceful, bringing her ever nearer.

And when she reached him, without any hesitation at all, she rose up on her toes, wound her arms around his neck, and claimed his mouth as though it belonged to her alone.

God help him if it didn't.

Without thought for the consequences, he closed

his arms around her and brought her up against him, enfolding her in an embrace that made the world seem right again. For a week, he'd barely slept, tossing about whenever he tried. He'd missed her so damn much. It took every shred of decency he possessed to not go see her, to not tell her how it was slowly killing him not to have her in his life.

Leaning back, she held his gaze and what he saw there nearly brought him to his knees.

"I love you," she said with clear certainty.

He slammed his eyes closed as emotions rioted through him.

"I'm not going through with my original plan. I won't claim this child as Lushing's. I want our son—or daughter—to be raised within your shadow, to know you for the wonderful man you are."

Knowing people were watching, listening, knowing he should take her elsewhere for this discussion, he seemed incapable of doing little more than staring at her dumbfounded. Gently, he cradled her cheek. "Lena, I can't give you—"

"I don't give a bloody damn what you can't give me. I know what you can give me, and it's more than enough, more than I deserve, more than I ever hoped for. And it'll be enough for our children." Her smile was beatific and radiant. "I know you love me. I saw the painting in your lodgings. Change the background to a small cottage and make me the happiest woman in the world."

Dropping to his knees, he pressed a kiss to her belly where their child grew. "I love you with all that is within me." He looked up at her. "Will you marry me?"

Countless sighs echoed around them as her smile

grew and her eyes warmed. "Oh yes, I'm looking forward to introducing you to the pleasures of marriage."

Laughing, he stood, swept her up in his arms, and began carrying her from the room amid cheers, claps, and adoring smiles. "No reason those pleasures can't begin immediately."

"No reason at all," she agreed.

"WELL, THIS IS a pleasant surprise," Connie said as she strolled into the small dining room, Flo and Alice in her wake. "You don't usually join us for breakfast."

"I have some news to share with you girls." And she wanted to do it before they'd had an opportunity to read any gossip rags, so she'd come down to wait for them.

"That sounds portentous." Flo wiggled her eyebrows suggestively before settling in beside Selena. Connie took a chair beside Flo while Alice came around to sit on the other side of Selena.

"It does mean there will be some changes," she told them.

"Do tell," Connie ordered playfully while a footman set plates of sausage and eggs before them. Selena's stomach roiled. She really needed to tell the cook to dispense with preparing eggs for a while.

"I hardly know where to begin."

"At the beginning usually works best," Flo said.

"Yes. Right. Well—"

"It's all over London that you kissed that Trewlove bastard!" The shouted words accompanied Winslow as he barged in, came to a stop at the foot of the table, and glared disbelieving at her.

"Is it? Well, it is what one does when one is to marry a man: she kisses him."

"I knew it!" Alice crowed.

Selena watched in stunned fascination as the twins removed a pound note from their pockets and dropped it into Alice's outstretched hand. "What's this?"

Connie rolled her eyes. "After our afternoon at the bookshop, Alice wagered us that Mr. Trewlove had more than a casual interest in you and that you would be wed within the year."

Selena could scarce believe her ears as she looked at her baby sister.

Alice merely shrugged. "They wouldn't have been silly enough to take my wager if they read romantic novels. The manner in which he looked at you matches the description of any hero who has fallen madly in love with the heroine. I noticed it right off, the moment we arrived."

"You certainly did a splendid job of not giving away your thoughts to me."

"In any good love story, the heroine must come around to realizing it on her own."

"All fairy tales aside," Winslow said impatiently as he pulled out a chair and sat, "it was rather poor planning on your part to reveal your tendre for the man so early into your pregnancy. It might cause the Crown to doubt the legitimacy of your claim that the babe is the duke's."

"You're definitely with child?" Connie asked.

She could not prevent her soft smile from forming or her hand from protectively flattening over her belly. "I am. However, it is Aiden Trewlove's babe, not Lushing's."

Winslow looked as though she'd rammed a lance the length of the table between two of his ribs. "You shouldn't have confessed *that* to them. The fewer who know—"

"I sent a missive to the duke's solicitor, Mr. Beckwith, this morning alerting him of that very fact and asking him to notify the Crown that no possibility I am carrying Lushing's heir exists."

"Have you gone mad?"

"I will not spend the remainder of my life living a lie. I will not have my child grow up believing another to be his—or her—father." She glanced at her sisters. "Which is the reason that I am here this morning at breakfast. I love you all dearly. Aiden and I will do what we can to see you in good marriages, but I must be honest. I think each of you will be a spectacular catch for any man who is smart enough to recognize what you have to offer. I believe you each have it within you to make a good match all on your own."

"You know we'd have never forgiven you if you sacrificed your happiness for us," Alice said.

Reaching out, she squeezed her sister's hand. "Thank you, sweeting. I do feel a bit guilty putting my own wants first. It's an odd sensation, as I've never done it before, but I think it will actually make me a better sister."

"You deserve to have a man who gazes at you the way Mr. Trewlove does. As much as I loved Lushing, he never looked at you as though he would die if he couldn't have you in his arms. The only other man who ever came close to looking at you that way was Lord Kittridge."

"Kittridge? I think you're mistaken there."

"No, I'm not. It was at Christmas. You and Lushing were playing a duet on the pianoforte. Kittridge was watching you with such yearning that I'm surprised you didn't feel it."

"Hmm." She couldn't imagine it, but other moments sprang to mind—she shoved them aside for later consideration. "Be that as it may, I don't want you girls to worry about your futures. My dower property in Hertfordshire will, of course, become Aiden's as the law dictates, but we are in agreement that you girls may live there. When you are in London, you may prefer to stay with Winslow as his residence is quite roomy. Although you are always welcome to stay with us. We will be setting up a trust for each of you, and the income from my trust will be split evenly between those trusts to go toward your dowry."

"You seem to have given this a lot of thought," Winslow said. "Without consulting me at all."

"I was going to come speak with you about everything this afternoon. If you are wise, you will accept my choice in husband and welcome Aiden into the family. You might even seek his advice regarding improving your financial lot in life."

He sighed deeply. "I don't think you truly understand what you'll be giving up."

"Ah, Winslow, I don't think you truly understand all I am gaining."

"You've created quite the scandal," Kit said.

It was a lovely afternoon, spring at its height. Selena had sent a missive to the viscount asking for an audience, and he'd suggested a stroll through Hyde Park during the fashionable hour. She knew he'd done it as a way to show London she had his support. A few people they passed scowled in disapproval. Some simply looked away. While she still wore widow's weeds, her recent actions confirmed she'd not bothered to observe the proper mourning period.

"Yes, I know, but I like to think Lushing would applaud me for rebelling a bit against Society."

He placed his hand over hers where it rested in the crook of his elbow. "I suspect he would."

"But it leaves me with a bit of a dilemma, and I was hoping you might be good enough to help with it."

"Whatever you need, Selena."

"It's our shared plot at the cemetery, you see. I love Aiden with all my heart and want to be with him through eternity. I want to lie beside him when I sleep at night and when I drift off into my eternal sleep. I realize you might marry—"

"I'll never marry." His voice held such certainty.

"You need an heir."

"Unlike Lushing, who had no one waiting in the wings, I have a brother who is next in line to inherit the title and properties. He'll do well by them, has already married and produced a son. So if he goes before me, the line is secure."

With his words, she was more certain than ever she had the right of things.

"In that case, perhaps you'd consider purchasing the plot next to Lushing in Abingdon Park, the one he'd designated for me. Before he died, he told me I wasn't obligated to make use of it, but I don't want to leave him there alone, and as the two of you were such dear friends—"

"How much?"

"I was thinking a shilling."

He stopped walking and faced her, his eyes soft. "Selena, he paid much more for it than that."

"I know. And perhaps I have the wrong of it, but I always felt he was happiest when you were about. As a matter of fact, it once occurred to me that if the law allowed it, he'd have preferred to have married you rather than me."

Abruptly, he dropped his gaze and studied his boots polished to a shine. Finally he lifted his gaze to her. "He was the love of my life."

"I'm glad, Kit, I'm glad he had you, that he knew what it was to be so loved. I cared for him, loved him even, but I was not in love with him."

"Few among the aristocracy marry for love. He felt an obligation to his birthright to provide an heir. Having been raised in an atmosphere where duty is everything, I couldn't fault him for his decision, even respected him more for it. Although he did worry that he'd done you a disservice."

"Our reasons to marry all involved responsibilities. I think we made the best of it."

"As I told you before, after you married, he was never unfaithful to you. Our relationship became one of deep abiding friendship, but nothing more. I was always grateful that you welcomed my intrusion in your life and allowed me to be part of your adventures."

"You were never an intrusion, Kit. I can't imagine how difficult it must have been for the two of you to never let the world see what you meant to each other. For a while, I kept Aiden and my love for him a secret and I've never known such despair. While

I am certain that Society will not embrace us fully and challenges await, at least we will face them together. I'm so sorry that you and Lushing could not have had the same opportunities."

"At least they no longer hang men who love each other, but imprisonment remains a possibility. Neither of us wanted that."

But still they'd been enclosed by a prison of Society that never truly allowed them to be free.

"The secret of your love remains safe with me. Should anyone ask, and it's none of their business, you were helping me out of a spot of bother by purchasing a plot that would otherwise go unused."

"He did love you."

"But he didn't desire me."

He shook his head. "He tried to, for the sake of an heir."

"I do miss him. He was quite possibly the kindest man I ever knew." She wound her arm through his, and they strolled on. "You will come to the wedding, won't you?"

"I wouldn't dare miss something that's going to be the talk of the *ton*."

IT HAD BEEN a small, quiet ceremony with only family and friends present. After all, she was still in mourning and wouldn't publicly disrespect Lushing any more than she already had with the kiss at the Elysium. That had been required in order to make her point: she was not ashamed to be seen with Aiden Trewlove.

It was a good thing indeed since her name was now Trewlove.

"Come here, Mrs. Trewlove."

Wearing only his trousers and a shirt partially unbuttoned, Aiden stood beside the huge four-poster bed in an incredibly well-appointed room that was part of a grand suite at the Trewlove Hotel. He hadn't wanted their first night as husband and wife to be spent at the club. He'd wanted her to have a special memory. She couldn't help but believe that every night with him would be special.

As she neared, he drew her into his arms, buried his face in the curve of her neck, and began nibbling. She moaned softly.

"Your brother seems to have grudgingly accepted me." He trailed his mouth over to the other side, creating delicious sensations as he went.

"That probably has to do with you and your brothers going over his books and suggesting ways for him to increase his income. I also think you lot terrify him, and he decided it would be wiser to dance with the devils he now knows."

He chuckled low, his breath tickling her ear. "Your sisters will make good matches, Lena." He straightened. "I swear it."

"All I really ever wanted was for them to have choices, choices I didn't have. I think your sisters showed them that they can be independent, live on their own terms. Perhaps they will each find someone to appreciate them. But they'll find happiness, I've no doubt. Now, I merely want to concentrate on making you happy."

"Then take off your clothes, woman. Because I know I'll find happiness with you in my bed."

Epilogue

*A*iden stood on the parapet and watched as his son—who would have been a duke if Lena had gone through with her plans—and his two daughters, who had followed in the years after the boy's birth, frolicked around the angel statue as the sun began bidding its farewell to day. The Duke of Lushing's properties had been placed on the market. With the money Wyeth had returned to him and the increasing success of his businesses and investments, he'd had enough to purchase Sheffield Hall. He liked to think the duke would have been pleased with the care he gave it.

He'd assisted the Earl of Camberley in making his estate once again profitable and it was now returned to its former glory.

Between Camberley, himself, and Selena's trust, they'd managed to provide impressive dowries for the twins, both of whom had made fine love matches. Alice preferred her books and lived in Selena's house in Hertfordshire, where she penned romantic novels with quite a bit of success. It seemed the world was in want of happy stories.

The Earl of Elverton had passed away three years after suffering apoplexy. The countess's esteem among the *ton* had risen because of her devotion to her husband during his prolonged illness. She often visited the Elysium and had recently taken on a lover several years her junior.

The new Earl of Elverton was a far better lord and man than his predecessor. On occasion, Johnny would meet Aiden and Finn at the Mermaid and Unicorn to share a pint. Sometimes they spoke of the past, but mostly they concentrated on the future, advising each other on investment opportunities and business ventures.

Hearing the door open, Aiden glanced over and smiled at his wife.

"I thought I'd find you out here," she said as she sauntered sexily over to him. Or tried to. Their fourth child was due to arrive any day now, and Selena's increasing made her a bit more wobbly than she would have liked.

When she was near enough, he pulled her in close, wrapped his arms around her, splayed his hands over her belly, and felt the kick of their child. "It's my favorite view." He kissed her temple. "Other than you."

She laughed lightly. "After all these years, you are still such a flirt."

"But I am and will always remain only a flirt to you."

Turning, she wound her arms around his neck, and he lowered his mouth to hers. He would never tire of kissing her.

The children's laughter floated up, adding to his contentment.

He'd always feared he'd be like his sire. But unlike the earl, for Aiden, only one woman would ever hold his heart, and he was the luckiest of men because he held hers as well.

Coming next:

Fancy's story

*A*s Fancy Trewlove embarks on her first
Season, she isn't nearly as intrigued with the
lords flirting with her as she is with the darkly
handsome and mysterious gentleman who
resides around the corner from her bookshop.